"*The Proof* combines the consp._____ *Code* and the hair-raising suspense of *Apollo 13*—all encaps...... mes-sage of faith, hope, and love. Protagonists John and Amy Wells provide a refreshingly believable, three-dimensional example of the real-life joys and struggles of following Christ in an increasingly secular world. If you liked *The Evidence*, you will love *The Proof.*"

—JOHN W. TANNER, Pastor, Cove United Methodist Church,
Huntsville, Alabama

"Don't start reading it if you have something else you should be doing. You can't put it down! It is nonstop action and suspense, but with an eternal significance."

—SAM WHATLEY, Christian magazine columnist and author
of the devotional, *Pondering the Journey*

"Austin Boyd continues his thrilling series with a mastery of suspense, symbolism, and surprise, taking the reader on a thrilling ride through space and life. A must read for military personnel and their families facing long, fearful separations."

—JOSEPH G. GREEN, III, Lieutenant Colonel, US Army (Retired)

"Austin Boyd has masterfully crafted a tale rich in symbolism and steeped in intrigue—challenging the reader to peel back layers of deception and to discern the forces energizing and motivating the antagonists. This is one of the most spellbinding and multifaceted nar-ratives I have ever read."

—CAROLYN BOYD, Ph.D., cognitive archeologist;
author of *Rock Art of the Lower Pecos*

"Once again the fulcrum of international and interplanetary events tests the limits of known science, challenging the faith and beliefs of a nation, and, in particular, one man—Captain John Wells. With this incredible thriller, Austin Boyd has proven himself to be one of the best new authors of this decade."

—DAVE BACIOCCO, Vice President, SAIC, Commander, U. S. Navy
(Retired), Former Staffer, Deputy Undersecretary of Defense for Space

THE PROOF

A NOVEL

MARS HILL CLASSIFIED BOOK 2

AUSTIN BOYD

LIVING INK BOOKS™

Writing Worth Reading™

The Proof

© 2006 by Austin Walker Boyd, Jr.

Living Ink Books, an imprint of AMG Publishers
6815 Shallowford Road
Chattanooga, TN 37421

Print Edition: ISBN 13: 978-0-89957-829-3   ISBN 10: 0-89957-829-2
ePub Edition: ISBN 13: 978-1-61715-382-2   ISBN 10: 1-61715-382-6
Mobi Edition: ISBN 13: 978-1-61715-383-9   ISBN 10: 1-61715-383-4
ePDF Edition: ISBN 13: 978-1-61715-384-6   ISBN 10: 1-61715-384-2

Cover design by Daryle Beam of Brightboy Design, Inc., Chattanooga, TN
Illustrations of Mars and Mont Saint Michel by Rosemary Williams

Unless otherwise identified, all Scripture quotations in this publication are taken from the HOLY BIBLE: NEW INTERNATIONAL VERSION® (NIV®). Copyright © 1973, 1978, 1984 by International Bible Society. Used by permission of Zondervan Publishing House. All rights reserved. Other versions include *THE MESSAGE* (MSG), Copyright © 1993, 1994, 1995, 1996, 2000, 2001, 2002. Used by permission of NavPress Publishing Group.

Published in association with the literary agency of Leslie H. Stobbe, 300 Doubleday Road, Tryon, NC 28782.

Printed in the United States of America
1 2 3 4 5 6 7 8 9 10 –B– 16 15 14 13 12

To Walker and Jody Boyd
Inspirational and loving parents who always encouraged me to write

Books by Austin Boyd

It Only Takes A Spark

The Evidence

The Proof

The Return

Nobody's Child

H_2O

ACKNOWLEDGMENTS

WRITING A NOVEL IS a team effort. Books start with ideas and rough drafts. Robert Zubrin's remarkable text, *The Case for Mars*, and a meeting with astronaut Story Musgrave, during my NASA astronaut selection interview in 1994, were critical sources of inspiration for the plot of the Mars Hill Classified series. My early plot found sound critique in my best friends, Dave Baciocco and Dr. Kelly Lynn. My agent, Les Stobbe, helped me shape those ideas into an initial contract with NavPress, and later with AMG for the second edition.

A cast of reviewers across the country have helped me tune the smooth draft of my novels to be ready for professional editing. First drafts were wisely edited by my journalist son, Andrew, who booted many scenes and characters out the door — and made this a far better book. My dad (Walker Boyd), Bill and Nancy Slagle, Jenny Frith, the Lynn family (Karen, Kelly, Emily, and Molly), Chris Kelly, Marv Price, Mary Ellen Harris, Marian Jensen, and many others provided crucial inputs to shape this story. My mentors, best-selling authors James Scott Bell and Davis Bunn, deserve special mention for sharing their critiques and insights on process, plot, structure, and character.

Editors are beyond valuable; they are as essential to a book as its cover. I am honored to learn under the five-star tutelage of Dave Lambert (Howard Books) and always look forward to solving the challenges posed by his detailed critiques as each novel comes to fruition. Jeff Gerke (Marcher Lord Press) refined many plot lines and chapters. Freelance editor Linda Nathan (Logos Word Designs) has a wonderful eye for refining the Christian voice of my characters. I am indebted to all of you for your editorial honesty, enthusiasm, and patience as I learn this craft.

Once the book is edited, the other half of the job begins, always driven by looming deadlines. Editorial directors Terry Behimer and Kris Wallen brought the first edition together at NavPress. Rebeca Seitz, my high-energy publicist at Glass Road PR, made it fun to tell the world about the book once it was in print. Warren Baker, Trevor Overcash, Rick Steele, and publisher Dale Anderson at AMG Publishers, Inc. demonstrated the vision and tenacity to bring this book series back into print.

"When do you find time to write?" many ask. With a fifty-hour-a-week job, a novel only comes to fruition when you take time away from something else. Cindy, my ever-patient wife, and my four children, gave up the six hundred hours of personal time that this book represents. I am forever indebted to my wife and kids for supporting me as, together, we forge a new career in writing.

Above all, I give thanks to God, whose wise counsel, Scripture, inspiration, and amazing grace abound to guide me in writing, and in life.

Austin Boyd
304 Broad Armstrong Drive,
Brownsboro, Alabama 35741
www.austinboyd.com

1

SIMON FLINCHED AS THE roar and snap of igniting solid rocket boosters boomed across Cape Canaveral. Alone behind a line of tall bleachers, the nine-year-old glanced at the Space Shuttle as it soared skyward, momentarily diverted from the mysterious wave of swaying reeds in a nearby marsh.

"T plus thirty, passing ten thousand feet," a voice boomed from big speakers in front of the people in the bleachers: his mother, uncle, and hundreds of strangers—important people, he'd been told. Simon watched for a moment, then jogged on toward the fascinating swamp.

Something large was moving in the marsh. As he ran closer, he could see a line of tall cattail stalks waving, probably pushed aside by some giant water creature swimming past. *Alligators!* Simon dashed to the water's edge, pulled off his shoes and socks, and stepped without hesitation into the black water. Sinking knee deep into muck, he crept between sharp blades of saw grass into the bog.

"Endeavor, you're GO at throttle-up," NASA's flight controller announced, his words amplified over the huge speakers before the VIP stands. Robert cringed.

"Roger. GO at throttle-up," the Shuttle commander replied.

Dr. Robert Kanewski, chief scientist for the robotic Mars Rover mission, held his breath as he watched the early morning launch. This was the moment when, twenty-six years earlier, Mission Commander Dick Scobee spoke Challenger's last words. Robert envisioned the pilot advancing the engines to maximum thrust. The deafening rumble and crackle of solid rocket boosters shook Robert's insides, but Endeavor's O-rings held one last time. Robert sighed with relief, reveling in the awesome power of the launch. Endeavor was on her way, carrying a crew of seven, including three astronauts headed to a new commercial space station and then on to Mars. Their mission: to confirm what his own robotic Rover had discovered only days earlier—irrefutable evidence of intelligent alien life on the Red Planet.

The winged spaceship arced majestically to the northeast, her long white plume like a massive stack of cotton balls reaching up to the sun.

"SRBs separating at this time," the voice of NASA announced over the speaker.

Moments later, Robert saw the reusable boosters split off to either side of the vehicle, their fall to the ocean retarded by parachutes. There would be no need to recover these boosters; Endeavor was the last of her kind. This was the Shuttle program's final mission.

Simon waded up to his waist in smelly water, heading toward the splashes and rustles in the reeds just ahead. He fondled a hank of bailing twine in his submerged pocket, brought all the way from the farm in Minnesota for this special day. He pulled it free, wrapping the cord around his hand just as his hero would. Now he waited, heart pounding, hoping the line was long enough. Favorite episodes of *Crocodile Hunter* raced through his head. No one would make fun of him again, not after today.

Moments later, the tall cattails parted ahead of him. Simon caught sight of the creature—and screamed.

Robert's pulse raced for minutes after the eye-watering launch of the first manned mission to Mars. He imagined the crew—including three people he'd helped train—heading to the interplanetary craft, Epsilon, a brilliant white cylindrical spacecraft docked to a new commercial space station in equatorial orbit. For the next 470 days, Epsilon would be the home of three modern Magellans headed across the solar system to investigate evidence of alien life. His own robotic exploration of Mars, history-making though it was, seemed pale in comparison to this magnificent venture.

"Robert? Have you seen Simon?" asked a freckled woman to his left, interrupting his daydream. Barbara, his sister. "He was playing under the stands a minute ago . . ."

Robert shook his head, frustrated that she'd broken his concentration. She stood and pushed past him, hurrying up the bleachers against the flow of the departing crowd. He turned to watch her scan the sea of people. The last time he'd seen his nephew was before the launch, at least fifteen minutes ago.

"Are you sure, Barbara? I mean, that it was just a *minute* ago?" he asked, huffing to the top of the aluminum stands to join her.

"Simon!" she yelled.

Robert's annoyance grew; his wandering nephew was nowhere to be seen. Then he spotted two shoes on the grass near a large wetlands area, about thirty meters away. In a flash, Robert forgot all the previous lost-child episodes, his only thought of Simon—of his vivid imagination and his passion for reptiles. He dashed down the stands, yelling over his shoulder. "The marsh!"

Behind him he could hear Barbara's feet pounding down the metal stairs in frantic pursuit.

The creature pushed through a clump of cattails into the open. It was a towering silver spider-like thing, with eight gleaming jointed legs that emerged from an egg-shaped body and descended into the moss green waters. Some manner of head rose from the front of the egg, like a football on the end of a silver snake-like hose. The head, barely hidden by the tall cattails, had one large eye and no mouth that Simon could see. The head descended to face him.

Simon couldn't move, his legs frozen in sucking black goo. His hands, shoulders, and knees shook out of control. A second scream lodged in his throat.

A moment later, other reeds parted to the right and left of the metal spider. There were three of them. He squeezed the braided twine in his right hand with all the force he could muster. He refused to run.

Simon gritted his teeth, pushed sweaty hair off his forehead, and bent to grab his right knee, his arm immersed to the shoulder. He pulled hard and freed his foot but lost his balance and fell face first into slime. *Mom's gonna be mad,* he thought. He regained his balance and moved within reach of the creature's closest leg, his heart pounding in his ears.

He leaned left and right, trying to see around the massive silver thing. *Maybe it* is *a spider from space,* he thought, remembering the stunning images of two spiders pursuing the American rover on Mars only a few days before. *Or maybe there's an alien inside a ship that's* built *like a spider.* Either way, his excitement and curiosity barely overcame his burning desire to turn and run.

The head thing followed his every movement, then looked to the left and right at the other silver spiders. Simon heard a noise, like a high-pitched cry in the distance, but he couldn't make it out. The other creatures heard it too, and all three heads elevated to the top of the cattail stalks, looking to his right.

Simon shook so hard that he could barely breathe. He forced himself to calm down, then extended his left arm, palm out. He reached up to touch what looked like a jointed aluminum bamboo pole, one of eight, that extended in a gentle arc from the creature's body. The leg was cool. As he touched it, Simon could feel the silver thing hum.

The spider didn't seem to like his touch; it retreated beyond his grasp, four long legs on each side pulling free of the muck in quick succession with a *shlop* sound. Simon waded forward, let one end of the cord fall loose in the water, and cinched it to the closest leg.

This is no alligator . . . and even if it was, 'gators only eat when they're hungry, he remembered. Memories of his Australian hero whipping ropes about snapping reptile jaws emboldened him as Simon tightened his first knot.

Robert reached the marsh first. He raced past a neat pile of shoes and socks and stumbled headlong into the slimy bayou. "Simon!" he yelled for the third time. "Answer me!" Stinging blades ripped at his bare arms as he pushed through clumps of saw grass, eyes darting as he searched for the boy.

"Over here!" he heard from somewhere to his right. *Simon's voice!*

"Simon!" Robert screamed again, stumbling through a thick mound of weeds. His shoes were sucked off his feet in the black ooze as he pushed through dense water lilies in the direction of the boy's voice. He could hear Barbara hit the water about ten meters behind him.

"Uncle Robert!" he heard, just ahead of him. "I've got one! Come see!"

Robert stood aghast, unsteady in the muck five meters from his tiny nephew, gasping for air, sweat sheeting off his face. Simon slogged slowly toward him, a short hank of braided twine cinched around the mud-drenched leg of a three-meter-tall silver tarantula that followed the boy's lead. Behind it, another two moved through the muck, their jointed silver legs making a *shlop-shlop-shlop* sound as twenty-four appendages slid in and out of the marsh mud. The three moved forward single file at the speed of Simon's proud progress through the green and black water.

Robert fought to get a full breath. The closer they came, the more his chest constricted. Barbara stumbled into him from behind, pressing through the last clump of weeds and nearly bowling him over. She fell face first into the green water. Robert helped his sister to her feet as she spat mud and gasped at the sight of her son with his bizarre captives.

"Simon!" Robert commanded, "Stop now. Let them go."

Barbara whimpered behind him. He gripped her hand hard to hold her back.

"I caught some Martians!" Simon said with a huge grin as he led the ominous trio.

"Simon!" Barbara screamed and pulled harder at Robert, as though pleading with him to let her go to her son. He relented, and the two struggled to free their feet of the mud, then moved toward the boy.

One silent minute later, Barbara stooped in slime-covered water, sinking to her knees at the base of the lead spider to take her son in her arms. He handed the twine lasso proudly to his uncle and hugged his mom.

Robert looked up at the stationary spiders ahead of him, their heads moving about crazily on long slender necks. One peered above the weeds in the direction of the bleachers, and another looked back along their line of advance. The lead creature lowered its head to confront him, one unblinking eye the only feature on its "face."

Robert pulled Barbara up from the dank water. "Move back," he said, motioning toward the shore behind them. She nodded in silence. Mother and son slogged a retreat to safety.

Robert waited. He could hear Barbara pulling Simon through the swamp, thrashing their way through tall reeds. "Uncle Robert!" Simon called. But Robert was alone now. He'd lived this moment remotely two weeks ago with Rover, his marvelous robot one hundred and fifty million kilometers from Earth. Rover had been cornered on Mars by two of these creatures; Robert faced three.

"Run!" Barbara urged from a distance.

Run? Not a chance. He stood still, grasping an insane hope that these creatures would behave like those on Mars. Peacefully.

He didn't have to wait long. "Claws!" Half a minute later, Simon yelled from somewhere behind. A pair of snapping pliers-like grapples on long appendages emerged from the belly of the lead alien, just as Robert and his colleagues had witnessed two weeks before in startling images from Mars.

Once fully extended, the claws coiled upward to the underside of the craft and reached inside the muddy pod—just like on Mars—and pulled an iridescent golden orb from its belly. It reached both flexible arms across the water and presented the polished sphere without hesitation. Robert extended his own arms, his pulse pounding in his ears. The alien seemed to be waiting on Robert's next move. Again, just like on Mars.

He took one step forward, Barbara's soft cries the only other sound in the wetlands. His hands trembled, poised at the edge but not touching the shiny grapefruit-sized offering. This was an exact duplicate of the Martian greeting nearly every human being in the modern world had seen at least once—many a hundred times—on the television in the past fifteen days.

A sudden pain stabbed his chest. *What's happening?* He ignored the sensation, his whole will focused on the historic importance of this moment.

Swallowing his fears, Robert clasped the sides of the offering. As soon as he grasped it, the orb transformed to a brilliant blue, a hue so intense that he turned his head to shield his eyes. The alien released its grip, backing away. Slowly, with the gift safe in Robert's hands, the searing blue light paled to a gentle azure glow.

The spiders crept backward a few meters, and all three heads again snaked to the top of the cattails. A piercing whine from the lead alien was followed by five loud tones in short succession, one each from the two spiders behind the leader and three more from somewhere deeper in the marsh. Then, with a soft *whoosh*, each of the spiders began to power up as though for flight.

Cattails and saw grass blew wildly around Robert as the propulsive blast of the aliens flattened weeds and sprayed water like the rotor downwash of a helicopter. Robert shielded his face with his right arm as the spiders rose, slipping their long tendrils free of the dark bog. In the distance, he could see three more spiders rise above the vegetation.

He wanted to watch it all, but chest cramps doubled him over. He clutched the sphere tight in his right hand. He couldn't breathe. Craning his neck, he looked up one more time, cringing from the pain he could no longer ignore. The alien craft rose in a triangle formation, the lead one followed by its two partner spiders and three more from deeper within the swamp flying behind them—1-2-3, pointed like a dart straight up into the sky.

A searing pain brought him to his knees. The blue orb slipped from his grasp and sank slowly in the murky water as Robert crumpled, chest deep. A hot spike seemed to drive itself through his left shoulder, numbing his left arm, and he fell forward. He heard Barbara scream once more as he gasped for air, then sank beneath the green scum.

"Welcome back," Barbara said, squeezing Robert's hand half an hour later. He lay immobile on a stretcher at the edge of the marsh. Emergency medical technicians lifted the gurney and began to roll it away.

"Barbara?" Robert whispered.

"I'm here," she said, trying to hurry along with the EMTs. "We almost lost you."

"My heart?"

She nodded. "Simon ran for help. I held you out of the water." She shivered, still shocked by how close they'd come to losing him. "He saved your life."

"I'm proud of him," he whispered. "Roped some aliens, too." He winced and squeezed her hand. "Must tell you . . . something," he said, struggling to speak as the EMT locked the gurney into the floor of the ambulance and hooked Robert up to a portable EKG.

"Be quiet, Robert. Save your strength. We have that blue ball they gave you. It's safe. Some NASA folks found it." Barbara returned his squeeze. "You made history today—*again*." Her tears fell on her brother's shoulder.

"Listen! Must tell Scott O'Grady . . . at my lab . . . no one else."

She nodded.

"They *spoke* . . . to me." She saw him glance at the EMT, as though waiting while the technician moved to the back to close the doors.

"The *aliens?*" she asked.

He nodded; she felt his hand tremble in hers. He motioned with his head for her to lean closer as the van started its diesel motor. "These words. Repeat them . . . to Scott."

He whispered into her ear. Barbara felt her skin go cold—then the EMT hurried her out the side door of the ambulance.

Robert leaned back, relieved. "Be sure to thank Simon."

She wiped her wet eyes and waved in silent reply as the door closed and the vehicle rolled away.

Robert's whispered message gnawed at her as she knelt beside her wet son and pulled him close. She'd always denied that aliens existed, certain that her brother's recent Martian discoveries were the result of someone's cruel hoax. Yet she'd seen the aliens today with her own eyes. Simon had delivered them to her. The proof.

And now her brother's desperate whisper had, in the course of only a few minutes, shredded her deep conviction that life had been created only on Earth—and validated the beliefs of eccentric groups that stood for everything she opposed. She wanted with all her heart to forget this message that testified against the very foundations of her faith—

We are many. Do not fear. We are the Father Race.

2

WEIGHTLESSNESS EMBRACED JOHN WELLS
like an old friend. John adjusted to zero-G better than any man alive, or so his doctors told him. Nearly fifty years old, the lanky astronaut with deep-set eyes and bushy eyebrows was something of a medical phenomenon: his sinewy body showed no ill effects from his recent record-breaking four-hundred-day stay in space.

The lack of gravity brought back a flood of memories of life on the International Space Station during that long stay: of zipping between crowded cylindrical modules crammed with pre-packaged meals and electronic equipment, of long work days repairing critical mission systems, of rousing talks over meals, and of sixteen glorious sunrises every day. Now on his fourth space mission, John again felt at home. And he felt that familiar twinge — the stabbing pain that he'd bottled up deep inside for many months — the realization that following his calling to space tore him away from those he loved most.

"Time to climb out of those Gumby suits," Colonel Melanie Knox, Endeavor's Commander, said over the Space Shuttle's internal communication system once they reached low Earth orbit. "You can come up to the main deck now."

"Roger that," John replied. Navy Captain Sean O'Brien, the big man seated to John's left in the Shuttle's windowless lower deck, unlocked and twisted off his helmet, then signaled for his partners to do the same. Dr. Michelle Caskey, the third party in the tiny hold, shook her hair free as she removed the helmet, her auburn hair floating up in the weightless environment. Sean, Michelle, John—and in a fashion, their spacecraft designer, Rex Edwards—were the future crew of the interplanetary spaceship Epsilon, aptly named for the fifth letter in the Greek alphabet. The Space Shuttle Endeavor would deliver them to Epsilon—America's fifth space-faring ship that followed in the tradition of Mercury, Gemini, Apollo, and the Space Shuttle. Five decades of manned space experience, and John and his two crewmates would need to rely on everything the space program had learned in that time in order to survive the most difficult manned space mission of all time: a manned mission to Mars.

The three astronauts shed their orange space suits in favor of pocket-rich cargo pants and matching polo shirts. Michelle buckled her trademark pink fanny pack around the base of her shirt and helped the others store their gear in the Shuttle's lower deck. Ready for action, the red-shirted trio floated through the access hatch to the crowded upper deck and cockpit area. John was first, and he looked out the small overhead observation window, amazed anew at the breathtaking blues, whites, greens, and browns of the planet rotating below him.

"Bring back a few memories, Hawk?" Sean asked as he floated up from behind. John's nickname—Hawk—came from his days as a sharp-eyed Navy pilot finding submarines the old fashioned way: visually. Sean's call sign was "Bear," and the handle fit him. Brown and gray hair covered the thick arms and neck of this big man. Shocks of brown sprang up like a hairy ascot from the front of Sean's polo shirt.

"Seems like just yesterday I was coming home," John replied.

"It *was* just yesterday," Michelle chimed in. "You've only had seven months to recuperate between the two longest space missions in U.S. history."

As the Earth rolled by, John nodded in silence, thinking back on those short seven months since his Space Station mission. They'd been difficult months as he, Amy, and his four children struggled with a decision to say "yes" to John's life dream—to visit another planet. Then came the frenetic training, the separation, the stress, and finally, two weeks ago, a mysterious alien confrontation on Mars. Until a moment ago, it had all been a blur.

"Hey! Earth to John," Michelle teased as she tugged on his shirt.

The secret dread John tried to rationalize away had finally broken loose from the little cage where he kept it hidden. He thought of Amy and four growing children who needed a husband and father more than they needed the fame of his space exploits. Ahead of him were nearly five hundred days in zero-G, including a lonely month in orbit while Sean and Michelle explored Mars, and nearly a billion kilometers of space travel. A billion kilometers that stood between John and home.

His family had endured the impact of what he'd always felt was a calling—an unshakeable lifelong tug at his spirit—to space exploration. Yet for the first time in a frantic seven months of postflight celebration and preflight preparation, John was forced in this quiet moment to confront the brutal reality that had long ago consumed his wife and kids. For the next sixteen months, Amy and the children were on their own.

Floating above his friends as they watched their home planet in silence, John again committed Amy and the children to God's care. He believed with all his heart what he'd promised Amy just days ago—*God will provide.* And yet, the dread continued to tug at him. This mission would put them—and his faith in God's provision—to the acid test.

"Robert Kanewski is dead," NASA's Mars Mission flight director said. Their ground-based leader of the mission, Dan Jefferson, spoke to the crew via radio only two hours after their launch from Kennedy Space Center.

"His sister, nephew, and a dozen others are in quarantine. We now have our hands on one of those glowing alien spheres—a duplicate of what the spiders handed to our Rover on Mars. It's crazy down here. Hundreds of people—including your families—saw the aliens lift off from the swamp. Robert confronted the spiders face-to-face. Pretty convincing evidence that we're not alone."

"But *how?*" John asked, floating with the rest of the crew in the upper deck area, a microphone suspended midair before them. He groaned inside at the pain Amy was surely experiencing in the media frenzy at the launch site—and perhaps at home. She deserved better.

"Heart attack got him," the flight director continued. "Robert had a history of cardiac problems. He was resuscitated once by paramedics, spoke a few words to his sister, then died on the way to the hospital. We're all in a state of shock; everybody knew 'Dr. Mars.'

"According to his sister, her nine-year-old son found the things in the swamp behind the VIP stands. Robert sent the boy back to land, but stayed in the swamp with the spiders—or aliens. To hear the story, the lead spider made the same presentation we watched on Mars—a shining sphere that went from gold to blue when Robert touched it. Once he accepted the blue ball, they lifted off. The spiders flew out to sea . . . then *poof,* they dove into the water and disappeared. Just like that."

"Where'd they come from?" Sean asked, his head cocked to one side.

"Must have walked up from the ocean," Flight Director Jefferson replied. "Found their tracks across the beach, past the vacant pad 39-A, all the way to the VIP stands. They crossed several kilometers of sand and marsh. No telling how long ago they came up. Security's been pretty tight along the coast for the past week."

"What about his sister and the boy?" Michelle asked.

"Devastated—and in quarantine. The docs locked them both up, along with everyone who touched Robert, the orb, or the boy. It's a zoo at Canaveral. All over NASA, in fact. From contamination hysteria to end of the world stuff. And the media are going nuts."

John heard Dan Jefferson laugh in frustration. "Be glad you're in orbit," he said. "We're getting mobbed down here. No one was prepared for this . . . least of all, Dr. Kanewski."

Sean spoke up after a long silence. "There's one major question that needs to be resolved, Dan. Are we still GO for Mars? I mean, if the aliens are on Earth now, what about the mission? For the record, of course, I want to go."

"Wondered when you'd ask," Dan said, his tone more somber. "We just checked with Jet Propulsion Labs. The images continue to arrive from Mars showing the alien craft next to Viking 1. We don't know what that means now that the alien craft are on Earth, too. It's possible—even probable—that today's sighting is some sort of a sophisticated trick meant to derail the mission. Since nothing has changed on Mars," Dan said, "the mission is still on."

| LOS ANGELES,
| CALIFORNIA

Malcolm Raines adjusted his clerical collar as the director counted down from ten. He popped his third antacid that day in an attempt to quell the stomach distress that plagued him each time he spoke in public. Bright lights behind the cameras made his audience almost invisible, but it wasn't the visitors in the gallery that he cared about. Nearly a billion people would hear his voice tonight on cable, through the Internet, and on the airwaves. This was his moment.

"Live from Burbank, California, this is Foster Williams . . . with news that could change your life! And what news it is! Aliens land in Florida, humanity heads for Mars, and a leading space explorer dies of heart failure after greeting interplanetary visitors!"

To Malcolm's right, his plastic host soaked up the adulation of the crowd. Malcolm could see the cracks in Foster's pancake makeup, the man's fake tan in sharp contrast to his perfect bleached teeth. Malcolm smiled at the camera as Foster gestured in his direction.

"You keep hitting home runs, Father Raines. You said we'd hear from the aliens, and it happened—on a historic day! Every one of your prophecies has been dead-on. Tell us more about the past week and what this morning's momentous visitation means." Foster settled into the deep couch and crossed his legs.

Malcolm nodded, gesturing with massive light brown hands as he spoke. "We are not alone, Foster. That much is clear. My prophecy in Phoenix last Saturday foretold today's remarkable events. I heard these words—audibly. 'Watch for us when you venture forth.' Endeavor ventured to the stars, the first step for humanity's initial foray to another planet, and—as promised—the blessed visitors have now arrived."

"Sounds like those 'visitors' stole your famous 'Venture Forth' tagline, Reverend," Foster said. Malcolm hated to be called "Reverend"; everyone knew him as "Father Raines." And Foster knew that; it had been a deliberate dig.

"Those were not *my* words," Malcolm said, narrowing his eyes at his arrogant host. "That phrase came from a revelation that God gave me more than a year ago—shortly after my first visit to your show, in fact." Malcolm paused, a scowl creasing his face. "As I prophesied, they have come to Earth at last. And we will see them *again!*"

Gasps arose from the theater seats beyond the blinding glare of stage lights. Malcolm knew that a hundred devotees, many from his World Inclusive Faith megachurch in Phoenix, Arizona, were here in hopes of some new revelation. He intended to deliver.

Foster leaned forward, looking noticeably uneasy. Malcolm had left this juicy tidbit out of their preshow coordination—on purpose.

"This morning, as their craft lifted off from the Cape—six emissaries rising majestically into the sun—I heard them speak audibly to my spirit. It was a remarkable moment, and I am honored beyond words to be God's oracle on Earth." He paused. "Their words were clear. 'We go to that place where life began.'" He paused a second time, flexing his fingers in trademark Malcolm Raines fashion.

"I predict that Africa—the land of my forefathers—is their next destination."

WEDNESDAY, AUGUST 1, 2012: CLEAR LAKE CITY, TEXAS

"You *already* tied 'em, mom," Albert insisted as Amy Wells double-knotted the laces on her son's sneakers for the third time in ten minutes.

The petite brunette looked up in surprise, jarred from a daydream of John's launch and flying silver spiders. "Oh. Okay. Hurry or you'll miss the bus," she said, kissing him on the cheek as she pushed him toward the door.

"You okay, Mom?" her oldest son Abe asked, holding the door as Albert ran out. "You look kinda—out of it—you know?"

Amy nodded and stood to watch her youngest son race to the curb and leap onto the church bus, headed to day camp. Abe shrugged and grabbed a hockey stick from the hall closet on his way out to join his friends who waited in the front yard. Amy stood at the screen door as he swung the stick and jousted with his buddies on their way down the street.

Amy held the door open a moment longer, watching the morning come alive in their brick-and-stucco neighborhood of Clear Lake City, Texas. They were a stone's throw from the Johnson Spaceflight Center in a modest house that had seemed large when she and John moved in thirteen years ago with only one child. Cicadas chirped and buzzed all around her, filling the background with their strange song. Life—albeit without John—was getting back to normal. Just a little.

Down the curved street, she could see her latest adversaries. Six television vans were queued up for the next run on her house in search of the latest tidbit of news to feed a nation of news junkies—faceless people and, she reminded herself, probably good people—but their addiction paid a rude army of news anchors and photographers to stand for most of the day on her walk. Amy shut the front door and locked it.

She pulled her long brown hair into a ponytail as she walked back to the kitchen. For a moment, she fought the never-ending urge to clean something, then picked up a rag and disinfectant and began to spray her countertops. For the third time that morning.

Half an hour later, Amy stood in front of the sink, her shoulders slumped. A tear ran down her cheek, unchecked, as she stared into the backyard, plagued by visions of spaceships breaking up in meteoric fireballs and astronauts marooned in Martian orbit.

Six-year-old Alice pulled Amy out of her nightmare, tugging at her pocket. "The toilet's stopped up again, Mommy."

Amy turned and smiled through red eyes, then knelt in front of her daughter. "Arthur used too much paper again?" she asked as she ran her fingers through her daughter's blonde curls.

Alice nodded. "Don't cry. Daddy's coming back. He *promised*," she said cheerfully.

"He *will*," Amy said with a sniffle and a weak grin.

Her daughter pulled at Amy's hand. "Arthur needs you."

Five minutes later, wielding the well-used plunger like a mock sword, Amy shooed a red-faced Arthur off to the den to join his sister and a waiting video game. Amy went to her own room, closed the door behind her, and collapsed in the soft embrace of her bed. She pulled John's pillow to her, burying her head in the soft down as she breathed in the last of his scent, a faint whiff of Old Spice aftershave.

She stroked the down pillow, as if rubbing her hands through the soft bristles of John's gray flattop haircut. She pulled it close as she prayed in whispers, crying out for solace and for strength. She pleaded with her Creator for wisdom—for understanding of aliens, prophets, and planets. She begged for endurance, and for freedom from her insane focus on control—freedom from obsessive cleaning. She prayed for some semblance of peace in her daily battle to manage her diabetes, her environment, the chaos, dust, clutter, kids, schedules, and daily emergencies. She prayed for balance, for strength—and she prayed for John.

Amy rose from the bed. She'd been here before—many times—and had learned to cope without John. It was time to move on—and to trust in God's constant provision.

"Alice! Arthur!" she called out, grabbing her baseball cap, Arthur's soccer ball, and Alice's jump rope. "Let's go to the park!"

3

THIRTY-SIX HOURS AFTER their launch, John watched from the main deck of the Shuttle as Colonel Melanie Knox made a slow approach to the immense Epsilon spaceship. Hovering three hundred kilometers above the equator, the huge craft reminded John of a sleek concept from a 1960s-era space picture book. This wasn't the Lego-like eclectic connection of cylinders and solar wings of the International Space Station. Epsilon was an entirely new experience. Despite his familiarity with the ship—and more than a thousand hours of simulators and study—he was amazed by the beauty of the craft.

Epsilon was brilliant—genius engineering and pure showmanship at a bargain price, moved to low Earth orbit in only three hundred days. She was dazzling—a luminous gem. Rex Edwards, the aerospace industry mogul and Epsilon's designer and builder, insisted that the interplanetary ship's exterior be a glossy reflective white. She sparkled like a snow-covered mountain in the sun of a bright winter day.

"Von Braun would be proud," Michelle remarked as she floated near John. He squinted as he watched Epsilon's slow approach through the Shuttle's cockpit window.

"Not just proud . . . he'd *love* it," Sean added. "No wonder Rex is the envy of NASA. She's *beautiful*."

The shiny new ship was a massive cylinder ten meters in diameter and nearly one hundred meters long. At the rear, two silver articulated engine nozzles would provide the thrust to send the crew from Earth to Mars. The long white cylinder was surrounded by tuna can-shaped refueling tugs that had launched from Rex Edwards's rocket complex on an island in the middle of the Pacific Ocean. Three Delta V Corporation astronauts floated near the ship as they topped off massive volumes of liquid oxygen and hydrogen to fuel the next sixteen months of space flight.

A massive curved shell swept across the forward end of the craft. Like an enormous *Star Wars* stormtrooper helmet spread thirty meters wide, the aero-shield would protect Epsilon during the fiery approach to Martian orbit, and would shield the super-cold cryogenic tanks from the sun. Thirty-meter long solar wings reflected the sun like a mirror, extending from either side of the cylindrical ship to provide a backup to Epsilon's fuel cells. It was the most complex spaceship in history, but remarkably simple in its design, a credit to the visionary engineer who had designed it with his own money.

"Looks like a big umbrella with wings," Sean said, floating to John's left.

John smiled, marveling that Rex Edwards had succeeded where others only dreamed. For the last fifty years, proponents of a manned mission to Mars had written about various concepts to reach the Red Planet. Now Rex made those dreams come true with an elegant-yet-simple craft. A craft fueled with enough propellant to take them to Mars and home, and with plenty to spare for fuel cells, breathing, and water. Enough water, in fact, to meet all their hydration needs and still ensure regular showers for the crew. An inner core of water tanks also provided cosmic ray protection to handle occasional solar flares and the radiation exposure of their return trip slinging around Venus.

Rex's approach to building the massive ship had been unique. He had launched his own space station to create a staging area for Epsilon. The world's first commercial space outpost sailed along in equatorial orbit, often snagging a new launch of propellant or supplies lofted by Delta V Corporation for this mission. Rex's components came from NASA's unused Space Station parts, Russia's Soyuz docking ports and modules, Canada's manipulator arms, and the unused Japanese Space Station laboratory, which he'd used to create his own three-man space outpost at a fraction of the money NASA would have spent. His was an eye-opening success for NASA managers who'd never understood the dynamics of a profit motive.

"Sunglasses?" Melanie asked as she offered Sean a pair of Oakleys. "Trade you. My house in Clear Lake — and Endeavor — for your place on this mission."

Sean extended an open hand to her over the Shuttle's center console. "The house, Endeavor . . . *and* your cherry red '64 Corvette. Then you've got a deal."

Melanie shook her head and turned back to her instruments. "Sorry, Bear. The Corvette's been with me too long." She feigned a frown and thumbed over her shoulder at John and Michelle. "Guess you're stuck with those guys."

✳

"What do you think, John?" Sean asked as the two men floated through Endeavor's crew lock into the sparkling Epsilon, two hours after Melanie flew a flawless docking maneuver.

"A little overwhelming," John said, gliding from the joint airlock into the massive spaceship. As the flight engineer for this mission, John had responsibility for every rivet, wire, monitor, hatch, and switch. The breadth of his duties was daunting. He had to keep it all working.

"What's intimidating about it?" Sean said as he patted a plasma control screen with reverential awe. "We know this baby better than any two guys alive."

"I'm not *intimidated*, Sean. I said *overwhelmed*. I spent my whole life trying to get here. Only three people were selected for this mission, and I'm one of them. That's *overwhelming*." John looked around him, drinking it in. "When you consider all the paths our lives could have taken, it's pretty amazing that we're here—right now."

"You always did use ten words when one would do," Sean said with a chuckle.

John knew Sean was only half-kidding. "Okay, Bear," he said. "This is so *awesome!*"

"Good," Sean replied. "I can understand that."

Navy Captain Sean O'Brien was a decorated Navy pilot, and, like John, on his fourth flight into space. He was a jet pilot, a test pilot, a veteran of combat operations in Bosnia and Iraq, shot at a dozen times, ejected from a jet twice, wild, untamed, and unabashedly blunt.

Sean's call sign, "Bear," fit him well. He'd tackle any problem with the ferocity of a grizzly—an unmatched single-minded determination to succeed that had carried him successfully through the Navy to NASA. But life as an astronaut had not always been rosy for him. In his first year as an astronaut candidate, Sean's devil-may-care attitude and one-man, can-do perspective was not what the astronaut corps needed or wanted. "Be a team player," he was told. He adapted in short order to become the best team player in the astronaut office — what astronaut Colonel Mike Mullane once called a "political astronaut." "Whatever it takes and whatever they ask," he'd said more than once. "A mission is worth any sacrifice." Sean was a survivor whose monogram read "SOB." The moniker fit him well at times, and he was sure his ex-wife would be the first to agree.

Sean ran his hands across the computer controls of Epsilon's command center, drinking in the odor of the new craft — like a new car smell, but more pungent. Around him the stars of deep space gleamed through the curved high-definition plasma video panels that surrounded the spherical flight deck and revealed the universe outside Epsilon's pressurized cylinder. The stars gleamed so clearly, in fact, that he felt he could reach out and touch the vacuum of space through this virtual window to the universe.

Sean strapped himself into the Commander's seat, facing forward in the direction of the "barn" — that portion of the cylindrical ship beyond the flight deck where Rex stored the Crew Return Vehicle and the Mars Lander, both tucked behind the sweeping aero-shield. The planetarium-like environment of the flight deck made it seem as though he was hanging on the front precipice of the ship, his feet dangling in space. He spoke a single command, and the lower half of the screens before him transformed into a "glass cockpit" — digital readouts displayed for all of the ship systems. He lifted his right hand, two fingers extended, signaling to an imaginary crew like a real-life Jean-Luc Picard.

"Engage!"

✳

Dr. Michelle Caskey was the crew's chief scientist and the perfect complement to Sean for this mission. Together, Sean and Michelle would explore the surface of Mars while John stayed behind in Martian orbit. She was the science-comes-first component of the crew, with no interest in how they got to Mars. She had a consuming passion to get her hands on rocks and search for alien life. The newly married wife of an airline pilot, Michelle might have easily graced the cover of a women's magazine as well as NASA's astronaut website. Her long auburn hair, hazel eyes, and pixie nose made her one of the most recognizable young women in America.

Michelle made no apologies for her gender. "Two Navy pilots and one attractive woman?" some media wags had asked months before. Michelle brushed off their salacious hypotheses with frank talk that won the hearts of the nation. "If you think one woman's too few, then send *three*. We'll get more work done that way."

No one in NASA, astronaut or other, knew more about planetary geology, biochemistry, exobiology, and organic markers in sedimentary rock than Michelle Caskey. In the world of science and initiative, she was an overachiever. Two PhDs, a patent, and a pilot's license were the "merit badges" that got her to a NASA interview. Now a space veteran, she'd been the ideal choice for Mars science. Her six months on the International Space Station with John proved she was able to handle stressful conditions in close quarters for long periods—and that she knew how to cope with men. Her medical feats, saving one life and helping to save another on the Station, proved her worth as the medical component of this crew.

Michelle drifted through the habitation module, in wonder at the remarkable upgrade in accommodations since her six months on orbit with John. On the Station, her personal compartment had been the size of a water heater closet. Here, she had the equivalent of an entire bedroom. Michelle gawked at how different this seemed — a compartment she'd experienced hundreds of times in Earth simulators. But floating into the middle of the voluminous living space, something she could never have done in Texas, was magical. Zero gravity gave everything a new perspective.

Along the curved exterior bulkhead of the ship she had two portals, each space-age porthole a meter in diameter, formed of thick optical glass that gave her a perfect view of the universe. Starlight made faint shadows on the bulkhead behind her as she gazed in wonder at a carpet of stars. Far out there, she could barely make out the red fuzz of a tiny round Mars.

She had her own bathroom! No more sharing a cramped toilet with three men. She had a *woman's* space toilet and her own shower. A space-age vanity lined what some would call her ceiling. This compartment would be her private getaway. Like a child first to the tree on Christmas morning, she floated from one amenity to another in her personal quarters, rediscovering her new home.

Michelle spied a pole of some sort poking out of the top of the quilted down cocoon that would hold her while she slept. She floated from the vanity to the sleeping area. It wasn't a pole at all, but a guitar neck hidden in a plush sleeping bag. And not just any guitar, but a Martin *Eric Clapton* signature six string, probably worth five thousand dollars. A gold-embossed note was tied near the top fret, with a simple inscription. "Sing to the stars. Your best friend, Keith." Her new husband must have worked a miracle to get this extraordinary gift on Epsilon. She closed her eyes, sure this was a dream.

When she opened her eyes a minute later, she was staring across the compartment at her own private office, complete with two computers and a strap-in chair, double plasma monitors, and a rack of her favorite technical books. Rex had even remembered her passion for drawing, and he'd mounted some of her favorite pencil and charcoal works on the walls around the king-sized living area. A large wrapped box, with a red bow, was secured to the computer "desk." She sailed across the room to retrieve it. Another gold-embossed card drifted above the box, labeled "Mich."

"For my favorite artist. Hurry home. Keith," she read out loud as she opened the envelope. Her eyes misting, she pulled off the top of the box to reveal a set of pencils, a charcoal set, and three thick pads of sketch paper secured with a metal spiral binding.

A tiny note festooned the top pad. "Capture Mars for me. I love you. Keith."

John ran his hand along the gleaming counters of the science lab, whistling an old country tune. He knew every system in this ship better even than most of those who'd built it. Epsilon was a phenomenon of engineering, and after fourteen years flying in NASA spacecraft designed in the seventies and eighties, the commercial sparkle and roominess of Rex's Epsilon was a pleasant change. He couldn't get enough of it.

John cruised through the viewing deck with its digital telescopes and communication equipment and headed to the rear of the vessel through the central access tunnel of the ship, itself an interior airlock. He eased through the last automatic hatch labeled "Systems Control." White bulkheads were arrayed with plasma panels, switches, circuit breakers, and meters. "Propulsion," "Environmental Systems," "Habitation," "Electrical," and a dozen other signs marked the well-organized space where each element of Epsilon's system had its backup control and electronics. He tapped a plasma screen, initiating a communication link to his crewmates on the primary flight deck.

"I'm ready," he said, connecting with the other astronauts by intercom.

For the next three hours, John, Sean, Michelle, and the three Delta V astronauts worked through hundreds of checklist items, completing the final acceptance test of the spacecraft. Every element of the ship performed without flaw—another oddity of Rex Edwards's uncommon engineering. The aging Space Shuttle could never match this.

Their tests complete, Sean and Michelle signed off the intercom and headed to other duties. Alone and free for the first time in two fast-paced days, John closed the hatch to the central access tunnel, sealing himself in silence to listen to the Spirit and to pray. He looked out one of the small portals in the compartment, watching the blue planet rotate slowly below. He caressed the thick circle of ballistic glass separating him from deadly vacuum, as though to touch Earth . . . touch home . . . and touch his family, so very far away.

Thirty-eight years ago, a special sense of destiny had placed him on the path to this place—a sense that he'd been called, since childhood, to make a difference. And in the developments of the past two weeks, John was certain that God had again spoken to his heart—clear words that he'd heard when he first learned of the silver alien spiders on Mars. Those words echoed again in his heart as he hung in the silence of the colossal Epsilon, his eyes closed in prayer.

I have called you for such a time as this.

4

"EIGHT DAYS — OR MORE," the shorter man said, his English flavored with a thick Russian accent. He pulled a cursor across the map on his laptop, measuring the distance from the submarine to tiny islands west of the belly of Africa.

Nick nodded, mentally adding the eight days left until replenishment, and another thirty-two days of submerged travel to his destination—Cameroon, West Africa—if they could remain undetected. It would be a much longer trek—and more harrowing—if the persistent American submarine rejoined the chase. His own sub, a reconfigured Russian Kilo with a special diesel and liquid oxygen propulsion plant, was the quietest on the planet. Nevertheless, the captain could do no more than three knots when submerged running on batteries. And they were almost out of power.

"Is our fuel ready in Cape Verdes?" Nick asked, pointing at the tiny island rising from the deep Atlantic.

"Da," the shorter man replied.

"Very well. Keep us clear of our American friends, Captain." Nick turned to a tall man standing beside him, the only crewman wearing jeans and cowboy boots. "The Americans have tailed us long enough, Tex. It's time we do something to slow their progress." Nick pointed to a special underwater communication device. "You know what to do."

NAVAL MARITIME INTELLIGENCE CENTER, SUITLAND, MARYLAND

"What's a CASREP?" asked FBI Special Agent Terrance Kerry. The trim African-American agent's close-cropped haircut and chiseled features fit the federal mold. He handed a printed message back to the female naval officer who'd brought him the bad news.

"It's a casualty report," replied Dr. Pestorius, the chief technology officer responsible for the advanced concepts cell of the Navy's classified Undersea Warfare Intelligence Group, or UWIG. "And it's not good."

"Meaning?"

"Meaning our sub called off the chase an hour ago due to a sudden—and unexplained—loss of lube oil pressure in their engineering plant. Their main shaft bearings are fried. It'll take two days on the surface to repair." Dr. Pestorius shook his head as he paced the operations center floor. "These kind of things don't just *happen*. Someone on that crew deliberately turned off the lube oil pumps. It *wasn't* a mistake."

"What are our options?" Kerry asked. "We can't afford to lose the Kilo. Not now."

"We've launched an aircraft," Dr. Pestorius said, touching a digital chart of the Atlantic as though he could absorb some special insight through his fingers. "But it'll be at least four more hours before our first plane from Jacksonville can be on station. That gives the crew a search area of about five thousand square kilometers. Challenging—but not impossible."

Dr. Pestorius touched the chart and the monitor responded. An icon over the northern reaches of the mid-Atlantic ridge showed the last reliable position for the Kilo submarine—and Elias Ulrich, aka "Nick." "We fight worse odds every day," the gray-haired doctor said, caressing the screen with his index finger.

Special Agent Kerry collapsed with a thud into a walnut chair at the head of the conference table. Two heavy doors with enciphered locks, four guards, and three blast walls stood between Kerry and Maryland's fresh air. Nearly three weeks in this modern intelligence prison had robbed him of sleep and sunlight. He rested his head on his hands.

"It's only a matter of time," Dr. Pestorius continued. "Ulrich and his team will realize we're not in trail. He probably needs fuel—and rest. His delay will give us a chance to get back in the game."

"You're the submariner, sir," Kerry said. "I just wish we'd rammed him—or done something decisive with our sub—when we had a chance."

"Admirable sentiment, Special Agent Kerry. But not a good move. We want Ulrich alive, not dead." He chuckled. "And you don't ram submarines on purpose."

"I'll take him any way I can get him . . . alive *or* dead," Kerry said quietly. "Now what?"

"Rest. We'll call you once the search aircraft is on station. Until then—"

"Until then, we're sunk. Thanks for your help, doc, but I won't be coming back for a while. I'm going to try another lead in Colorado. You keep the heat on Ulrich. I plan to visit his old friend—General Boomer Fredericks."

"'No bucks, no Buck Rogers,' someone once said," quipped Rex Edwards, addressing his television host via a remote connection. "As Robert Zubrin once opined about Mars, 'There can be no progress without a goal.' Since the greatest obstacle to our reaching Mars was politics, I accepted Zubrin's challenge. I spent my own money to get the program off the ground."

Edwards gestured with his hand toward the camera. "I built Epsilon as a speculative venture," he said, pausing. "And now she's ready. Tomorrow she'll leave Earth's orbit for Mars."

"It all happened so fast," the host commented off-screen.

"Yes. Three hundred days. From the modules I'd already assembled at my Palmdale production facility, then shipped to my Baker Island complex in the Pacific, and finally launched to orbit. No other company was ready when NASA went to contract. I couldn't lose."

"However you did it, Rex, it was a gutsy move," the talk-show host said from her Los Angeles studio. "Let's continue the tour." The scene cut to the ship's interior and an image of John floating before a small hatch.

"Over to you, Captain Wells. Tell us what you've been up to the past eleven days, and show us around," Rex said, his face displayed in the upper right corner of the Fox and Friends television broadcast as he emceed this real-time remote tour of his magnificent spacecraft. Resplendent in his trademark red bow tie, Rex was an intimidating sight. A massive weight-lifter neck emerged from a button-down collar just a few centimeters below a bulldog jaw and a thin smile.

John's grin and "aw shucks" demeanor contrasted with Rex. "Yes, sir. Glad to. As for the past week and a half, we've been completing the final system checks and stocking of Epsilon, getting ready for our departure to Mars. We topped off the last of the propellant today. Come on. We'll look around," John said as he waved to the camera.

"Follow me down the central access tunnel. We're leaving the rearmost compartment, the systems control deck—moving past the exercise deck, the crew galley and food storage deck—past the habitation deck—we'll visit my compartment in a minute—and past the science and communication deck—to Epsilon's cockpit." After a fast scoot up the interior tunnel, John was at the automatic hatch leading into the spherical flight deck.

"Our first stop on the tour. Before we enter, Rex, did you want to say anything about the design of the central access tunnel? About cosmic rays and solar flare protection?"

"Thank you, John. Epsilon's cylindrical body is ten meters in diameter and has a three-meter-diameter central access tunnel—or CAT—running the entire length of the ship's center. This tunnel, configured with automatic airlock hatches, feeds into each compartment. Besides being an access way, the CAT enables the crew to seal any compartment in the event of a hull breach, yet provides access to the entire ship. You can't do this on the Space Station. A pressurization problem on the Station will shut off an entire module—and permanently isolate its opposite ends.

"Tanks surrounding the CAT store enough water for five liters per person per day on a five hundred day mission. That same water provides protection from solar flares and what we call 'single proton events.' In a pinch—with high radiation or loss of pressurization—the crew can survive in this tunnel. Sort of a space version of a tornado shelter."

John spoke. "We call it the cave, Rex. Hope you don't mind."

"Not at all, John," the magnate replied, his gaze steely, "but that *cave*, as you call it, might just save your life one day."

"You okay?" John asked.

Amy was alone with John on their last private video teleconference—a wonderful luxury—before Epsilon left Earth orbit for Mars. She wiped her eyes and took a deep breath. "No. I'm *not* okay. It's time for me to be honest."

He appeared to clench his jaw as he looked down, silent. That was his sign that he was waiting—ready for her to let him have it. It was his resigned face.

"You know what, John? I agreed that you should go to Mars because I knew how important it was to you. I know how you feel led to be part of this mission—part of the space program. But I hate it—and I always have. On top of that, I'm royally ticked off at you for going. Yes, I prayed about it months ago, I felt a peace about your going, and I said you could go—but the human and imperfect part of me—that part I've got to live with every day—really wishes you'd stayed home. Call that inconsistent if you want; I don't care. It's how I feel." She pulled her knees up toward her face from her seat on the floor before the monitor and breathed deeply, trying to calm her wild pulse.

"Do you remember that call you made to me from Athens years ago? The day you learned you'd been selected for the astronaut program?" She looked up, hoping he'd respond. John nodded. "I was standing in front of the bay window at our house in Maine," she continued. "It was snowing. As you told me the good news, I felt proud and scared at the same time. For *both* of us. I still can't shake those feelings . . . like a sense of *loss*."

John was silent.

"Aren't you going to say anything?" Her voice rose.

"I'm trying to find the right words."

"What words, John? We've left a lot unsaid these past few months, dancing around an issue that we both needed to discuss—but didn't. I initially agreed with this mission—but, there are many days that I regret that decision, fickle or not. Before you leave orbit, I need some closure—I need to *know*—do you feel that? A sense of loss?" She searched his eyes. "Please, John. I need to know your heart. I need your complete honesty."

"Amy, there's no—there's no sense of loss, as you call it." He appeared to take a couple of deep breaths, as though gathering his thoughts. "I'm glad you're being honest, although I'm not happy to hear how you feel. But at least we're being straight with each other. You're right. We dodged lots of issues we should have talked about."

He coughed and looked away from the camera for a moment. "As for this mission—the risk doesn't concern me. I know it's always on *your* mind—but it's not on mine," he said with a shrug. "Maybe I'm too close to it. I do feel stress over the separation, though. Leaving you all—for so long and going so far away—" He spoke slowly and looked down again. "You know what rips me apart every day?"

"What?"

"How can I be so convinced that this mission—my being an astronaut—is in God's will when it takes me away from the very family He commands me to care for?"

After a long pause, she spoke: "John . . . do you feel so strongly about this calling from God that you would . . . well, you'd go—even if you knew it meant you wouldn't come back?"

His face took on a weird look, as though suffering great pain. He looked away.

"What?" she asked, her voice cracking. "I asked you a question,

John Wells. We're in this *together.* I deserve an answer."

"I just wish you hadn't asked."

"Why? You said you're broken about being called to space because you have to leave us. So, would you go . . . even if you knew it meant you might not survive?"

John looked into the camera, his eyes misting. "Yes, Amy. As much as it hurts me to go—as much as it hurts *you* for me to leave—I'm convinced God led me to this point, for a reason I still don't fully understand. So, yes—I *would* go, Amy—no matter the cost."

SUNDAY, AUGUST 12, 2012: EPSILON, LOW EARTH ORBIT

Sean and John occupied the left and right seats of the flight deck sphere, with Michelle in the middle, as the countdown neared zero.

"Endeavor's clear," Melanie Knox said from the Shuttle, trailing safely twenty kilometers behind Epsilon.

"Copy that. Propulsion systems are GO and navigation has a good lock. Ready to rock and roll, Houston. Just give us the green light and we're outta here." Sean flashed a thumbs up at his crewmates, who returned the gesture.

"Epsilon, you're GO for Mars transfer orbit. On your mark."

"Copy that, Houston. On my mark. Three . . . two . . . one . . . main engines firing—now!" Sean touched the command button on his panel, opening valves in the cryogenic tanks filled with liquid hydrogen and oxygen. Sparks flew in the two main engine nozzles as the dam opened to thousands of liters of the bitterly cold liquid fuel that would combine in the combustion chambers of the two engines and form an explosive gas mixture in the burners. A plume of blue-white flame erupted from each nozzle, joining into a single flame that streamed three hundred meters behind the great white vessel. The vibration of igniting engines rumbled through the ship with a kick in the pants for the riders as Epsilon leapt forward.

"On our way!" Sean yelled. The engines drained the cryogenic tanks at a staggering rate as a deep rumble and low frequency vibrations shuddered through the ship from one end to the other. The thrust shoved the three astronauts backward.

"Copy that, Epsilon! Two beautiful flames!" Melanie said over the radio.

Sean watched the controls with a practiced eye, wary of any possible malfunction that would spell disaster. There was no room for error. He looked at John, to his right, who made the sign of a cross over his heart as the jolt of the booming engines continued to press them into their seats. Stars gleamed on the spherical displays.

"Delta-v now six point five kilometers per second. Six point eight." John recited their increase in velocity over nominal orbit speed, passing the magic value "seven point eight"—the signal that their extra velocity was sufficient to fling them free of Earth's gravity.

"Thirteen point nine!" John exclaimed several minutes later as the ship's automatic controls shut off the giant engines. The sudden loss of acceleration released the three astronauts from their positions, pinned in the seats, and they floated in their straps. In an instant the craft, now hurtling toward Mars at nearly seventy-five thousand kilometers per hour, became quiet, as it would be for the next six months.

"Houston, Epsilon. Delta-v thirteen point nine," Sean radioed. He punched the air in celebration. They had blown past Earth's escape velocity and were headed to Mars. At the other end of the solar system.

ATLANTIC OCEAN,
WEST OF THE CAPE VERDES BASIN

"American is back," the sailor said in halting English, pointing at a sonar data screen. Tex nodded. It was another sixty hertz acoustic signal, just like they'd seen in the Caribbean two weeks ago.

"P-3C aircraft," Tex drawled, examining the squiggle on the monitor depicting the acoustic signature of the airplane's engines and propellers.

Tex moved off in search of Nick, stooping under the pipes and valves that protruded from the overhead of the tiny Kilo submarine. He found his boss in the officer's mess, poring over a set of digital charts of the West African coastline.

"The Navy's on top of us, Nick. It's a submarine hunter," Tex said matter-of-factly. "We pulled the snorkel as soon as we saw his radar. Acoustics confirmed the aircraft just a minute ago."

"Options?" Nick said, bending over a digital map of Cameroon. He didn't look up.

"We can maintain our course to Cape Verdes and refuel. But if we stay down here at three knots until our batteries go, then pop up and snorkel, the whole world will see us. The liquid oxygen is almost gone. We're gonna *have* to snorkel in about twenty-four hours."

"Other options?" Nick asked, looking up, a gold earpiece of his reading glasses dangling from his mouth.

"Yeah. Now that the U.S. submarine is off our tail, we should reverse course. Make this game a little more interesting. And then play our trump card." He drew a line with his finger on Nick's map, pointing toward the east. "We're too predictable right now."

"I like that. Tell Victor to reverse course and get deep for twelve hours.

Then we'll turn north for another twelve. They'll still be sweeping the route toward Cape Verdes, and we'll be long gone."

Nick turned back to his laptop, scanning maps of the west coast of Africa for the right place to fuel a customized Russian submarine in the employ of an American terrorist—probably the world's most searched-for person since he'd escaped Nicaragua at the cost of dozens of Americans' lives. He was, no doubt, even more in demand after setting up Iranian terrorists as the fall guys for his brutal attacks on Washington where thousands had been killed or injured. Nick set down his glasses, stood, and began pacing.

A minute later, he turned to the intercom unit and summoned Tex and Victor to their consoles in the control room.

"Yeah, Nick?" Tex responded over the speaker.

"Change of plans. Turn the active acoustic cancellation system on *now*, and reengage Air Independent Propulsion. When we've thrown off that sub-hunter aircraft, turn southeast until the diesels run out of liquid oxygen. And stay below the thermocline. As soon as we lose them, we'll run straight for Guinea Bissau." Nick hesitated. "And Tex?"

"Yeah?"

"They'll throw everything in their arsenal at us. Be vigilant."

5

"BRUSH YOUR HAIR," Amy commanded as Arthur passed through the kitchen.

"You just brushed it, Mom," Arthur protested. "Remember?"

"Not likely." She pointed toward the bathroom. "March!" She turned back to her digital glucometer, sure her blood sugar was too low.

"Didn't you just check that?" Abe asked, slurping another spoon of cereal.

"No," Amy snapped, pressing the electronic device against her finger.

"But I just saw you do an insulin bolus." The hurt look on his face pained her. "I'm trying to help, Mom . . . we *all* are."

Amy tilted her head, and then looked down at the tiny insulin pump clipped to her waist. It showed she'd taken two units of insulin four minutes ago. She replaced the glucometer in its usual place on the counter, her hand hesitating on the unit, unsure what to do next.

"Is this okay, Mom?" Arthur asked, pointing at his hair as he emerged from the bathroom. Amy nodded with a blank stare.

Four feet came bounding down the stairs like a boulder rolling over the steps, accompanied by shrieks. "Stupid!"

Albert flew through the kitchen, half-dressed, with Alice hot on his heels, her hair unkempt and tears streaming from her eyes. "It's mine!" she yelled as she pursued her laughing brother. "Give it back!"

Amy stuck out an arm and collared young Albert, who was clutching an old green beanbag frog. As Alice caught up she pummeled him with tiny fists. He laughed even harder as her screams intensified.

"Alice! Albert! Stop it!" Amy shouted. "*Please!*" she implored as she noticed Abe and Arthur skulking away into the den.

"Give it back!" Alice cried in a rage.

Amy screamed a single high-pitched "*STOP!*" as she tore the toy from Albert's grasp and threw it against the wall. The beanbag split and black-eyed peas scattered everywhere—peas that Amy had carefully forced into that frog forty years ago. Alice watched in shock, her bottom lip quivering as tears rolled off her cheek.

Amy gasped. Her favorite toy from her own childhood, now the most precious of possessions for her daughter, lay in ruins on the floor. Alice raced from the room and up the stairs bawling.

"Alice, please. I—" She turned to Albert, her voice a hoarse whisper. "Go to your room."

"But . . . what about church?"

Amy shrugged, then felt the tears begin to flow down her cheeks, one or two at first, then a flood. Through the blur, she knelt—too hard, her knees complained—and felt around her for the soiled cloth of the disemboweled amphibian, then held it to her cheek. She crawled across the linoleum, gathering up black-eyed peas, then gave it up and slowly sank onto the floor, dimly aware of the sound of Albert's footsteps as he ran from the room.

WEDNESDAY, AUGUST 15, 2012: PALMDALE, CALIFORNIA

Rex Edwards stood motionless, arms crossed, surveying the activity twenty meters below him from a clear squat cylinder suspended above the center of his vast manufacturing facility. The solid glass cupola, ten meters in diameter, allowed Rex to survey every element of production in his plant. A clear acrylic conference table and matching chairs were the only furniture in the room. Plasma screens ringed the top of the glass walls displaying live images from the manufacturing floor and every phase of spacecraft construction. No stair or door broke the perfect cylinder of glass.

A quiet hum behind him announced the arrival of his guest as the ceiling parted in a spiral of interlocking translucent panels.

The transparent elevator car descended through a hole that opened in the floor below her. Adrienne gasped as the floor seemed to disappear, and then pulled her skirt tight to her legs when she saw the probing eyes below. The near-invisible elevator descended into the glass cupola and came to rest. The other occupant, a thin woman in a fitted black jump-suit with jet black hair to her waist, touched a plasma panel to open the elevator door.

"Welcome to Delta V Corporation, Ms. Packard," Rex Edwards said as the crystal access silently rotated out of the way. He waved around the room. "Please, be my guest."

Adrienne stepped out of the magical car, and it rose back into the ceiling with her escort, translucent ice-blue tiles spiraling closed behind it like a camera lens. Only a dot remained to mark the access. *Amazing,* she thought as she gawked at the unique ride. The quiet reporter struggled to regain her composure.

"That was my idea," said Rex, gesturing toward the ceiling. "I wanted the Crystal to have no apparent access—in or out." He waved his hands in an arc about the room. "I think I succeeded, don't you?"

She forced a smile and pushed long blonde hair back over her shoulder. A single solitaire diamond in her wedding band sparkled in the brilliant light as she extended a thin hand. "I'm sorry, Mr. Edwards. I was so taken by the sights that I didn't introduce myself. Adrienne Packard, *Aerospace News.* Thank you for the exclusive, by the way. I'm sure our readers want to know more about the business—and personal side—of your success."

Rex smiled. "Glad to oblige. I'm pleased that you came, Adrienne."

Her fingers were crushed in his grip, but she didn't flinch. "It's my pleasure, sir. Thank you for asking for me by name." She glanced around the glass room—then back at Rex, who seemed to be looking her up and down.

"Please, be my guest," he said, waving toward the glass wall.

Adrienne walked toward it, hesitating near the edge as though it were a cliff. The invisible floor unnerved her. She gasped and retreated to stand on a large Persian rug. Rex moved to the conference table, pouring a cup of coffee from a clear thermos.

"Sugar and cream, correct?" he asked as he offered her the cup. "You can see it all from here, Adrienne. The headquarters of Delta V Corporation." His hand motioned left to right as he waved around the glass circumference. "Design, laboratory development, manufacture, test, shipping, contracts, and finance." He turned to face her. "Simple . . . but effective."

Adrienne shook her head. "You understate a significant feat, Mr. Edwards. Five years ago, you were your only customer. Today you dominate the space transportation market. Truly amazing."

Rex walked to the wall and wiped a smudge from the glass with an embroidered handkerchief. "Please, call me Rex. And thank you, Adrienne. You've just made my day." He smiled and gestured to a pair of clear chairs behind her. "Would you like to sit down?"

"I would," she said, settling into the seat. Rex pressed a remote control, and the glass darkened to a smoky haze. The factory floor was only dimly visible. Perspiration rose on the back of her neck, her fear of closed spaces at once gripping her. Mr. Edwards seemed a little too anxious to darken the room.

"Let's get started, shall we?" she asked, her pulse quickening as he sat down directly in front of her. She pushed her hair back again, took a deep breath, and opened her digital notebook, trying not to appear overwhelmed. She'd never been comfortable alone with a man other than her husband. "Tell me about your family, Rex." She looked at her notepad, trying to divert her concentration away from his frequent stares.

"Ah— the personal touch. I'm a father. A son, Rex Jr., and an adopted daughter. Sonya. Eight and seven. My wife died several years ago."

"Two children? Are they here?" Adrienne asked, looking around for pictures. There were none.

"No. They stay at my launch complex in the Pacific. Private tutors, only the best. Sonya is a whiz at math. She was a little waif in a Romanian orphanage for Gypsy children when I found her. And Rex— he has lots of his dad in him." He waved his hand. "But enough of that. Let's talk business."

"Okay," she said. "Tell me about Delta V, Rex. Let's start with the logo." She pointed behind him.

Rex stood and walked to a super-sized corporate emblem painted on the glass. "Great question. Delta, the Greek symbol for 'difference,' and V for 'velocity' combine to create an abbreviation in rocket science that represents the difference in velocity—known as *delta-v*—imparted by firing a propulsion system in space. With sufficient delta-v—extra speed—you can break free of the Earth's gravitational pull and go to Mars, or even escape the solar system. The more delta-v you have, the faster you go." He caressed the emblem with his hand.

"A red V overlays the top of the black delta—a triangle—with a blue globe in the center of the intersection, all of it superimposed on a field of brilliant white. The V is red for the glowing rocket nozzle, the globe blue for Earth, a planet of water. The black delta symbolizes space. With water I make the magic elixir of my business—rocket fuel of liquid hydrogen and oxygen. Three atoms—two of hydrogen and one of oxygen—combine to make the molecule that sustains all life, and sends us to Mars."

"Fascinating," she said. She took a deep breath, regaining her calm. "You know, if you pulled the bottom of the V down just a little more, you'd have a Star of David—six points—with a blue globe in the middle."

"The Star of David is purely coincidental, I assure you. But the six points are deliberate. They represent six degrees of freedom for motion in aerospace—motion in three dimensions, along with pitch, roll, and yaw. Life has its constraints. I like that."

"Interesting," she said, staring at the emblem.

He crossed his arms, and his gaze bored into her. "Adrienne, about that Star of David comment. Are you religious?"

She watched the veins in his considerable neck bulging above a red bow tie. "Do I have a belief system?" she asked. "Yes. But devout? No. Why do you ask?"

He shrugged. "I'm amazed at how often people infer a spiritual message in something as straightforward as a logo or a random occurrence. Like you just did."

She forced another smile, ignoring Rex's attempt to change the subject. "It was simply an observation. Nothing more." *He's touchy about spiritual issues,* she reminded herself and made a quick note on the digital tablet. "Tell me about your secret to success, Rex. How did you become such a powerhouse in aerospace?"

He laughed. "Fair enough. I'll let you sidestep religion for the moment. My secret sauce? Simplicity, risk, and incentive." He tapped the glass wall with the ham of his fist. "I build hardware and fly it. No bloated government studies, just good solid engineering. I use proven technologies, finish my projects ahead of schedule, and deliver on cost—fixed price."

He looks like a bulldog in a suit, she thought, her tension easing a bit. *A bulldog who talks with his paws.*

"I don't lose sleep over risk. I build in a reasonable measure of redundancy and accept occasional failure as the cost of doing business. I focus on incentive. I challenge my employees to exceed their grasp, and I reward them handsomely when they do." Rex folded his hands smugly. "Those are the fundamental tenets of my business."

Adrienne looked up from her notes. *Why does he stare at me like that?* She pulled her skirt down again as she glanced back at the tiny glass dot in the ceiling. "Was there a tipping point that led to your success?"

"An epiphany? Yes," Rex said as he turned toward her. "Ten years ago we began to research reactive propulsion technologies—using liquid hydrogen and oxygen. We found a way to get 30 percent more thrust out of a kilogram of cryogenic fuel. That technology made transporting rocket fuel into orbit a profitable business venture. All I needed was a reliable base for launch operations, so I built an enterprise on Baker Island in the South Pacific. We use a Russian nuclear reactor for the power to distill fresh water from the ocean and then break that water into hydrogen and oxygen. I launch rockets with the fuel I make from the ocean. The islands are on the equator where I can reach orbit at a lower cost per kilogram than anywhere else on Earth. As a byproduct, I mine trace quantities of gold and precious metals from seawater and I export drinking water. Simplicity, Ms. Packard, has its rewards."

Rex began to pace about the periphery of the room. "I'd like to ask you a question, if I might?" He stopped for a moment and stared at her. She matched his unflinching gaze.

"Are you acquainted with a group known as Saint Michael's Remnant?"

She shook her head. "No. Why do you ask?" *More religion. Here goes.*

Rex gestured with his hands as he walked. "I said earlier that I don't read spiritual messages into random events. I deal only in probability—in what I can measure. That's why I asked you about Saint Michael's Remnant. Consider the images coming from Mars showing spider-like craft, then the appearances of alleged aliens in Florida last month, the string of correct prophecies from Malcolm Raines, and the predictions of this group known as Saint Michael's Remnant, which I'll explain in a moment. It is improbable—in the extreme—that the intersection of these independent events and predictions is attributable to chance."

Then why bring it up? she wondered.

He walked from display to display, appearing to consult manufacturing statistics as he spoke. "Saint Michael's Remnant traces their heritage to Mont Saint Michel, the famous tidal island near Normandy in France. Christian tradition states that the Archangel Michael appeared to a French bishop thirteen hundred years ago, inspiring him to build an oratory on the ninety-meter-tall island rock. It took five hundred years to complete the abbey . . . twenty generations of singular dedication to a common cause." He was silent a moment as he peered through the smoky glass.

She watched him in silence. *There's more to this than aliens and spaceships. He's passionate about something—but what?*

"Saint Michael's Remnant says that the visit wasn't from an angel, but from an alien race—a race of beings *just like us,* seeking believers who would set themselves apart, building a sanctuary for worship and contemplation, until the visitors returned. The descendants of the first Remnant still worship in secret on Mont Saint Michel. I've recently learned that they have physical proof of the alien visit—a mysterious golden orb presented as a gift thirteen hundred years ago by what they call 'the Father Race.'"

"Really?" she asked. "I mean, they have this—proof? Is it in France? Have you seen it?" She began to write quickly on the tablet, anxious to capture every word. She forgot his probing eyes.

"Wait! I remember them now," she said. "This is the sect in France that says that when we start cloning humans, and reach other planets ourselves, these visitors—what you've referred to as 'the Father Race'—will return to Earth."

"The same," he said. He smiled, his eyes locked with hers.

She studied him carefully. "I see where you're headed with this," she began, "but surely you know that this alien thesis, or one very much like it, underpins dozens of certified UFO frauds."

"Open your mind, Adrienne! With all that's happened in the past year—in the past *month*—isn't it possible that Saint Michael's Remnant is correct?"

His stare was penetrating. She looked down at the notebook and pretended to write. The sweat rose on her back.

"If they are correct, Adrienne, then we *must* go to Mars. The Father Race is waiting."

He's nuts. Adrienne quit taking notes and stared beyond Rex at the glass. "I guess it's possible. . . ."

"And *probable.*" Rex moved toward her, his hands and speech speeding up. "Consider their two conditions—spaceflight and cloning. Humans have sent dozens of spacecraft, all tainted with microbes, to Mercury, Venus, Mars, Pluto, asteroids, our own Moon, and the moons of other planets. We've drilled our spaceships like seeds into the gaseous innards of Jupiter and Saturn. We've flung spacecraft beyond our own solar system and developed all the technologies we need to live on another planet. We've cloned dozens of animal species, mapped the entire human genome, and—if you believe some reports of clandestine genetic engineering in China and Italy—we've had human clones in our midst for nearly a decade. Based on that evidence, the necessary conditions could soon be met."

Adrienne stared beyond Rex, caught up in his speculation. It was a compelling line of thought, but it required signing on to incredible assumptions.

"Either that—" she said with a sudden shiver, "or—"

"Yes?" he asked, folding his arms, with his right hand to his chin.

Adrienne stared at him in disbelief. *He's interviewing me, not the other way around.* "Or," she began, "*we* have become the Father Race."

Rex smiled again. "An interesting prospect, isn't it?"

6

"AMY?" JOHN PLEADED. His face on the screen spoke to an empty room. "Please, Amy. I need you. And I want to help."

Outside their computer room, Amy sobbed, his every word breaking her. But she couldn't turn back to him. Not now. Not after all he'd said in the past two weeks.

"Can you hear me? I don't know if it's the comm link or you. But my equipment tells me the connection is good. Please forgive me, Amy. You've misunderstood me. I simply was saying that if you'll call Dr. Lynn, he might have some idea about what's been bothering you. It's okay to see him. I want you to be happy—*and* well."

She heard him sniffle, a sure sign he was near tears himself. She'd walked out of the teleconference ten minutes ago, planting herself in the hallway, listening to his voice, praying he wouldn't hang up, but too proud to return, all mixed up in this incredible stress some fool had once called, "being the lucky wife of an astronaut."

Amy's heart began to beat erratically as she imagined John so far away, feeling the pain in his plaintive voice.

"I love you, Amy, and I'm sorry I hurt you. But please, please don't tune me out." He hesitated a moment as if hoping she would respond. "I'm going to pray, okay?" she heard him say. "If you're out there, and I hope with all my heart that you are, would you pray with me?"

MONDAY, AUGUST 20, 2012: COASTAL ISLANDS, WEST OF GUINEA BISSAU, AFRICA

"We're about ready to go, Nick," Tex said, his thumbs hooked under a broad leather belt studded with silver diamonds. "Tanks are topped off, and we've moved all the fresh provisions in through the water lock."

Nick watched the line of sailors moving shrink-wrapped bags of food and supplies down the passageway from the forward lock, his ingenious design to bring supplies from the surface using a system of cables, divers, and a wet-dry airlock on the ship. His special Kilo-class submarine could be completely provisioned underwater in a few hours, including diesel, liquid oxygen, and drinking water. The intelligence satellites searching for Nick wouldn't find him today. His black leviathan lay on the bottom, twenty meters below the keel of a rusty supply ship in Nick's employ.

"What did Victor say about our departure?" Nick asked.

"In about an hour. He knows we're pressed for time," Tex replied, his eyes on the line of men moving the last of the parcels, dripping with seawater after their automated transfer from the ship above.

"Tell Victor to lay in the course to Cameroon," Nick said. "Remind our friends up there that we've got an appointment we can't miss."

TUESDAY, AUGUST 21, 2012:
COLORADO SPRINGS, COLORADO

"My retirement ceremony was canceled. But you already knew that, didn't you?" the tall, pudgy man asked, his speech slurring badly. One side of his face was immobile, a line of drool forming at the left corner of his mouth. General "Boomer" Fredericks lay in Cardiac Intensive Care, under the watchful eyes of a nurse taping yet another sensor to his skin. Special Agent Kerry stood at the foot of the bed, silently taking notes.

"I gave you a statement last year. So leave me alone. After a heart attack, stroke, and a quadruple bypass, I'd hoped you'd extend me some respect."

Kerry stood ramrod straight. "I'm sorry, general, but I *do* have official business here. And you know why I've come."

"No idea. Surprise me," General Fredericks said, wincing as the nurse adjusted his IV.

"Elias Ulrich," Kerry said. "Perhaps you know him by his alter-ego, 'Nick.'" He hoped the general's reaction would confirm his suspicions.

The general's eyes widened, then he turned his head. Drool rolled down his left cheek. With Fredericks's head hidden behind the nurse, Kerry lost sight of the man's eyes, and he moved to keep the general's facial expressions in view.

"Ulrich was drummed out of the Air Force years ago," the general said, his speech slow and garbled. "I should have locked him up, but I granted him a dishonorable discharge."

"Why?"

"Why *what*? Why let him off? Or why was he drummed out?"

Kerry could see his agitation rising with the blood pressure and heart rate values on the monitor above the bed. The nurse, an FBI undercover agent, glanced at Kerry with a "please be careful" expression as she left the room.

Kerry nodded and continued, looking occasionally at the EKG and the newly installed monitor. "Ulrich maintains he was innocent—that he was framed by you. Says you went to Cripple Creek with him, unlawfully forced him to leave his post and drive you to a gambling casino, and ordered him to retrieve gambling dollars from ATMs with government credit cards. He says you were in the sedan with him when you crashed—that you were *both* drunk—and that you escaped from the car to blame the entire night on him."

"You don't have to recite the proceedings, Kerry. I remember the court martial. He lied and the court threw the book at him. I argued for his freedom, based on his stellar prior record. He should thank me he's not spending the rest of his life in Leavenworth."

"Perhaps. Have you heard from Ulrich—since the trial?"

"No," he said, pawing at the drool with his good hand. "He appealed his dishonorable discharge all the way to the Secretary of the Air Force. Denied. He could be dead now for all I care. And I *don't* care." Fredericks struggled to move in his bed, one side of his body immobile. "I trusted Ulrich. He failed."

"Perhaps . . ." Kerry began, watching the medical device. A small series of foil patches on Fredericks's forearm, finger, scalp, and chest were connected to a portable polygraph unit disguised as a heart rate monitor. The polygraph results wouldn't be admissible in court, but they'd give Kerry the start he needed. The lie that Boomer Fredericks had just told—proclaimed by bold squiggles as he denied hearing from Ulrich—was the first confirmation that a connection existed between Nick, General Fredericks, and last year's attack on Colorado.

"Trust me on this. Ulrich is alive," Kerry said, watching the heart rate monitor. "And we know that he's been in touch with you—

recently." The monitor spiked again and stayed high.

General Fredericks's eyes were wide. "You're lying," he said, his half-paralyzed mouth trying to sound forceful. "Never heard from him since the appeal." Fredericks closed his eyes.

"He e-mailed you," Kerry said. "In fact, I have copies of every message. Want me to read them?" Kerry bumped the bed to jostle him. The monitor spiked again.

"Must be a mistake," Fredericks said in a hoarse whisper. "Like I said — never heard — from him."

"That stroke must've wiped out your short-term memory, general," Kerry said. "Since you claim to have never heard from him, I'll just contact the others." Kerry held a silent hand up to the FBI nurse who'd returned in response to the accelerating heart rate. She frowned as Kerry waited on a reaction.

"What others?" the general slurred, his eyes still closed.

Kerry bent over and whispered in the general's ear. "The mothers of your three illegitimate children, that's who. Women waiting for child support that you never paid. Women anxious to tell us things about you that you might want kept secret. You're in this up to your neck, old man. Better hope that memory of yours improves. And fast."

The polygraph spiked wildly and the general's heart raced. The EKG became erratic, triggering an alarm.

"Mr. Kerry, you need to go," the nurse said, entering the room. "*Please.*" She gave him a gentle push toward the door. Kerry saw the general open his eyes as he left the room.

"Very well. We'll be in touch, General. Don't run off."

Five minutes later, the nurse FBI agent met Kerry. "You could've killed him! His heart rate — *and* his poly — are off the chart."

Kerry nodded, smiling as he put a cap on his thumb drive, the tiny plastic device loaded with electronic files of Fredericks's heart rate, galvanic response, skin temperature, and other physiological indicators. "Too bad I can't use this in court."

"You might get to," she said, handing Kerry an attorney's business card. "He just asked me to call his lawyer."

SATURDAY, SEPTEMBER 15, 2012: EPSILON, TRANS-MARS INJECTION ORBIT

Mars filled the screen of John's high-resolution digital telescope with amazing clarity, glowing brighter than he'd ever seen it on Earth. A brilliant white cap was visible on the pole of the planet, and the rough gash of the Marineris valley could be seen, even from here. John adjusted the magnification, driving the focal point toward the prominent four-thousand-kilometer-long feature, the solar system's monster version of the Grand Canyon. He clicked the "send" icon.

"Check this one out, guys. Valles Marineris is as wide as America and seven kilometers deep. It's a tectonic crack—made in the crust when Mars cooled, like your mom's cheesecake splitting when she takes it out of the oven."

Seventy-five million kilometers away and four minutes later, Amy and the children watched enthralled as the image appeared on their video conference monitor. This was John's contribution to Abe's eighth-grade science-fair project, and his son copied the images to the computer's hard drive every time John refreshed a picture. Amy watched from the back of the room, a warm glow rising deep inside her.

It was almost as if John was home again, walking his kids through the magic of space with his unique ability to make even the most complex subject seem simple and engaging. From planetary geology to orbital mechanics, John had a down-home way of describing his work. Capturing the interest of teenaged Abe was remarkable. The other three children sat rapt before the screen.

The recollection of walking out on her teleconference with him a month before haunted her: leaving John hanging on a video link, talking to an empty room, begging her to connect with him. She was filled with praise that God had restored John to her and taught her a valuable lesson as well. Never again — no matter how upset — would she do such a thing. Total separation from a loved one, she realized, was as close as you could come to hell on earth.

Abe saved another picture, and then the screen changed to John's face. "That's it for science tonight, guys. Let me talk to Mom for a minute, okay? I need to hear her voice."

"I met with Dr. Lynn again today," Amy said when they were alone. "Sharon Walters went with me, for moral support. You were right — much as I hate to admit it. He was very gentle with me. And he said to tell you hello. Anyway . . . my problem is called obsessive compulsive disorder — OCD." She laughed a little. "He says that people like me tend to clean a lot and that we're always checking and rechecking things. Sound familiar?"

Eight minutes later, John's response was gentle — a strong voice from a man who understood her so well. "You *do* clean all day — but don't let it bother you. We all have our foibles. I forget stuff. I overdo things. I don't know how to relax. Did he recommend any particular treatment?"

Amy had prayed much of the day, hoping John would understand her point of view. "He did," she said, smiling as she fought the compulsion to wring her hands. "He prescribed Paxil." She hesitated and took a deep breath. "But I've done lots of thinking and studying about this in the past week, John. Sharon and I have talked about it a lot, too. She's been a godsend, you know. I have a peace about this affliction . . . that is, a peace about *why* I have it and *what* I need to do." She took a deep breath and continued.

"I think this is my thorn, John, like the apostle Paul talked about—something that I have to learn to live with. I could take the medication. In fact, I plan to for a while. But I feel like it's also a call for me to put my total trust in God, and let Him work in me, too. This disease might be something to remind me to depend on God every day. Maybe He'll give me the strength to grow out of this problem—and leave the meds behind." She paused, sure that John would want to confront her determination to abandon the prescription after a time. But she wasn't going to be dissuaded. He responded minutes later. She hated the delay—and it would only get longer as the mission wore on.

"He wouldn't prescribe medication without a good reason, honey. I want you to get some relief." He paused, like he did when he was trying to convince her of something she didn't want to do.

"Cooperating with Dr. Lynn takes nothing away from your spiritual response to the illness, Amy. That medication isn't an antibiotic. You don't just take it for a few days to kill an infection. You might need to take it for a long time, and sometimes people with your disease are the most resistant to take what they need. So please listen to Dr. Lynn. I'll pray about it with you, from way out here. I love you, and I'll support you—whatever you choose."

She smiled, relieved that John could understand.

"I'm going to work through this, John. I think I knew what my problem was a long time ago. I've just been in denial. I promise I'll try to be objective about the meds and listen to the doctor. With God's help, the family's, Dr. Lynn's—and yours—I can . . . *we* can . . . get through this."

SATURDAY, SEPTEMBER 29,
2012: PHOENIX, ARIZONA

"Hoya!" Malcolm Raines exclaimed to a packed house in the Veteran's Memorial Coliseum in Phoenix.

"HO-YA!" resounded over sixteen thousand loyal followers packing the arena, here to follow their mentor and Georgetown Hoya basketball idol, Dr. Malcolm Raines. Near the stage, three rows of tall teenage basketball protégés, all mentored by Malcolm and coming to him from disadvantaged homes, echoed the response with "MAGIC!" They knew him better as the legendary former Orlando Magic power forward who'd found his way from a backwater Louisiana upbringing to the international stage, including Oxford and a doctorate in philosophy. He was the only dad they knew—and Malcolm was a part-time dad to thirty-two of them.

Behind them, the sixteen thousand of his faithful rose to their feet and followed the enthusiastic boys' lead.

"MA-GIC!"

"Soon!" Malcolm's voice boomed into the miniature mike wrapped around his head. "Very soon we will hear from them again . . . from our brothers on Mars . . . the very same who made the glorious presentation to Viking last year . . . who met one of our scientists two months ago. I have news—a message kept secret until today!"

Gasps and murmurs followed by a sudden hush met this special revelation, part of the nightly shock Raines delivered to his overflow crowd. Not since the Toronto Outpouring had people packed a nightly service in such overwhelming numbers. The arena had been booked for the past six weeks.

"Their message? They are *coming*! To Africa!" He raised his arms. "You have heard me say it before. To Africa, land of my fathers. Where life began—Africa, where we will meet our progenitors."

He paused, hands clasped over a large Bible. "But there is more," he said, picking up the Bible. "I bring you another level of truth, revealed to me alone by our fathers. I have heard their message to humanity—a message that speaks of our origin—mysterious knowledge hidden for ten thousand years! I encourage you—open your minds for the coming herald! Hear now their message to me this very night!

"We are many. Do not fear. We are the Father Race."

7

"**LIVE WITH US FROM** Ivory Coast is our correspondent Nuja Almadi, with late-breaking coverage of new alien sightings."

A television image of the African continent loomed before Amy, who'd been surfing the news shows while she waited for the kids to come home. An elegant Middle Eastern woman appeared, her curly shoulder-length black hair covered by a modest scarf.

"This is Nuja Almadi, reporting live from the capital in Abidjan, Ivory Coast. Today at eight p.m., there were numerous sightings of silver spider-like craft at locations throughout this West African country. Here in the political capital at Yamoussoukro we have reports of low-flying craft landing on grassy fields and roads. A digital video by a Baptist missionary shows what is thought to be an alien craft as it descends into a crowded soccer stadium."

As the reporter paused, a jerky video showed one of the spider craft landing on a brightly lit soccer field. Children and adults scattered in several directions, their screams audible in the background.

"As you'll see," came the reporter's voiceover, "a head or antenna emerged from the front of the body. The spider walked rapidly across the field, panicking players and spectators. One child, in a race to escape the advance, fell as the craft closed in on him. I caution you, the next segment of this video is graphic—yet incredibly historic."

A terrified African boy about ten years of age lay screaming on the ground below the silver spider while the eight-legged creature towered over him. It pinned the terrified child to the ground on his back with a spear-like leg, as though shoving a two-meter-long silver index finger into the boy's chest.

"The arrival of the spider and others like it—and the capture of the child—happened in less than a minute. As you are seeing now, the craft freed the boy and retreated. While people rushed from the stadium, the craft squatted, leapt into the air, and flew away, joining two others in flight and rising above the field in a triangle formation. The child is in quarantine while being treated for minor surface wounds and severe shock. World Health Organization and NASA officials are headed here to investigate evidence from the landings and evaluate possible alien contamination at sites throughout Ivory Coast.

"These sightings occurred in at least five locations around the capital city, always in well-lit areas near sporting events or refinery operations. Ivory Coast is in a state of emergency as military officials attempt to quell widespread panic. Are these the aliens we have seen on Mars and in Florida? Will they be back? From Abidjan, Ivory Coast, this is Nuja Almadi, reporting live, for CNN."

"You nailed it again, Father Raines," Foster said. "They came to Africa. Just like you predicted."

Malcolm Raines nodded, his chin resting on his hands in silent contemplation.

"In Phoenix you predicted the coming of the Father Race. Was this it?"

Raines shook his head. Then he sat up straight and pushed back from the commentator's table.

"No, Foster. This is not what I expected. I *was* right—they did come to Africa. But God has revealed much to me tonight—about this event. I am convinced that the great awakening is *yet* to come."

"Where then? And *when*?" Foster asked. Raines was sure he was fishing for the next bit of news bait to keep his viewers tuning in.

"I can tell you where, but I do not know when," Raines said, shaking his head again. "However, I am certain that, when it happens, it will be a historic reunion." He removed his round gold-rimmed glasses and toyed with them. "The Father Race has returned, that much is sure. We will meet them at the peak of Mont Saint Michel, just as the adherents of Saint Michael's Remnant foretold. We have only to await the proper day.

"As I have told my followers, Saint Michael's Remnant believes that the Father Race will return when we have demonstrated an ability to cross interplanetary space—as our astronauts are doing now—and when we have mastered the genetic arts of cloning, transgenics, and reproductive choice."

"Explain what you mean by 'genetic arts,' Father Raines."

"Of course. Cloning, the first genetic art, represents our ability to reproduce an exact duplicate of an organism—an exact twin. Progressive nations have already embraced human cloning, from embryonic stem cells to complete humans. The oldest clone, whom I have met at a secret site in Italy, is eight years old today."

Foster's eyes went wide. "Human clones?"

"Yes, they are still children," Raines said. "There are many more scattered across northern Italy, France, Eastern Europe, and China. For those innovative researchers not intimidated by the tough talk of international sanctions, there are great medical and financial rewards in the successful cloning of human beings. It is a natural and logical extension of medical developments in reproductive health and fertility treatments. A decade from now, many will ask what all the fuss was about."

Foster shook his head, his eyebrows raised. "And transgenics?"

"It is the second of the blessed genetic arts, our ability to transfer genetic structures from one being to another. Researchers have been doing this for a decade, beginning with such relatively simple demonstrations as placing a jellyfish's gene—one that causes it to glow in the dark—into a rat. This is an important art—not one intended simply for parlor tricks like glowing rodents. Transgenics allows us to modify parent DNA with the best feature of another creature or plant, such as disease or drought resistance, and make a better organism—and not just plants, but potentially human beings."

"A human and animal genetic mix?" Foster asked, as though incredulous.

"Yes. There are genetic traits in some animals that would significantly improve the human species. Some detractors call this a 'chimera,' or a human-animal mix. I call it *opportunity*—an enhancement of the human genome."

"We could debate that one all night, Father Raines. But what about the other art—reproductive choice? Haven't we had that for some time?"

"Do not fall into that trap, Foster. I am not talking about the common—and fallacious—use of the word 'choice.' Everyone can choose whether or not to reproduce. I'm talking about the art of actually choosing *how, when,* and *what* we reproduce. This art's foundations began with in vitro fertilization, then sex selection, and now our ability to pre-screen embryos for defective genes—imperfections we cannot allow to proliferate through the human gene pool. Using reproductive choice, we can cull out physiologic failures and seek genetic perfection. As I say, this is an *art*—an ability to create and refine, rather than simply reproducing at random. Somewhere out there, we will find a descendant of the Father Race with no genetic imperfections. That is our reproductive goal. A beautiful thing, don't you agree?"

"Some would *disagree* with you. Back to Saint Michael's Remnant. Why the visitation at Mont Saint Michel?"

"The Remnant believes the return will happen on the Mount, as promised thirteen hundred years ago. They are worshiping around the clock in preparation for the great arrival. And I intend to be there when the Father Race returns." Raines put his glasses back on. It was time to bring this interview to a close, before Foster pressed too far.

"When?" the host asked.

"I do not know, Foster. When the time comes, I am certain I will hear it in my spirit. Until then, we need to be ready. That day will come like a thief in the night." The camera light to his left blinked off, indicating a commercial break, the end of the interview, and a strategic reprieve for Raines. The voices in his head were back, and he needed some quiet time—alone.

Like a ringing in his skull, or the sound of blood rushing within his ear, he could hear them speaking again. Raines left Foster mid-stage and hurried away.

Suddenly there was quiet, the lull that always preceded their closing words. He clutched at a doorjamb, head lowered, eyes closed, desperate to snatch the whispers from the air.

His heart leapt as the final words rang in his ears. The Father Race would return. And he knew precisely when.

MONDAY, OCTOBER 29, 2012: SUITLAND, MARYLAND

Kerry was beginning to feel this would never end. Yet another cycle of presenting his passport, scanning his retina and palm, then following a tight-lipped escort through a bank of guards, monitors, and locked doors—just to reach the inner sanctum and hear that common refrain: "We haven't found them yet."

Kerry felt a long way from the late July debacle in Nicaragua when Ulrich and his three key men had slipped away, killing more than twenty American Special Forces. Kerry's successes interrogating the rest of Ulrich's team, captured in seven countries across Central America, failed to stir him as long as Ulrich was still loose. He stifled a yawn, fighting the fatigue of his latest trip from the covert CIA facility that held Ulrich's band in Panama's remote Pearl Islands. He placed his palm on the last reader, and the door opened with a hiss. The positive pressure of the sealed room exhaled its cool breath on him.

"Welcome back, Agent Kerry," Dr. Pestorius said, extending a hand from his seat at the table. A cane leaned at his side. "Forgive me for not standing. I'm not the same on my feet since I returned."

"Returned?" Kerry asked.

"A quick trip to the African continent. Lost my footing on a stair. It's not serious."

"Africa?" Kerry asked, his eyes scanning the ultramodern operations center, a true-to-life Tom Clancy setting.

"In search of Ulrich," Dr. Pestorius said slowly.

Elias Ulrich, now confirmed as leader of the most widespread terror attack on the United States in history. Leader of nineteen handpicked men who—Kerry had learned through the last three months of interrogations—had operated invisibly in the United States for two years as they'd planned and executed the March 21, 2011 attack.

Enormous and anonymous resources backed Ulrich, or Nick, as his men knew him. He was a remarkably adaptive man who'd managed to escape a nationwide dragnet, set up residences for over a year in countries ranging from Belize to Colombia, and move untold millions of dollars through small Central American banks undetected. The American public still had no idea he existed. His cunning move to pin the March 21 attacks on al Salah and Iranian money—jihadists who had truly operated undetected in the U.S.—had managed to cover his tracks for a time. It was almost as if Ulrich had done America and law enforcement a favor, blaming the attacks on Islamic extremists who were, in fact, developing far more dangerous plans than the explosive attacks Ulrich had used to decapitate Washington and Colorado Springs.

Kerry was silent, his eyes again scanning the periphery of the ultraclassified operations center. With the nation now in a limited war with Iran over terror cells and nuclear programs, President Manchester's attention on the real perpetrator of the attacks was starting to wane. His focus on the upcoming election, only a week away, and the rebuilding of Washington, the Pentagon, and military infrastructure in Colorado, had the administration's attention fully occupied. Manchester and his vice president, Lance Ryan, campaigned on a theme of Mars and "tough on terrorism." Exposing Ulrich would defocus the nation. It was unlikely that the administration would ever admit Ulrich's involvement. Rebuild, punish the Iranians, and move on.

America needed a reason to attack Iran, a justification to stall radical Islam's development of weapons of mass destruction, and to counter their growing missile threat. Ulrich, in an oddly patriotic way, had delivered the motive. Now the intelligence community, aided by the Navy and Kerry, had to find Ulrich on the sly. *Nick's story might never be told,* Kerry thought.

"Where *is* he?" Kerry demanded. "After more than two months of no contact, I'd begun to lose hope."

"I understand," Dr. Pestorius answered. "You'd like to personally be on the man's trail. But you depend on us—and our naval systems—to track him. Were I in your shoes, I'd feel the same way."

"*Where,* Dr. Pestorius? I need to know."

"Very well. Nancy?" The tall retired admiral pointed toward the main display at the front of the nerve center. His military assistant directed a remote control at a monitor displaying a map of Africa's western coast.

"I found it interesting," Dr. Pestorius began, "that on the day of the previous sightings in Florida—July 30—Reverend Raines predicted the next sighting would occur in Africa. Two weeks later, we lost track of Ulrich, headed toward that continent. Africa is a big place, and the fact that Ulrich headed that direction means almost nothing. Except that we know he *stopped* there. South of Ivory Coast, in fact."

"You knew he was in Africa? No one called me—" Kerry protested.

Dr. Pestorius raised his hand and continued. "We learned this only a week ago." He pointed to the map. "From detailed analysis of a classified network of remote acoustic sensors throughout the Atlantic, we've determined that soon after our submarine called off the chase, Ulrich turned due south. The reason our aircraft lost him that day—and that our sensors on the mid-Atlantic ridge also lost contact—was this."

Dr. Pestorius nodded at his aide. She pulled up a display of what looked like an audio signal, a mass of squiggles flowing from left to right, with a sudden decrease in amplitude in the middle of the screen.

"He has a remarkable technology that can cancel his submarine's acoustic signature. In a sense, his equipment renders a cone of silence around the Kilo submarine. This is a very advanced technology, one that—let's just say—has been 'under development' for years in our country—and in Russia. Mr. Ulrich, it would seem, has some very well-connected friends. Or he's a genius."

"Or *both*," Kerry said as he stared at the screen, processing the revelation. The Russians had repeatedly assured President Manchester that they'd do everything in their power to help locate Ulrich and had denied any connection with the man. Someone was lying.

"Can you process that 'cone of silence'—or whatever it is—and *find* him?"

Dr. Pestorius smiled. "Excellent insight, Kerry. Yes, we can do that. And we have." He waved a laser pointer at the digital map of Africa. "He was in Guinea Bissau for a day. My hunch—he kept the Kilo under a cargo vessel to avoid detection."

"Where is he *now*?" Kerry asked, frustrated.

The screen changed to a detailed map of West Africa, from Ivory Coast south to Cameroon.

"We don't know. He stopped in Cameroon for fuel and supplies. Then this." The screen indicated a detailed track of a submarine operating south of Ivory Coast. "He was at this location this morning. Sit down, Kerry. There's more." Dr. Pestorius waved to a chair.

"I returned from Cameroon last night. We got this photograph from a CIA intelligence operative." He flipped over a page-sized glossy image of a Russian Kilo submarine, but with one major difference. A massive blue-gray structure, shaped something like a whale, sat atop the submarine behind the Kilo's sail. It was ugly compared to the sleek submarines he was used to. In the photograph, a thin man matching Kerry's expectation of an older Elias Ulrich stood on the top of the huge fixture, waving at a rusty merchant vessel.

"We have some ideas about what this structure is on the rear of the submarine," Dr. Pestorius continued. "My favorite theory says this is a massive mini-sub, one that would provide Ulrich maneuverability for extended covert operations."

A frown crossed Dr. Pestorius's normally engaging face. "No submarine we've ever tracked has exhibited this Kilo's acoustic silencing. The implications are extraordinarily serious for our national security. With Ulrich's acoustic signal cancellation and his demonstrated ability to foil even our best antisubmarine forces, this enemy could penetrate any harbor and evade any defense—with abandon. We don't have the ability to fight this quarry, and we must stop him as soon as possible. We can hope that there is only one submarine with this capability. Somehow, though, I doubt that."

He pushed a sheet of paper toward Kerry, labeled on the top with bold red letters—MAR. "You've just landed in the middle of the Navy's most classified special access program, Mr. Kerry. Please sign this." He handed the agent a pen.

"Codename MIRADOR. Consider yourself briefed."

8

"HOW I SPEND MY off-duty time is none of your business, John. And what you do on your own time doesn't concern me. So drop it," Sean said, his face red and jaw clenched.

"You're half right. Anywhere else, Sean, your free time *is* your business," John replied, trying to measure his words. "But we're on display up here. So let's not give the public something to make a scene about, okay?" John was strapped into his flight engineer's seat on the right side of the flight deck while he and Sean practiced maneuvers for the arrival in Martian orbit in less than three months. Sean swore at him and went back to the checklist, ignoring John's comments as he huffed loudly.

A minute later, he left the checklist adrift and went after John again, the tone in his voice even more acid than before. "What happens on deployment stays on deployment, John. An old Navy pilot tradition, remember? And don't give me any of your 'goody two-shoes' God talk.

You're as much a hypocrite as the next guy. I've seen the way you ogle her. So give it a rest. Michelle and I are both adults, and we know what's expected of us." He turned back to the control panel.

John swallowed several retorts that Sean deserved. "I hope so," he said, pointing at an eyeball-like device on the bulkhead before him. "Because with all the cameras around here, our lives are an open book."

THURSDAY, NOVEMBER 22, 2012: CLEAR LAKE CITY, TEXAS

Amy reached for her glucometer. The tiny finger prick reminded her that this was the fourth blood sugar test she'd done in the last hour. She set the meter down without even reading it, wiping at her forehead and sweeping back her bangs. She bowed her head for a moment, praying herself through the testing compulsion, and then went back to work.

Today was Thanksgiving. A turkey was in the oven, the cornbread stuffing was finished, salads were ready, and pies were baked. Her parents would arrive from Pensacola within the hour, and the Walters family would arrive after that. All she had to do was finish the table setting—and carve the meat.

She looked at the long carving knife on the tray before her. How many times had she sharpened that knife in the past week? Half a dozen? More? She remembered just how John stood when he took the knife to the sharpening stick, the long strokes, and his constant nibbling at the meat as he sliced it. But not today. Perhaps her dad would tackle that chore.

Amy wiped the counter clean again with spray cleanser. Obsessive compulsive disorder—OCD. She turned the acronym over and over in her mind as she looked at the bottle of pills in the window sill. Her *new* disease, as if diabetes wasn't enough. She had to conquer this problem, to force it into submission, just like the diabetes. Then she looked at the faded cotton rag in her hands, the same one she'd cleaned the counter with twice that morning. She turned from the prescription bottle and sank into a kitchen chair, frustrated.

"Common compulsions," Dr. Lynn had told her, "include washing, checking, touching, and counting. Your obsessions might take the form of excessive doubt, perhaps doubt regarding John's mission or imagining that you're losing control. When you catch yourself doing this I want you to realize that it's not your fault, and it's not due to a weak or unstable personality." That was encouraging.

"But I'm not normal, am I?" she'd asked. "I feel like I'm having a case of mental hiccups—urges and thoughts that won't go away."

"You're normal," her girlfriend Sharon had assured her. "If you didn't have some kind of hang-up, you'd be the odd one." Sharon shared her own struggles with anxiety. "Life's complex, kiddo. We all deal with it. I'm here for you, like you are for me."

Amy bowed her head over clasped hands, confessing that she could *not* control this on her own—the obsessive-compulsive nature that sought to destroy her from the inside. She would put this in God's hands, with Dr. Lynn's help. Amy rested her elbows on her knees, placing her head in her palms as she began to whisper her concerns. Victoria, Alice's calico cat, purred at her feet while the warmth of the aromatic kitchen embraced the two of them.

THURSDAY, DECEMBER 13, 2013: EPSILON, TRANS-MARS INJECTION ORBIT

"Halfway there," Sean said as he, John, and Michelle completed a battery of system tests and a final course correction en route to Mars.

"And only twelve shopping days 'til Christmas!" Michelle added. "When are we putting up the tree?"

"Tonight," John stated, deadpan. "I have a surprise I've been stowing away."

"You didn't?" Michelle said with a gasp. "You brought your *wife?*"

John finally let go the belly laugh that Michelle had been trying to pull out of him for the past month. "I made a deal with the administrator—right after I learned I was on the crew. Sold him on the idea of a Christmas show from deep space. He loved it. The tree's artificial, complete with zero-G ornaments. I think you'll like it."

Sean stared ahead. His mood had grown more sullen each day. Was it Sean's response to the isolation and monotony of deep space—or a bad case of Christmas blues? As for John, this was the season of Advent, his favorite time of year—building up to Christmas.

"Why the long face?" Michelle asked Sean, placing her hands on his shoulders. She was determined, John thought, to inject some holiday cheer into the crew.

"I wasn't informed about the tree," Sean said with a frown. "Why?"

"Lighten up, Space Commander," Michelle joked, massaging his tense muscles. "It's *Christmas*. John did us a huge favor. So relax. It's okay to have a little fun. Now—where is it, you sneak?" she said, releasing Sean and turning to John. "My decorating bug's getting the best of me."

Sean broke into a big smile as he pointed at their lone female crewmate. "Never took her for the nesting type. Did you, John?"

"Very funny, Sean," Michelle said as she floated out of the compartment into the central access tunnel. "Very funny."

SUNDAY, DECEMBER 16, 2012:
HOUSTON, TEXAS

The television talk show was on the big screen of Mars Mission Control in Houston as Malcolm Raines dropped the bombshell. "Mid-afternoon on March 21, 2013, the Father Race will return atop Mont Saint Michel."

Marv Booker, NASA's associate administrator for manned space flight, jerked his head toward the huge CNN image of Malcolm Raines. "Is there any chance that he's right? That there's really a Father Race—whatever that is? And that God talks to him audibly?"

Dan Jefferson, the flight director, shook his head. "No, he's a fruit-cake if you ask me, Marv. But with his record, I'll bet my next paycheck that those spiders show up right on time—on March 21, if that's when he says it'll happen."

"Who's feeding Raines this stuff?" Marv asked. "Don't tell me God's behind Raines, or I'll find you another job."

Dan was silent for a long moment, then spoke. "I have a theory, Marv. Actually, it's not *my* theory. There's someone I want you to meet."

"Don't keep me in suspense. I'll have a billion questions to answer after the White House digests this latest alien revelation."

Dan smiled and leaned toward Marv. "You need to meet this fella. Name's Terrance Kerry. He's a special agent for the FBI. Came to see me yesterday to find out more about the analysis on the alien sphere. He shared what I thought was a preposterous proposal. But now I think he's on to something."

"What *about* that glass ball thing? Did they ever figure it out?"

"After all the nondestructive tests came up negative, someone sug-gested cutting it in two. That got nixed by the National Space Council.

Said it was 'too valuable.'"

"So?"

"So they did some other tests. Can't tell you what they call it, but the experts claim it's purely chemical. Like the juice in a firefly's tail, but it responds to slight changes in surface charge. The aliens hand it off, the sphere discharges in the hands of the recipient, and the chemicals inside flash blue."

Marv shook his head. "Beyond me. I'll stick with rocket science. What about the FBI guy? What'd he say?" Marv asked.

"Said 'everything's not what it first appears,'" he replied, pointing toward Raines's lingering image on the screen. "Like that kook. You need to meet Kerry and hear him out."

EPSILON

"I don't think our Christmas show will have the same draw that Raines just did," Michelle said, adjusting a bow on the two-meter-tall artificial tree in Epsilon's galley as she nodded toward a news monitor. On Earth, the tree would appear to be mounted sideways on a wall. But the plastic ornaments didn't care in zero-G, tied with bows to the green limbs.

The dining area was festooned with decorations, a cheerful reminder of the season of celebration back on Earth. Michelle had immersed herself in the tree, decorations, and garland like a kid. Her enthusiasm for decorating the dining area had proven contagious. Even Sean had enjoyed the opportunity, much to John's surprise—and, apparently, Michelle's.

John adjusted another sheep in his magical attempt at a zero-G nativity set. Arrayed in the middle of the compartment, Mary, Joseph, the baby Jesus, and a dozen props all floated together in a remarkable decoration that could be viewed top-down or bottom-up. He struggled to keep a sheep from bumping into the cradle. This was much harder than getting seven carrots to spin in sync, his claim to fame up to this point.

"Anybody taking bets on when we see those spiders next?" Sean asked as he sent one of the shepherds tumbling to the end of the compartment with the sharp flick of a finger.

"Hey!" John objected with a smile. "Pick on someone your own size."

Sean shook his head. "I think all those stimulants fried his brain."

"Who? Raines?" John asked.

"The same. Chemical man. You ever hear how Raines got into this religious stuff?" Sean asked, retrieving the toy shepherd.

John shook his head.

"D'you?" Michelle asked.

"Yep," Sean replied as he helped to set out more decorations. "He was a graduate student at Oxford. American professional basketball star with a blown knee, but he wasn't much of a scholar, to hear the reports. I read that he started popping Adderall to stay awake—to 'concentrate'—or so he claimed."

"I remember," Michelle added. "Adderall was popular with college students."

"What's Adderall?" John asked.

"Stimulant," Michelle added. "Sort of like Ritalin, the medicine for ADHD. But this is different. It's a mixture of methamphetamine salts. Potent stuff."

"And easy to get. So he's popping Adderall like he's King Kong," Sean continued, "and sooner or later, he overdoses. He was in some kind of séance one night. All of the philosophy students were on stimulants doing a 'meaning of life' thing, when he had this vision of aliens and what he called 'humanity's final reckoning.' He became a one-man religion that very night—at least, that's what I read on the e-mail from Marv Booker a while ago."

"That all of it?" John asked.

"No. After that he went full out for this alien stuff, and his wife couldn't take it. He bailed on her and set up a storefront church, such as it was, in Sedona, Arizona. He was there preaching to himself for nearly two years before anyone noticed him. His mentoring of boys from broken homes is what got him a national stage—not his wacko religion. Good three-point shooter, by the way."

"So I'll take your bet," John said. "Ten bucks says we see spiders before March 21."

"You're on!" Sean exclaimed.

"And you're *busted*," Michelle said. "There are aliens on Mars. We'll be there in February—or have you forgotten?"

"Pay up," John said, laughing.

Sean shook his head, red-faced. "You cheated."

"Naw. I was just playing with you," John said. "But I'll tell you what *will* be happening around March 21. We'll be together again and headed home."

Sean's smile disappeared and he narrowed his eyes. "Hawk. You've brought that up three times today—and a dozen this past week. What're you picking at?"

"Nothing," John said, his pulse quickening. "Just gonna be glad to see you both get off the big red rock safe and sound—and join up with me again."

"No," Sean said, drawing a little closer to John and his zero-G nativity. "There's more to this than you're admitting. So spit it out. What's eatin' you?"

"Nothing," John insisted.

"You're a rotten liar, John," Michelle said. "So you'd better ante up. As the crew's medical officer, I insist."

John pulled away from the nativity and the two of them, shaking his head. "You're overreacting. Let's not make an issue of something that's not one, okay?"

"Whatever," Sean said, as he turned with a shrug and went to a locker for a snack.

Michelle's eyes were locked with John's, like a lioness searching for the first sign of weakness in her prey. John's pulse quickened all the more.

"You're not being honest, John. I can't tell what it is, but I know you pretty well. So you'd better come clean. If there *is* a problem, we need to fix it." She pushed away, headed to her compartment, John presumed, for her rest time. She stopped at the central access tunnel, watching him.

"You're starting to sound like a man, Mrs. Caskey," John said, calling after her. "I'll tell you if I need your help fixing something."

"You just *did*, Hawk. I can read you like a book."

A NASA psychiatrist had once challenged John to write down the one dark secret he'd never confessed—the fear that turned his blood to ice. Now that same fear gripped him in his stomach, forcing a plug of acid up his throat. His pulse pounded like a drum in his head.

John drifted in the central access tunnel—the cave—cut off from the greenery of the decorated kitchen and the spacious portals in his compartment. Like a garbage compactor closing in on him, the three-meter-diameter tunnel seemed to squeeze in. His breath was shallow. He fought a sudden nausea and racing heart with all the will he could muster.

John could still see that dreaded shrink in front of him during his astronaut interview—"What is your deepest secret?"—the question scrawled on a whiteboard in the barren evaluation room. *Confess a fear? Never!* What was it a squadron safety officer had once said to him? "The mark of a good pilot is he never admits his mistakes." John hated that saying; it was the kind of thinking that killed people. But when interviewing for astronaut, perhaps it was good advice. He never confessed his fear—to the doc, his wife—or himself.

He swallowed hard, forcing his stomach to settle. He could see the one word on his paper, a sheet he'd shredded, then crumpled and flushed away. *The secret that Sean and Michelle can never know. Please get me through this, Lord!*

As he prayed those words, John could remember what another astronaut aspirant had said as she described her personal horrors in the claustrophobia test of the astronaut interview week.

"Did you ever get so scared," she'd asked, "so scared that you just needed to *feel* God's presence? Not praying, just basking in the realization that He's there—and His presence is the only thing keeping your reality together?"

Claustrophobia had never bothered him—sealed in a tiny canvas ball for hours. But the experience had terrified his friend. Unlike John, she'd been honest enough to share it.

And now *John's* reality was falling apart. He willed himself into the system control compartment and sealed the hatch, consumed by the irony of his actions. He'd isolated himself in the absolute rear of the ship to escape his deepest mind-numbing fear. And here he was, just where he was terrified to admit that he could never stand to be for long.

Alone.

9

TUESDAY, DECEMBER 18, 2012:
EPSILON

"PSYCHOTROPIC MEDICATIONS?" John asked, his eyes wide as he and Michelle floated in the galley area over the breakfast vestiges of space waffles and juice. "For me?"

Michelle watched him carefully, wanting to assess his emotional response to the suggestion. "I haven't prescribed anything, John. What I'm saying is there are some specialty medications that may help."

"You think I have a problem?" he asked, his eyes narrowing into a squint.

She moved closer, laying a hand on his arm. He didn't flinch when she touched him, and she held on, releasing the rail above her. His skin was warm. "We've been out here four and a half months. It's another two until we reach Mars. As the crew medical officer, I'm supposed to isolate behaviors and treat problems that affect our mission. You're a candidate." She paused. "That's not so bad, by the way," she said, lowering her eyes. "I'm a candidate, too."

She looked up at him after a moment, still holding onto his forearm as she floated closer to him. John's puzzled look told her that she wasn't getting through. "I'm lonely, John," she explained. "Hard as that may be for *you* to understand. And it hurts." She looked away and released him. "I've been taking some things—antidepressants and oral hormones—since the day we left."

Part of her ached for him to reach out to her, to take her by the hand or hold her. To talk. She squeezed her eyes shut for a moment, determined to control the tears that had wracked too many of her nights these past weeks. When she looked back toward him, John's puzzled expression was gone, his gaze clearly focused on her legs.

John hated himself for the thoughts he'd just allowed to flood through his mind. And, worse, he could see from the expression on Michelle's face that she knew exactly what he'd been thinking.

"Why are you looking at me that way?" she asked slowly as John's eyes came up to meet hers. She grabbed a rail and pulled away from him, shaking her head and blushing. "This is *too* weird," she said as she tried to pull down the legs of her loose khaki shorts. He looked back down as she tried in vain to hide her thighs.

His skin hunger on this remote mission was getting the best of him, especially faced with a woman who, he was sure, had just confessed her own intimate needs before him—in a roundabout sort of way—and then denied it. He wasn't stupid; "oral hormones" was just another term for the Pill.

He hated himself for his natural desires, hated the recurring need to force the passion demons back into a little box—in a deep secret place where he bottled up the physical nature he'd fought so hard to master. It was a nature he'd spent his entire adult life trying to run from. That brief fantasy of Michelle clung to him with seductive claws. He shook his head hoping the lingering mental image of her might dissolve.

"You misunderstood me, Mich. I was surprised about your medication, that's all."

"You're a lousy liar, John. I can guess what was on your mind," she said, sounding hurt as she again lowered her eyes and tugged on her shorts. "I'd hoped you were different . . . but you're not."

"No!" John blurted out. "Well—maybe I *do* have occasional thoughts I regret. But we all do, right?" He moved toward her. "Please, Michelle. I apologize. You've read too much into this."

She held her position, clinging to a handhold, the red gradually draining from her face. "Maybe you're right," she said, cocking her head, "although I'm pretty sure of what I saw in your eyes. But—apology accepted." She tried to smile, then chuckled nervously. "Don't ever lay that lecherous look on me again, though. You hear me?" She pulled at her shorts once more. "However, I have to admit," she said with a slight smile, "part of me is honored that you notice."

"Like you said—this is too weird," John said, shaking his head. "But as long as we're on a touchy subject, there *is* something we need to talk about."

She smiled. "Agreed. Now, about your problem—"

"Let's not go there yet," John interjected, moving close enough to touch her. "I need to ask you something." A voice deep inside screamed for him to back up, and he moved away slightly.

"Shoot."

"This is not going to come out easy any way I say it, so I'm just going to say it plain. There have been many times in the past month when I've gone looking for you—or Sean—and you've *both* been gone.

At the same time." He paused, watching her expression. "And it wasn't a rest cycle—for either of you."

He could see the red rising in her round face. The volcano was about to erupt. "You told me you're on the watch for situations that could lead to trouble. So, are you and Sean one of those powder-keg situations that we need to address?"

✳

"No!" she exclaimed. "How can you even think such a thing?" She was sure her eyes flashed fire as she spun around and headed for the access tunnel. She'd find Sean and confront him. Immediately. This was *his* fault. He'd said something to John; he *must* have. She should have known better than to crew with two men—testosterone-pumped Navy pilots at that. The tears she'd tried so hard to squelch began to run.

"Michelle! Wait a minute. If you're going to find Sean, don't blame him for what I just said. He reacted the same way you just did. Nearly punched me out, to tell you the truth."

She turned back toward him before she escaped the galley area, her face in spasms from frowning so hard. Her heart pounded like a drum, the beats in her temples threatening to explode. "Don't you care a thing about my feelings, John? I just told you that I'm lonely—desperately lonely for some companionship that is far beyond your selfish 'I'm too busy' ability to supply."

She felt the liquid pain break free from her eyes, and she did nothing to try to stem its flow. "I came to you for help, John. For that, the thanks I get is you undress me with your eyes and then accuse me of sleeping with Sean."

She swiped at her eyes with the back of her hand. "If I can't turn to you, where can I go?" She shook her head, looking down again. "There's nothing going on—no fantasies about you, and no hanky-panky with

The Bear. But I *do* need to talk." She looked up again. "Can you possibly understand that?"

John exhaled that long drawn-out breath that she'd come to hate, shaking his head as he looked away, blushing. Then he spoke in a low tone—his "I'm frustrated to the limit" voice. She wanted to slap him for what he'd implied earlier, yet hug him for caring enough to ask and keep her accountable. Her mind was racing in a thousand different directions, so she just hung there, paralyzed and waiting. Aching to be touched.

"I *do* understand, Mich. I'm not trying to pry into your personal life—even though it sounded like it. But you said yourself that there are trouble signs we need to isolate to ensure mission success. I took a chance—shared a deep concern—and I offended you. I'm sorry. Please forgive me for being so blunt—and for looking at you the way I did." He extended a hand. "Friends?"

The hurt part of her held back while her heart screamed for her to reach out. She finally slipped her hand into his and held on. *Please don't run, John. Not this time.*

Michelle knocked on the hatch to the flight deck after dinner was over. She and Sean had eaten alone, theirs a cold conversation over a hot chicken cordon bleu. John had said he was too busy to join them. She suspected he hadn't wanted to face either one of them for a while. *No wonder.*

The sliding hatch didn't open when she touched the plasma panel, meaning John had locked it—or that they had a deadly decompression in the flight deck. The door slid open a moment later with a barely audible *whoosh.*

John was waiting on the other side, examining the screen of a large personal digital assistant, an Earth PDA on steroids, so to speak. He looked up as she entered.

"I'm sorry if I overreacted this morning," she said, settling into a handhold near his seat. "You were right—to share your concerns with me, I mean. Your conclusions were dead wrong, but your motive—for us and the mission—was right on." She hesitated. "You were brave to ask."

John shrugged, smiling a little. "No apology necessary. I stuck my foot in my mouth. *Both* feet."

Michelle nodded slightly, wondering if she'd misread him, if his intentions and gaze hadn't been as lewd as she'd assumed. It didn't matter now. She was dealing with facts, and her deep emotional needs a hundred million kilometers from home were creating havoc—for her and for her crewmates. And as much as John might not want to hear it, she feared that his mental health was on the line, too.

"Why'd you lock the hatch, John?" she asked.

"I needed to be alone."

"That's normal. Social withdrawal can be healthy if it helps you to refresh yourself and establish boundaries, but it can also lead to loneliness." She changed handholds to move closer to him.

John looked up at her, letting the PDA drift momentarily. "I'm not on the verge of a space anxiety disorder, Michelle." He grabbed the PDA again and began to write on it with a stylus. "I'm sorry I missed dinner. You can put away your drugs. I'll be fine."

Michelle debated how much further to press this. She'd seen a side of John today that he'd never exposed, a raw human side below the veneer of busy astronaut, overworked space repair man, and devoted family man who tried his best to live a righteous life. She was sure that today she'd seen the whole man—including his prurient physical side. Now she knew he was three dimensional, not the prudish "glass is half full" godly optimist that she'd always assumed him to be.

He kept his nose to the engineering notebook, fiddling with switches in the cockpit. She knew the ship—and John—well enough to know he was trying to escape. She could see it now, a complex defense mechanism at work in him that sought activity and withdrawal as an outlet to deal with conflict, isolation—and, she suspected, temptation. She'd give him some room tonight, and come find that whole man again another day. Michelle slipped out without saying good-bye.

John was staring at the ever larger rust-red image of Mars amid a field of stars when the communication system chimed an hour later. The flight deck's display screens were in exterior camera mode as he hung on the precipice of the solar system, enthralled by a billion suns shining before him, most of them millions of light years away.

The second ding of the comm panel got his attention. He shook off his concerns and selected the incoming message. A high-priority communication waited, addressed to him, labeled "eyes only." The sender was his old friend, FBI Special Agent Terrance Kerry. For a moment in his thoughts, he was back on the Space Station, swapping ideas with Kerry as they attempted to break the case of the national terrorist attacks—two unlikely partners, agent and astronaut. All thoughts of Michelle and today's embarrassment evaporated as John downloaded the message to his PDA—the half screen, half clipboard that was his primary engineering tool on the ship. The opening line of Kerry's e-mail made his heart jump.

John. I need your help.

I know you haven't heard from me since before the launch. Life's been pretty busy here, and the chase is getting

*interesting. The Ulrich case has taken a turn into some
black-world corners of the Navy, but Dr. Pestorius has given
me the green light to get your insights.*

*We followed Ulrich's Russian-bought Kilo submarine to
the mid-Atlantic but lost him in late October. We pinpointed
him in Cameroon, West Africa, for a time and have images
of his sub. See attached file. Notice the large structure on
the rear that looks like a whale. Presumed minisub with a
huge seam down the middle on top, as if it would open like
a clam.*

*We were able to process Atlantic hydrophone arrays to
track Ulrich's progress up the coast of Africa. This guy is so
quiet that our aircraft and subs can't hold a constant track
on him. We lost him a month ago off the Straits of Gibraltar.
All of us presume he's in the Mediterranean or that he gave
us the slip and headed into the North Sea, or the Barents.
Read the summary below. I need to know if you see a pattern
and need to know where you think this case is headed. I have
my own theories but require your insights right away.*

John scanned down the rest of the bulleted message, picking out
dates, numbers, and other evidence he'd had at his fingertips a year ago
but had not connected.

- *Projected date by Malcolm Raines to meet the so-called "Father
  Race": March 21, 2013 (3-21-2013)*
- *Alien waveform transmitted by the golden probe that you
  imaged last year from the Space Station breaks down into an
  audio signal of twenty-one whole notes spread across three
  octaves. (3-21)*
- *Alien sphere presented to late Dr. Kanewski was measured to be*

a volume of 321 cubic centimeters and weight exactly 321 grams.

- *Attached images of alien craft departing Florida in echelon for-mation shows three abreast at the rear of the echelon, two abreast in the middle, and a lead (3-2-1). Same formation seen in attached imagery from the Ivory Coast sightings.*

- *You reported from Space Station report sighting laser transmis-sion from the alien probe, occurring in three different spectra, cycling for twenty-one seconds each. (3-21)*

There is a clear 3-2-1 numeric pattern in the NASA data. Dan Jefferson shared it with me when I asked him about his thoughts on the latest Malcolm Raines prediction being the same date as the terrorist attack—March 21. Here's the clincher: we're finding connections between the alien pattern and the terrorists. To wit: attack date March 21, 2011. Alien sighting in Florida on the same date that we located Ulrich in a submarine a thousand kilometers south in the Caribbean. Alien spider-craft sighted in Ivory Coast on the same day we had Ulrich in a different sub a thousand kilometers to the south. Why is Ulrich one thousand kilometers south of both landings, underwater, and his attack date the same as Raines's alien arrival date? It's almost too convenient. Maybe we've got a copycat here, but remember that Ulrich and the attacks came first. Who is imitating who?

John's eyes fell to the bottom of the message.

If there is a connection, alien craft and terrorist, then there are at least two possibilities. One, Malcolm Raines is on to something. The aliens, whoever they are, attacked the United States. That's a theory you proposed as a joke last year, if you recall. Ulrich is an alien—or he works with them—which might explain why he attacked our space surveillance system, why none of Ulrich's people knew anything about his background, and why he keeps giving us the slip every time I think we've found him. Maybe that crazy Raines has missed a key point—the Father Race already lives here and Ulrich is one of them. It's too wild to consider, but we have to evaluate all the options. I'm no fan of Raines, by the way.

The second option is this: The terrorists created the aliens and, by extension, the requirement for your mission. That option does not bode well for you.

10

"A DELANNOY NUMBER?" Dr. Pestorius asked, thrusting his finger in the air. "Yes! John's a genius!"

Special Agent Kerry stifled a laugh. There were times, like this, when he was sure military intelligence personnel had lost all touch with reality. Kerry had no idea why Dr. Pestorius was so excited, much less how this revelation could help find Ulrich. Lieutenant Commander Slagle sat to his left, entranced. Together they watched the esteemed PhD in antisubmarine warfare hobble about the room, his broken ankle just beginning to heal.

"It was brilliant for you to get John's insights, Kerry." The tall doctor drew a large four-by-four matrix with sixteen interior squares on a whiteboard.

"Delannoy was a Frenchman, a student at L'École Polytechnique where military officers received a scientific education. He dedicated his life to science, particularly mathematics. He was an active member of the French Mathematical Society and a brilliant amateur mathematician who made great contributions to the field of array theory."

"Forgive me, Doc, but how on Earth do you know all this?" Kerry asked, shaking his head.

"Ah! Good question. Monsieur Delannoy published a work in 1886 on how to use a chessboard—his term for an array—to solve mathematical problems. My work in antisubmarine warfare specialized in matrix algebra and array computations—such as arrays of hydrophones on the Atlantic seabed. Clever guy, that Delannoy."

"How does the number 321 figure in, sir?" asked Lieutenant Commander Slagle.

"See this array I've drawn on the board? Think of it as a small chessboard. Or a map grid. Delannoy devised a formula to prove a finite number of steps exist from the board's bottom left to the upper right. As it turns out, if you only take steps to the north, to the east, or diagonally northeast, there are exactly 321 different paths transiting from the bottom left to top right of a four-by-four matrix. Our magic number is the fourth entry in the Delannoy series—3, 13, 63, and 321. As the array expands, the number of possible steps increases from there."

He began writing numbers on the board and talking faster. "But see here? There's only *one* Delannoy number . . . in fact, there's only *one decreasing sequence* of three consecutive numbers in all of mathematics . . . that does what 321 does. Watch. All of these numbers *multiplied* together yield the number six. And all of the numbers *added* together also equal six. And you can't reduce or expand that series. All fail the test—21 or 4321—and so on. *In all of creation*, only 321 has these properties—a decreasing sequence of three consecutive numbers whose sum or product are the same. It's unique, like hydrogen or the speed of light or pi."

"What about 123?" Kerry asked.

"Same math properties, but not decreasing. It has to head toward zero, like a count down."

Kerry shook his head. "I think we've lost our focus in this hunt, Doc. How do these numbers lead us to an alien nation or to Ulrich?"

Dr. Pestorius turned around, capping his erasable marker. "Ulrich is giving us the clues we need. How did you say he communicated with his men in Central America?"

Good point, Kerry thought. *Now we're getting somewhere.* "It was steganography, Doc. Embedded code hidden deep within text, Internet files, HTML commands, and all of it spread through covert websites around the globe—mostly in Russia, China, and Central America. It was the most complex code system of its kind we've ever seen."

"Therefore, just the kind of man you'd expect to hide his objective in numbers. Would you agree?"

"I would," Kerry said, "if—and only if—we're making the correct mental leap tying Ulrich to the alien sightings. If not, this conclusion will send us on a wild goose chase. We can't afford that."

"Ulrich picked the original date, my friend—3-21," Dr. Pestorius said. "The alien revelations all came *after* his attacks. I find that fact particularly troubling."

Kerry nodded, brightening at the thought there may yet be a thread of hope. Mathematics, of all things, might lead them to the man. Or to the aliens.

Or to both.

TUESDAY, JANUARY 1, 2013: COLORADO SPRINGS, COLORADO

"Where did you find him?" Kerry asked, standing over a corpse in the morgue of Colorado Springs' Memorial Hospital.

"Hanging by his neck off the Bijou bridge," an FBI agent said. "Just down the street from the Clarion Hotel. We'll have an autopsy ready in the morning."

Special Agent Kerry pulled the sheet back to inspect a large scar down the middle of the cadaver's chest. He replaced the sheet, turned, and nodded to the technician to remove the body.

"Anybody been to his apartment yet?" Kerry asked as they walked out of the morgue.

"Yeah. It's under police lockdown. They don't think this was a sui- cide," the second agent replied.

"They say why?"

"Aside from the fact that he could barely use one side of his body and could never crawl over the edge of the bridge to kill himself?" the second agent remarked with a sarcastic tone.

"Just asking," Kerry said, shoving his hands deep in his pockets as he walked slowly down the corridor. "He'd been out of the hospital for quite a while."

"That's true. There was another e-mail, like the ones we intercepted from Ulrich when he was in Honduras. Same tenor, same threats. I'd say Ulrich is back to his old tricks." The young agent handed a stick of gum to Kerry as they shuffled along. "If Fredericks did frame him, as we sus- pect, I'd say Ulrich had his ultimate revenge."

"And then some. What did the e-mail say?" Maybe his quarry slipped up and left the critical clue to close the noose.

"Said to meet him at the Clarion Hotel . . . that they needed to settle an old score. Apparently they did." The agent handed Kerry a short medical form. "The general was sauced, by the way."

"Figures," Kerry said as they walked. "He spent lots of time with a bottle. But it doesn't add up. We thought Ulrich was on a sub headed into the Med or up north—and now he's in Colorado?"

"We haven't had a reliable sniff on Ulrich since October. He could be anywhere."

"Have you been briefed on Ulrich's history after Fredericks railroaded him for that drinking incident?" Kerry asked.

"No. Why?"

Kerry stopped at a corner of the hallway, watching for prying ears. "The day Ulrich lost his last appeal, he showed up in London. Valid passport. He dropped off the net for years, until we connected the dots after his escape from Nicaragua."

"Where'd he go?"

"St. Petersburg, Russia. To some world-famous school for clowns, if you can believe it. And he apparently got in deep with the Russians. He took a post in Moscow, presumably with the circus. On the surface he's doing a clown gig, but he's also working the Russian submarine angle at the St. Petersburg shipyards."

"If he could move that easily and avoid detection, then that might explain how he slipped into the country to kill Fredericks. Could have come ashore anywhere."

"Bingo," Kerry said. "Have the police circulated Ulrich's picture?"

"No. You said to keep his name out of things."

"Good." Kerry looked down at the news clipping still in his hands. *Four star general found dead under Bijou bridge. Foul play?* Kerry added the months—nearly twenty-two—he'd been on this trail. He could almost imagine Ulrich falling into his grasp, but he knew it would never be that easy.

"Lay low," Kerry told his understudy. "Let Ulrich stick his head up; then we'll pop him."

Rex Edwards was alone, the glass cupola hanging silently above a vacant manufacturing floor late at night in January. The Crystal hummed with the quiet whisper of computer fans supplying cooling air to hundreds of processors and dozens of monitors throughout his nerve center. A CNN broadcast droned in the background. He pointed a remote control, and monitors around the Crystal sprang to life with new video live from Epsilon. These were NASA's direct feeds that only Mission Control could follow—or so NASA thought.

Rex turned toward one of the monitors, images of Michelle's private sleeping area, then Sean's, and finally John's. Everyone was awake and working. Bored by the lack of an interesting venue, Rex flipped back to Epsilon's system status screens where he could monitor the mission every step of the way to Mars. Voyeurism had become his consuming passion. Using the ship's deep-space communication system, there was no aspect of activity on Epsilon that he couldn't see. The CNN broadcast caught his attention, and he instantly shifted from space voyeur to news junkie.

"It's been a mistake from the beginning," said one female panelist with a French accent. "Long-duration space missions, with a mixed crew, are a terrible mistake."

"Ridiculous," said a second woman. "No data support that conclusion."

"Not true! NASA studies, MIR lessons learned, psychological profiles of crews wintering in Antarctica—they're all long-duration missions in isolated environments. Those lessons show that you need a balanced culture to survive for long periods of time. Mature pair-bonded couples are critical to crew morale and mission success. We all know that emotional and physical intimacy will enhance the crew cohesion. Oui?" She winked at the British-accented host.

The host smiled, too savvy, Rex thought, to let this Parisian hot-blood sucker him in. She continued. "But NASA only sent three astronauts—one of them a young woman, along with two aggressive dominant males. Since when is this balanced?"

The other female panelist huffed. "The most valid data are what we are observing at this very moment. The great experiment is working."

"What about Monsieur Wells?" the French woman protested. "He's alone for a month. Who will care for him? This mission is a recipe for disaster."

The second panelist interrupted again. "Presumptuous hyperbole. Wells has the nation's space endurance record. If anyone can take it, he can."

"This is real life, not a Rambo movie," the French woman objected. "The man has never been alone—desperately alone—for a month. Does solitary confinement mean anything to you? We should have followed Robert Zubrin's advice—launched a larger crew to Mars and stayed for eighteen months."

"Ladies," said the talk-show host as he interrupted them, "let's recall that this mission was flown out of necessity to gain quick understanding of the alien craft on Mars. It's a small crew, a quick mission, and a timely return; just what we asked for—and paid for. Every astronaut was well tested during tours on the Space Station and MIR. Two are married."

"Married or not, we have a dangerous petri dish with this mix of men and women," said the French woman. "We'll regret the day we stranded an astronaut in solitary confinement on the opposite end of the solar system. I hope that Captain Wells has an iron mental constitution. He'll certainly need it."

"Ridiculous!" Rex said, flipping the show off and returning to his secret view into Epsilon. "Everyone up there is just fine."

SATURDAY, FEBRUARY 9, 2013: CLEAR LAKE CITY, TEXAS

"I'm not as strong as all of you might like to believe," Amy said, standing before a packed women's group at her church, most of her slight frame hidden behind a garish podium. Her brown hair fell below her shoulders, held back with a single clasp.

"I suffer from a disease called obsessive-compulsive disorder, or OCD. And I have a husband who hears a calling that I can't completely understand. Either one can ruin your life if you let it. I almost did." Her friends' nods of support calmed her. *Here goes.*

"John's Navy deployments were hard. Besides the OCD, I suffer from diabetes, which requires incredible discipline to control. If you're a diabetic with OCD, you can go *overboard* with control. I did—when John left on frequent trips to do classified flight test work or chase subs around the Mediterranean. During his absences I'd be so focused on regimen that every minute of every day was planned, every surface cleaned, and I watched my food intake to the gram. That's no way to live.

"I learned a lot in those early years in the Navy. I learned about *myself.* I used to think my depression over John's absences was *his* fault, that my problem with obsessions—before I learned about OCD—was *his* fault—the result of having to deal with so much of life on my own, whether that was a new baby or moving to yet another house. But over time I realized that difficulties are normal in life. And *my* problems—while more traumatic during John's absence—are ultimately *my* problems. Not John's.

"Some of you might have OCD, others diabetes, but you all have at least one gremlin you're dealing with. If you didn't, you probably wouldn't be here, searching for healing and redemption. I don't advocate ignoring your doctor or tossing your medications, but I do have a message of healing and hope that goes beyond professional consultations. It's a message that has been burned into my soul since John left for Mars.

"My message is this: God provides. It's that simple. *God provides.* He can take you through any challenge. I'm not saying He'll do away with your problems and make your life perfect. It's conceited to expect God to spare us difficulty. But I can cope—through Christ—with all of the situations that life deals me. He strengthens us to cope *and* to endure. And He provides—if you trust Him completely.

"For the first few months John was gone to Mars, I fell back into my old ways. Flying the Shuttle or spending time on the Space Station is one thing. Flinging yourself to the end of the universe is quite another. I was mad at him, and I worried—all the time, every waking minute, and even into my dreams. I still worry. A lot. I got over being mad. It just ate away at my insides until God changed my heart—over time.

"Problems are part of living. You may have marital discord, suffer from depression or anxiety or eating disorders, or even be a triple dipper like me—with diabetes, OCD, and a spouse who's marching to a different beat. Perhaps you've endured cancer or lost a job. Or lost a loved one. In all those trials, Christ is the same friend and counselor, an immense source of strength. I go to Him in prayer every day, asking for others before myself, asking for Him to change my heart, to help me see problems through the eyes of others and to give me strength. I don't ask Him to take away my troubles; instead I ask Him to make Himself more real to me in the midst of my trials."

Amy moved to the side of the podium, picked up her contemporary language Bible, and thumbed to her favorite passage in Philippians. "Here's what Scripture says. It's balm to my soul."

> *Don't fret or worry. Instead of worrying, pray. Let petitions and praises shape your worries into prayers, letting God know your concerns. Before you know it, a sense of God's wholeness, everything coming together for good, will come and settle you down. It's wonderful what happens when Christ displaces worry at the center of your life.*

11

"DON'T LOCK THE BACK DOOR," Michelle said, hugging John for the first time he could ever remember. "We'll be back late. But we *will* be home."

John returned the squeeze. It felt good to hold another human being—and to be close to Michelle. For a fleeting moment, he wished he'd been more personable and available to her as a friend during the six-and-a-half-month voyage. But in his heart, he knew it was better that he not get too close—for both their sakes. Michelle held him in a prolonged embrace, then kissed his cheek.

"For good luck," she said, releasing him and darting through the airlock into the access tunnel to the Mars Lander.

John saw Sean watching the good-bye from the airlock portal. He felt like Sean had become almost possessive of Michelle in the past weeks—for whatever reason. John hated that dynamic of their recent crew life and pushed away thoughts of what might be wrong. He wasn't going to ask Sean—or Michelle—any more questions. He would let this issue of their private lives die—he hoped. Sean floated across the compartment and thrust out a hand.

"You'd better be here when I get back, Hawk," he said. "I'm depending on you."

"Ditto, Skipper. Bring me some trinkets. Maybe a T-shirt that says 'Mars.'"

"Sorry, pal. I'm out of cash." Sean squeezed John's hand and placed another hand on his forearm, his smile fading. His eyes locked with John's. "Seriously, though, I know you wanted with all your heart to make this trip. I really do wish you could go with us. I *mean* that." Sean squeezed his hand again and then looked away as if there was something he didn't want John to see. After a moment he released the grip and turned for the airlock. Soon Sean was out of sight, floating through the hatch into the lander's spacious interior.

The crew had tilted Epsilon's broad aero-shield out of the way, then backed Columbus—as they dubbed their capsule-like craft—out of its hangar, the cylindrical storage shed located forward of the airlock and flight deck. Sean then had repositioned Columbus alongside Epsilon at a joint airlock node. For a week after entering Martian orbit, they'd mapped the planet, configured systems, run diagnostics, and practiced final maneuvers for the landing. All was ready.

John looked out a viewing portal adjacent to the airlock and saw Michelle and Sean through a window in the lander. In silence, he watched his friends slide into their Mars pressure suits to prepare for the fiery descent to the surface. He pulled the massive, weightless hatch closed and checked Epsilon's pressurization. As the door sealed, he felt that familiar stab of pain that had robbed him of peace since their launch in late July. The hiss of pressurization, like the reverse of opening a soda can, was the spark that set his insides churning. It was official now. He was by himself.

"Columbus is free. Thrusters engaged." Sean's voice was steady, always the cool one in times of stress. The big lander looked like an Apollo capsule atop its own cylindrical base, and that combination sat on six flexible landing struts attached to an aero-shield. Small gas jets moved Columbus away from Epsilon. The two crews were officially separated.

John knew these images were making the long twenty-minute trip to Earth. In two months, Mars would be at its farthest from Earth in many years—2.4 astronomical units. Three-hundred-sixty million kilometers. They couldn't be any farther from home.

NASA and the world watched as Sean and Michelle slipped free of their home on Epsilon and prepared for the dangerous plunge into Mars's atmosphere. Occasionally John waved to the flight deck camera, hoping Amy and the kids were watching—but there was no possibility for conversation. With a communication roundtrip of more than forty minutes, NASA had wisely delegated all landing responsibilities to Sean. John would act as safety observer, and NASA would stay quietly out of the way—for the first time in history. There was no other way to do it—Houston was too far away to exert control—and John was glad for the autonomy that separation provided.

Mars rotated below him with a grandeur that kept pulling John back to the window or to the Mars view on the large flight deck screens. Sitting between the wall of spherical displays was like sitting in a balloon high over the Martian desert; he felt he could reach out and touch the planet.

"Fifty meters out, Sean. You're pulling away nicely. We have a clean data handoff from Epsilon to Columbus. The orbital parameters should be on your screen soon."

"They are. Copy all."

An hour later, all systems operating at nominal condition, John passed the final command. "I have you on vector now for insertion, Sean. Let 'er rip."

Michelle answered, her voice brimming with excitement. "Copy. Orbital burn in thirty seconds . . . mark."

Half a minute later, Michelle called again. "Firing now." A long orange spike-like plume emerged from the top of Columbus, showering sparks of burning solid fuel as it slowed the lander. They quickly dropped behind John's orbit, descending far below him.

The ache inside John demanded to be heard. He thought back to shutting the airlock hatch earlier that day; it had been like closing the final door in his private struggle. There was no going back. Any chance he might have had to see Mars, in person, disappeared with that final pressurization seal. Michelle and Sean were on their way. Without him.

His only ride to the planet fell away until it disappeared. He'd traveled more than four hundred million kilometers to the orbit of a planet he'd always dreamed he'd visit. And now he watched his friends take the ride of their lives into history, to the surface of Mars. In that moment, he understood, perhaps like no other man in history, how Moses felt standing atop Mount Pisgah after forty years of wandering in the wilderness, gazing into the Promised Land he was destined to see—but never reach.

Licking tongues of orange and red trailed back from the perimeter of the eight-meter-diameter aero-shield as the lander careened into Mars's outer atmosphere. Michelle was bathed in flame. All around her, through the portals at her three, six, nine, and twelve o'clock positions, she could see nothing but the glow of the fiery aero-shield, burning itself into oblivion in front of them on the plunge toward the surface. Glowing bits of expended heat shield whipped by the portals as the flames wrapped the ship in a blistering cocoon. Michelle imagined they must look like a giant meteorite as they ripped into the planet's thin carbon-dioxide atmosphere.

Electrodes on Sean and Michelle registered their pulse, respiration, and skin temperature, data that Michelle monitored as she scanned the instruments. Her bouncing view of the digital displays rattled her more than she'd expected, and she fought to keep her gaze moving from medical data to system functions and back to medical. But the turbulence increased to a penetrating vibration. Like a luggage strap buzzing in the airstream on a car's roof, the noise increased until it seemed to be sawing into her spine.

"This wasn't in the simulation, Sean. What is it?" she asked, trying to sound calm. Perspiration ran down her neck under the collar of her pressure suit. She couldn't do anything about the sweat. She was sealed in, helmet and all.

A heartrate alarm beeped in front of her. She reached forward, fighting the increasing G-load of the descent, and canceled the alarm. She was sure Sean had seen it. She willed herself to calm down. The intense vibration increased.

"Something's loose out there, Mich. No idea what it is."

"I was hoping you'd say 'system nominal.'"

"That noise is *not* nominal."

She saw him turn toward her, trying to get a look at her face. "You okay?" he asked.

Her voice cracked, but she steadied it. "Ready as ever. Ignore my heartrate alarm. All systems still GO. Landing video will be ready as soon as we pickle the aero-shield and deploy the chute." She gulped as they seemed to hit a bump in the rollicking ride. The flames increased in their intensity. The buzz ground her teeth, and her heartrate alarm beeped a second time.

Sean reached over and laid a gloved hand on the arm of her suit for a long moment. "It'll be done soon, Michelle. Get ready to grunt."

The vibrations were now so piercing that Sean had the sense of an electric palm sander welded to his forehead. He scanned his instruments again for some sign of the problem, seeking a way to fix it. But this fault defied him.

Sean had trained almost a year for this day, and, except for the intense vibrations, he relished the rough ride down through the carbon dioxide shell of the Red Planet. This was the crowning moment of his aviation career. He began to grunt, out of habit, as the G-load increased—a natural reaction to years of beating the blackout during high-G maneuvers in the F-18. As the force of gravity continued to rise, he settled into his seat like old times in the Super Hornet. He spoke in short bursts, grunting against the deceleration.

"Starts buckin' . . . now, Mich . . . You gotta . . . grunt, girl . . . Focus."

He scanned to his right, making sure she was conscious. The sudden G-load, something he'd handled easily on Earth, was a huge stress today after two hundred days of space flight and zero gravity.

For the next few minutes, they rattled and grunted through the worst of the deceleration. The flames began dissipating, and, as the craft slowed in the thickening atmosphere, the vibration also began to die. He glanced at Michelle's heart rate, glad it was dropping. "You still okay?" he asked, his voice warbling from the violent bouncing. She stretched out a thumb. *Probably ready to puke,* he thought, remembering his own barf session after his first high-G maneuver.

"Standby high-altitude chute deployment." His hands moved across an array of panels. "Get ready for a strong snap."

Moments later he felt like someone kicked him in the seat as the first drogue chute opened in the hot trail of the descending craft.

"Stand by. Here comes the next one . . . now!"

A second jolt slammed them much harder as five huge canopies scooped at the thin atmosphere, straining to slow their descent. Sean punched the air in jubilation just after the pounding punch of the five chutes. Columbus began descending more vertically, the G-loads now dissipated.

"Twenty kilometers downrange," Michelle said, as though accustomed to riding a wild roller coaster wrapped in a two-thousand-degree fireball with a chainsaw bolted to her ear. "Stand by to cut the shield." She reached forward and commanded the release of their nearly spent ablative aero-shield. "Bye-bye, baby." She punched the plasma switch.

"Video up yet?" Sean asked.

Michelle had hoped he'd say something historic or motivational after such a death-defying ride. But that was Sean. Not much of a communicator. He *was* a pilot, after all.

"Landing site's in range. Acquiring imagery now."

"Check. Gear extended, solid lock on all six struts," he said. Soon afterward, her video displays came to life. One showed five monster zinnias stretched tight above their ship. Another video acquired the landing site in the distance as they continued screaming toward an alien planet, its plain speckled with NASA's toys and alien spiders, but devoid of human life.

"Michelle," Sean said in a firm voice. "Pass me the imagery of the primary site."

Sean's voice had changed—lower, slower, and with an authority she'd not heard since leaving Earth's orbit. In her helmet speaker she could hear him take a deep breath. His heart rate had jumped fifteen beats a minute in the past thirty seconds.

"I need that image *now,* Michelle."

Michelle touched her plasma screen and patched the image of their landing area to Sean's display. "What is it, Sean? Lock on is correct. I don't—" She choked mid-sentence as she saw the video image again. She turned to Sean, sweat gleaming on his face.

"Begin video acquisition of Alternate Site Alpha," he said, his hands moving in a flurry over his command panel. "I'm altering the descent profile—now."

Michelle marked the alternate landing site with digital crosshairs on her monitor, a spot two kilometers southwest of their original landing zone. The surface was coming up fast; they were only minutes from touchdown. The expanding rock-free area planned for their landing grew in size, and as the resolution improved, Michelle stared in disbelief at two spider-like craft, distinct silver eight-legged somethings, walking from the Viking site toward the original landing area. The capsule would land before the spiders arrived, but it would have fallen on top of them had Sean not deviated to the alternate site. Her skin crawled as she watched, all memories forgotten of the rough ride from orbit. The spiders were crystal clear in her video, advancing on pointed silver jointed legs that crossed dust and rock toward their intended touchdown zone. It was as if they'd known that she and Sean were coming.

Attitude control jets and their descent engine fired as Columbus settled into its final five thousand meters of transit to Mars's surface. Sean shook his head to dislodge sweat running into his eyes under the helmet.

Gravity and stress worked him harder than he'd been tested since his first carrier landing twenty-five years ago. He loved it.

"Final descent protocol. Thrust vector nominal. On target for Alternate Alpha," he said into the helmet microphone.

"Roger ball," John replied, a reminder that both were Navy pilots and Sean was lined up on approach, as though following the "meatball"—the multicolored stack of lights—that would direct him to a perfect three-wire landing on the deck of the USS Eisenhower.

"What?" Michelle asked.

"'Roger ball.' Navy talk for 'on glide path, on glide slope.'"

"If you say so. The video shows no major obstacles. You're cleared for approach." She paused. "And those spiders are still moving our way."

He shook more sweat free, straining to see through stinging eyes and the dried salt staining the inside of his visor.

"Fifteen hundred meters, nominal profile," Michelle said in a stressed voice as he scanned the instruments and she monitored the alien greeting committee.

"They're stationary now, Sean. They've stopped their advance toward the site. Altitude one thousand meters—mark!"

Sean made last-minute thrust adjustments to slow the descent of the craft, and two minutes later, his retro engine firing at maximum, the craft settled perfectly on six gangly legs. The big engine blasted pristine talcum powder-like red Martian dust all about them. The roar of the descent stage quieted, the *whoosh* of the vernier control jets was gone, and all movement stopped. For a brief but memorable moment, no one moved or said anything. The sun shone through a portal to Sean's left. Mars lay solid under Columbus as Sean keyed his communication link to John and to Earth.

"Houston, this is Mars Base One. Columbus has landed!"

12

"**PRUDENT PRIOR PLANNING** precedes perfect performance," Marv Booker said as he addressed the large audience of news reporters and government officials at the space center. As the associate administrator for manned space flight, he was the lead NASA bureaucrat handling the press. Marv was glad to be home in his old stomping grounds near LaMarque, Texas, and even happier to be preparing for a historic first step on the Red Planet. Marv shared the podium with Rex Edwards, Jack Schmidt, the director of flight operations, the Johnson Space Center's Director Greg Church, and Dan Jefferson, the Mars Mission flight director.

Rex Edwards reached for a microphone on the white cloth-covered table that stretched out before the men. "Prudent prior planning, I might add, Marv, that was conducted by Delta V Corporation in the design of Epsilon and Columbus. It was a flawless landing for a *reason*—I anticipated every contingency." Rex settled back in his seat, and Marv continued with his response to queries from the press.

"Thanks, Rex. I should have qualified my earlier remarks. Clearly, the advance planning by Delta V Corporation made today's success possible. Next question?"

A reporter near the back waved at Marv, catching his eye because of her height and calm demeanor. "Yes, ma'am. In the back."

"Adrienne Packard. *Aerospace News*. Can you comment on the high-pitched vibration that Captain O'Brien and Dr. Caskey reported yesterday during the descent?"

"I'll take that," Rex said, taking the microphone again. "Hello again, Ms. Packard. Glad you could join us today. The vibration was caused by a loose linkage between the aero-shield and lander. The ferocity of the reentry set up a harmonic vibration, but it had no adverse impact."

"A follow up, please?" she asked.

Rex nodded.

"Now that the crew is on the surface, and the alien craft have—shall we say—come over for a look, how will you protect the lander should there be a confrontation?" A murmur rippled through the audience, and Adrienne responded immediately. "It's not such an outlandish proposition. We do have images of children pinned to the ground by these things—whatever they are."

"Agreed, Ms. Packard," Marv responded. "The truth is that our crew does have self protection. I'm not at liberty to discuss it in this forum. But you can rest assured there is a 'plan B.'" Marv frowned as more voices suddenly chimed in.

"*Please*, ladies and gentlemen," he said, raising his hands. "We don't anticipate any difficulties. The Rover was met peacefully by the alien craft. Dr. Kanewski apparently had no conflict with them, and neither did his nephew, a young boy who led them with a hank of bailing twine. The child in Ivory Coast suffered no permanent harm or apparent contamination. I assure you, measures will be taken with the utmost concern for crew safety. Nevertheless, there is a reasonable expectation that this meeting will be historic—*and peaceful.*"

SATURDAY, FEBRUARY 23, 2013: EPSILON, MARTIAN ORBIT

John configured the wraparound screens of the flight deck to display a panorama of the dusty rock-strewn Martian plains surrounding Columbus. Supplying a second set of eyes for Sean and Michelle using the camera mounted on top of the lander, he provided a stunning view of the surrounding area. It looked like a Martian parking lot with all the robotic craft. Someone at JPL once commented that Mars was a robot junkyard, considering all the missions that had crashed into the planet or died over time. John would do everything in his power from his remote vantage to make sure there were no more failures.

Chryse Planitia, the wide, low plain surrounding the Viking 1 landing site, was strewn with small rocks, thousands of them, the size of basketballs or smaller. The jagged gray rocks, many of them volcanic in origin, lay in a bed of red dust, powdery drifts driven against the base of every stone by the light carbon dioxide winds that blew across the bone-dry planet. JPL estimated that there had been ponds of water—acid-filled, red-tinted shallow pools—as little as two million years ago. There was no moisture apparent now—at least, not yet. But Michelle would soon be on the hunt for signs of water—and life.

The panorama ranged from a ruddy rust red to reddish orange. After only a few minutes in the surround-view display mode, John began to realize how much he missed the color green. The deep, thick green of St. Augustine lawns, tall fragrant green pines, and the lush, succulent green of West Virginia hay fields. Here, on Mars, there was only dry dust, dark grey rock, and red—everywhere dusty rusty red.

Except, that is, for one spot to the northeast of their location. There, two silver eight-legged spiders waited. Beyond the silver, he could see Rover's gold metallic covering and the white of the ancient dirty Viking Lander. The plains were crowded with landers. Five of them, including the manned capsule.

"Columbus, Houston." NASA was calling. It was time. "Mission Control confirms you are GO for EVA. Be advised that Raines predicts the craft will make the first move. We're not endorsing him, but he's been correct every time. Take appropriate precautions, as detailed in your briefings. Carry a big stick. *Read back, over.*"

Great, thought John. Those last three words added forty minutes to the wait. *Twenty minutes for Houston to hear Sean and another twenty for us to hear them say they heard us.* This could take all day if every command required a read-back confirmation. But perhaps it was worth it. After all, Malcolm Raines did seem to have the gift. If the aliens were hostile, an extra forty minutes to be fully coordinated probably wasn't a bad idea.

And "carry a big stick"? Was that Houston's idea of secure communications? They might as well tell the world what was about to happen. The space-age spider-killing version of a shark bang stick, up to this point a classified element of the mission meant for dealing with recalcitrant silver aliens, would be in Sean's hands as he stepped out. But Houston didn't have to tell the world about it.

No one wanted to think about, much less debate, the consequences of an armed struggle on Mars. Just as two years ago no one had wanted to discuss the potential that the arriving alien probe might possibly be coming into orbit when John and his crewmates were on the Space

Station. John realized he was starting to sound like a conspiracist. Imagine the intergalactic headlines, he thought, if they muffed this Martian weapon thing. "Humans assault friendly arachnids on Red Planet. *Homo sapiens* armed and dangerous."

COLUMBUS LANDER, CHRYSE PLANITIA, MARS

"You all buckled up, Mich?" Sean asked, tapping his helmet and then hers. She nodded.

"All set. Thanks for your help," Michelle said, patting his helmet in return.

"You're welcome. Got everything?"

Michelle nodded again. "Spider repellant, core sample tool, a spade—and this lamp." She waved a NASA space flashlight in his direction. "I'm set."

"Then let's do it," Sean said, with his usual blunt lack of flair. He moved out of the eight-meter-diameter living and science area into the airlock.

Michelle joined him, closing the motorized access door behind them. Sealed inside the tiny space, Michelle felt a sudden twinge of claustrophobia. "I'm fine," she replied when Sean rested his hand for a long time on her shoulder.

"Better not plan to argue with me," Sean said as the lock decompressed—words she hoped weren't being recorded for posterity. Neither astronaut wanted to read later about committing some verbal gaffe in the last minutes before stepping into history.

"I don't *agree* with you, no. But I won't argue. I'm honored—you know that. But don't you dare do this to be chivalrous."

"Shoot no, little lady. This is *history*. This gesture will get me a date with any woman on Earth."

Michelle turned toward him, aware that he was trying hard to punch her emotional buttons—and he'd succeeded. She chided herself for any concern about what Sean thought about other women. She was married—what did she care? Yet, for some reason, she *did* care.

She tried to force her personal thoughts into the background. The last two months had exposed personal weaknesses she'd never dreamed she was vulnerable to. Today, of all days, she needed to be rational and not driven by emotions.

Sean moved to the exterior hatch as the lock pressure equalized to the cold Martian environment. Her heart pounded as Sean began to crack the access door.

"Houston, I'm opening the hatch now."

Michelle knew this was a ruse, and after he said it, Sean waved at her. His distinct intent was to have a woman touch the soil of the new planet first. Few people remembered that Buzz Aldrin was the second man on the Moon, but many knew him for his commitment to space exploration. Sean had said many times he'd rather be remembered as Buzz than Neil Armstrong.

"If *you* go second," Sean had said to her last night as they watched for the small rocky moons, Phobos and Diemos, from the seclusion of a darkened lander, "you're so quiet that the world will forget you—forever."

"Quiet?" she'd said with a laugh, playfully pushing him away from the portal.

"Yep. You're a shrinking violet. A true Martian wallflower. So you're definitely going first."

Now Sean gave *her* the playful push—toward history.

"It's all yours, Mich. I'll cover you," Sean said, pulling the big spider-killer pole alongside him. "Ladies first!"

CLEAR LAKE CITY, TEXAS

Amy adjusted the volume on the television to hear better over the chatter of four hyper children. The only children of Martian explorers. As the moment drew nearer for Sean and Michelle to step out of the airlock hatch for the first time, she checked her watch, straining against the limitations of light speed. About now, her friends were stepping on the surface of Mars, and she had to wait at least twenty minutes to see it.

She tried to focus on the news report, but her mind kept drifting back to John. She ached for him—to touch him, to have his fatherly influence part of their family again, to talk and to laugh—and she ached for *him*, knowing he'd give up almost anything to be in Sean's shoes. Or his Mars boots.

The medication had worked, and she wanted to share that news with him in person. She'd told him, but you had to live with her to see the kind of changes taking place in her life. The kids could tell. Life was more peaceful, between the regulating effect of her medication and her surrender to God's control of things beyond her own. Amy squeezed Alice's hand and turned her attention back to the newscast.

"We will watch Captain O'Brien through four sets of eyes today," the commentator said on the news broadcast. Amy's heart raced as though she were watching the drawn-out climax of a thriller movie. "Rover is watching from a perspective beyond the alien spiders. As we have for the past months, we'll also be watching the still imagery transmissions from the alien craft—two of them—both squatting, as you can see, very close to Columbus. And this perspective," he said, showing an image of Columbus and the landing area from atop the tall craft, "comes to us from the telescoping mast above the ship. With it you can see to the northeast and, two or three kilometers away, the silent Viking 1 lander."

Amy watched the automatic panning of the camera as it zoomed in on the soiled Viking 1, part of the dusty Martian landscape for the past thirty-seven years, a lonely white sentinel that had observed thousands of blue sunsets and pale yellow skies. The images shifted to a close-up of Columbus's partially opened airlock hatch, as viewed by the still camera of an alien. Whatever the spiders saw, so did humanity, their signals monitored through the deep space network. Wherever the spiders went on Mars—but curiously, not on Earth—humans managed, through some unexplained capability, to go along for the ride.

"These next pictures from Rover show just how close the spiders have approached Columbus," the commentator explained. "The arrival of the Mars Rover seven months ago added a new dynamic, giving NASA an ability to take a camera—Rover's camera—directly to the alien and Viking landing site. When Rover landed that harrowing morning in July last year, she was forced into an escape across the plain, running from pursuing twin alien craft. The two aliens hemmed Rover in against Viking 1 with nowhere left to turn, and their cameras provided an unparalleled look at the chase through the perspective of the two pursuers. That day ended as it did for Dr. Kanewski in Florida, with the presentation of a golden orange-sized sphere that changed color to blue as Rover grasped it in a mechanical claw."

A second commentator chimed in as Amy saw the hatch fully open on Columbus. "This is truly an uncanny sight, watching the aliens—and watching them observe us. We have both perspectives. Engineers at the Jet Propulsion Laboratory have been receiving these still-image transmissions, in a modified Viking 1 format, since our first pictures came from Mars in 2011. Wait! Captain O'Brien, the first man on Mars, should be going down the ladder very soon. Perhaps within a few moments."

The network stitched all four perspectives together on the television. Long distance video from Rover, a close overhead shot, and two stills from the spider craft. The long-range view from Rover was less clear. NASA would bring her in from the rear if some defenses or her camera were needed, the commentator explained.

Malcolm Raines's voice rang in Amy's memory, his latest glory-stealing prognostication that "they will make the first move" setting her nerves on edge. She watched with her kids and the rest of the world as she waited for Sean to step into the open and for the alien craft to respond.

She got only half of what she'd expected.

Rover's camera showed a figure in the door. "He's there!" Amy exclaimed, pulling Alice closer. As she said it, he turned to his side, extending an arm toward a smaller figure and helped her, in a clumsy white Mars explorer suit, to reach the ladder. Michelle would set foot on Mars first!

"What?" Abe protested, rising up on his knees.

"It's perfect!" Amy blurted, pulling Abe back down to a sitting position so that she could see.

"Ladies first?" Abe asked in a mocking tone.

"And don't you forget it, young man!" Amy responded, pinching him playfully on the shoulder. "What a gentleman!"

"Whatever . . ." Abe said.

As Michelle turned and took hold of the ladder, no doubt handling gravity and the bulky suit with some difficulty, the two still images from the aliens began to change in perspective.

"Spider one and two are moving!" the first commentator said in an excited voice. "It's confirmed by Rover. Her video shows them closing on Columbus!"

NASA had programmed such a sophisticated level of autonomy

into this mechanical rover that it would have begun to move at the first sign of alien action. Only moments later the Rover's video imagery began to jerk, a clear sign that she was closing in.

Michelle descended the ladder first, with Sean following, carrying a long yellow and red pole. The spiders seemed to be moving faster now, as imaged by the Columbus camera. Rover's camera was bouncing, unable to keep the two astronauts in focus as she rolled along the uneven terrain.

In a brief lull of commentary, Amy reacted in shock to the movement of the spiders. Albert spoke up in a strong voice. "It's okay, Mom, they just want to say hello."

13

"SPIDERS ARE ON THE MOVE, Sean! Forty meters and closing. Get off that ladder!"

John tried keeping his voice calm, but failed. He watched the advancing spiders, measuring their distance with a laser range finder mounted on Columbus's telescoping mast camera. John was the eyes and ears of the mission from his orbit six hundred kilometers above the planet. Using a small data relay satellite they'd placed in a Mars stationary orbit when Epsilon first arrived, he was able to communicate with Columbus as his ship circled the planet.

Michelle stepped off the ladder, Sean five rungs behind her. She turned toward the approaching silver craft, then back to Sean to help him to the surface.

"Thirty meters. You've got about two minutes—max," John said.

"Copy. I'm off the ladder," Sean said, his huffing a sign that the

Mars gravity and space suits were something to contend with after six-and-a-half gravity-free months in space. John was sure that their day and a half acclimatizing to Mars's reduced gravity hadn't been enough. "Spider repellant armed and ready," Sean said, panting.

John watched Michelle stop and face Sean. "They *distracted* us, Sean," she said. "We forgot to say something!" Michelle turned toward the alien craft, now twenty meters away and moving steadily forward on pointed legs.

"Later," Sean said. "After we put this problem behind us."

"We'll do it now!" Michelle insisted. She took hold of the giant bang stick, planting it firmly in the soil as Sean held on, and pointed toward the camera on top of the lander. Sean's gaze followed her point. "For America ... and for the human race ... in the spirit of discovery."

"Great. Now turn around," Sean snapped.

The two craft stopped their approach at ten meters. Sean and Michelle stood near the ladder, the pole in Sean's hands ready if the closest spider threatened. He would shove it into the alien underbelly, exploding a large shell to cripple it. Sean could flip the pole over and have the other end shoved into a second spider in a moment if need be. John prayed as he watched, hopeful they would never need that precaution.

Michelle spoke, calmer than either of the men. "They've stopped, Sean. I'm going forward."

"Let's just wait and see what happens."

John watched Michelle turn to Sean. "We've gotta take our lives in our own hands," she said. "We can't be asking permission for every action, remember?" She faced the spiders. "I'm going forward. Are you with me?"

"I could order you not to," he said.

"You could," she said, moving a step closer to the visitors as the spiders began to advance.

Sean gave her a small shove. "You're right. Go ahead. I've got your six."

✳

Michelle fought to calm herself and ignore the sweat that soaked her cooling undergarments. She shivered as the salty wetness chilled her inside the suit. Her hands shook a little as she reached inside her left leg cargo pocket and pulled out a small baseball-sized item. It just fit in the palm of her gloved hand, and she made sure that Sean couldn't see it from his vantage behind her. He'd know soon enough.

Michelle moved toward the pair of slow-moving spiders. Their ellipsoidal pod-shaped bodies measured a good two meters to the tops of their backs, and their heads on gangly snake-like hoses accounted for another meter of height. Michelle felt dwarfed. Each spear-like spider leg sank into red dust. Michelle had seen how sharp those leg tips were in images from the Ivory Coast and from the pursuit of Rover on Mars seven months ago. Forty meters beyond the spiders, she saw Rover stop, the robot's ungainly wheels and elevated mast in sharp contrast to the sleek silver creatures before her. Her hand palm down, Michelle extended her arm and took another step.

"You're pushing your luck, Mich."

"Stay behind me to my right, Sean. Keep our insurance ready. Remember, these guys have done nothing but give gifts—up to this point."

"Your call. I'm a pilot, not a negotiator."

Michelle could occasionally see the yellow and red banded pole out the side of her visor and Sean following immediately to her right and one step back. He was poised to ram the high explosive into its guts if a spider so much as sneezed on her. She forgot her sweat-soaked chill for a moment, warmed by Sean's protection.

Hand extended, Michelle approached within two meters of the alien pair. She raised her left hand, palm out in greeting, then turned her right hand over. A clear globe was balanced in her palm.

"Where'd you get that?" Sean said, his voice gruff. She could imagine what the controllers in Houston would say twenty minutes later when they saw what she'd presented. This time delay to Earth was a blessing, in a way. She and Sean were on their own — for now.

"Didn't want to come out empty handed," she said, staring straight ahead and wondering if the spiders, or whatever intelligence was behind them, could hear her talk — or even understand her. "John gave it to me. Seemed appropriate." She held her arm stiff, hoping for a sign of recognition from one of the creatures. The one on her left began to move forward, and as it did, its partner stepped back, relinquishing the lead.

"Be . . . careful . . ." Michelle heard John whisper, measuring his words as he watched from the other side of the planet. "Rover's ten meters out if you need her."

"Copy. See the grapples, Sean? They're descending. Just like they told us might happen. And they're pulling out an orb!"

"They'd better not play footsy," Sean said. "I'd rather not have to use this thing."

She could see the tip of the pole to her right, poised for the explosive thrust. Rammed into the body of the spider, a five-centimeter-diameter charge would ignite and force a depleted uranium explosive round into the body. Or so the Army had assured them. She had no desire to spray alien guts all over the place. "Hold on, Sean. Watch!"

With her arm starting to quiver, Michelle willed herself to remain calm as two metal grapples on long flexible hose-like arms snaked into the underbelly of the craft and pulled out what she'd dreamed of for months: A brilliant golden orb the size of a large orange shone like a miniature sun in the grasp of the alien. The two grapples clutching the sphere flexed from under the belly out toward her and extended the prize to within a few centimeters of her own hands. With remarkable dexterity, the right grapple took the orb in its clutches, holding the gift toward Michelle. She lowered the palm of greeting and extended her own arm, hesitating just a finger's width from touching the ball.

She'd seen it a hundred times on the replay of Rover's encounter, the moment of contact when the orb would flash a blinding blue, then dull to a warm azure glow. *It killed Dr. K,* she thought, *and my heart's about to explode.*

Michelle reached further and connected with the golden ball. Despite the reflective gold-tinted sun visor, the flash nearly blinded her. She saw Sean pull the pole back, as though momentarily startled. She stood her ground.

As her eyesight gradually recovered, Michelle lifted her arm and placed her own fragile gift in the empty grapple of the alien. As though gifted with a human's delicate sense of touch, the spider gently grasped the glass globe and lifted it. A head that looked like a football on the end of a silver hose, just as little Simon Kanewski had described, descended from a meter above her and regarded the interplanetary gift. Then, with one unblinking eye on its front, the head moved down within half a meter of Michelle's helmet, as though trying to peer through the reflective tint of her visor, but instead seeing its own reflection. Michelle could see herself in the glassy eye of the spider. The head withdrew, and the grapples came together, carefully lifting the clear globe into its belly. Then the craft stepped backward.

Michelle relaxed.

"What is it, Mom?" Arthur asked. The family was sitting on the floor in front of the television in the den, and Sharon Walters had dropped by to watch history unfold with the America's most famous space wife. Amy and Sharon leaned forward, straining to make out the glass-like globe filled with white, green, and red in Michelle's hand, far away on another planet. The object was unlike anything she'd ever heard John describe for the mission.

"What in the world is that?" Sharon asked.

Amy knew she'd seen the globe before; she wracked her brain for some idea where.

"Maybe it's a weapon," Abe offered.

"Could be," Amy responded, "but your dad never mentioned this. Perhaps it's just what it looks like — a gift."

Alice jumped up and put her finger on the screen, to the boys' protests. "No! I know what it is!" she cried.

"Sit down, Alice," Abe said. "Let's watch."

"What, Alice?" Amy asked, reaching for her excited daughter. "Do you know?"

"Uh huh!" she exclaimed, pulling her mother toward the television.

"You do?" she replied in surprise. She put an arm around Alice and stared at the sphere in the grapple of the spider.

"You gave it to me! For Christmas!" She turned to her brothers and Mrs. Walters, her voice filled with glee. "It's a snow globe!"

"You want to interview *me*?" Amy asked a few minutes later, incredulous. "But why?"

"For starters, you're the only mother married to a Mars astronaut,"
the voice on the phone said, "but more to the point, I heard about your
talk to your church group. You've got a message—call it a voice, if you
want—for millions of women who are struggling with untold pres-
sures. Somehow, you manage to hold it all together. People need to hear
that."

Amy shook her head in wonder.

"What? What is it?" Sharon asked, coming up behind her from the
den and the Martian show. "Did you say *American Moms Magazine*?"
She was bouncing on her toes, all ninety pounds of her tiny frame alive
with emotion. "This is *huge*!"

Amy smiled and pushed the effervescent Sharon back toward the
den. "Ms. Behimer, I'm incredibly honored by your offer," Amy said,
"but can we talk about this a little later? The astronauts are on Mars, and
I'd really like to watch. I promise, I'll consider your offer. And I do want
to share my testimony if it will help other women cope."

"Amy! Go, girl!" Sharon shrieked as Amy hung up the phone and
hurried back to the den. "You'd better do this, you hear me? People
need you!"

EPSILON, MARTIAN ORBIT

"You did it!" John exclaimed to Michelle on their internal communication link once they'd returned to the base of the lander. It was painful to watch the activity on the planet's surface and realize he could
never join them.

"Uh-huh. That snow globe will have their scientists guessing for years about us," she replied, holding the blue alien sphere with two hands as she and Sean watched the spiders retreat toward Rover and Rover back up to maintain a safe separation.

"I kind of like it," Sean said. "Has sort of a retro feel to it. Like that wacky movie where they carried a galaxy around in a cat's necklace," he said. "But I still don't understand how you happened to have that on you. And why the water in it didn't freeze in this cold. It's forty below."

"It's *alcohol*," John said, butting in over the radio. "I told Mich I thought it would be a nice touch. And there's still something we need to consider," John said as Michelle reached the ladder with the azure orb in hand.

"Yeah, what's that?" Sean asked, putting a foot on the first rung.

"Do you really want to take that alien thing inside?"

"Ooh—good point," Sean said, stopping his climb. "We have no idea what it is."

"You're right there, John," Michelle said, stopping her walk to Columbus, and holding the orb in front of her. "This could be a Trojan Horse."

PHOENIX, ARIZONA

Malcolm Raines stood ten meters tall, a giant video image on the supersized screen in his massive coliseum church in Phoenix. "Welcome to the Race of Fathers!" he began in a scratchy baritone. He felt like he'd been speaking for days, but it didn't matter—the immense overflow crowd was a double methamphetamine jolt, energizing him for his ministry and mission. "Today we have made the *second* great step!"

The crowd rose, applauding, then sat down at his gesture.

"The first great step—*master the genetic arts*. We have made great strides in this area, yet there is still so much to do. The second great step, *carry our seed to other planets*. Did you see tonight? Did you notice, as we replayed the day's historic events, that it was Eve, not Adam, who placed the first foot on the next planet? The fertile womb of womankind was first to Mars—Eve—the bearer of life! And she received the perfect sphere, the shining blue.

"First the Father Race presented their gift to a machine, to Rover—seven months ago. Then to man, the late Dr. Robert Kanewski. And they reserved the greatest honor, the finale, for *woman*. Did you notice that of the three recipients, only *she* gave a gift in return? Remarkable! We have taken the second step. We have met our makers on another planet. Only one step remains!"

Raines strode across the stage and bowed to a guest in the front row. Newly inaugurated Vice President Lance Ryan, in his second term and flanked by four expressionless secret service agents, nodded in return.

"They will meet us, in less than a month, on Mont Saint Michel. There we will commune with these emissaries and learn their final message for us." He swept his hand in a wide arc. "Now! Go into the world! I give you this new commission, to share the news of the Father Race, to invest yourselves in the genetic arts, and to prepare!" He was finished and the thunderous applause began.

Raines stood still, arms raised, smiling broadly, immersed in the celebration of his vision. While three astronauts took America to Mars, he had plans to embark on an even bolder mission—a foray into the genetic core of humanity. He had all the support he needed in the front row—access to the highest levels of government. This was his time.

The Father Race would be proud.

✳

"I am honored, Mr. Vice President," Malcolm said in his private conference room later that evening. "It is good to have you with us again, sir." He gripped Vice President Ryan's hand like an old friend.

"You, too, Malcolm. You've accomplished some amazing things. Impressive service, by the way. Now, down to business." He handed over an official envelope, with the vice president's seal on both sides. "These are your 'friendly' contacts — everything you'll need to accomplish your plan. Control this information in the strictest manner possible — or we'll both hang. Understand?"

"Thank you, sir. I understand. The Chinese laboratories are ready to begin work on the DNA profiling. They await only my shipment of tissue and blood samples. And funding."

"Full genetic profiles, right?" the vice president asked.

"Yes. We have purchased twenty million tissue and blood specimens to date. I can have another two million tissue donations available within a month. And the Chinese want to start processing immediately."

The vice president clapped his hands. "Perfect! We'll have a whopper of a DNA database for genetic research. I'll make sure the seed money is there. After that, you'd better deliver." He nodded to a grim-faced agent who spoke into a cuff mike. The other thee agents stiffened, ready to spring.

"Look at the payoff," the vice president said as he headed for the door. "Your gene bank — and your bank account — will be overflowing if this comes together. You may even find that perfect defect-free Father Race guy you've been searching for. I don't give a rip. I just want those profiles. We're going to put America on the biotech map. For good."

Raines nodded as his guests prepared to depart. "You will be pleased, Mr. Vice President."

The veep waved at the dour agents who made an immediate circle around him, heading out the double door. He spoke back over his shoulder.

"Venture Forth, Malcolm. You pull this off and we'll *both* be on a billionaire path to genetic perfection."

EPSILON, MARTIAN ORBIT

John touched the screen in his compartment, lingering over Amy's image on the computer monitor. How he longed to touch her, to hold her in his arms, and to play with his kids. He closed his eyes in thanksgiving for Amy, for the children, and for his many blessings, then prayed prayers of support for Sean and Michelle and for their hearts.

He slipped into the soft sleeping sack and curled naturally into the classic fetal position for a sleeping astronaut, arms floating free in front of him, bent slightly at the elbows, his knees drawn up a bit toward his chest. He willed himself to clear his mind, the activities of the day ricocheting inside his head: Sean and Michelle waking up to their second day on Mars, preparing for their first EVA and a possible confrontation with the spiders. The aliens moving in just as Raines had predicted, and their gift of the classic gold orb, the third such presentation. Then Michelle's gift of the snow globe that he'd given her two days before.

She'd carried through as he'd asked, and the thought brought a smile to his face. The little miniature world would frustrate the alien scientists—if they existed—when they tried to decipher the deep spiritual significance of a winter ecosystem, with a miniature house, sleigh, and blizzard. He could imagine some foreign race stating that humans can shrink and encapsulate life-forms. That was the beauty of his present. And now it was inside the craft—listening.

He shook off the memory of the day he'd received the globe from Special Agent Kerry, and the lengths he'd gone to in order to sneak it onto the ship. Director Church would undoubtedly be mad that he hadn't been consulted. John would take a slap on the wrist in stride. It was worth it.

His brain simply would not shut down as he rolled in zero-G, seeking a comfortable position. Somewhere between wake and sleep, his mind still in overdrive but his body demanding rest, an idea nibbled at the edge of his consciousness, trying to tickle his mind awake long enough to register, to remember. Dreams and reality mixed, until suddenly his eyes popped open, the inspiration on his lips.

321. Kerry's magical number *did* have more meaning, much more, than he'd realized days earlier when he'd sent his first analysis to Kerry with ideas for how the motif played in this drama. Why the number—and its significance—popped into his head now, he could only wonder.

AD 321. A famous day in the annals of Christendom, the year in which Emperor Constantine decreed that no work be done on the *first* day of the week—Sunday in modern vernacular. Thus began the battle of the Sabbatarians, a divisive religious debate over why Sunday—the first day—was holy and Saturday—the last—was for work. 321—the year it was decreed that the Holy Day would be celebrated on the same day of the week that God spoke the universe into existence.

John stripped himself free of the sleeping sack and pushed over to the computer in his private compartment, searching "321." What had Kerry said? 321 cubic centimeters and 321 grams. That was the density of water: one gram per cubic centimeter. The density against which all other densities on Earth were measured. If it was an exact duplicate of the orb on Earth, then the aliens had given Michelle a perfect blue sphere that was the color and precise density of water. Why?

The first day of the week, the day of creation, the modern Sunday, established as holy in AD 321. A brilliant blue sphere the density of water. The speed of sound at sea level on Earth—three hundred twenty one meters per second—possibly important to a silver craft that communicated through sound using three octaves and twenty-one notes—again, 321. And the Dellanoy number. What of that, and the uniqueness of the number sequences? It was all too perfect—but what was the common clue? Speed, volume, density, mass, timing, and direction. Like jumbled jigsaw pieces, all the parts stared back at him.

Fatigue weighted his eyelids, and he could no longer maneuver the dense maze of data. He turned off his screen and floated back to the sack, crawling in and shutting down his busy brain, this time in only moments. He was finally at peace. There was a clue waiting for him. He'd let his head process the problem while he slept and hit it again in the morning.

Minutes later, John began to dream. Vivid, colorful, combative dreams. Dreams of a Trojan Horse.

14

**SUNDAY, FEBRUARY 24, 2013:
CHRYSE PLANITIA, MARS**

"THEY'RE GONE!"

"Are you sure, John?" Sean asked, grumbling and nursing a sore shoulder as he spoke on the radio. "When did they leave?"

"That's John? The aliens left?" Michelle sat up, awake.

Sean rubbed a bump on his head while she crawled out of her sleep sack. He'd jumped out of his bunk and fallen on his face, forgetting gravity in deep slumber. He handed a headset to Michelle and sat down next to her on her bunk.

"I woke up about half an hour ago," John said. "I uploaded the files from the Columbus camera. They left last night."

"It's *still* night," Sean said, his voice raspy.

"Not for long. Sunup's in half an hour, and I'll make a direct overhead pass with the telescope just after that. I haven't called Houston yet."

Sean stood and walked to each of four glass portals. The alien landers were nowhere to be seen. Rover sat where they'd told her to park, fifty meters northeast of the lander.

"Go ahead and call Houston," Sean said. "Mission Control will want to know what's up." He rubbed his face hard, the two days of stubble demanding attention.

"It'll take about an hour to hear back from them."

Sean removed the headset and ran his fingers through his short gray hair. He stared at Michelle who stood adjusting her clothing carefully and slowly. Her vestibular system was as messed up as his was, and she leaned against his shoulder to steady her wobbling. He breathed deeply, enjoying the faint scent of her skin lotion as she took her first step of the morning.

EPSILON

"Got 'em," John said out loud. Now that he'd been alone for three days, he was discovering that he talked to himself all the time. Maybe that was natural. Amy said it was a sign of old age. But he was probably just lonely.

The alien craft were five kilometers southeast of Columbus, crouched close together. This overhead pass by Epsilon was perfect. He kept the telescope system running at maximum magnification to capture all he could, zooming in for remarkable detail from six hundred kilometers.

His pulse quickened as he saved the high resolution images, calculating the time until the aliens and Columbus rotated into view of the Earth and when he would be on the other side of the planet. He'd only beat them by twelve minutes. In that dozen extra minutes, he had to hope his e-mail would find Scott O'Grady so that he'd be listening when

Mars rose. This might be Earth's last chance to record the aliens' transmissions. The spiders could be gone soon.

"They're five kilometers southeast of you," John said, watching his friends get suited up. Michelle's lack of modesty as she put on the thermal undergarments—part of her insistence that she was "just one of the guys"—made John wonder how Sean kept his mind on his job. John struggled to avoid watching her—and was partially successful.

"Did you tell Pasadena to stand by for images from the spiders?" Sean asked, pulling on his Mars suit pants.

"I did. You ready to get the Mars Maneuvering Vehicle on the road?"

"The MMV is ready," Michelle said. "We checked all the diagnostics last night when we dropped it from the parking bay."

"Good," John said. "My recommendation is to scoot downrange five kilometers as soon as possible. If they're leaving, like Raines said they might, then we need to get imagery and some samples right away."

"Copy. We'll be rolling inside an hour. Columbus out."

A little more than an hour after his first call, John heard from NASA. "Epsilon, Houston. A data file is headed your way, patched to us from Scott O'Grady at Pasadena. The encryption key of the day is Alpha-Mike. Houston out." John made a quick note on his PDA and entered the encryption data at the flight deck communication terminal.

Houston's voice transmission was repeated three times, and an e-mail with the identical message hit John's inbox about the same time. While the large data file spooled in from across the solar system, he turned on a special laptop he'd connected to a data port on the communication panel. After three password screens, he entered the encryption key. The laptop's screen came to life.

John's heart fell as he saw the data. As he'd hoped, JPL's Scott O'Grady had recorded the still pictures transmitted by the departing aliens. Those imagery signals, relayed back to John from Earth, confirmed his worst fears. Months of classified work by Dr. Kanewski, the National Security Agency, and other federal organizations had found information—never revealed to the public—encoded in the side lobes of the aliens' high-data-rate imagery signals.

No one on Earth suspected that the alien data stream represented anything but images of Mars. No one, that is, but Scott O'Grady, who'd taken over this deep black classified program after the doctor's untimely death.

John had used Michelle to place a covert transmitter inside an alien—a Trojan Horse. Only a handful of people at NASA and NSA knew what the device was. Their "snow globe" was really a high-tech recording instrument, a digital "mole" that mined high frequency information emitted by transmitters and microprocessors. If the alien craft had any information to share, the beacon slipped into its belly could record it. That information was then encoded as a rider on the sideband of the alien's imagery signal—the same signal transmitted to Earth in this morning's communication window.

After John's call, JPL was ready to record those transmissions, and now John could see the proof for himself. Their suspicion—that the spiders were sending back more than pictures—was now confirmed. Someone was communicating with the spiders from Earth. And the aliens were answering.

"Just how do you intend to stop them?" Michelle asked as the MMV sprang to life, its fuel cells producing enough electricity for thirty kilometers of travel at normal speed — perhaps half that at the chase speed Sean needed to tag the spiders. She wasn't convinced this escapade was possible. Sean was a cowboy at heart, and this mission demanded more calm than he or John exhibited today.

"Remember Kanewski's nephew?" Sean asked as he settled into the seat of the cramped Martian version of an SUV, a small protected cab atop a boxy vehicle rigged with eight articulated wheels.

"The boy? Yeah, but — "

"I'm gonna rope it," Sean said, pulling a length of high-tensile cable out from under the seat. It was part of their equipment for winching in and out of tough situations. "John says it's a matter of national priority that we scan them before they leave. And he's right. If they do leave, then we have no data to support or refute Raines's statements about alien life. We must have proof."

Michelle nodded, completely amazed that, clad in a white space suit on the surface of another planet, she was about to go on a high-speed chase, dodging basketball-sized rocks and churning through red powder, to attempt a hasty digital scan and metallic analysis of giant silver spiders.

Two hours later, after a rough ride, they sighted the spiders. The aliens stopped and turned as Sean gained on them, their football-like heads whipping on the ends of flexible masts.

"They've spotted us, John," Sean said over his comm.

"How much cable do you have?" John asked.

"Twenty meters. And two clasp hooks."

"Good. I recommend you toss a line over one of them. I'll bet the other guy stays nearby."

"And if they *don't* like that?" Michelle asked, her voice shaking. "This isn't a rodeo, John. Our lives are at stake."

"That's why I've got the bang stick," Sean said, patting the red and yellow-striped cannon behind her. "You complete those scans and samples. I'll take care of the rest."

Half an hour later, the MMV pulled up close to the rear alien while both of the spiders watched their approach. Sean lumbered out of the MMV, missing the flexibility of zero-G and wishing his suit was more agile.

"Get pictures, Mich! And bring the sample kit," Sean commanded, huffing across the soft red dust toward the closest spider. He pulled the cable with one hand and held the pole in the other. "Remind me to tell you how crazy this is, John," he said as the first sweat began to drip into his eyes. Next time he wouldn't forget to wear his sweat band.

"I'm right behind you, Sean. Be careful," Michelle said.

Sean approached within two meters of the closest spider. Without hesitation, he coiled the flexible cable, a heavy snap hook attached to the end, and lofted it over the tall body.

"You gettin' this, Mich?" he said, panting. "Top of the pod's about my height—call it two meters. Head's another meter above that."

"Copy. Watch out for those grapples we saw yesterday," she said as she videoed Sean struggling against the bulky suit, huffing and kicking through the dust toward the spider's opposite side.

"Got the clasp. Throwing it back . . . through the . . . legs!" Sean stumbled back around the confused craft, pulling the cable that ran between the spider's jointed appendages. "Used to rope giant tarantulas as a kid," he joked, breathing hard as he snapped the clasp over the metal rope.

Sean flashed a thumbs-up sign and hustled toward the MMV. "You ready? He might not like it when I take tension."

"Eighteen minutes 'til the first images of you hooking 'em up are on the Web," John said. "Try to get 'em scanned before Raines sees this. I'm sure the spiders are transmitting."

"Roger that. Taking tension," Sean said, engaging the winch motor. Within moments, the winch pulled the noose tight, hitching the MMV permanently to the departing space arachnid—seven kilometers away from Columbus.

"We're committed, Hawk. Get in there with your stuff, Michelle." Sean grabbed the pole and hustled back toward her as best he could in the dusty soil, ready to fire a depleted uranium round into the spider if it reacted.

It did react, its head suddenly dancing about, seeking the cause of the restriction. *If that head had snapping jaws*, Sean thought, *I'd have already fired the round.*

"Spider's stuck," he said. "The MMV's holding. See if you can sneak in for a metal sample, Mich. I'm ready with the pole."

"Here we go," she said, approaching the spider's back side, away from the MMV and out of the alien's sight.

"Other spider's headed this way, Mich. Move fast!"

"On it," she said. With clumsy space gloves, she opened a small kit and removed a paint scraper-like device with a matchbox-size receptacle attached under the blade. She swiped hard at one of the legs. The diamond-tipped blade sheared off a light sliver of metal. Sean half expected to hear the thing cry out in pain as he watched, but it didn't react.

"Hit it again," he said, watching her, the roped spider, and its approaching friend now only sixty meters away.

She did. Another sliver fell into the box attachment. She laid the scraper back in its aluminum case, snapping it shut.

"Don't forget to scan!" Sean said, turning toward the approaching spider, whose head was popping like the end of a bull whip. The first spider continued straining at the cable, hopelessly lassoed to their vehicle.

"Here goes. Don't let him get an arm on me!" Michelle pulled out a device resembling a policeman's radar gun and moved in close to place her scanner's head against the body. "Firing now!" she yelled.

We're almost out of time, babe, Sean thought. "Twenty meters 'til we have company. Fire again if you can!" He moved clumsily to intercept the second creature, which stopped, then tried to step left or right around Sean as he countered its movements. His delaying tactic couldn't succeed forever.

"Ten minutes 'til Earth sees their images!" John called from Epsilon.

"Claws!" Michelle screamed, trying to position the handheld device for a second internal scan. During his dance with the second spider, Sean looked to his right as two hoses with fierce grapples on the end emerged from the belly of the captured craft.

"It's coming for you," he yelled.

Before she could react, the first spider's head turned toward Michelle. The fast-moving pincers snaked toward her and ripped the electronic device from her hand.

"Michelle!" Sean screamed as she ducked to miss a jointed leg swinging toward her. She stumbled, and a second pincer grabbed her boot and jerked her feet out from under her.

"Hang on!" Sean yelled, holding the pole with one hand and reaching toward her. Michelle kicked her boot free of the clutches of the spider and clawed at the dusty Martian soil as she crab-scrambled backward away from the roped alien, her bottom to the ground.

"Give me a hand!" Michelle cried, scooting beyond the grapple's range.

"Back to the MMV!" Sean said, waving the pole in the second spider's face. Then he grabbed Michelle's suit at the shoulder, jerked her up, and pushed her toward the MMV. "Cut the cable!"

Michelle plodded through the dust and pulled herself into the cab. "Free!" she said as she threw a switch that severed the cable for emergency purposes.

Sean whacked aside another claw with the end of the pole. "Hurry!" Michelle screamed as the second spider turned on him. Sean dove right again and backed up toward the MMV.

"Put it in reverse, Mich!" He thrust the pole at both spiders, then turned and ran as best he could toward the MMV. The spiders stayed put as he fell into the rover. Michelle slid across in the seat.

"Drive!" she said, gripping the silver sample box from her metal scraping.

"No argument there," Sean said between labored breaths.

"Eight minutes!" John reported over the radio. "Are you both in the MMV? I can't see you."

"Safe and sound. We're outta here," Sean said. Sean cut the MMV wheels, whipping the vehicle into a reverse turn, and then put it in forward drive. He made the fastest escape he could along the tracks they'd made through obstacles, leaving behind twenty meters of light metal braided line. They were headed at high speed back to Columbus. He could see Michelle watching the two spiders over her shoulder as he made the escape.

"They're moving," she said at last. "*Away* from us." She turned back in the seat, patting Sean's thigh with a gloved hand. "Enough excitement for one day."

"We're alive," Sean said, panting, "But we failed. All we got was video and a sliver of metal."

"Much better than that," Michelle said with a cheerful voice.

He looked at her, barely able to make out her smiling face under the reflective gold of her visor. "What d'ya mean? They took our scanner!"

"Scanner, yes," she said, "but *I've* got the data." She dangled a tiny computer chip on the end of a light cord tied to her wrist. "Insurance. If they got the gun, I made sure the lanyard pulled the memory chip free. Let's get back to my lab. We got what we came for."

15

"**THIS IS WHERE I EARN** my paycheck," Michelle said, hunkered over a mass spectrometer on the science deck. "John'll tell you—I can do *anything* except fly rocket ships."

"I believe it," Sean said, watching her manipulate the complex analysis suite.

"I just wish I had my lab back home." She moved between the equipment and her computer, transferring data for further analysis. "I need chemicals to do this right; there's so little metal in those scrapes. The scanning electron microscope and ion mass spectrometry are probably our best choice."

"Whatever. Learn anything yet?"

"I have. Are the spiders returning?" She looked up at Sean leaning over her shoulder and she moved to the right. He got the hint.

Sean stood up and walked the deck's perimeter, looking out each of the four portals. "Nothing moving out there, Michelle. Rover's patrolling around us at about one hundred meters. That's one amazing robot. John will pass over in another hour, and we'll get some overhead imagery."

"What about Houston?"

"We're all waiting on you."

"I get the message," she said. "So here's my first assessment. Based on the coloration of the body and the head, I presumed the entire exoskeleton to be polished titanium."

"Expensive."

"Depends on how you see it. Titanium costs a bunch because of the refining process, but it's a prevalent element in the solar system."

"What else?"

"It's not just titanium. It's actually an alloy—which makes sense. Pure titanium is too ductile—it bends, you know? This one's what we call a near-alpha alloy. You probably wouldn't see it in the U.S. Most of our alloys are alpha-beta, or near-beta. Like the MMV; it's built of grade 23 Ti-6."

"English, please?"

"Sorry. Our titanium alloys are usually 5 to 6 percent aluminum. The most common titanium alloy in aerospace is what we call Ti-6—6 percent aluminum. This is *not* Ti-6, which is a relief. These guys weren't made in the USA. But there's more."

Sean stopped pacing and approached. She hoped he'd keep his distance.

"See that spike on the spectrograph? It measures the element distribution profile, and it's a jewel for determining low concentrations of trace elements. The aluminum number is just 2 percent. Then there's this spike—*manganese*—very rare in a titanium alloy. And there's none of the usual tin, zirconium, vanadium, nickel, or molybdenum—

nothing. Just manganese and trace elements. That bothers me."

Sean pulled up a stool and sat down at her side, pouring over the spectrograph. "Why would you expect the other elements?"

"Mostly because I *always* see them. But that's the point here, right? These guys aren't from Earth. Or so we thought."

"Why manganese?"

"The crystal structure, like I said, is near-alpha alloy. Combine titanium with manganese, and you get outstanding corrosion resistance, which explains how they do so well in this caustic dust and in the ocean. Superior heat transfer capability, good for space flight and hostile planets. And great strength. But it's not what the manganese *does* that concerns me."

"Then what?"

Michelle faced Sean, holding a sheet of research printed via the communication link to Epsilon's main computer. "Look at this. Granted, we've never seen an alien before, right? So these craft could be made by a race of beings at least as smart as we are, and they know how to manufacture and machine titanium, right?"

Sean nodded.

"So riddle me this. Why is it that, halfway across the solar system, an alien lander is made of a titanium alloy *identical* to one from Earth? Why an alloy made in *only* one country on Earth, and then only in limited quantities? Why, of all the elements you could pick from the periodic table, would an alien race choose this *specific* titanium and manganese formulation?" She pointed at the top of the paper, labeled "OT-4-1."

Sean scanned the page, his jaw dropping.

"Now do you understand why John's been so coy with us today? If we were back home and you asked me to analyze this sample for you, I could tell you *exactly* where it was made."

Sean made a low whistle. "Either the alien race that made those spiders picked this formulation completely by accident. Or—the 'aliens' bought their supplies on Earth."

Michelle nodded. "Titanium alloy formulation OT-4-1. It's an *exact* match. That thing is Russian."

EPSILON, MARTIAN ORBIT

"Call Houston yet?" John asked an hour later as he poured over Michelle's research on the flight deck's big screens.

"No. There's more to this, John," Sean said in a stressed voice. "And we think there's something you're not sharing with us. We wanted to come to a little understanding before we break the news." He paused. "Last time I checked, Hawk, we were a team."

John sensed the quelled anger in Sean's tone. And he couldn't blame him. John had kept a lot of secrets lately. "You first, Sean. I'll tell you what I know in a minute."

"Are they on the move?" Michelle asked, interrupting the standoff.

"Yes. And no. I've covered most of the area. The orbit took me close enough to scan within one hundred kilometers of you, and they're gone. I mean *gone*. From this altitude, I can't see tracks, but with another pass tomorrow, I can probably look for scorching, presuming that they took off with some sort of rocket. But we have to assume that they can fly around on Mars just like they did on Earth."

"Which means they could be anywhere and return anytime," Michelle said, exasperated.

"Maybe they *can* fly around," John said. "But somehow I don't think they'll be back. I've been in touch with JPL, and they haven't seen any signals from the aliens since you followed them." John tried to change the subject. "What about the scanner?"

"Open the third file I sent you," Michelle said. "It's nonconclusive. I didn't have time to get a good seal with the scanner, so the image is fuzzy. The MMV's surveillance unit registered lots of electronic activity, but we'd expect that. And the infrared scan function saw heat sources inside the pod. It was too fast, and the skin too thick, for the scanner to resolve properly."

"Anything nuclear?" John asked.

"Some," Sean replied, his voice still strained. "We ran the radiation monitors the entire time they were near Columbus and during our approach this morning. Very low readings. They're probably using radio isotope thermal generators—RTGs—just like on Viking."

"And you weren't confusing those readings with Viking's radioactive emissions?"

"Viking's dead," Sean said. "But you knew that. So, cough it up, Hawk. What *else* do you know?"

John was glad, for once, that his friends were on the surface and he in orbit if Sean lost his temper. "Shift to a secure comm channel, Sean. Make sure you cut the video connection to your data recorder—and to Houston."

"Stand by." A minute later, Sean returned, his voice distorted by the encryption system joining the two ships. "I'm back. No more delays, Hawk."

"All right. For starters, that snow globe was not some toy I stowed away. The black plastic base was a complex surveillance system designed to pick up low-level electronic emissions from microprocessors and data busses. If the landers *weren't* aliens—if they used electronics like we do—then we'd get important confirmation that this is a colossal hoax."

No one spoke from the Columbus, the impact of his news settling in.

Then Michelle said, "I wish you'd shared this with us earlier, John." He knew her well enough to read the hurt in her voice. "I might have kept the snow globe, and the spiders would be gone. Where would that leave us?"

"Up a creek, that's where," Sean said. "You gambled with an entire mission *and* your precious data."

"I agree. But it was a chance we had to take."

"We?" Sean asked.

"I can't divulge any more. Later perhaps. But I did have a reason to keep you in the dark."

"And that was?" Sean asked, his anger loud and clear.

"Malcolm Raines," John replied. "He supported the selection of the two of you and pushed it all the way to the vice president. You had ties to Raines. And that meant you might be compromised."

"You flew all the way to Mars suspecting we might be part of some cover-up—a mammoth plot to fake aliens on Mars?" Sean yelled. "You think I'm one of that preacher's pawns?"

John waited a moment, hoping Michelle was trying to cool him off. "No. Not at all, Sean. The implication was, if Raines wanted you in, there was a reason. No one pinned any of this on either of you."

"The globe. What does it do?" Michelle asked, changing the subject.

"It records things using background electromagnetic energy to power it, like from the alien's S-band communications. Very advanced. And, it radiates a signal impressing its data on the side lobes of the alien S-band communication link. When they send pictures, we can pick off the results of the globe's analysis."

"And?" she said.

"And the globe reached the same final conclusion that you did. The operating system is advanced beyond what we've seen in commercial systems, but here's the kicker. All the emissions we intercepted were digital—a 64-bit code just like we use in our microprocessors. And when you translate their binary into higher level code . . ."

"Let me guess. It's in ASCII format," Michelle said.

"Bingo," John replied. "The 'alien' computers are programmed in English."

MONDAY, FEBRUARY 25, 2013: CLEAR LAKE CITY, TEXAS

"So, what now, team?" Greg Church asked the next day. The Johnson Space Center director huddled in a private conference with the CAP-COM Jake Cook, Scott O'Grady from JPL, and Dan Jefferson, flight director.

A fifth group member spoke first, FBI Special Agent Terrance Kerry. "Sir, if John got independent confirmation this is a hoax, then we need to suppress the news and see where this plays out. Otherwise, whoever set up this ruse will run."

All heads nodded.

"I've been in touch with John," Kerry said. "We've shared some items the rest of you aren't aware of."

"You've what?" Director Church blurted. "How?"

"Sorry, sir. When John and I began these discussions during his Space Station flight, he devised a protected laptop video teleconference capability. We've talked quite a lot in the past eighteen months. I have him to thank for deciphering some very complex evidence." Kerry paused. "The guy's a pretty inventive fellow."

"Maybe. What did you two share?" Scott asked.

"He put me on track of some of the terrorists. That's all I can say."

"For crying out loud! How'd he do that from the Station?" Director Church pushed back from the table and crossed his arms.

"John has a strong military space background, sir," Dan Jefferson said. "And he has a knack for solving puzzles. That's why we picked him."

"I remember," Church said with a hand flip. "Go on."

"John once hypothesized that the aliens might have caused the 3/21 terrorist attack. He was just joking at the time, but his point was valid. There might be a connection between the terrorist bombings and this hoax. If in fact this *is* a hoax."

"How else do you read it, Kerry?" Director Church asked. "They flew to Earth and bought their parts at Radio Shack?" The other men suppressed a laugh.

"Anything's possible. Remember, Raines said—"

"I could have gone all day without hearing his name," Dan said.

"Me, too," replied Church.

"Let's suppose Raines is right," Kerry continued. "Take this to the limit. What if there really *is* a Father Race? What if this Father Race set up a scam to get us moving—off the planet and headed to Mars?"

"That's preposterous," Church said. "You've been smoking too much FBI evidence."

"Is it preposterous? I'm trying to get you to think of all the possibilities. We absolutely *cannot* expand the circle of those with need to know beyond this room. So it's up to us to figure it out . . . right now. What are the possible implications of our evidence? Option one, the Father Race is real, they got us headed to Mars, and Raines is right."

"Give me another option," Church grunted.

"The Russians did it," Jake said. "We know now the lander's material was a unique Russian formulation. Although the computer code is in English, which could mean it was programmed here — or . . ."

"Or in India," Scott said. "They could have farmed the code out under the guise of another project. The Indians do code for everyone. The Russians could've hired them as a cover."

"Good! That's what I'm looking for. Brainstorm," Kerry said.

"Maybe *we* did it," Church said, looking at the ceiling. "NASA or someone in the Administration set all this up to get the nation moving. Same as the Father Race theory, but we did it to ourselves —" he laughed — "unlikely as that may be."

Kerry continued. "It could be someone else. Not Russia, not the U.S. Maybe Japan or China. John suggested once that the Chinese had much to gain by shutting down our space surveillance system during the 3/21 attacks. He said they could've placed one or more nuclear devices in orbit to blackmail us later."

All eyes turned on Kerry. He knew they were not military men but was sure they all understood space. The specter of a nuclear war, with multi-megaton weapons raining down at random, was too terrible to imagine.

"Maybe it's not *any* of them," Scott proposed. "Back to your first theory. It's not a government, not aliens, but maybe a person — or small group — who did this. Saint Michael's Remnant has a lot to gain if they're proven right."

Every eye was on Scott.

"Go on," Church said.

"That's about it. Maybe the Remnant has something to gain. But who cares? We're on Mars," Scott insisted. "We went there to find aliens. And we *found* them — but they left. We also went there to do good science. So let's make this the most productive manned mission ever, and then get our crew home. It's a win-win, right?" Scott looked around the room. "Treat this like a huge favor. Kerry finds his bad guys; we go to

Mars. Nobody else needs to know."

"People may die," Kerry said.

"People die every day, Agent Kerry," Director Church said. "If this is a hoax and some crazies go off the deep end, what do we care?"

"You're nuts, Greg," Jefferson said, crossing his arms.

"Let me finish," Church replied, frowning at his flight director. "Scott's *not* right about keeping this a secret. We're on Mars and the mission is successful, true. But we have nothing to lose by exposing the hoax—if indeed it is a hoax. However, we can't prove that—yet."

"I like this logic better, thank you."

Church shrugged. "I don't care whether you like it or not, Dan. It is what it is. I propose a middle ground. We sit on the data for now and gather more information. The spiders might still be on Mars somewhere, for all we know. And anything could happen in the next three weeks. Bring those samples back to Earth, and we'll evaluate all of the data." No one spoke.

Church stood up. The meeting was over. "We keep it quiet for now," he said as he walked away. "I have no desire to tackle Malcolm Raines and his church without solid proof."

Kerry dialed his cell phone as he whizzed along I-45 headed north to Houston.

"This is Shawnda," a voice said, answering the CIA red phone he'd dialed with his classified cellular phone. Kerry lowered the phone and glanced at the display. "Top Secret." The link was solid and he had a covered line.

"Shawnda. It's Kerry."

"I'm glad you called," she replied. "We've got that file you asked for."

"The background on the Remnant?" Her analyses for the Agency were some of the best, and whenever he called, she found a way to deliver.

"The same. Are you going to come get it, or do I have to find you?" she asked with a chuckle. Kerry's heart sped up.

"Headed your way, girl. Be in DC in five hours. Can you meet me at Langley around seven tonight? We've got some more options to consider."

"I'll be waiting, Terrance. Travel safe."

16

"WE'VE BEEN HERE FIVE DAYS and you're vacuuming already?" Sean said, completing his last data logs at the science console. It was time to rest. Seven blessed hours of sleep—at last.

"I'm not going to live in a pigsty, Sean," Michelle shot back. "This Mars dust could kill us, for all we know. And I'm *not* doing this to be domestic."

Sean stood up and turned off the lamp at his station. He walked to Michelle. She pointed the wand of her space-age version of a hypoallergenic vacuum at him in jest, as though aiming a pistol. He rested a hand on her shoulder.

"I didn't mean to imply that, Michelle—about being our housekeeper. I know this is a science mission . . . we're under lots of stress and under a microscope—" He glanced at one of many cameras arrayed about the compartment and lowered his voice. "But you've been very distant since we got here. I don't understand."

Michelle turned on the vacuum and spun around, free of his touch. "Please, Sean. Not now."

John floated in his Extravehicular Mobility Unit—EMU—looking down on Mars, far below. He couldn't see Epsilon. It seemed so long since he'd accidentally drifted beyond sight of the ship. Perhaps days ago. He'd lost touch with time. He shook his head, trying to clear the cobwebs, struggling to move in zero gravity, but his limbs felt frozen in place. He looked down on the planet, somehow able to see Columbus from this great distance, and two space suits far away. Michelle and Sean, outside the lander, waving up at him. He tried waving back, his arms frozen to his side. He tried yelling, but his mouth wouldn't open; only a garbled *mmph* cleared his throat through sealed lips. He longed to be with his friends and ached to see his family.

The vista below began changing colors, morphing from rust red to deep blue, then green, with splotches of brown and fluffy white. Hundreds of kilometers below, Earth rotated. He could see the massive sprawl of Houston, Galveston Bay, and even make out the edge of the Johnson Space Center. He tried to turn, to see the International Space Station that would surely be behind him. He was alone, drifting free in orbit about his home planet. He'd lost his friends. He tried again to scream for help, but no sound came out.

He saw Amy and his children, as though he were hanging over his house in a space suit. They were in the back yard, standing around the grill, Abe flipping meat on the fire, Alice in the swing set he'd built two years ago, Arthur and Albert throwing a football. Amy stood on the patio, looking up. John tried hard to wave, but she only stood there, her hand shielding her eyes from the sun.

He began to cry, just sniffling at first, then deep sobs. Salty tears ran down his cheeks, and something told him that wasn't possible. In zero-G tears should float free. He fought the fog in his head, struggling to understand. The planet drifted below, the greens and blues giving way to red, Amy and the family disappearing, and the planet falling away until it was just a speck in the distance. John gave a mighty heave to reach out, to catch the planet, and to pull himself home.

The sack ripped, his arm flailing free. John awoke, drifting in his compartment. He opened his wet eyes, little diamonds of water floating around him.

"Amy?" he called, his voice a solitary sound in the silence of Epsilon.

No one answered. He was alone.

John left the lights off and floated to the portal in his compartment. *My stateroom,* he reminded himself, reminiscent of his first assignment on an aircraft carrier. He hung by a handhold next to the glass portal, staring into the dense cloud of stars composing the Milky Way galaxy. The brilliance of the heavens glowed on his skin.

"This is a spiritual attack, Lord," he said. "There's nothing for me to fear in being alone. I know that. I know it in my head and I know it in my heart, but I can't shake this—this—need for a sense of belonging. I'm separated from everyone I belong to. They're on the planet below me, or on a planet I won't see again for months. Right now the people I care about are just voices or videos. I need to *hold* someone and be *held*. I need your strength—because I don't have the strength to fight this thing."

John imagined that he saw all the way to the center of that swirling ring of stars, billions of kilometers away. "You spoke all those stars into existence, Lord. In the snap of a finger, you made them all." He closed his eyes, discerning the light through his eyelids, so bright were the heavens.

"I can stay busy to avoid the pain, and when I do, I shut you out. But if I shut you out, you're there anyway, aren't you?" He chuckled as he opened his eyes. "Like the stars. Whether you see 'em or you don't, they're still up there. Every night."

A college girlfriend's favorite verses came to mind as he watched the starlight again through closed lids. *Where can I go from your Spirit? If I go up to the heavens, you are there. Even the darkness will not be dark to you; the night will shine like the day, for darkness is as light to you.*

John laughed and pushed away from the portal, headed back to his ripped sleeping sack. "You're *not* nuts, Wells," he yelled. "Fruity, compulsive about work, maybe too driven, but you're not nuts." He slipped into the sack, yelling at the walls again. "And you're *not* alone."

He pulled the zipper up halfway, leaving his arms free, and closed his eyes as he sank rapidly into slumber. "Good night, Jesus," he said quietly, moments before he began to snore.

WEDNESDAY, FEBRUARY 27, 2013: WASHINGTON, DC

"There's no question, Kerry," the voice on the telephone said. "We found what we were looking for. Come up to Maryland and I can tell you more about it."

Special Agent Kerry stared at the colorful space calendar on his office wall in downtown Washington. A Christmas gift from his attractive—and single—new friend at CIA headquarters. "SAIC—Mission

2013" was emblazoned above the image of a Mars Lander and suited astronauts probing red soil. Below it was a hand-scrawled "23" on today's date—his countdown to March 21, the coming of the Father Race according to Malcolm Raines.

"I can be in Suitland in an hour, Dr. Pestorius," Kerry replied. "Anything else you can tell me on this line?"

"No, but your theory would seem to be proving out, Kerry. They're right where you said they'd be."

SUITLAND, MARYLAND

Kerry planted his hand on a scanner at the Naval Maritime Intelligence Center, then flashed his identification card to a guard he'd come to know as Manny, a retired school teacher on duty defending the Navy's deepest operational secrets. Proceeding to the classified operations hub in the center of the fortified building, he wondered how many men and women had walked these halls, never to divulge what they had seen or done.

All the players were in their usual places when he opened the positive pressure door to the electronic vault, like rejoining a James Bond movie after an advertisement. A *whoosh* of air hit him as he entered the large, well-lit room.

"Hello, Doc. Hi, Nancy," he said, waving at the retired admiral and his ever-present aide. "I'm back."

"We've missed you, sir," Dr. Pestorius said, rising. "Thank you for coming so quickly. Coffee?"

"Please," Kerry said, plopping into a modern office chair and pulling up to the conference table, now covered in multiple images of the mysterious Kilo submarine and its bulbous housing. He lifted a large-format picture, studying what looked like a whale affixed to a submarine's back. "Ever figure this thing out?" he asked, pointing at the odd fixture.

Dr. Pestorius smiled. "We hoped *you* had," he said. "All our analysts say it's a big minisub, meant to carry a large payload."

"You don't sound convinced."

"I'm not. I'm interested in your theory at this point. You have an excellent intuition for the improbable."

Kerry set the photograph down, rose, and walked to a large paper map on the wall of the ultramodern center, a throwback to earlier days before computers and monitors. He pointed to Europe's Atlantic coast.

"Okay. I'm betting—before you tell me what you've found—that he's operating somewhere between the north African area here—" he said, pointing to northeast Morocco—"and here." He moved a finger along the English Channel to the southern reaches of the North Sea. "And I'd bet lunch at the Capitol Grill that he shows up *here* around March 21." He tapped a tiny island on the coast of France labeled "Mont Saint Michel."

Dr. Pestorius was wide-eyed. Kerry saw him glance at Nancy and two watch standers listening to the conversation. Without a word, Pestorius waved to a petty officer at a terminal and pointed toward the large display screen at the front of the room. "You amaze me, Terrance. You really do. Look at this." He moved forward slowly, resting on his cane, and motioned to a map of Denmark.

"We got a one-second acoustic contact on Ulrich three weeks ago. He was sneaking past Helsingborg, Sweden. Seems he was in the Baltic and thought he could leave without us catching him. We had a sub waiting in the North Sea on patrol and tried getting his trail, but he slipped again. Until yesterday." He pointed at the western coast of France in the Bay of Biscay, south of Brest.

"We can hear him again, for whatever reason. He's nearly silent, but now there's a transient signal that we're able to process. It seems his active acoustic cancellation has ceased to operate. Considering how long he's been on the run, I imagine he's not too pleased." He pointed to the map. "They're still south of Brest."

"Off the coast of France?" Kerry asked.

Dr. Pestorius nodded. "Just like you said." The older man smiled at the female aide to his left. It was as if they had a mutual bet about what Kerry would say each time he visited. These intelligence types gave him the creeps.

"Would you mind sharing the rest of your theory?" Dr. Pestorius asked. "You've pegged it so far."

"It's not *my* theory. I've been depending a lot on John Wells."

"John? You're still in touch with him about this?"

Kerry nodded and tapped a tiny dot on the coast of France. "We call it the 3-2-1 theory. You and I talked about that number in December."

"I remember."

Kerry moved over to a whiteboard. "Goes like this." He began writing a list as he spoke.

"Terrorist attack on 3/21. Found the terrorist manifesto in box 321 in Falls Church Post Office; 321 explosive points used to bring down the DC area bridges; 321 was the side number on the red Cigarette boat that Ulrich had pier-side in Roatan, Honduras — the same one we blew up when we went after him." He turned toward the room. "This is just the beginning. It gets stranger."

Kerry made a second column. "Look at this. The orb mass is 321 grams; volume is 321 cubic centimeters — the density of water, by the way. There's a clue there that we haven't broken yet. There are three octaves in the alien audio communication scheme, with twenty-one distinct tones. The alien spiders fly in chevrons of 3-2-1. The probe that John's telescope observed last year during its transit past Earth showed a repetition of three laser transmissions lasting twenty-one seconds each. And there's more, all of it pointing to 3-2-1."

He faced his small audience. "John once proposed that these aliens might've been the reason for the attacks. I thought it was a joke at first, but it's almost like someone is sending us a message in this 3-2-1 symbolism. John says 321 is a numeric acronym for the 'Space Coast,' and it is the telephone area code for Cape Canaveral. Like it's a sick riddle to link the alien craze to the terror campaign.

"321 is also a pointer to DNA work and cloning. That Delannoy number thing is used as a predictor for DNA sequences—used by groups that support the same cloning the Remnant talks about. And he told me about some other linkages that start to make sense in the context of some sick, quasi-spiritual, terror-alien conspiracy. Stuff that tied back to AD 321 and the beginning of the Christian Sunday worship day. Weird religious stuff like that. The more we look at it, the more it looks like something Raines would preach about. The numerology is *everywhere* in this investigation."

"It's all circumstantial," Dr. Pestorius said.

"Is it?" Kerry asked. "Ulrich sent an e-mail to General Boomer Fredericks, who was killed the next day, hung by the neck with exactly 321 centimeters of rope. I'm telling you, it's *not* circumstance. And we've gotten one more revelation this week. You remember that paper you had me sign? Code name 'MIRADOR'?"

Every eye in the room locked on Kerry when he spoke that code name, a word he couldn't utter outside the massive vault door. Dr. Pestorius nodded.

"Why would Ulrich have been in the Baltic, sir?" Kerry asked.

"We presume the submarine went to St. Petersburg for provisioning. Unfortunately," Pestorius began, looking at Nancy, who shrugged, "we have no satellite imagery of their appearance dockside. No acoustic contact, no visual sightings. Yet it makes sense. St. Petersburg is where they built the boat."

"Russia then, correct?" Kerry asked.

"Of course."

"And we know Ulrich has strong ties to the Russians through his time there, time in St. Petersburg when he was ostensibly studying with the circus. He spent most of his years after the dishonorable discharge in Moscow or St. Petersburg."

"Correct. We've been over this. What's your point?"

"My point is," Kerry said, writing on the board again, "that we have another data point tying us *directly* to Ulrich's adopted country. One that is *not*—as you say—circumstantial." He watched them staring at the board and puzzling over the significance of the last entry in the alien column.

"OT-4-1? What does that mean?" Dr. Pestorius asked. Kerry erased the entry then faced the group.

"It has a double meaning, we think. For starters, it happens to be the titanium alloy formulation of the metal legs of the spiders on Mars. A very special alloy formulation." He snapped the cap shut on his marking pen with a distinct *click*. "An alloy identical to one made *here*," he said, turning and touching the map: "Russia."

Dr. Pestorius dropped into his chair before his aide could offer a hand. "No, Nancy. I'm fine." He looked toward Kerry then back at her. "We must tell him."

"Let me finish first," Kerry said. "OT-4-1 is a real alloy. You can find out all about it from a metals dealer. But the designation also has a double meaning; it's a modified affine cipher for 321. We saw this exact cipher in Ulrich's steganography when he was communicating through the Internet. Most of the time he'd use words with no numbers mixed in. You place a numeric value on each letter—O is the fifteenth letter, T is the twentieth. Take the product of those two—300—then multiply the difference—or 5—by the next number, 4, to get 20, then add the last number, 1. Voila, 321. You get the same numeric value with words like 'gulf,' or 'vane.' The symbolism in his communications is too prevalent to call it 'circumstantial.' It's everywhere."

"But don't most ciphers use A=0 and Z=25?" Lieutenant Commander Slagle asked.

"Yes, but Ulrich was always consistent in this practice."

Kerry leaned across the table toward Dr. Pestorius. "What I have shared with you today is known only by you—and four other people. It must stay in this room."

"And it shall, just as what I have to say in reply must remain within MIRADOR security channels. You'll be quite amazed."

Kerry sat.

"The whale-like attachment on the rear of the submarine," Pestorius continued. "We have some space-based thermal imagery from yesterday, taken when it surfaced for only minutes in the Bay of Biscay. Look at this." He pointed to the watch petty officer, who commanded a short video clip.

A grainy movie began playing in green monochrome shades, light and dark shapes that were clearly a submarine's outline. Then Kerry saw it, the outline of the large structure on the sub's rear. It began opening, a single dark expanse gradually splitting in the middle, the bright light-green of heated sources exposing the barn's insides.

Six distinct blobs, front to back, were parked in single file. The infrared video zoomed in, and it was now apparent. Each blob had eight warm appendages extended, with a primary heat source in each blob's center. After a minute, one blob moved off the submarine, as though flying away. The movie stopped. Dr. Pestorius turned in his chair toward Kerry, gesturing with his cane across the table. "See? You were right. There was a reason Ulrich has been near all the sightings. And I understand there's one sighting yet to come—March 21. Correct?"

Kerry stood, nodding, amazed at what NMIC had uncovered independent of him and John. "Then there's only one conclusion, as I see it. The terrorists . . . and the aliens . . . are one." He traced his finger along the Normandy coast. "And the Father Race—whoever that might be—is coming."

17

MICHELLE SAT NEAR ONE of the four portals on Columbus's habitation deck. She couldn't sleep. Behind her, Sean lay a few meters away, his heavy breathing barely audible above the whirring ventilation system. She watched his chest rise and fall. They'd been roommates for a week on Mars and had only ventured out twice. Once for the landing and greeting the aliens, another to chase the retreating spiders. Other than that, Houston had kept them bottled up, human sardines in a tiny gold lander.

As she watched him, her thoughts drifted to Keith, so far away. She'd spent less time in her marriage to Keith, far less, than she had been with Sean. After months of travel to Mars in close proximity to this self-made man, she'd come to know every aspect of his personality and had seen him exposed, perhaps for the first time in his fifty-five years. She'd penetrated his rough exterior to discover a sensitive man afraid for others to see his frailties. His vulnerability drew her to him as a friend. And more. She sighed, realizing her thoughts of Keith always led back to Sean. She turned to the window.

The sun would rise soon, and she waited on the blue ring that often surrounded Sol as it shone through the dusty atmosphere. She longed to go out and explore. Sean would find a way to break the NASA logjam, or they'd go out anyway. He was like that—defiant and take-charge.

The sun's first rays peeked over the rocky ridge beyond her window. White frost was barely visible in the early morning light where it crested the dark gray rocks scattered across the landscape. Windswept red dust made miniature drifts against those rocks, first seen thirty-seven years ago when Viking 1 came to Chryse Planitia—The Plains of Gold on Mars. As the sun rose, patches of frost began to sublimate in the thin carbon dioxide atmosphere. Outside, the temperatures rivaled the worst of Antarctica back on Earth. By midday it would be balmy by comparison.

The MMV—their family car—sat within view below her window. Beyond it, Rover—like a trusty family dog—waited, as she had for months while they transited the solar system to see the alien landers. Michelle wondered about the alien evidence that brought them here, whether this might be the ultimate cosmic joke: *The progenitors lured us to another planet to entice mankind into interplanetary travel.* The thought of being a pawn in the hands of a mysterious master race offended her.

Michelle stood and walked over to Sean's bunk. She knelt beside him and watched him snore, his breath warm on her cheek. The lander's chill after a bitter cold night made her shiver. She placed a silver reflective space blanket over Sean, then left him, undisturbed. She walked back to her bunk, wiggled into her sleeping sack, and curled her knees toward her chest. She wiped away the moistness in her eyes, then felt for her wedding ring, and turned the diamond under her finger. She buried her head in a soft pillow, her sobs muffled in the early morning calm.

EPSILON

An hour after sunrise and ten kilometers southwest of Columbus, John found it—absolute proof. A blackened area in the normally pristine soil. One large circle, hardly distinguishable, marked the landers' departure. The site was three kilometers beyond where Sean and Michelle had confronted the landers on their escape. Somehow the landers had lifted off—perhaps together. Sean and Michelle would have to investigate.

He keyed the mike.

"Columbus, Epsilon. Time to rise and shine. I have something for you."

No answer. He waited a few minutes longer, then tried again. NASA had scheduled their wakeup a half hour from now. His friends weren't normally this hard to roust. "Columbus, Epsilon. Anyone awake down there?"

Still no answer. He selected the Columbus video feed, but it showed only the science module. The video in the habitation module was turned off. *That's a first,* he thought. They'd agreed to keep the video feed up 24-7 for just this contingency; if no one could hear them, at least John or NASA could *see* the problem. He tried again a minute later.

"Columbus, Epsilon. This is John. Of course it's John. Why'd I say that? Anyway, if you guys are sleeping in and left the hab video off to get some privacy, that's nice and all, but I have important news. So wake up and answer the call. *Please.*"

A minute later, Sean came on, sounding groggy. "Sorry, pal.

Overslept. We're up. Keep your pants on, okay?"

"Good morning to you, too. Ready to work in the MMV today?"

"Could be."

"I found what we were looking for," John said, watching the hab video channel that was still shut off. He waited to see when they'd bring it on.

"Where?" Sean asked.

"Three clicks southwest of where you roped the big one a few days ago. One large distinct plume circle. Is the MMV ready to roll?"

"It is. Ship the coordinates and the images down, and we'll be ready in a couple of hours. I'll call Houston. I'm not taking 'no' for an answer this time."

"Images are in your queue, Sean. And I agree—we came to explore Mars, not just sit on it. Where's Mich?"

"Getting washed—her turn. It's been a while for both of us. I was sleeping in. Sorry. I'm hanging out in the science module to give her some privacy."

John clicked the mike twice to indicate he'd gotten the message. The image from the hab deck remained blank.

He switched the video feed back to the science module.

Sean wasn't there.

MARS

Michelle sat to Sean's right in the MMV. In the distance she could see the large circle of blackened soil John had spoken of. They passed a long snake of silver cable, the severed wire from their winch that fell free of the spider as it walked away. On the navigation screen, the MMV icon was almost on top of the coordinates John had provided. They'd arrived—and with NASA's blessing. She touched Sean's suit with her left glove and pointed ahead. He nodded.

Their lightweight suits were a far cry from the stiff EMU and ORLAN suits that Michelle had grown accustomed to on the International Space Station. At least Mars had a semblance of an atmosphere, which meant they didn't have to fend off the absolute vacuum of space. And the temperature extremes were more like Earth—deep winter in Antarctica. It was an environment that allowed a more flexible and adaptable suit. She liked it. She hated NASA's standard white color, though. After only two EVAs, hers was stained with red soil. That's what NASA wanted, apparently—so that they could see what to clean off the suit after each EVA.

Sean stopped the MMV only a few meters from the five-meter-diameter black circle. It wasn't much, and Michelle wondered how John had found it from six hundred kilometers above.

"I've got the sample kit ready," he said. "Let's get started."

"Whatever," Michelle replied. She didn't move.

"Well?" Sean asked, turning in his seat to face her. "You coming?"

Michelle scribbled something on her note board and held it up for Sean to read. "*Comm secure. Now.*" She watched him switch radios, fingering a wrist control to silence his communications with anyone but her.

"It must end here, Sean. Please. I meant what I said this morning."

"How do you just turn something like this off? I'm not a lightbulb."

"And I'm not a *light switch*," Michelle countered. "I love *one* man, Sean," she said, glad the reflective gold visor hid her face. "And his name is Keith."

"Right. And he's nine months away—at best. Do you really think we can both go that long—as friends? After all we've been through?"

Michelle placed a hand on his shoulder. "We have to, Sean. The entire world is watching."

"You're right there." He turned away, shaking his head. "Never in a million years would I have imagined myself in this situation. The shrinks told me it was a possibility—a rebound from the divorce and the result of close contact for weeks. I told them they were nuts—that for me, the mission is and always would be everything." He made a sound like a short laugh. "The *mission*. That's why Debra left."

Michelle touched his shoulder. She wanted to hold him, but also felt the urge to remain silent. She compromised. "Me too," she said gently.

Sean faced her. She could see her helmet and the distant Martian horizon behind her in the spherical gold reflection of his visor. "I don't understand," he said.

"I mean just that. '*Me too*'—the shrinks told me to watch for the same thing. They said I was sometimes desperate for affection. And I didn't listen."

Sean nodded slowly, looking back toward the plume site they'd come to investigate. "I never mentioned this," he began, his voice muted. "Because it insulted me—hurt my pride. The psychiatric profile on our crew predicted this would happen—but not with *me*."

She released her grip. "I've *seen* the profiles. What are you saying?" Her heart rate quickened. She was glad Sean couldn't monitor her physiology today.

"You never saw this part. And I think you can figure out what I mean. But it didn't matter in the end. Politics beat the psychiatrists, and they sent the three of us anyway."

She started to interrupt, but Sean turned toward her and put a glove on her arm. "Let me finish, okay? Part of me always knew what John told us the other day—that we had major support from Raines, from the director — and from the White House. Politics drove the selection process, and NASA turned a blind eye to all the other issues — like what you and I are dealing with right now."

Michelle shook her head. "No one trusted *me*?" She wanted to run, to hide from Sean and NASA, to hide from the world and the people watching her with video cameras. From all of them. They'd *expected* this of her, and she'd delivered. Reality television, interplanetary style.

"No, Michelle," he said, squeezing her forearm. "You read me wrong. The profile said that a man and a woman who knew each other as well as — as well as you and John — might . . . Well, you know."

She turned back toward him and laughed in a strained way. "Just goes to show how little those shrinks understood us, doesn't it?"

"It does. And for my part," he said, laying his glove on hers, "I have no regrets."

Michelle clenched her jaw, forcing back the first words that came to mind. *Maybe you don't regret it, but I do.*

"We are where we are, Sean," she said. "Please, let's end this now." She paused. A radio call from John saved her from herself.

"Hello? Hello?"

"Our conscience is calling for us, Sean. We need to go."

Sean shrugged and turned away from her.

"Hey, you guys. I see you're up secure comms. Everything all right down there?" John's voice reached out from the other side of the planet every time they were quiet, it seemed. Michelle wondered how he was handling the loneliness. Sean was right. She did know John, very well. For a brief moment she wondered — were the shrinks right about her and John? The thought that she was so predictable chilled her.

Michelle switched circuits and pointed to Sean to do the same. "We're here, Hawk," she said. "About ready to take the samples. Your coordinates were dead on."

"Of course they were," he said. "I've got the best eyes on the crew."

"You used to," Sean chimed in as he climbed out of the MMV, "when you were forty. You wear glasses now, pal."

The mike clicked twice.

Michelle climbed out of the MMV and stood in the red dust. She could see where the pointed legs had pierced the soil. A ring of black marked the location of the launch. Somehow, the spider-like landers had lifted off, presumably headed to orbit based on the size of the large blackened area. "They must have gone together. There's only one well-defined plume ring," she said, kneeling down to sample the soil.

"There was nothing on those spiders to make a plume burn like this," Sean said, kneeling to scoop up the heavily charred dirt. "Something major—like our lander—did this."

"The blackened soil on the edges might give us a good idea of the temperature of the rocket plume," Michelle said. "But the center will probably yield some chemical constituents to classify the propellant." She looked back at Sean who was slowly circling the site looking for other clues.

"Got something," he said, going down on both knees in the rocky soil.

"What is it, Sean?" John asked, watching them both with the video from the MMV.

"Michelle's gift. Seems they didn't like tourist stuff."

"What do you mean?" she asked, twisting in her suit to face Sean. He had a black fragment in his hand. Molten glass dotted the blackened ground, and the base showed evidence of some micro-miniature electronic parts, all fried in the inferno of the spider's rocket.

"It's the snow globe, Hawk. They left it behind. In pieces."

The MMV's articulated wheels took the rocky terrain in stride as Sean and Michelle rolled back to the lander. Rocks ranging from the size of basketballs to baseballs were strewn across the plain. It made for tough going, finding a dirt path between the obstacles. Michelle was sure that was why whoever designed the alien spider landers had used eight pointed legs. The spiders could pick their way without difficulty through the minefield of rocks that frustrated her and Sean in their wheeled conveyance. Fortunately, they rolled over most of the rocks with the eight wheels independently suspended and adapting to the terrain. Their progress was slow but steady—about five kilometers per hour.

The sun turned midday, and the temperature rose. At the hottest time of day they would be basking in 50° F weather. By night, when they sought refuge in the lander, the temperature would plunge to minus 220° F. Michelle adjusted her internal temperature using the controls on her wrist, then continued her conversation with Sean. "I think we should try the crater to the north. It's pristine and nonvolcanic. We should get some good background samples there."

Sean half-shrugged, half-nodded, and turned the MMV to the northeast.

"We're headed northeast, John," Michelle said, keying her communication to John who was passing low on the horizon at the moment.

"Copy. I have some news for you guys when you're ready. We'll need to go up secure comms."

"Shoot," Sean said. "We've got an hour to kill before we reach the crater. What's up?"

"More information from back home about the alien landers. Seems they think they've located the six spiders that lifted off from Canaveral just after we did."

"No!" Michelle blurted.

"The same, we're pretty sure. My FBI friend says they're hanging out south of France."

"Why?" asked Sean.

Michelle punched him in the ribs. "You know. Raines said the Father Race would show up at Mont Saint Michel on the twenty-first. About three weeks from now. We'll be headed home by then."

"There's more. The six spiders are apparently riding on the back of a submarine. A Russian. Lots more we can discuss when you get back to the lander, but the evidence of a Russian setup seems to be mounting."

"But why?" Sean asked as he bounced along over small rocks. "Why influence us to spend, build, and fly all the way to Mars and beat them here? Why lose all that national prestige?"

"Maybe they thought we'd fail," Michelle said, adjusting her position in the lawn-chair style seat for comfort. Comfort was a relative term. She felt sick at her stomach from the topsy-turvy ride, but didn't want to think about what it would be like to vomit in a space suit.

"Perhaps," John replied, "there's *another* option."

"You're a born conspiracist, Hawk. But lay it on us," Sean said, steering around another boulder.

"Slow down, Sean," Michelle pleaded. "I'm a little green."

"Okay," John said. "Raines has been making a big deal about this Father Race bunch. What if they're already here? If we look like 'em, how would we ever know, anyway? Suppose they do live with us, maybe even mate with us. Maybe *they* built the landers, and then flung them out here as some kind of bait." John paused. "Which makes us the fish."

"They call that 'chumming,'" Sean replied.

"And it works, doesn't it? We're here."

"John?" Michelle asked. "I hate to bring this up, but do you remember the medications I left with you?"

"Can it, Michelle. I'm not hallucinating. But I *am* spending quite a lot of time talking to intelligence analysts back home. That's the only place I'm at risk of falling into alternate realities—working with intel spooks. Trust me. I'm *fine.*"

"Okay," she replied, unconvinced.

"Is there any more to this that we ought to know about, John?" Sean asked as he rolled around the top edge of a shallow crater.

"Yes," John continued. "What if they baited us out here for a reason other than meeting their landers on Mars? Why did they cut and run right after we got here? That makes no sense."

Sean stopped the MMV. Michelle shrugged as he looked at her. She had no idea what to make of this. Or of John.

"What are you *not* saying?" Sean asked, his voice gruff.

"Someone—something else—wanted us out here. For a reason."

Michelle's stomach heaved, and she swallowed chunks of the morning meal that tried to come up. Acid burned her throat and she coughed.

Sean reached over to her. "You okay?"

She nodded then turned her head for a swig of water from her hydration port. "Yes. Okay. Stomach's upset, that's all. And what John said brought to mind a history lesson I learned a long time ago."

"That was?" John asked.

"Magellan. He set out to discover a route around the world. But he never came back. He died at the hands of natives in the West Pacific. Maybe we were brought out here for the same reason—to blaze the route. But our return wasn't ever part of the plan."

18

"I'M NOT HUNGRY," Michelle said, rising from their small table—a combination dining area, food preparation counter, and science area. Sean shrugged and picked through her breakfast remains for meat.

"Have you heard from John this morning? He usually calls by this time." She peered out at the dusty landscape beyond the portal, then turned and watched Sean, wondering how he could eat what reminded her of green eggs and ham. "D'you hear me? What's with John?"

"Guess he's busy running those mapping surveys. We're doing our part. Why bother him?"

"Something's wrong. I could hear it in his voice last night."

"You're playing nursemaid again. He's a grown man. He can take care of himself."

"Easy for you to say, Sean. You're down here—with company,

gravity, and a chance to explore Mars. Remember that John's only seeing this from a distance. He might be depressed."

"You talked with him about that. He knows what to take." Sean stuffed the plastic containers into a compactor and wiped his mouth on a sleeve. "Besides, only wimps and women get depressed."

"You are such a Cro-Magnon sometimes. Depression is a real illness, and men get it too."

"Not me. And no man I ever met."

"Maybe none that ever *admitted* it. But you're right—if John thinks like you do, he might not take what he needs. It's time for plan B."

"What are you going to do? Fly up there? Just leave him be. He's fine."

Michelle smiled. She'd anticipated John's withdrawal. Once—a long time ago—she'd been down the same path. If he was determined to resist the medical help, it was time to alter his mood with food. And she had just the plan.

"Baked 'em myself," Michelle said, watching him on video. "From scratch."

"They're delicious! Why didn't you tell me about this chocolate stash sooner?" John shoved in a fourth brownie.

"Figured there'd come a day when you were missing home or missing us. I wanted to surprise you. Do you like 'em?" Michelle's voice lilted. It was the first joy she'd felt in three or four days, despite the history-making trip and Martian experiences. "Thought if I baked you enough and froze them in separate pouches, you'd have plenty to last on orbit."

"I could eat them all in one sitting!" he said, as she watched him dive into a second pouch for a fifth rich, dark-chocolate treat.

"No! Don't do that! *Ration* them. I left you enough for four a day until we return. No pigging out. Promise?"

"You're probably right. Too much chocolate gives me a stomach-ache anyway. I'm sure glad you called." He paused. "I really needed this."

More than you know, she thought, wishing she were able to talk face-to-face. There was so much she wanted to share.

SATURDAY, MARCH 2, 2013: EPSILON

"I should probably stop talking to myself," John said out loud early in his new morning. The whir of ventilation fans was the only reply.

John hugged the quilted down sleeping sack a moment longer, then bolted from his zero-G bed. It was good to feel normal again. For the past week it seemed he'd been sinking deeper into a funk. Yesterday morning had been his low point, refusing to get out of bed despite NASA's calls, wake-up alarms, and the maddening *ding* of priority message notifications sounding throughout the ship. Only Michelle had managed to rouse him.

He'd known yesterday what his problem was all along, but refused to acknowledge it. He'd been hiding from himself—and from his dilemma. Michelle would have diagnosed it as depression. He smiled at how she loved to psychoanalyze him. And treat him long distance with the blues-busting benefits of chocolate.

"I hate to be alone, Michelle," he pronounced, looking up at a camera and pretending to be in her care. "I know dealing with loneliness is a problem common to all isolation missions, whether in space or in Antarctica. Loneliness can lead to depression. And yes, ma'am, I understand how to treat that."

He smirked and turned around, pretending to be Michelle. "But John, you know that loneliness unaddressed will continue to manifest signs of depression even after you begin medication." He spun about again.

"Yes, I understand that, Doctor. Thank you for your diagnosis. May I have another brownie?"

None of the psychobabble he'd heard about isolation had helped as much as that call from Michelle, and her stash of special treats. There was something, after all, to that talk about the serotonin-inducing qualities of dark chocolate—the "chocolate high." Nature's own antidepressant. The only side effect was that too much choco-happiness kept him awake at night. And made him fat. But he could work off most of those side effects with an extra hour a day on the stationary bike. Someone cared about his situation, the chocolate cheered him up, and—for the first time in ten days—he felt *happy.*

Today brought another special treat. "Shower day, John-boy! Just you and me." There was plenty of water to shower lightly every day, but John saved it for a soaker every third day. He whistled while preparing for this space-luxury. As he entered his bath area, a small card taped to his mirror stopped him cold.

1 Corinthians 1:8-9: He will keep you strong to the end, so that you will be blameless on the day of our Lord Jesus Christ. God, who has called you into fellowship with his Son Jesus Christ our Lord, is faithful.

He stared at the card a long time, his heart aching over lost opportunity. How long had it been? Three days? A week? It had been *nine* days—nine days since he'd taped up that latest verse, his failed attempt to memorize a verse a day while alone in orbit.

"I'm sorry, Lord. You were here all along, holding out a hand." He hadn't shaved in three days, another Wells first, as he'd sunk deeper into his malaise. With no trips to the mirror, the card had gone unread—and unpracticed. He wondered if any NASA shrinks watched him today as he stole a glance back at the camera. The audio and video were always live back to Houston, the price of being alone. Someone had to watch over you.

John pushed over to his desk unit and pulled out the entire stack of memory cards, his towel and shower vacuum hose trailing behind him. He pinned the cards around the mirror—all twenty-eight.

"You *are* faithful, Lord, just like Paul promised. With your help, we're gonna beat that depression." He pinned the last card to the mirror with flair. "I don't care if NASA and a planet full of shrinks *are* listening. I'm gonna talk out loud all day. To Jesus."

SUNDAY, MARCH 3, 2013: MARS

"I've never seen it before. I'm not saying it's not of Earth origin. Just that I've never encountered anything like it," Michelle said, looking through a digital microscope at the soil particles. "It could've been a man-made rocket. The residue has some of the chemical precursors I'd expect from a solid rocket burn. But this test is nonconclusive."

"It *could* be, right? Earth origin, I mean," Sean said.

"I told you, it's *possible*. The large plume circle suggests that a single large craft took off—and perhaps carried both spiders with it. But whatever made that plume ring was some kind of new solid rocket. The soil burns have hints of chemicals in them that would be consistent with an Earth-built rocket motor. But all I can tell you is that it was *not* a methane-oxygen or hydrogen-oxygen engine. Other than that, the samples will have to go to Earth for more detailed analysis."

"In other words, it's a bust."

"*No!* What is it with you lately, anyway Sean? We came all the way to Mars to explore the planet and to determine where those spiders came from. Now they're gone. But this voyage—and my analyses—are definitely *not* a bust."

"You took that the wrong way, Mich."

"I took it the way you said it. I can't read your mind."

"Good thing, too."

"What?"

"Good thing you can't read minds. You wouldn't like what you see."

"And what's that supposed to mean?"

Sean walked to the communication console, as though he had something important to do. She knew better. He was on a roll and wanted under her skin in the worst way. He was about to achieve that.

"It means," he said after a long lull, "that you—like most people—probably wouldn't want to hear what others think about you. In this case, what I'm thinking right now."

"I'm strong. So lay some of that on me, Bear. I can take it." Michelle turned in her seat, arms crossed, her soil samples forgotten.

Sean faced her, his face red. "You asked for it. The last few days you've been real testy. On edge. I don't know—like it's that time of the month or something."

"I'm *not testy*—and even if it *was* the 'time,' that's none of your business."

"Maybe it *is* my business."

"What makes you think so?"

"Michelle, we're depending on each other to stay alive. You can't fly this thing off this rock without me, and I can't analyze anything except a good meal. We need each other. In more ways than perhaps you're willing to admit."

"We've had this conversation, Sean. It's a dead issue."

"For you, maybe."

Michelle turned back to her analysis. "It's been fun, Sean. The last seven months with you have been truly memorable. And the next nine will go even better if you spend half as much time thinking about your future as you spend thinking about me."

Michelle pointed over her shoulder toward their radios. "Send a message home, big guy. Tell 'em we can't conclusively determine the type of rocket engine used to extract those spiders. My analysis is on its way. And ask 'em to send a cold shower on the next resupply mission." She looked at Sean. "You need it."

"Sure. I'll send your message for you," he said. "I'd love that shower—*any* shower in fact. And while they're at it, maybe NASA can send me a partner who's not such a tart."

SATURDAY, MARCH 16, 2013: NEW YORK CITY, NEW YORK

Malcolm Raines had shown that he could pack any auditorium in the nation, and Madison Square Garden was no exception. The monstrous arena overflowed with crowds watching him on huge video cubes. An entire section was packed with his protégés—basketball hopefuls—young men he'd brought who looked up to Malcolm for a brighter future. Tonight he would offer them spiritual hope as well.

"Five days from today," he said, "I will stand on the sacred mount in western France with my arms raised in adoration and expectation. Join me in spirit and welcome the coming of the Father Race!"

Raines's face was soaked in perspiration from an hour of exhorting the crowd and spinning his prophetic visions for humanity. With only five days to go, interest in alien life, the history of Saint Michael's Remnant, and the Mars mission was at an all-time high. The tall "Priest of the Heavenlies," as he had recently come to be known, stood at the center of the stage near the west end of the arena. Hands on the lectern, he bowed his head in silence. The crowd hushed.

"Humanity will soon come to completion. After a thousand decades of development and maturing, and a thousand decades of growing pains, we are ready. The day of the Father Race is at hand.

"Tonight each of you stands at a spiritual threshold, a life-changing moment, and you must make a decision. Will you place your faith in truth you can see? Or cling to old stories of a man-God? I offer you something you and I can touch—a Father whose representative will soon stand in our midst on the holy mount.

"I offer you the opportunity to realize your inner potential—the seed of the Father Race within you. Nietzsche was right; Christianity is a religion of slaves. It has taken us as far as it can. Under its leadership our eyes are clouded. But soon we will achieve the goals set out for us. And when that glorious day comes, we will have reached equality with the Father who set us on this Earth." Applause started, but he raised his hand and remained silent for over thirty seconds. Then the voice came, the famous deep baritone that heralded news from across the galaxy—the voice of the alien nation. The Father Race would again speak through him. Raines was riveted, like some hand gripped him from inside, his body stiff as he stared up at the lights.

"Be still! We are coming." The disembodied voice paused and the arena was silent. "Study our number. We are *six*."

Raines slumped—a result of what he'd once termed "near exhaustion from communing with eternal beings"—into the embrace of two aides. An assistant held a portable microphone, and he began to speak again, this time in a raspy voice. "Six! Did you hear? Man's number is six. God needed six days to complete creation."

He waved off the aides, staggering back to lean on the podium. "Six! Do you understand this significance? The meaning!" Raines picked up his ever-present Bible and waved it. "It is all in here!" He thumbed to the first book.

"Genesis—the origin of man. Chapter *six*. 'The Nephilim were on the earth in those days—and also afterward—when the sons of God went to the daughters of men and had children by them. They were the heroes of old, men of renown.' That is the Father Race! Among us then—and I proclaim in your hearing tonight—they are among us *even now*.

"Evidence of our Fathers transcends the ancient historical records of distant civilizations. These Nephilim were titans—and *tradition* proclaims their existence worldwide. That tradition is vitally important, for many religions have carefully eliminated any record or memory of the Nephilim, demonizing our Fathers as fallen angels or bestial beings. But they were none of these. They appear in the Dead Sea Scrolls—towering beings who mingled with the women of earth. They were known as the Angels of the Heavens . . . Sons of God . . . Uranus, great primeval god of the sky . . . Titans, the sons of Uranus and Gaia, mother earth . . . and raksasa of Indo-Asia. Evidence of the existence of these tall master beings pervades our history. They were the *Father Race*. They are coming. Indeed, *they are already here*."

Raines stepped away from the podium, his strength restored, and walked to the edge of the dais. "Be wise as serpents, my friends. Divine the presence of the Father Race. Their number is six."

Half an hour later, Raines dismissed his aides, stepped into a private dressing room, and locked the door.

A young woman in a slick black jumpsuit, ebony hair falling to her waist in a single ponytail, stood waiting. "Stunning presentation," she said in a low voice, pulling Malcolm close and nestling her head into his chest as he towered above her.

"You are my oracle—my power," she said as she wrapped herself around him.

Malcolm looked down and smiled, reveling in her incredible strength. He placed a hand under her chin, tilting her face up toward his.

Red lips whispered the words he longed to hear. "You are my Titan," she said. "My raksasa—*you are Nephilim.*"

Malcolm nodded, smiling down at her.

"I am."

CLEAR LAKE CITY, TEXAS

"That's us, Mom!" Alice said.

"Alice! You sneak. I thought you were asleep. Lie here a moment longer, sweetie, and then we'll go up to bed." The boys were asleep, and Amy fought to keep her eyes open, exhausted from a day of soccer tourneys.

The late-night replay of Raines at Madison Square Garden fascinated, yet deeply offended, her. He was spinning doctrine and Scripture in such a convincing way that she felt she needed to go back to Genesis just to confirm that what he said was true—or false. What had her pastor said just last Sunday, quoting Paul's letter to the Ephesians? "Then we will no longer be infants, tossed back and forth by the waves, and blown here and there by every wind of teaching and by the cunning and craftiness of men in their deceitful scheming."

Raines—and his message—were the epitome of deceit.

"I said . . . that's *us*, Mom!" Alice repeated groggily. Her little eyes were wide open.

"Go back to sleep, honey. This isn't a show I wanted you to hear."

"I *was* asleep, for a while. But then I heard the Raines man. He said 'they are six.' *That's us!*"

Amy's mouth dropped open and she stiffened.

"Right mom? Three boys, a mom and dad, and one girl—me! Three plus two plus one. That makes six."

The children were asleep as Amy typed her message to a widening e-mail list of women who turned to her for support. The broad network of women just like her, capable professional women all in the role of a mom, was an expanding audience to proclaim God's healing—and to counter the deceit of the world. Tonight, Amy took on the lies of Malcolm Raines in her latest posting. Tomorrow, hundreds of women would read it, distribute it to other women in their churches, and write back with encouraging, challenging, and insightful responses to Amy's concerns and opinions. The process stretched her and it felt good.

"Our father is not Nephilim," she began as she wrote her evening missive. The quiet house filled with sleeping children embraced her, and her heart was filled with praise.

19

"GOD IS NOT THE author of confusion."

Pastor Jim McGehee made a fist for emphasis. Amy wished John were here to share these critical days when she felt the world was making an all-out assault on her faith. John always had a fresh spiritual view on breaking news, and he would want to be in the thick of this false gospel of Malcolm Raines. *Thank you for keeping my John safe,* she prayed silently.

"People all over the world are flocking to Mont Saint Michel—but why?" He raised his hands in question. "To find out more about where we came from? About our Maker? To meet Him? The curious on that island won't find God if they go looking for a Father Race. Because there *is* no Father Race. Those are hard words, but we need truth these days, not media-inspired false prophecy. This great stirring is *not* from God."

A few parishioners shouted "Amen!" Amy could hear whispers

rustle through the pews. Few, if any, in this church would give Malcolm Raines the time of day after his blatant "God within you" presentation last night in New York. Among those who studied their Bible, Raines's philosophies and prophecies failed miserably.

"I'd like to address Malcolm Raines point by point. His statements in New York bring us to the brink of our faith, as he himself says. But his path will lead you the wrong way."

Amy closed her eyes and began praying for Pastor McGehee as he recited the litany of Raines's spiritual errors. She prayed for Alice and the boys to understand the gravity of these days. And she lifted up John, thankful for His care—and petitioned for John, Sean, and Michelle's safe departure from Mars, less than a week away. *Please, Jesus.*

"'Because you have seen me, you have believed,' Jesus says in John's gospel. 'Blessed are those who have not seen and yet have believed.' Malcolm Raines calls on us to place our eternity in his hands, to believe in him and in his cause because we can *see* these spiders—proof, he says, of the coming of a Father Race—tall beings he says are like us but who supposedly seeded humanity on our planet ten thousand years ago. Don't believe it. Malcolm Raines's ravings pale in comparison to the living Lord whose actions I observe and experience every day. Remember, our God is *not* the author of confusion. He would not set up a mystery like this in order to draw people close to Him.

"Has Christianity taken us as far as it can? Perhaps. Raines might be right on that account." Amy sat up, pulled from her prayers by the murmurs about her.

"Surprised you, didn't I? I say this because we *don't* put our faith in Christianity as a religion. Raines is right on this count. Christianity can only take us so far. But *Christ* can take us all the way! We need to invest ourselves in a relationship with the risen Lord Jesus. If organized Christianity fails, it will be because we've taken our focus off Christ and put it on mankind and tradition. We will fail when we put our focus on men like Raines—or some towering race of beings."

Usually, services in this church were quiet—but today, Pastor McGehee's comments elicited several "Hallelujahs" and a dozen "Amens."

"And the Nephilim! What about them?"

Here it comes, Amy thought.

"Malcolm Raines must think us fools to connect six alien spiders with proof that an unseen alien race represents the fallen angels of Genesis chapter six—the fallen angels who came to Earth and consorted with human women. Remember, God is *not* the author of confusion. Raines's numerology—'our number is six'—is pure divination. It's from Satan—not Jesus—lest anyone mislead you. That kind of symbolism, searching the Scriptures, names, or events for numeric patterns and clues, will lead you astray. Read your Bible!" he said, holding his own Bible in front of him with both hands. "You don't need numbers and symbols to find God!"

Amy wanted more material to counter the lies being spread among her own friends. But the clock was the pastor's enemy. He began to wrap it up, to close their church's live television hour.

"Raines says that equality with God *is* something to be grasped. He claims that you can realize the God within you because you have the seed of the Father Race. That's one of the oldest lies told by the enemy—that we can be like God or be equal with God. Don't believe it for a minute. You will fall into the trap of self-worship and lose your focus on the saving grace of Jesus Christ. God *is* in you, yes—but *only* if you ask Jesus in."

"Allow me," Rex Edwards said, offering Adrienne a hand off the bullet train at Caen.

"Thank you, Rex. I swear, I'll never travel in heels again." She smiled at him, lifted her bag, and swept long blonde hair over her shoulder as she stepped on the platform.

The high-speed rail from Paris and the first-class airline passage across the Atlantic were special accommodations she'd never before enjoyed. The more time Adrienne spent with Rex, the more comfortable she felt around him, and the more she was amazed at his span of control. Her apprehension, alone in a room with him months ago at his Palmdale office, had all but vanished. And the more she saw of the man's personal side, the more she found herself drawn to him. She was quickly losing her journalistic objectivity—and rationalizing away a failing marriage.

"Bonjour, Madame. Monsieur." A tall, slender woman of about twenty emerged from the crowd and proffered her hand. Jet black hair cascaded to the middle of her back, lying like an ebony mane over a skin-tight black jumpsuit. Deep red lips set off the perfect tan of her face.

"Thank you," Adrienne said, taking the hand of the Mediterranean goddess. "Have we met?"

"Yes, you have in a way," Rex replied with a chuckle. "This is Monique, Dr. Raines's personal assistant."

The young woman released Adrienne's hand and bowed toward Rex. "Welcome sir, as always," she said, in English heavily accented by what Adrienne assumed to be native French.

"Monique's twin sister, Antoinette, was your escort when you visited me at my corporate office. I recommended Monique highly to Malcolm last year. He was wise to accept my endorsement—she's very good at her job."

"Oui. I have Monsieur Edwards to thank for this position. And my skills. He cared for my sisters and me for many years." She gazed at Rex for a moment, her eyes locked on the powerfully built man, shorter than she by a head, as though gathering control of her emotions. "We owe him a great deal. He is the only father I have ever known."

"Really?" Adrienne exclaimed, turning toward Rex. "Don't tell me you've known her since she was a little girl?" Rex's compassionate side got deeper by the day, a facet she'd need to reveal in her next article. This was brilliant.

Rex waved his hand, anxious, it seemed, to be on the way and free of the subject.

"I'd like to hear your story, Monique. Is that okay, Rex?" Adrienne asked as they started to walk. "It's a wonderful angle on you and the business." She touched his arm as they walked. "Two children at home, and others you've helped along the way. It's remarkable!"

He shook his head. "Thank you, but no. Monique and her sisters are doing quite well. The media exposure would only pry off old scabs for many people who don't deserve to be hurt." He pointed down the platform, and Monique nodded, signaling four porters who retrieved their bags within moments.

"We are so glad you've come to join us," Monique said as they proceeded toward a waiting Mercedes limousine. "Father Raines waits for you on le mont."

Two hours later, after moving through six roadblocks and past hundreds of gendarmes, the limo finally arrived at Mont Saint Michel's new parking area. The most visited site in France, the ninety-meter-tall granite mount rose like a tall boat at low tide from the midst of an endless mud flat that stretched beyond their sight.

"We must walk from here," Monique said. "We will take the new pedestrian bridge." She dismissed the head porter: "Take the bags directly to the hotel."

"Where's the causeway?" Rex asked. "We used to drive up."

"There are no longer car accesses. That road," she said, pointing to a narrow bridge, "is for logistics only. The rock causeway was removed five years ago to allow the tide to remove the silt and restore the island to its natural state." She waved her hand across the mud flat. "The tide will be in soon. Twelve meters today. Very fast. You will see."

A shuttle took them across a short bridge spanning most of the mud flat. They alighted from the small car for a walk across the final kilometer. The graceful new bridge curved westward toward the ramparts of the thousand-year-old structure, and then sloped gently down to an earth platform. At the base of the island, they walked the final few meters to the Porte de l'Avancee, through a narrow castle entrance, and up to the island's sole cobblestone street. The steps ascended steeply ahead of them, lined with gaudy tourist shops at the point where they entered the village. Gendarmes seemed to be everywhere, controlling the access to the city, the bridge, and lining the walk up the mount.

"Father Raines has arranged for a room for each of you at Le Relois Saint Michel, a five-star hotel." Monique smiled at Adrienne, and then nodded to Rex. "Adjoining rooms, as you requested, sir. Father Raines will meet you in his suite for a late breakfast on Wednesday."

Adrienne blushed, but Rex seemed unfazed. He nodded to Monique, who turned to lead the entourage up the narrow cobbled street by foot.

"I'm sorry if I embarrassed you with the room arrangements, Adrienne," Rex said as they stepped carefully across the uneven stones. "I took the liberty of requesting adjoining rooms to simplify—how shall I say this—the logistics of our stay. This hotel is a maze of rooms, and Mont Saint Michel will be a madhouse in the next forty-eight hours. I believe you will be impressed by the accommodations."

Adrienne walked slowly on the rounded stones, placing a steadying hand on Rex's arm as she negotiated the ancient street in heels. "No apology necessary," she said with a smile. "I know how to lock the door if I need to."

"Rex Edwards is here. With some reporter from *Aerospace News*. Name's Adrienne Packard."

"Got it," Special Agent Kerry said into a microphone on his headset. He looked down on the mount from the cockpit of a small jet circling above the mud flats and jutting rock. A few boats lay in the mud, awaiting the deadly tide. The smart ones had departed, and these would surely be swamped as the next tide raced in. The devastation had become a twice-daily occurrence, onlookers trying to hold a place in a boat, but swamped by a raging wall of water. He could see the streets of the city below him and the narrow entrance where his two agents had been covertly scanning the face of every person entering the city for the past two weeks. Linked by satellite to a massive data library in the States, they had near-instantaneous facial recognition of many of the people entering the city. Soon he would have a complete database on almost all who attended this circus, only three days away.

"Keep up the watch. You know who we're looking for. And get a bug on the reporter. I want to know where she and Rex are at all times."

"Thought they were the good guys?" the radio voice responded.

"They are," Kerry replied. "But they're guests of Raines. Where they go, we'll find *him*."

"One more thing," the voice continued.

"Yeah?"

"The tall woman with the long black hair. From the limo. We've seen her before somewhere. In the States. You know her?"

Kerry looked at the images in the photos, pulled via satellite from the FBI database in Quantico, Virginia. He squinted at the low-resolution image of the black-clad woman in front of the two Americans. "No. Don't recognize her."

"She's Raines's aide. With him everywhere back home."

"So?" Kerry asked.

"So, this is the first time she came by the camera." The voice hesitated. "But that's not what's so interesting."

"Then what?" he growled, nausea tugging at him as the plane banked to keep the mount in sight.

"Her identity," the agent said as though stating a question. "She's got at least ten of 'em. And every one comes with a passport. She's either a drug dealer or she's got a bunch of sisters."

MONDAY, MARCH 18, 2013: LONDON, UNITED KINGDOM

"We did as you asked, Mr. Kerry," a British agent said with a thick Scottish brogue. Kerry smiled, remembering a teacher years before who'd spoken with the same melodic English. Kerry liked it here. The Ministry of Defense was much more laid back than the ultra-classified days he remembered at the Navy's intelligence center. He always enjoyed working with MOD. Stuff got done when he came asking the Brits for help.

"We agree with the assessment of your associates in the States. This woman has many faces and many names—or else there are many of her exact likeness." The agent tilted his head to one side. "Considering how many aliases we found, mate, the latter option is quite impossible."

"Did you query the database—without the hair?"

"Yes. We removed hair as a screening option, and even aged her face older or younger to see what additional candidates we could pull up. You understand, of course, that we were searching a global database of all passports, public officials, and criminals. That effort got us another five aliases—and one new subject." The agent handed Kerry a sheet of paper with a printout of a passport photo and biographical data. "Do you know her?"

Kerry stared at the agent, then the paper. "Only one? Surely there's a world full of women with some resemblance to the lady in black."

"Apparently not, sir. Do you know this woman?"

Kerry looked at the page, shook his head, and then handed the picture back. "Should I?"

"Thought you might," the Brit continued with a shrug. "The computer thinks she's an exact match, but much older."

He pointed at the weathered face on the page. The black hair was different, shorter and wiry, and her face appeared wrinkled from years of smoking. Her pancake makeup was cracked by long lines and crow's feet, with deep ravines that coursed across her face.

"We checked her out. A big fish in your NASA organization, she is. Wicked temper too, I hear. Dr. Felicia Bondurant, director of your Jet Propulsion Laboratory."

Kerry stared at the picture a moment longer and then made a note in his pocket notebook. "Do me a favor, will you, Seamus? Check with MOD and find out if this woman has any daughters."

20

THE MMV ROLLED OVER rocks all morning in a mind-numbing series of bumps and heaves that made Michelle sick. She was amazed that their "Little Engine That Could" hadn't failed yet; it survived every obstacle Sean tackled.

"Don't puke, babe," Sean said, staring at the crater rim ahead. "I'm gonna dump over that lip and head down into Snoopy."

"Snoopy" was part of Sean's naming convention for local landmarks. He refused to use the proper Latin and Greek terminology established years ago. After her initial objection, his nicknames had begun to grow on her. Now it was fun. Craters got their names from *Peanuts*. Rocks were based on the *Wizard of Oz*, the largest being the Wicked Witch, a spectacular bedrock outcropping at the northern reach of their explorations. Potential water and geologic sites, her favorites, were named for Disney characters. That was her choice.

Another bump jarred her out of her daydream as Sean plowed over the sand-like rim and pitched headlong down the powdery red slope of the crater. Michelle choked down the stuff rising in her throat. She'd thrown up once in the suit a week ago, in a situation just like this. It hadn't been a pretty sight, and they'd rushed back to the lander just before vomit plugged a critical air intake for the recycling unit. "Never again," she'd promised herself. Today was her last ride.

The MMV approached the bottom. This was the largest crater they'd yet explored. On a previous trip, Michelle had planted at its base some special data-collection equipment to measure the daily frost of water ice that sublimated away each morning. This deep crater was more protected from sunlight than any other spot they'd found — perfect for capturing ice and with strong potential for containing water, if there was indeed water here to be found.

Millions of tiny nodules resembling blueberries lined the crater floor. First identified by the rover Opportunity years ago, the blue hematite nodules formed in water's presence. They littered the bottom of what had once been a pool of water. Michelle had driven spikes to the bottom of the pit to measure subsurface moisture and drilled several core samples in the crater to map the subsurface strata. This would be her last trip to Snoopy — her favorite crater.

She stepped out on weak legs. Her stomach roiled. Sean jumped out and headed for the equipment. She'd hoped he'd show some concern for how she was feeling, but he moved on.

"Any special instructions before I yank this thing out?" he asked, standing over the monitor and its spike. "Although I'd prefer to leave this rod in the ground, if you don't mind."

"We can leave the spike. Just let me download the data." Michelle walked slowly to the site and pulled her digital field notebook out of a thigh pocket of the Mars suit. She could write on it with a stylus, connect all her equipment to it, and communicate to the lander and their Mars-synchronous satellite with it. Even send e-mail to Earth—if she didn't mind waiting forty minutes for a response. She paused, crossing the fingers of her bulky glove. "For good luck!" she said, patting the top of the spike. In all likelihood, it would be one more "dry hole." But if not . . .

If not, then everything mankind knew, or thought they knew, about this planet would have to be reconsidered.

She removed the data line from the spike's side, inserted it into her digital notebook, and retrieved the data. The sensor's discovery flashed on the screen.

She read it, digested it—and then closed her eyes, waited a moment, and checked it again.

"Eureka!" she yelled. "It's wet!"

"What?"

"Moisture, you dummy! At the bottom of the spike. Not much, mind you. But it's *there*. Probably some ice crystals bound in the strata, about two meters below the surface."

Sean shuffled over.

"We found it, Sean! Water! On Mars!"

"That's not much to get excited over," he said, peering over her shoulder at the display. "We get frost every night."

"Right. And it's gone by sunup. But this is *permanent*."

"We'd need a backhoe to prove it."

"No, we don't. We have this data. The spike shows that the ice—or whatever—is there. It's what we've been looking for, Sean. There might be some extremophiles living down there."

"Maybe. All the same, wish I had that backhoe. Or a longer drill."

"We don't. Do we have any more of those little flags left in the MMV?"

"Yeah. One. You want to dub this baby?"

"Absolutely. It's our first subterranean moisture on Mars. And a possible site for life." She pulled a sample bag from her resource kit. "I need you to pull that spike, Sean. And when we do, I've got to collect whatever's on the end. We might get lucky and find an organism. You never know."

"You're a romantic. But I'll get it out." He moved over the spike, grabbing the hand holds welded to the long rod for just this task. "And what name," he asked as he grunted, "will you give this . . . location of historic . . . geologic . . . and life-sustaining . . . import?"

Michelle shook her head, amazed that such a cynic had made it this far in the space program.

Sean wiggled the spike, grunting until it released. She promptly wiped the end with a filter strip and sealed the sample in a plastic bag. "Perfect!"

With her sample stowed, she took hold of the large spike and raised it like a sword above the hole in the soil.

"I hereby dub thee *Mickey*," she said, planting her last miniature U.S. flag in the soil.

MONT SAINT MICHEL, FRANCE

Special Agent Kerry peered out his hotel room window. The panorama of the old abbey-city below was breathtaking. He'd allowed himself precious little time to enjoy the sights as he'd chased Elias Ulrich around the world these past two years. Staring out at the beauty of this centuries-old granite monument to Saint Michael made him realize how much of his life he'd given up. Yet, perhaps, for not much longer.

He felt, like a sixth sense, the nearness of some conclusion in this case.

His phone rang.

"Kerry." The special cellular phone showed that the connection was a top-secret line. To Suitland, Maryland.

"Hello, Agent Kerry. This is Dr. Pestorius. We've got a good track on Ulrich, fifty kilometers west of you. Navy patrol aircraft picked up Kilo 960 this morning, headed in your general direction. It all seems to be coming together."

"How'd you find him? I thought you couldn't hear the sub."

"Doesn't matter—we're on him now. He's loitering like he's waiting on something—or someone."

"I've got full surveillance here, Doc. I have visual at all entrances, roving agents, and a full suite of electronic intelligence. But you need to stand off enough to let him do his thing. If we spook Ulrich at the last minute, we might never get another chance."

"That's the instruction I passed to the Navy reconnaissance aircraft. They understand. Just keep your eyes open, Kerry. The closer we get to the twenty-first, the more things will heat up."

MARS ORBIT

"Systems check out perfect," John said. "I'm ready for you to come home anytime."

John, Sean, and Michelle ran through the launch practice and systems checks in preparation for the liftoff from Mars in two days. He displayed images of his friends in full size on the flight deck screens. A digital family.

"Now that the tests are over, I have some news. Change in plans," Sean said.

"What's that?" John asked.

"We leave tomorrow."

"A day early?" John asked. "Why?"

"I've been talking with Houston over the past three days," Sean said. "Headquarters says the world's going nuts over Malcolm Raines and his Father Race appearance on the twenty-first. They have two concerns. Believe it or not, they don't want to be upstaged by Raines. They said to leave early and be heroes. Let whatever happens in France play out."

"What's the second reason?" Michelle asked.

John could tell she was miffed. She'd been left out twice—by John with the alien investigation, and now by Sean.

"If something really wild happens on Saint Michael's rock," Sean said, "we need to be safe and sound in orbit. Who knows? Houston gets zapped with a death ray by a returning horde of alien warships. They don't want to take any chances." He paused. John could see Sean turn to Michelle.

"We're done here. We leave tomorrow. Get the ship ready for us, Hawk."

CLEAR LAKE CITY, TEXAS

"Mom!" Abe yelled. "It's Mission Control!"

Abe ran into the kitchen where Amy was decorating for Albert's birthday party. He skidded to a stop, a portable phone in his hand. Images flashed in Amy's mind of another call—the one telling her John would be in orbit another six months on the Space Station. She prepared for the worst.

"This is Amy. Who's calling?" She struggled for breath.

"It's Jake. Everything's fine, Amy. I wanted you to know before this news hits the press. We're bringing Sean and Michelle off the planet a day early."

"Are they okay?"

"They're fine. We're just taking some precautions. All this hype about the twenty-first in France and the two-year anniversary of the bombings . . . we want to get an early start. Thought I'd let you know."

Amy felt that maddening blip in her heartbeat, a momentary pounding. It had been happening too often lately. "We'll be ready. That's Albert's birthday. He'll be excited."

"Good. Expect the press. You know the drill."

"Only too well, Jake. I'll have the boys spool up the neighbors. They protect us pretty well. What time will they lift off?"

"Our noon, Amy. About nineteen hours to go."

MARS

A blue halo surrounded the sun's setting disk on Michelle's last day on Mars. She felt the chill of the rapidly cooling night as her suit sought to compensate and keep her comfortable. She had about an hour of air left while they completed their last MMV survey of the area. Viking 1 was their last stop. Four weeks ago they'd retrieved the two orbs presented by the spiders to Rover last July. Now she was here to say good-bye.

Michelle walked around the ancient lander, placing her gloved hands on Viking like a parting handshake. She lingered at the digger arm, still extended and plowed into the ground where it had stopped in 1982. She dusted off canister-like devices, experiment packages long since silenced by time. The antenna dish, dusted with red powder, pointed into the setting sun. Four hundred million kilometers away, on a straight line through Sol—Earth's star—Keith was waiting.

Michelle tied a plastic-sealed card to the antenna stanchion at eye level—just high enough for other bipeds to see. Inside the clear sample bag, bold red letters said "Read Me." Her words to the next explorer were these: "Michelle Caskey. March 19, 2013. An explorer who came to find out about life beyond Earth, but learned much more about her own life in the process."

She doubled the knot and stepped back. Her last EVA on Mars, her last sunset, her last day as a Martian, all came down to this moment. A lifetime of trials, of competition and study and work, missions on the Shuttle and Space Station to prepare her, and months of travel—all culminated in this moment, in this place. Aliens or a hoax had drawn them to Mars, and they'd stayed for a month of frustrating searches for life. At this moment, the only new life she could find was what she brought: herself.

Michelle took one more bag from her suit and tied it below the first on the gangly pole. The second card was labeled "For John." She was breaking the cardinal rule: Do Not Leave Biological Material on the Planet. But it was only fair. John had missed this amazing opportunity. He'd stayed behind in orbit, for them. A sample of his hair was hermetically sealed inside a block of resin within the pouch. She smiled as she stepped back and said good-bye to Viking 1, patting some of the dusty gold insulation material as if for good luck.

The dark began to consume them, and Sean waved in the direction of their home. She nodded, both astronauts silent in this, their last moments walking on Mars. Michelle looked back at her little gift tree as she prepared to ride the MMV to Columbus. She could see the two bags tied to Viking, one with a special letter to any visitor who might happen that way. The other a personal confession that John would never see.

"You all packed up?" John asked in his last evening chat with Columbus and his friends. Tomorrow at this time they'd be with him. John floated in the galley, finishing his last supper alone. He'd saved one frozen brownie to celebrate that special event.

"We're set. Systems are all GO," Sean said. "Old Rex built us a good ship, no doubt about that. Remind me to tell him."

"I will," John replied. "We have a big teleconference scheduled tomorrow evening, prime time East Coast viewing. You can tell him then."

"We'll be ready. Did you miss us, John?" Michelle asked.

"Like losing an arm. It's been a lonely month. I spent some time repainting your bedrooms while you were gone." John laughed. "Yours is pink, Michelle. You'll love it."

"Very funny," she replied. "How are Amy and the kids?"

"Doing great — she says. You never quite know with Amy, though. She doesn't like to talk about problems. And it's hard to converse real-time from this far away. E-mail is better."

"Yeah," Michelle chimed in. "You say 'I love you' and then wait forty minutes to hear 'I love you, too.'"

"You guys call home too much," Sean said with a frown. "There's an old Navy jet pilot rule — one a prop jock like you wouldn't understand, John. Only call home when you hit port. Every month or two. Give people their space, and they'll give you yours."

"Whatever floats your boat, Captain. That doesn't work for me."

"Me either," Michelle said. John could see her shove Sean from the back. "There's something else we need to discuss," she said. "About Mickey Mouse."

"Come again?" John said.

"Michelle finally found some faint indications of moisture," Sean said, "and a definite salt concentration at the bottom of Snoopy crater. She got a bio sample, and we're analyzing it now. Named the site Mickey Mouse."

"I'm hoping I found some extremophiles, John," Michelle said. "That's why this early launch could hurt us. We might have *finally* located something. We need to stay another day and check it out more thoroughly."

John waited a minute before he responded. "How far is Mickey Mouse from Columbus?"

"Four kilometers—too far to go back," Sean said. "Look, guys. We went to Snoopy three times looking for methanogens in the rim. Nothing. Tried three times in the crater's bottom for water. Again, zip. Then, on our *last* day, we found a trace of water. That's great. But we're done. Accept it."

"Couldn't we run some more core samples? *Something?*" Michelle asked, shaking her head.

"I hear you, Mich, but we've been here nearly a month. Houston told us to get off this rock before all you-know-what breaks loose back home. So we go."

"I understand, Sean," John said, trying to facilitate what was obviously a sore subject. "Why don't you finish your bio-sample analyses tonight, Mich? If there are no organisms in the sample then this isn't an issue. Right?"

"We'll know in a few hours," she said, dejected. "My samples are incubating now."

John understood her disappointment. This was why she'd come to Mars, to find water and life. Now, on the eve of her greatest find, she had to pack up and go home.

"You know the drill, Michelle," Sean said, waving his hand dismissively. "Even if you did find something, some naysayer would claim you contaminated it and want another sample. So where do we draw the line? We're out of time. We're leaving tomorrow." Sean huffed and left the mike in her hands.

In the monitor, John could see Michelle beginning a slow burn. "Let's deal with this a step at a time," John said quietly after Sean left. "Run the tests and let me know your findings. I'll call Houston and tell them you're on the cusp of a major find. Maybe I can get them to reconsider."

She nodded slightly. "Sean won't like that. But thanks."

21

SEAN'S SNORING WAS REGULAR. After four weeks as his roommate, Michelle had no doubt he was down for the count. The sleeping aid she'd added to his dinner hadn't hurt.

Michelle disconnected the egress alarm before venting the airlock, hoping he wouldn't hear the pumps and wake. She forged ahead, breaking every rule in the book. Sean would kill her. But if she was right, it wouldn't matter. Their trip to Mars would not have been in vain.

Michelle went down the ladder she'd first descended a month before, making history then in more ways than anyone had realized. She carried so many secrets right now—and she didn't want to die with all of them.

Standing on Mars for her last time, she turned to see if the portal remained dark. It did. She relaxed.

The MMV's electric drive came to life: 42 percent battery charge level. It would have to do.

Four kilometers would take forty minutes. Another hour to drive a spike, download the data, pull the spike, and take a bio sample. Then another forty minutes to drive home. Three hours tops. Sean would still be in the sack, she'd be home free, and they'd have the confirmation they'd searched for this past month. Proof of life on Mars.

As she drove, a billion galaxies reached down to touch her, bathing her in a pale blue light. Somewhere out there, Keith was waiting. "You're so far away," she whispered, aching to be home. "On the opposite side of the solar system."

An hour into her bumpy ride toward Snoopy, Michelle realized her folly. Sean drove like a maniac on the rocky terrain, but her careful plod in the pale starlight had only taken her two kilometers. The worst was yet to come, and the charge meter read 32 percent. Her stomach churned, anticipating a faster, more dangerous ride.

As she sped up, bounding across rocks, she remembered that the night had started with a lie. Sean had gone to bed sure there were no bugs in the Mars dirt. But that wasn't what she'd seen. The cultures had failed, true—but as she scanned them she realized why. Columbus's warmth and oxygen atmosphere had assassinated the cold-loving anaerobic creatures.

On her last scan with the electron microscope, she hit the jackpot. Distinct evidence of archaea, one of the three domains of life, phylogenetically distinct from bacteria and eucarya, the rest of the life kingdom. She found them all together, clinging to a single particle of moist soil: *methanogenium frigidum,* a lover of dark frozen environments, and the super microbe *deinococcus radiodurans,* a polyextremophile known to withstand space, nuclear cold, and oxidative environments.

Michelle's spirits lifted as she saw Snoopy's rim. She glanced at the gauge: 25 percent charge. She forced her thoughts back to the samples.

Two archaea, each able to survive in hostile extremes, and almost zero probability that she could have contaminated the sample with such rare life-forms. She'd wanted to scream, discovering the biology find of the millennium. But she knew what Sean's answer would be—he'd stay locked in Columbus to blast off for home. No matter what.

"This is insane. I'm out here all alone," Michelle said loudly. The MMV pitched over the crater's rim, plunging down the steep soft soil and crunching over hundreds of blue hematite nodules.

An hour later, she had a meter-long substrata probe driven into the soil. She leaned against the MMV, sweat sheeting off her face, consumed by the nausea and dizziness that hit her at least twice a day now. Two and a half hours had elapsed. She was behind schedule. *If only Sean wasn't so hard-headed. We could've done this together.*

Half an hour more and she had uploaded the first confirmation. Moisture. It *was* real. Given enough days and muscle power, she and Sean could have mapped this entire crater's substrata. They'd found Mickey Mouse too late.

Michelle tried to pull up the spike, but it wouldn't budge. She braced her feet and pulled with all her might. Nothing. *Use your legs,* she told herself as she tugged, moving the stake a little. Again, she squatted and pulled. Again, a centimeter of retraction at best. The end of this probe might hold all the secrets she needed. She couldn't fail.

Michelle fell against the MMV's front bumper, exhausted, her gloved hand resting on the new spool of wire Sean had replaced after he lassoed the spider. *The wire! A winch!*

In a flash, she reversed the cable, playing out enough slack to reach the spike. With a clasp hooked to the metal rod, she climbed in the MMV and engaged the winch. It took the slack, tugged a moment, and then stopped. By itself, the motor was no match for the friction of the embedded spike. Reversing the MMV, she backed up gingerly, tugging on the cable. Again, the vehicle stopped. *How did he do it?*

Then she remembered, Sean giving a good heave after wiggling the spike. Michelle slammed the MMV into reverse and jerked on the spike so hard she feared she'd break it off. The stake leaned over slightly. She'd broken the ground's friction lock. Again, she engaged the winch, and the motor strained as it pulled the long brass spike free of frozen Martian ground. Half an hour later, the job was done. Another half hour and she'd be on her way.

Michelle wiped tip samples on a bio-filter, then sealed and resealed the moist filter paper. She slid the end of the spike into another sample bag, placed it in the back of the MMV, and packed her equipment. She looked at her watch. Three and a half hours. Her oxygen was fine for now—but not for another two hours.

The MMV churned in the loose soil and nodules, slowly cresting the rim. In the distance, across a dark plain, she could see the blinking beacon of Columbus. For the first time that night, she shivered in the cold.

Bore sighted on the blinking light, Michelle plowed ahead Sean-fashion, her lights bouncing all over the rocky path. After an hour of the punishing travel she checked her power level: 10 percent. And still more than a kilometer to go. The cold numbed her arms and shoulders. Her feet felt like blocks of ice.

Michelle willed herself not to dwell on the problem. She knew exactly what was wrong. Her suit had charged only a few hours, and the cold night, nearly 220 degrees below zero, was causing her thermal control system to work overtime to keep her warm.

Thirty minutes later, she'd lost all feeling in her extremities and could barely turn her head. She pushed her hip forward, forcing the lame frozen foot to depress the drive pedal.

Half a kilometer to go. Normally she'd have been able to walk from here. But she couldn't walk now. It was impossible to concentrate with all the shaking. She dropped the steering handle, then couldn't will her arms to rise. The beacon flashed steadily before her, just beyond her reach. The numbing cold pulled her eyes closed. *If only I could rest, just a little*, she thought. *I'm almost there.*

She began to pray—like John had told her.

MARS ORBIT

"I can't sleep. Might as well work," John said, unzipping the sack. A great day was ahead, a chance to bring his friends home. He was wired. And he'd quit worrying about talking to himself. *Just don't talk back.*

John floated to the flight deck to watch the stars as Epsilon slipped behind the planet. Sunrises here weren't the breathtaking events that they were orbiting Earth. But the dark sky and its stunning panorama of galaxies was marvelous to behold. He turned off the flight deck lights and sat in the dark, as though on the precipice of creation, the universe spread before him.

Someone moaned, a barely perceptible voice. John flinched, looking for the source. Another sound, like the tender whimper of a little girl. On speaker.

John checked the comm panel. He was tuned to the Columbus frequency, as always. And the EVA frequency. Another moan.

"Who is it?" John asked into the mike. "Sean? Michelle? Are you there?"

No response. Another moan.

"Columbus, Epsilon. Come in *now*. This is John. Columbus! *Answer up!*"

No response.

He listened and called a dozen times over the next two minutes. At last a gravelly voice responded.

"Hold your horses, John. I'm here. What's wrong?"

"Sean? Are you okay?"

"I was 'til you woke me up. Are *you* okay? It's four in the morning, John."

"I heard voices."

"Voices? Man, you *are* going nuts."

"This is no joke, Sean. I couldn't sleep, so I came up to the flight deck. I heard it three times. Sounded like a moan. Is Michelle okay?"

"She's asleep. Where I ought to be."

"You're sure?"

"Yeah. Right over—Michelle! She's gone!"

| MARS

She dreamed of ice cubes and standing naked in the snow. Cold showers at camp and frostbite on a snowmobile.

She willed her eyes to open and saw a beacon before her. It was pulsing bright as though calling her the last step home. Her eyes shut. She still saw the light, somehow. *Why?*

She heard a whisper, deep inside, someone calling her. She willed herself to answer.

"John?"

＊

"She's calling!"

"I *heard* her!"

"You've gotta suit up, Sean! Find her!"

Sean ignored John, sure of what had happened. He rubbed his face to wake up, feeling sluggish, like he'd been drugged. He headed for his EVA suit and the fastest dressing job of his life.

He heard John calling Michelle on the radio. Her dull moaning response was like repeated stabs in his gut with a dull oyster-shucking knife. Michelle was in serious trouble, somewhere out there. And she'd called for *John*.

Sean's anger fanned into a rage. She'd outwitted him, drugged him, turned off the egress alarm that would've betrayed her, and slipped off alone in the dark of night only hours before their departure.

Worst of all, Michelle had sought John first—and John had been the one to notice she was missing. Sean knew he had no right to claim her—still, he felt she was his to protect. The ire boiled in him, most of it directed at John.

He descended the ladder and his heart sank. The MMV was gone.

Sean jogged around Columbus, his flashlight waving, seeking the MMV's tracks. Every track made since their arrival seemed to stare back at him, pulling his attention in wrong directions. *She must've headed for Snoopy, and more samples.* He took off on foot to the north.

"John?" he heard again through his helmet speaker, the dim voice barely moaning the name. His heart pounded from exertion and fury, from jealous rage. He plunged into the night toward Snoopy crater, his flashlight bouncing as he struggled across the rocky plain. He hated John. Hated him for his goody-two-shoes religious perfection and for pulling Michelle's heart just when Sean needed her most.

"Michelle!" John said, "Sean's coming for you. Can you hear us?"

"Michelle! I'm headed . . . for Snoopy crater. . . . Is that . . . where . . . you are?" Sean sucked air, trying to yell over John's voice and run in the bulky jointed suit. His head told him he was a fool. His heart said "go!"

"MMV. Five . . . hundred . . . meters," came a husky reply.

"I see her!" Sean yelled, nearly tripping on a large jagged boulder. He cursed, centimeters away from certain death if his suit ripped in a fall. His bouncing flashlight reflected in the gold visor. A hundred meters more.

"She's in . . . the MMV . . . I can . . . can get to her." He shook his head violently to sling the sweat out of his eyes.

Two minutes later, Sean was at Michelle's side. She slumped in the seat, as if frozen in place. He waved his light across the control panel. Four percent charge. Enough to get home.

"Michelle!" He shook her shoulder, gently bent her arms to grip her torso and move her out of the seat. In the glow of tiny red lights below the gold shield he could see the outline of her face.

"Sean?"

"I'm here, girl. Hang on."

He pulled Michelle into the passenger seat and belted her in. Moments later, he was driving. The bitter cold Mars buggy began moving in slow motion toward the distant strobe.

"Michelle! Stay with me, babe. Almost there."

"How far, Sean?" John asked, frantic.

"Shut up." Sean spit out the words. "Michelle, it's *Sean*. Can you hear me?" He shook her.

"Sean?" John asked again.

"I said *shut up*." He cursed again and whacked her helmet with his right glove. "Answer me, Mich. Now! Do *not* sleep. Wake up!"

She moaned. He slammed her helmet with his fist. She moaned again.

"Sean?"

"That's my girl. Talk to me. What'd you find?" He flailed across the rocks full speed.

"Spike . . . samples."

"Tell me more, baby. Did you find life?"

"Yes . . . archaea. I—"

She was silent.

Sean thumped her helmet again and rapped her on the shoulder, steering the bucking cart left-handed. Less than a hundred meters now. He could pull her to safety if he had to.

"Found . . . life-forms."

"More, Michelle. Tell me more. Gotta get the life-forms home." He glanced in the back. She'd tethered four bio bags and the spike to the rear deck.

"Home," she whispered.

"Yes, Mich. We're going home. I promise. Hang with me, girl." Sean jerked his head to clear his wet eyes. The salty stuff wasn't sweat this time. He couldn't remember the last time he'd cried. He couldn't lose her, he just couldn't. "We're there, Mich. You're okay. Hang with me. *Please*."

"I've got the lock ready, Sean."

John's voice had been silent for some time, Sean realized. "Thanks. Gotta get her up the ladder. Wish you were here."

"I am, Sean."

Sean skidded to a stop at the base of the ladder, 2 percent showing on the charge panel, with a glaring warning light. He'd reposition the rover later. Right now Michelle needed warmth.

He raced around the MMV and threw her over his shoulder like a pillow, turned in the soft soil, and scaled the ladder in seconds.

"I'm in, John. Pressurizing."

"Roger."

A minute later, the inner hatch opened, and Sean pulled Michelle into the science deck. He laid her flat on the metal deck and removed her helmet. Her face was pallid, her body stiff and immobile. He rubbed her cheeks, calling her, his tears dripping on her face as he pulled it close. "Michelle!"

Her eyes opened and the faintest of smiles crossed her lips. Her breath was soft but regular. Sean pushed her auburn hair out of her face and put a finger under her jaw, seeking her carotid pulse. Her eyes closed.

"Don't go to sleep, Michelle! Talk to me." He began stripping off her suit, gloves, and boots, and rolled her over to unzip her from the lobster shell-like suit and its oxygen and thermal controls. He slid her out of the dirty white garment and carried her to her bed in the upper habitation deck, where he covered her with all the warming material he could find and then began rubbing her hands and feet. She opened her eyes, some color in her cheeks, and smiled again, her gaze meeting Sean's.

"I'm sorry, Sean . . . I thought . . . I could . . . make it."

"Don't be sorry. I saw your stuff. I'll bring it in. You just rest. I need a copilot today, okay?"

She smiled a little more, her teeth showing beneath purple lips. "Okay. Just give me . . . some time."

"All you need, baby. All you need."

Her hand took his in a feeble grip. "Thank you, Sean—for what you did." A tear pooled in her eye and rolled off her cheek. "Thank you—for saving us."

22

"**I HAVE EVERYTHING I NEED,** and I can touch anyone I want," Rex said, profiled sharply against the Gothic backdrop and the Gulf of Saint Malo. A "Foster's World Special Edition," broadcast from France, brought the world a perspective on Rex Edwards that few had ever seen. Adrienne wrote the copy, and Foster recited it like it was his own. Columbus's crew would leave Mars in a few hours, and Rex looked ready-as-ever for the next leg of this great adventure.

"You can monitor the launch and all of Epsilon's systems? From your hotel?" asked Foster Williams.

"That's not so unusual, Foster. This is a digital world, even in Normandy. I brought all the satellite connectivity and computing power that I needed, but I found ample satellite bandwidth here, thanks to Saint Michael's Remnant. I've created a virtual office on Mont Saint Michel with a solid link back to Palmdale. If I'm needed for some reason—by NASA or my own staff—then I'm here."

A shallow sea stretched into the distance behind Rex, who sat on his hotel room veranda. As the camera panned back, a broad array of monitors, computers, and assorted office duplication equipment filled the screen.

"Why retreat to this island in France, Rex?" Foster asked from Los Angeles. "Why not stay home for the big day and participate from your operations center? Or from Houston with NASA?"

Rex laughed and shook his head. "Reliability and simplicity, Foster: My systems *work*. And—I have complete faith in Captain O'Brien and Captain Wells. They'll handle the Mars launch and the join-up very well." He pointed toward the sea. "But more to the point—our visitors will arrive here at the mount in two days. I intend to be on hand when they arrive."

MARS

"You ready for this?" Sean asked Michelle, leaning toward her in the command seat of the Columbus module. Her nausea was back, but she forced a smile and nodded. The strength and calm in Sean's voice settled her. She was safe now and headed away from Mars. Toward home.

Sean waded through what seemed an hour's worth of complex system checks. They would only get one chance to do this right. The rocket motor was ready to send them into a high Martian orbit. With no off switch. As Rex liked to say, "Some risks are worth taking, and this is one of them." The liquid-fueled rocket would be ultra reliable; it would wait an entire mission for its brief moment of fame, and then start when they needed it. And—in rare cases—it could fail catastrophically. But it was worth the risk—at least it was for Rex. And the taxpayers. *No worse,* she thought, *than the risk of going out alone at night on Mars.*

"Columbus, Epsilon," John said, calling from somewhere far above. "All systems are GO. Ready when you are. The first launch window's approaching."

"Columbus is ready." Sean flashed a thumbs up, and she returned the same. She stared through the grating of the deck below into the science and dining area. Her precious samples waited in deep cold storage for an evaluation. That critical analysis would have to wait until they were headed home with John. They had plenty of time. And she was sure she'd found the proof they required—proof of life on Mars.

Seven minutes later Sean threw the switch, and Columbus roared to life. The craft accelerated slowly for a fraction of a second, then pushed rapidly to more than four times gravity and exploded into the Martian sky. On the monitor she could see Rover's images of their ignition and liftoff, the trusty wheeled robot that had served them so well for a month taking pictures from a few hundred meters away. Rover would remain behind and watch—and eventually die. Months or years from now, her solar cells would cease to function, and like her great grandparent Viking 1 before her, she'd settle into an eternal series of frigid Martian days and nights.

Rover's camera followed the blue and orange blaze as Columbus rocketed away from the Red Planet. Sean called out altitudes and flew the craft, monitoring the automatic processes, ready to take over at any moment in manual mode if needed. He patted Michelle on the shoulder as if to reassure her. His touch felt good. She hated this rocket ride, but would never admit it.

"Got a visual!" she heard John say later on the comm circuit. "You're right on time!"

"Roger that, Epsilon," Sean replied. "Columbus has slipped the surly bonds of Mars. We're headed home."

JOHNSON SPACE CENTER, HOUSTON, TEXAS

"Praise God," Amy said out loud from her seat in the VIP deck of the Mars Mission Control in Houston. From her left and right, friends and family reached over to touch her arm or squeeze a hand. Yet Amy had no one on Columbus. In front of her, Keith Caskey punched the air in jubilation, his parents at his side—all the family Michelle had. To Keith's left, a lone woman, Sean's ex-wife Debra O'Brien, nodded in silence.

Before them, on Mission Control's large screen, they watched Rover's images of the liftoff twenty minutes after it actually happened. Columbus flew into a yellow sky, ending its last day on Mars. Cheers erupted from Mission Control and the gallery. An inset video on the screen showed Rex Edwards with the sea behind him at sunset monitoring the launch from his hotel in France. Malcolm Raines sat to his left in the makeshift studio. Amy wished Raines had been left out of this celebration.

"In sixteen days," the Mission Control announcer said, "Mars will be at conjunction—the farthest point from Earth in its orbit about the Sun. This video has traveled almost four hundred million kilometers—and twenty minutes—to reach us today."

His commentary did nothing to make Amy feel better about the mission's safety. She prayed silently for John as he waited for his friends. Somewhere out there, two-and-a-half times as far away as Earth was from the Sun, her John waited. Soon he would be headed home.

Amy watched Debra O'Brien in front of her, alone, barely responding to the events of the day. As the jubilation and cheers died down, and everyone listened to the chatter of John and Sean discussing flight parameters, Amy approached the solitary woman. "They made it," Amy said, extending her hand. "I'm so glad."

Debra wore a gracious smile. In her mid-fifties, she'd divorced Sean near the end of his Mars training. It was an ugly separation, one that some media fed upon as Sean took on the leadership mantle of a historic mission and also found himself in the public eye, even when he strayed. And NASA's golden boy strayed often. Amy wondered how the stoic Debra held up all those years.

"I know John is glad for this," Debra said. "It had to be a lonely month."

"It was. He probably didn't confess to anyone at NASA how tough it was on him. But he told me. He really missed Sean and Michelle."

"Yes," Debra said as she stood at her seat in the gallery. "But he'll have eight months to get over that."

Amy smiled slightly. "I'll be so glad when this is all over." She paused. "The kids and I have been praying for you, Debra. We'd love it if you could come over again sometime—like you used to."

Debra shook her head. "Thank you, but those days are past, I'm afraid. This mission—and life here—is over for me." She opened her purse and retrieved a magazine clipping. "I wanted to let you know what an impact you're making by being vocal." She pointed to the clipping as she unfolded it. "America's Moms: Amy Wells" was emblazoned across the top of the page. "You've captured an understanding of separation that I never understood all those years with Sean. Don't stop talking about stress and pain, Amy. There are lots of us out there who don't know how to get through the next day, but we won't admit it. Your encouragement is making a huge impact."

She took Amy's hand and squeezed it. "You were always there for me in the dark times. Thank you." Debra sighed, her eyes red and wet. "Do everything you can to stay out of my shoes, Amy. And help others avoid it, too." With that, she released Amy's hand, closed her purse, and said good-bye.

"Contact!"

John's voice cracked with emotion as he announced the return of his friends and the safe join-up of the Columbus module. After a six-hour chase, the two craft were one at last. Columbus, a short can-like ship, nestled alongside the cylindrical Epsilon, like a roll of toilet paper lying adjacent to a roll of paper towels. A docking collar joined the two.

"Lock!" John said, confirming Epsilon's grip of the Mars Lander. "Pressurizing now."

From his seat in the flight deck he watched the video transmitted from within Columbus, showing Michelle and Sean raise their hands in celebration, then pat each other on the shoulder. For the first time in a month, both were weightless. Their images were winging to Earth, and twenty minutes later the rest of humanity would celebrate with them.

"We can open it now," John said. "I'm headed your way."

Fifteen minutes later, hatches opened, seals confirmed, and check-lists tucked away, John tumbled into Columbus's tight confines, whooping like a high school mascot at a championship basketball game. "You did it!"

Sean and Michelle removed their helmets and embraced John in their bulky suits. John noticed the red dust everywhere; a fine coating hung in the air now that the ship was weightless. Their suits were stained and scuffed, and Michelle was more haggard than he'd ever seen her. Sean had a look of extreme relief. And no wonder. In the past fifteen hours, he'd saved Michelle's life and flown the first-ever launch from the surface of another planet. More than enough stress for one day. "You're the hero of the day, mate." He clasped his friend's mitt.

Sean shrugged. "Did my part. I wasn't about to leave her behind." He nodded toward Michelle who watched both men with a glow that John hadn't seen in her eyes in a long time.

"I'm sorry I put you through that, Sean. *And John.* Never again. I promise."

"I'll hold you to that," Sean said with a smile.

"Sneaking out at night again, young lady?" John said as he gave her a clumsy hug.

Michelle held him tight and whispered into his ear on the side away from Sean. "You and I need to talk."

WEDNESDAY, MARCH 20, 2013: MONT SAINT MICHEL, FRANCE

"One more day," Rex said to Adrienne. "A moment I've been anticipating a long time. The return from Mars." He pointed at the sunrise. "They're directly out there, Adrienne, on a straight line through the Sun, but half again as far from the Sun as we are from it. On the opposite side of the solar system. We couldn't see them with a telescope if we wanted to; that big star's in the way."

Adrienne and Rex stood together in the Oratory of Saint Hubert, a pinnacle on the northwest side of Mont Saint Michel. He'd led her out here through a maze of granite passageways and cobbled paths, as though he knew this abbey and quaint village by heart. The waters below them shimmered in the morning light.

Rex pointed down, directly toward the rising sun, at the green forested north slope of the mount. "Can you see that long stairway? The steep approach from the sea up through the trees? That's the only way in or out tomorrow afternoon. Now that the French have removed the rock causeway, we're cut off from the mainland twice a year by the highest of the tides—a proxigean spring tide—due to the rare alignment of the Sun and the Moon, both pulling the sea into the Gulf of Saint Malo."

He gestured from the sea toward the mount's top. "The Bishop of Avranches built the first chapel right there, on top, in the year 708." The ancient Benedictine abbey rose dramatically above the rocky, cone-shaped islet. Around it, the village nestled within the confines of crenellated granite ramparts and tall stone towers.

"The first abbey was improved, buildings fell in, others were burned, attacked, abandoned, razed, and rebuilt again for thirteen centuries. It survived the Norman invasion, but the French Revolution turned it into a prison. The island is riddled with catacombs."

Adrienne marveled at the Gothic architecture as Rex pointed out every detail of this most visited historic site in France. The no-nonsense aerospace engineer she'd met in California had a romantic flair for history, maps, dates, and numbers. He'd regaled her with the centuries-old story of Mont Saint Michel since their arrival, speaking of the ancient stairs and the rest of the mount with a passion, as though he'd been raised here. She touched his arm. "When did you say the spring tide was tomorrow?"

"*Proxigean* tide. That's different—bigger—than a spring tide. It's a good word for your article, by the way. It will send most of your readership scurrying for their dictionaries. My data predict it will occur just before three tomorrow afternoon. A fifteen-meter wall of water will rip across those mudflats at twenty kilometers an hour—the speed of a galloping horse. Pilgrims headed to the island once had to walk across those treacherous flats, often dotted with quicksand. When the tides came, they were usually swept away. A thousand years ago, you came out here by boat—or you walked out here with a good measure of faith."

"How much faith do *you* have?" Adrienne prodded him lightly in the side.

"Faith in what? My abilities? My spacecraft? Or some religious icon?"

"I know where you stand on spiritual faith, Rex. I didn't mean it that way. How much faith do you have in this mission? I heard what you said to Foster. But admit it: you've taken a risk leaving the States at a crucial time. Even considering that operations center you built in your suite."

He chuckled and looked back to the sea. "I gave you credit for understanding me better than that vaporhead Foster Williams. I have *total* faith in my spacecraft. We launched safely from Mars, didn't we? They didn't need me. If I hadn't built my ships to be ultra-reliable and triply redundant, I might be losing sleep. My design is simple. It works. Like a can opener—the manual ones are hard to break."

Adrienne looked across the flat sea, imagining a wall of water galloping in at the speed of a racehorse, and her, in deep wet sand, slogging to escape. Her last question had come off like that—quicksand.

"I admire that," she said.

"What? Faith? Or simplicity?"

"Confidence. Quiet assurance that you've done your best and needn't fret all the problems that could occur." She sighed. "I could use a dose of that confidence sometimes. I'm always worried someone will dislike my writing, or that it isn't perfect."

"It *isn't*, Adrienne. Nothing's ever perfect. Question is: Is it good *enough*?" Rex put a hand on hers where she'd rested it on a weathered stone rail. "Life's too short to second-guess your decisions, Adrienne." He turned toward her. This was the first day she could remember seeing Rex without his red bow tie. And the first time they'd physically connected beyond a cordial gesture. Her heart quickened.

"You do your best," he said, slowly. "And you move on. *Never* look back."

Adrienne shook her long hair in the sea wind. She squeezed Rex's hand and smiled. "No looking back. You have quite a way of speaking to issues under the surface, don't you?"

"Absolutely," he said, taking her hand in both of his. "I'm perceptive."

23

WEDNESDAY, MARCH 20, 2013:
MONT SAINT MICHEL

MALCOLM CLASPED REX EDWARDS'S hand with both of his own in greeting. The ex-basketball star-cum-religious icon dwarfed Rex, yet neither man seemed to notice. Adrienne thought it curious. They behaved like old friends at this brunch on the eve of the Great Awakening.

"Father Raines," Rex said with feeling. Then he gestured toward Adrienne. "May I introduce Ms. Packard, from *Aerospace News*? She is accompanying me on—shall we say—an immersive reporting assignment. Quite an insightful young woman."

Raines bowed! How long since she had seen that gesture? Adrienne blushed and extended her hand. Malcolm's massive mitt swallowed her fingers, and she pulled them back quickly, then eyed the nearby buffet, the aroma of the French variant of bacon drawing her.

"I have read your work, Ms. Packard," Raines said, a broad smile above the cleric's collar and resplendent purple robes. He seemed in no hurry to eat. "Succinct articles. You capture the essence of your subjects quite well."

The blush deepened. Adrienne nodded toward His Immenseness, her private term for the towering Malcolm Raines, and stepped closer to Rex, where she felt safer. They were on Raines's turf in a palatial hotel room, two floors above their own. Servants waited at every door.

"Please!" Malcolm insisted, pointing to a table set for four. "Have a seat." He turned to Rex. "I trust that your accommodations are acceptable?"

Rex smiled, one of the first that Adrienne could remember seeing. "Exquisite. You have excellent connections with the locals."

Malcolm nodded. "They know me well." He changed the subject. "Tonight the crew leaves Martian orbit headed to Earth, correct?"

"Seven more hours. I anticipate no difficulty," Rex replied.

If they're going to chat like this all day, I'll die of hunger, Adrienne thought.

Malcolm turned toward her. "Ms. Packard, are you enjoying your visit to Mont Saint Michel?"

She nodded. "Please, sir, call me Adrienne. And yes, I am. Rex is a marvelous guide." She turned and smiled at Rex, who seemed oddly at ease here.

"Wonderful. I trust you'll join Rex and me tomorrow for the big event? The great visitation?"

Her heart quickened. *The place of honor and a front row seat on history?* "I'd be most honored, Father Raines. It would be the opportunity of a lifetime."

Malcolm smirked. "The opportunity of *four hundred* generations, my dear. But I suggest that if you are here for immersive journalism, then you need to do more than *observe*. We grasp the inner knowledge best through participation and experience. Tomorrow you will have such a chance." Malcolm motioned to a waiter, who began preparing the plates, including a fourth for an unnamed guest. Malcolm ignored him, gesturing with his long fingers. "Adrienne, this inner knowledge I speak of is a mystical comprehension of the ultimate reality—what some in my body of believers refer to as 'esoteric' knowledge."

What's he talking about? Adrienne wondered. She canted her head, one eyebrow raised, and tried to capture Malcolm's last words on her notepad. The table was now crowded with hot food, and the aroma made it hard to concentrate.

Rex laughed. "You lost her, Malcolm. You lost me too the first time, remember?"

"Ah, yes. Let's try again. Join us tomorrow, Adrienne, because you will be able to experience truth, not just read about it. Experience is the ultimate arbiter of truth, don't you agree?"

She canted her head again, then shook it. "No. I don't agree at all. But I understand those who believe that's how it should work. I've been taught that truth doesn't have to be experienced for it to be truth. You don't have to fall off a building to believe that gravity exists."

Malcolm laughed and gestured to Rex. "A thinker, Rex! I am glad you brought her along—but my apologies. I have monopolized the conversation."

"Not at all," Rex said, sipping some fresh coffee. "Let him have it with both barrels, Adrienne. Let's not dodge this issue because, frankly, I like where he's going with this. If you can understand him, you'll be better able to describe me."

She shrugged, feeling like she was being set up. "Okay." She found some notes on her personal digital assistant. "You said recently in Phoenix that—I'm quoting one of your sermons—'Spiritual liberation is found in hidden knowledge. You will not find life's secrets within the life-negating constrictions of orthodoxy.' What's that all about?" She looked up, unsure if she understood her own question. Then she focused on her coffee to break Malcolm's unrelenting gaze.

"You're right, Rex. She *is* an insightful woman." Malcolm beamed. "You have quoted the essence of esotericism, Adrienne. Gnosis—the inner knowledge of our own divinity—is what we all seek. Orthodox religion sends us on a path to salvation through a creator, or through works or meditation, but my people embrace the belief that salvation is through *relational and experiential understanding*. Thus, liberation—our salvation—is found in the hidden knowledge of life, what we have to experience and discover in a relational manner, not what we read in books written by dead apostles."

She pointed her stylus at him, eyes narrowed. "But you also said that—hold on—here it is. You said, 'We must evaluate and embrace all religious traditions, and through them we will find a universal foundation.' How can you denigrate 'dead apostles,' as you call them, and still experience this universal truth your organization speaks about?"

She looked at Rex, seeking to gage his sensitivity to her cornering the meeting. He smiled over the rim of his coffee cup and waved her on. *He likes watching me perform.*

Malcolm was quiet, his hands pressed together, and fingertips to lips.

"Often, my dear—" he began.

Don't call me that.

"—we argue about issues that are simply different interpretations of a single reality—the one true reality. I apologize for that comment about dead apostles. They are all part of the differing appreciations of divine mysteries. But more to the point—and this is important for you to experience tomorrow, not just observe—*you* have a problem."

Adrienne sucked in her breath, her coffee cup lifted halfway to its destination. "I beg your pardon?"

Malcolm shrugged and Adrienne turned toward Rex. *What does Rex think?*

"It's not a serious problem," Malcolm continued, "but you are so locked into semantics that you have missed truth—and can never experience this inner knowledge. You are what my professors at Oxford would call an 'exoteric.' I caution you that you can go through life with this rigid, limited mindset, but true spiritual liberation is only found through our inner divinity. Every soul is but a drop in the divine ocean, my dear—and our path is the return through hidden knowledge to the Father Race. Until a few months ago, we knew nothing of the Father Race's spider-like landers. That knowledge was hidden. Now it will be revealed to us through our galactic Fathers."

Adrienne set the cup down, her attention focused. "Be that as it may, Father Raines, I fail to see where your hidden knowledge is of any value to the world as long as it's *hidden*. And once it ceases to be hidden, you can no longer revere it because it has been revealed. I might be exotic—or exoteric—whatever. But I know this. You're speaking in riddles, and you'll surround yourself with controversy at some point if you can't articulate a truth that the common man can understand."

Malcolm nodded, his smile fading. "Perhaps. We are locked in a battle of semantics. Eventually one of us will miss the spirit of truth. I am certain that person is you."

"Why is that?" She set her notebook aside. *This is getting personal.*

"Adrienne, I seek the highest principle of Being where we merge with the unknown and unknowable God. What we call the *pleroma*—or fullness. The highest of three layers of being and of the multiple layers of truth. Tomorrow, representatives of the pleroma will be in our midst."

He stared into her eyes with a power she'd never seen during his television appearances.

"Open your heart, my dear, and experience the Father Race to the fullest. God and you are one being. That's the ultimate knowledge."

There was an awkward pause. It stretched.

"Perhaps we should eat," Rex said, eyeing Adrienne. "We can continue this discussion over the meal. Malcolm?"

Raines nodded, a frown subsiding. Adrienne was sure Rex hadn't anticipated her diving into a discussion like this with such vigor. If so, he'd underestimated her. Rex waited while Malcolm motioned to the head servant. They spoke in whispers at the end of the table. *What's going on?*

"I'm sorry," Malcolm said. "We have one more guest joining us. She has just arrived from the States."

"I'm sorry," Rex said, "I didn't—"

Malcolm stood and Rex followed his lead. Adrienne shrugged and raised an eyebrow in surprise as the suite's main door opened. Moving quickly, his purple robe flowing, Malcolm greeted the new visitor.

A tall woman in her early sixties entered the room and embraced Raines warmly. Her jet-black hair looked stiff in its semblance of a short, wiry perm. Her powdered face was marked like a target with a red bull's-eye on a field of white; her bright lipstick, applied too far beyond the edges of her lips, was comical. Adrienne could see the beginnings of a skunk stripe. This woman needed hair dye. Every morning.

"Malcolm!" the woman blurted. "Thank you for arranging for me to join you. What a wonderful gift!"

"Felicia?" Rex said, stunned at the new visitor. "I thought you were staying in Pasadena for the launch."

She smiled, holding Raines close with both arms, staring up at his face. "JPL can survive without me, Rex. It's in Houston's hands now. Besides—" she released Raines and followed him to her seat across from

Adrienne—"Malcolm said I could use your operations center to stay in touch if necessary. Thank you for that offer." She seemed to wink at Raines.

Rex's face reddened above the bow tie. Adrienne had traveled with him long enough to realize why. Rex didn't like surprises. *They must know each other. Well.* Rex turned to Malcolm, jaw set in defiance and eyes narrowed.

"Perhaps we should introduce our guest," he said, gesturing to Adrienne.

"Yes! Allow me to introduce Dr. Felicia Bondurant. Director of NASA's Jet Propulsion Laboratory."

Adrienne stood and extended her hand. As she did, she glanced toward the servants closing the ornate French doors. Beyond the portal stood another black-haired woman. Raines's aide. Monique.

Amazed, Adrienne's mouth dropped open as she watched Monique peek in, then disappear. All eyes were on Felicia, and Adrienne was sure no one else had seen the young woman. The similarity between the two women was eerie—despite probably a forty years age difference.

"Adrienne? You look surprised. Have we met?" Dr. Bondurant asked.

"No—no. I'm sorry. We've not met. How do you do?" She glanced at Raines, all smiles, holding Felicia's hand. Then she looked back at the door. The servants had closed it and stood guard, awaiting Malcolm's next command.

She released Dr. Bondurant's hand as they both sat down. "It's just that you . . . you remind me so much . . . of someone else."

"Really, my dear? Who?"

WEDNESDAY, MARCH 20, 2013:
MARS ORBIT

"Houston, Epsilon. We are GO for trans-Earth injection. Initiating countdown now. T minus two minutes."

Sean and John sat on either side of the flight deck, with Michelle in the middle, as they completed the final acceptance checks prior to launch from Martian orbit. Michelle felt secure sandwiched between these two men she knew so well. One her protector, the other her close friend. Her thoughts drifted to Keith as she worked through the checklist items, and she was sure her two crewmates must have someone in mind, too, as they completed the final preparations. They were so far from home, and no one spoke of the dangers of this final critical step in their journey. *We all know what's at stake. Especially me.*

Other than the launch from the surface, this would be the most dangerous maneuver of the trip. If the engines failed leaving Earth, they would have, at worst, been marooned in Earth orbit until a return craft could take them home. In a pinch, with a failure of the retro-burn by the engines as they arrived at Earth, they could aero-capture in Earth orbit, albeit higher than they'd like, and get a ride back to the planet. But at Mars, there was no margin for error. This operation had to work right the first time.

"Navigation's got a lock. Tanks are primed. Ready when you are," John said a minute later, his voice steady and strong as though he did this every day. "I spent a month tuning this baby up while you were gone. She's ready to go."

He actually enjoys this, Michelle thought.

"Then what're we waiting for?" Sean said. "Let 'er rip."

"Roger that," John replied. "T minus forty-two seconds, gas generators spooling up now."

Aft of systems control, in the propulsion bay, gas generators ignited at John's command, forcing massive quantities of hot gas into the turbine ports of the liquid fuel pumps. In less that half a minute, the pumps were operating at full speed, ready to take on the months-old load of cryogenic fuels supplying the demand of Epsilon's three main engines. Michelle could see the diagrams in her head after months of training on every function. She understood the ship's systems, but she had no desire to fly it.

"T minus fifteen. Sparks." As Sean spoke, John commanded the aft sparks to ignite the mixed hydrogen and oxygen in the liquid fueled engines. Five seconds later, two super-cooled fuels spewed through automatic gate valves, mixing in each engine's head. A volatile fuel mixture spooled through a kilometer of nozzle tubing, expanding as it transited to the combustion chamber.

"Ignition!" John sang out. Michelle felt a strong push from behind. Both nozzles roared to life. On the monitor for the aft video, she could see long blue plumes streaking from the rear of the ship. Epsilon blasted forward, gathering speed.

"Delta-v updates on thirty-second intervals, Mich," Sean requested as he and John monitored the function of the engines and the ship controls. Michelle recited the increasing speed as they counted toward Mars escape velocity. She continued counting beyond that to the delta-v they needed to coast to Earth in eight months.

Less speed and they'd miss Earth. Too much speed and the same result. Catching Earth as it rotated around the solar system was like shooting at birds, she'd been told. You have to lead your shot. Earth was on one side of the solar system, far beyond the Sun. Mars was diametrically opposed on the other—the unusual conjunction that made this mission so hard at this particular time. Like being at six o'clock on the dial and shooting at the three o'clock. If they did it just right, Earth, falling from twelve o'clock, would be there right when they arrived. Except for one small detail, John would argue—"the solar system rotates counterclockwise."

"It depends which way you look at it," Michelle had countered once. "If you look at the solar system from below, it rotates clockwise." As far as she was concerned, her metaphor worked.

The tanks drained at a staggering rate, consuming half the remaining load of bitterly cold fuel. Epsilon accelerated smoothly, rumbling and vibrating, gathering speed, pressing the crew into their seats. Then, in an abrupt automatic shutdown, the engines quit. The rumble and rattling ended, and somehow Michelle missed them. It would be a long eight months of perfect stillness heading home.

"We're on our way," John reported, as the three astronauts floated in their straps. "Trans-Earth injection complete."

24

THREE-AND-A-HALF million visitors clambered up the gaudy tourist street from the medieval entrance of Mont Saint Michel each year. It seemed to Adrienne that every one of them was here right now. Were it not for the elegant, black-haired Monique, who had spirited Adrienne to the weathered granite stone cloisters north of the ancient abbey, she never would have found her way in this mass of humanity—or found Rex. From her hotel room, she'd been able to see thousands of people lining the beaches across the mud flats, and she knew that billions more watched over a dozen media outlets.

Ten meters to her left, Raines presided in French over his latest news conference. He had provided her a seat with the international media, behind the VIP area. Rex and Felicia sat at the head of the VIPs, but Rex looked none too pleased sharing his space with Felicia. Adrienne was still amazed at the facial similarities she'd noticed last night between

Monique and the wrinkled pancake-makeup lady. Except that Monique was slightly taller. And enviably beautiful.

Raines had said that the alien visitors would come from the west, but for some reason Adrienne continued watching the north. So engrossed in the space reverend were the media and Raines's groupies that only she saw the racing sea.

Adrienne left her seat to walk to the cloister's edge. She wondered if the others sensed it, but they were glued to Raines. She watched the water race toward them. The crowd in the abbey gardens, below her position, were pointing to the sea. The proxigean tide, a rare spring surge of fifteen meters or more of water caused by the Moon's alignment with the Sun once every eighteen months, was roaring across the mud flats toward Mont Saint Michel. Soon it would seal the island off from the rest of Europe. Chills raced down her back.

A buzz raced through the network crews as they also moved to the cloister's edge. Dozens of other reporters, realizing what was happening, pressed her against the stone railing. There was nowhere she could go. She looked for Rex, who caught her eye and headed through the crowd toward her. Adrienne looked at her watch. Two thirty.

Like a tidal wave racing toward the island, the sea roared into the mud flats surrounding Mont Saint Michel. Below, she could see the occupants of the few remaining boats bracing for the onslaught. She could hear the boaters' screams as the galloping tide rolled over the fifteen or twenty small boats that had braved the outgoing sea hours ago and waited for the coming alien visitation; all were swamped. Helicopters swooped toward the mount, hovering above the devastation as brown water roiled across the mud flats. The brightly painted boats were now just so much flotsam, some with panicked people still clinging to them. In a matter of minutes it was over, and the only screams came from the mount, the visitors reacting in horror to the devastation below. Adrienne turned her head, her eyes meeting Rex's as he finally reached her. She buried her face in his shoulder without a word. The media around her snapped pictures and continued to film the recovery of bodies by arriving French police boats. She'd seen enough. Rex escorted her to her seat.

"I need to go back to Raines. Will you be all right by yourself?"

Adrienne nodded, her head down. She stared at the stone patio for a few moments, then looked up. "Go, please Rex. I'll be fine. It just happened so fast. They never had a chance."

Rex nodded. "They were warned, Adrienne. If you need me, wave. It's going to get crazy very soon."

She nodded, glancing back at the stone railing and the gawkers. Her stomach turned.

Half an hour later, the gendarmes had directed people back to their seats, where they waited patiently alongside the purple-robed Priest of the Heavenlies and the Archbishops of Saint Michael's Remnant.

"Come sit down with me," Rex entreated.

"I'd rather watch from a distance, if that's okay. They're landing in the garden, right?"

"Raines says so. I'm sure he'd give you special approval to leave your seat and go back to the rail. If you need me, shout in English," Rex said, returning to his place of honor. She stood and began to work her way back to her left, to her original spot by the ancient stone rail.

Suddenly the crowd hushed. She turned to see the Remnant priests waving their hands to silence the crowds in the abbey and on the slopes below. Raines stepped up to an ornate microphone on the dais at the cloister's south end. He cleared his throat and stretched out his arms to quiet and reassure his flock. Adrienne had seen huge picture screens scattered through the city and knew that right now those screens bore Raines's towering image. He spoke three words.

"They are coming."

✳

Adrienne checked her watch. Three twenty-one.

On the twenty-first day of the third month of the year. Thirteen hundred years after the Bishop of Avranches heard the voice of Archangel Michael saying, "build here and build high." Or so the Bishop had claimed. Rex said it was a myth, but a thousand years of Benedictine monks vehemently disagreed.

Adrienne reached the cloister's edge and watched the sky. A thick sense of expectation hung in the air. The weather felt heavy like rain, adding a sense of foreboding. Rex mentioned that morning that the low pressure system sweeping in from the west could raise the tide another thirty centimeters. The Moon, Sun, and the weather lifted the sea until it cut off Mont Saint Michel from the mainland, only a few kilometers away.

The first scream pulled her eyes from the sky to the water's edge ninety meters below her. Looking due north from under the sweeping arches of an ancient stone cloister, she saw the first one arrive. Raines had been wrong. The advance came from the sea.

At the base of the stairway that descended Mont Saint Michel's forested north slope, a silver, eight-legged craft emerged from the still green waters and stood, dripping wet on the granite landing. Even from her vantage point ninety meters above the ocean, she recognized the creature. Eight spear-like legs clambered up the worn rock steps just as a second pod emerged from the jade sea behind it. Then a third. Screams echoed around the mount's base as Raines's faithful ran for safety. Adrienne saw many escape the steep stairs, leaping into the rocky, thickly forested slope on either side. A few brave souls near the stairway's bottom attempted to touch the climbing spiders, but the lead spider brushed them aside.

"*La Paix! Soyez Calmé!*" Raines commanded calm from the front of a U-shaped gallery surrounding plush red carpet. Like the patron saint of alien appearances, he raised his hands to calm his flock. Adrienne imagined that he was displeased that his prediction — the aliens' arrival by air in the lower garden — hadn't come true. His frown showed it, but surely the tall self-centered man she'd met over brunch was too proud to admit he was wrong.

Remnant priests stood beside him mumbling in French, working their alien version of worry beads through aged hands and humming an escalating twenty-one tone chant in unison. Reporters jumped from their seats and pressed to the rail, again pinning Adrienne against the stone wall.

"*Calmé vous!*" Raines bellowed. "*Restez tranquille! Ils sont arrivés!*" Adrienne knew enough French to understand he'd said something like "Sit down and shut up! They're here!" But in a nice formal French kind of way.

"They will be among us within moments," Raines said, changing to English as he looked into a bank of a dozen cameras. He had a language for the masses at Mont Saint Michel and another for television. "Their number is six. For us, they venture forth."

That did it. Like a triple Howitzer across Mont Saint Michel, the mind-numbing *boom-boom-boom* chant began: "Ven-ture Forth."

Special Agent Kerry stood, entranced, at the edge of the abbey gardens a few meters below the cloister. Only fifty meters below him, six of the wet silver things were climbing steadily up the rock steps in perfect cadence to the gut-rumbling chant. They'd come from the water — as he'd predicted. He knew Ulrich's submarine sat somewhere northwest. And Ulrich — he was sure — was here.

Kerry looked back into the multitude. People crowded the gardens behind him, hoping to see the spider craft. He maximized the volume of his micro-miniature ear implant and listened to his agents chattering throughout the city and near Malcolm Raines.

"That Bondurant lady is next to Raines," one said. "She's the one the Brits found in the database."

"She's not moving," Kerry said. "She's with Edwards and the other VIPs. Keep them in sight."

Images of every person on this forsaken rock, including the recently arrived Dr. Felicia Bondurant, were safe in a database somewhere. Video surveillance of every gathering area was being sucked into an orbiting aircraft just below the cloud layer far above him, beyond sight or hearing. But that knowledge didn't quell his unease. All the data pointed to this time. Soon—very soon—Nick the terrorist would show himself.

Kerry looked down again. The six creatures were nearly to the top of the stairs, headed for the landing just below the cloister. Then he saw her, the blonde reporter, standing at the rail. She was frozen as if in a trance.

They were advancing straight for her. Adrienne's heart seemed to smash a hundred times a minute against her ribs, demanding that she run. But she willed herself to stay. Rex had joined her again, leaving the side of Father Raines at last. She was glad he was near. *It's as if he came to protect me.*

The silver body closest to her reflected the mid-afternoon light, dried salt staining an otherwise perfect mirrored surface. They were so close she could hear the long silver legs, jointed in four places, *click* with an eerie staccato sound as forty-eight spear tips contacted the rock steps in unison with the chant of tens of thousands. Onlookers bailed off the stairs to avoid being swept aside by the tall craft.

The first spider reached the landing just below her, its football-like head swiveling on a silver hose of a neck and scanning the crowd in the abbey garden to its right. As it did, a sea of onlookers fell over themselves in sudden retreat to escape the alien's brief approach. She saw one black man at the front of the crowd stand his ground, his eyes locked with hers.

The craft passed abeam the man, who kept a hand under his jacket. Then a second alien passed, and the line of silver turned left, ascending a short stair, headed her direction. The crowd's chanting behind her quieted, although the numbing cadence continued elsewhere. Raines raised his hands, his amplified voice booming over speakers and televisions across the world: "They have arrived. Welcome the Father Race!"

Adrienne felt Rex tug on her arm to let her know he was leaving, then release her and work his way back to the place of authority near Father Raines.

The aliens climbed toward her, straight up the steps. In all of Mont Saint Michel, Adrienne Packard could not have picked a better place to stand. Gendarmes controlled the majority of the observers, keeping them away from the cloister, and most of the media had now taken their seats. She was in the path of the first alien cresting the stair. Her digital camera clicked away.

"Make room!" Raines bellowed, and the throng behind her eased back.

The first creature topped the stair, stooped under the arch, and entered the granite cloister. It stopped within arm's reach of Adrienne.

Raines bellowed in French. "*Bienvenue mon Père! Nous sommes à votre service.*"

Something about father . . . here we are . . . for your pleasure. This would be hard to follow if it was all in French. But then, why speak English at France's most visited site?

A second alien craft ducked under the arches, then a third. The remaining craft stopped in the garden, adjacent to the black man who wouldn't run. Silver heads danced wildly on long silver necks, looking left and right, craning over the cloister wall and peering toward Raines. The lead alien lowered its head within a meter of Adrienne's face. She stifled a scream.

A deep, incredibly amplified bass voice spoke from the craft's body, as though the pod were itself a massive sub-woofer: "Adrienne." Her legs wilted, and another reporter caught her under the arms as she staggered.

"*Nous sommes revenus.*"

"We have returned," the fellow reporter whispered as he helped Adrienne to her feet. "How do they know your name?"

Kerry refused to move. This was his chance. From beneath his jacket he pulled a small silver clam-shaped device. Every agent carried at least one today, sculpted the exact radius of the side of the bulbous pod body, and mirrored to match. With all eyes on the other craft, he reached out and pushed the device against the rear alien's back. The spider must have sensed his touch; it lifted its head toward Kerry. He backed away beyond reach of the pointed legs. The alien regarded him a moment, then turned back to face the cloister, and Raines.

"Top Dog, this is Kerry," he said into a cuff mike, trying to look like he was wiping his face on his sleeve. "Beacon's on number six. Acknowledge."

"Copy, Kerry. It's transmitting."

"All stations. Expect them to leave by sea. Keep an eye out for Ulrich. He's on the island, or maybe a boat offshore."

His task completed, Kerry moved behind the last alien to get a better view of the woman on the landing. The alien had spoken to her, and she hadn't run. He was sure he'd have soiled himself had he been in her shoes.

✳

"*Votre temps est venu.*" The ear-splitting bass of the lead alien addressed the most resplendent of the purple-robed bishops, the Master of the Remnant. The old man fell to his knees, weeping. The other priests followed his lead, as did some of the crowd. Adrienne watched in amazement. The French reporter hung on her arm. "'Your time has come.' Perhaps he means the old priest."

The lead alien turned to Raines, only a meter away. With remarkable dexterity, the spider seemed to kneel before the tall purple-robed African American. It remained in a kneeling position until Raines, too, bent at the waist, and then went down on one knee. They stood up in unison.

"*Vous avez entendu notre voix,*" the alien rumbled. "You have heard our voice," it repeated in English. "You proclaimed the truth. Do not fear. We are many." The alien bowed again in the direction of the old priest, repeating in French, "*Vous avez proclamé la vérité. Ne craignez rien. Nous sommes beaucoup.*"

Raines nodded to the priest, who regained his feet and stood abreast the Priest of the Heavenlies. Raines began to speak in unison with the booming bass of the spider.

"We are the Father Race." The amplified combination of both voices shook Adrienne's insides, and sweat broke out on the back of her neck. She knew this feeling. Raw fear.

"You met our brothers on the red planet," the alien said. "You have received us on the blue planet. Our brothers across the veil of stars are anxious for you to venture forth. Why do you tarry?"

Raines moved forward to the alien, placing his hand on the front of the pod. The creature's head bent down face-to-face with him.

"Representative of the blessed one. *Le représentant de celui qui est béni*," Raines said as he bowed his head toward the spider. "You are the hidden knowledge—the ambassador of the higher world and its divine mysteries—the pleroma. We will tarry no longer."

"You have spoken well," the spider said, its voice booming. "We bring you word from the adepts and encourage your mystical understanding of the ultimate reality."

As though they had rehearsed, the two knelt in unison again, then stood.

"The prophecy is fulfilled," Raines said, gesturing to the Master of the Remnant. "Come!" He gestured to the priest. "*Venez!*"

The old man moved toward the alien, his hands shaking. A fellow priest helped him along.

Fierce copper-colored grapples dropped from under the leader's pod, whipping about like mad snakes on the ends of two silver segmented hoses. Screams arose from those closest to the creature. Raines raised his hands for quiet. The grapples danced in all directions, then reached up into the body. When they emerged, a brilliant golden orb in the spider's clutches gleamed almost like a powered light, not a reflection. The spider offered the orb to Raines who deferred to the Master of the Remnant, standing at his left.

"We are here to proclaim the unknown and unknowable God," the alien said. "The highest of all beings. We invite you to learn the core realities. To explore our heavens. If you search, you will find us."

The elderly priest reached out two wrinkled hands and touched the perfect sphere. The blue flash that followed nearly blinded Adrienne. The priest turned his head reflexively, but held tight, and the alien released its grasp. Adrienne had recovered enough to use her digital camera, amazed at the repeat of the scene on Mars with the Rover and Michelle Stevens.

"*Il faut que nous diminuions afin que vous croissiez,*" the alien said, shifting back into French. The reporter behind her, also shooting multiple shots, whispered again as he zoomed for a closeup. "We must diminish that you may flourish."

"Thanks," Adrienne whispered back, her eye focused on the alien through her view finder.

"*Regardez au delà de vous-même. Explorez les fonctionnements intérieurs de votre sgénétiques. Ensuite, joignez vous à nous.*" The alien bent down in a third and final bow. Raines followed its lead, along with the Master of the Remnant. The spider began retreating, *clickety clacking* on the cloister's centuries-old stones.

The reporter behind her took hold of her blouse and tugged on her gently. She was directly in the path and had never noticed. "Look beyond yourselves. Explore the inner workings of your seed. Then join us," he said. "So you'd better back up or you will—join them." She looked around and caught his wink as he released her blouse. "You do not speak French, yes?"

Adrienne shook her head "no" and turned back to watch the spider. The craft advanced toward her as the others descended the stairs. When the leader came abreast of her, it stopped, its head curled down to face her. She stifled a second scream. Adrienne could feel a hand steady her in the small of her back. She shook violently within reach of the towering silver alien.

It spoke to her once more, but in English. "Adrienne, our sister. Proclaim the universal truth."

✳

"I see him!"

Kerry put his hand to his ear, only two meters from the departing leader.

"Where?!"

"He's not on the rock! He's in a boat! North northwest, one hundred meters off the shore. An ocean racer. I'm sure of it—Ulrich!"

Kerry spun about. Sure enough, one hundred meters out in the choppy sea was a Cigarette ocean racer, similar to the one he'd chased months ago off Nicaragua. How had he missed it? He yelled into his cuff mike.

"Chopper! Bring in the French. Now!"

Behind him he heard a French police helicopter lifting off the beach, beating the air as it homed in on the island.

The lead alien turned back toward Kerry and boomed at him. "You desecrate our temple! Leave now." Then it and the others moved ahead rapidly until all six stood on the stairway to the sea. The line stopped, and the lead alien raised its head again. The combined volume of all six spiders speaking in unison nearly burst Kerry's eardrums.

"Venture Forth!"

Between the six screaming aliens and the island full of wild chanting Remnant worshipers, she could barely hear. She watched the silver craft lift off the steep staircase one by one, only a third of the way down the mount, the piercing *whoosh* sounding like half a dozen accelerating jets at takeoff. They peeled off Mont Saint Michel in a flight of mirror-like flying craft led by the top alien and soon formed an echelon above the mount: 3-2-1, a triangle pointing up into the sky. The chant increased as everyone worshiped, with one voice, the Father Race departing above them.

Adrienne saw the black man by the stone railing of the abbey garden, wiping his face or speaking into his arm, she wasn't sure which. When he turned to face her, she was sure. He caught her eye, talking rapid fire into his sleeve.

She knew that look from her many days covering federal events. This was an agent.

✳

"Where's the sub?" Kerry yelled, bounding down the stairway two steps at a time toward the sea.

"About a hundred kilometers due north."

"Get a diver in the water where the boat departed. And stop that red boat."

"Police intercept headed that way. Divers in the water in less than one minute."

Kerry stumbled on the slick granite steps and fell into the edge of the woods, then jumped up and raced on.

A police boat roared around the northeast corner of the island. It was fast, but no Cigarette. Kerry's heart sank. He was at the landing as the boat pulled up. Offshore, he saw a diver, then another, fall from the chopper into the sea where the red boat had been moored.

"*Vite!*" Kerry yelled, pointing to the racing Cigarette headed out to sea. His limited French made the point: "Go fast!"

"*C'est une cause perdue,*" the boat captain said, jamming the boat's throttles forward and shaking his head. It *was* a lost cause, and Kerry got the point. In a few minutes, the Cigarette was long gone.

"Helo status?" Kerry yelled into his mike ten minutes later. The engine roar was almost too much to hear the response.

"On him. Going north fast."

Kerry signaled the captain to turn around. "Helicopter!" he yelled, pointing into the sky and then at the boat. The skipper nodded, smiled, then yanked the boat into a hard turn, aiming back toward the island.

Kerry looked up. The six alien craft had swept out to sea followed by a swarm of television choppers. As he watched through high-powered binoculars, the spiders swooped down low over the water, hovered, and stopped just above its surface, about ten kilometers east of Kerry's position.

Kerry tugged on the captain's sleeve, pointing toward the aliens. The man smiled and complied, hauling the boat into another hard left turn.

Less than a minute later, the image through his binoculars bouncing as the boat roared across the water, Kerry watched the six silver craft drop into the ocean. As he'd predicted. The captain was soon over the very spot where Kerry thought they'd disappeared.

Nothing. No ripples, no craft. No aliens.

And — no Ulrich.

"Top Dog, this is Kerry. Do you have a track on them?"

"Negative. No signal, Kerry. We've lost them."

25

"MALCOLM RAINES WILL BE unstoppable now," Sean said as the three astronauts drifted in front of the big spherical screens on the flight deck.

We can stop him, Michelle thought as she poured over the data she'd uncovered on Mars. "Someone has to go public about this. About my metallurgical analysis—the OT-4-1. We can't leave all those people in the dark."

Sean didn't respond. John shook his head.

"What? What am I missing here?" she protested. "Most of humanity believes that six aliens just made the visit of all time to mankind—but we know where they came from!"

"Do we?" Sean asked. "I mean, *really?*"

"Russian titanium!" Michelle blurted out. "Remember?"

"It's a Russian formulation, Michelle. But we have no proof they're

Russian-made," Sean said.

"And they program their robots in English? What about *that*?"

He shrugged. "You've got me there. For the record, I agree with you. But the problem is that it's NASA's business to bring any and all data forward—not our responsibility," Sean said. "We're not going to undercut the director and the agency with a press conference—or press *leaks*—from orbit. We've told NASA what we observed. Now we leave it up to them. My rule stands." He stared at her, and she knew what he was thinking. She'd violated his edicts more than once. He probably didn't trust her to leave this one alone.

"Was that Bondurant and Edwards I saw in the last video shot with Raines?" John interjected, trying to change the subject. "Both of them?"

Michelle nodded. "The same."

John was scratching his chin with a faraway look. "Did you notice what time the spiders came out of the water?"

She smiled. "Figured *you* did, Mr. Conspiracy Buff. Three twenty-one."

"Adds up to six, like all the others. Six aliens, even the year—2013—adds up to six. There's a clue in all that. We just haven't found it."

"There were only two of the spiders on Mars. How do you explain that?" Sean asked. "I think you both need to chill out a little and stop reading more into this than is there. We're not getting paid to ana-lyze . . . just to observe and report."

"Maybe you are. Not me," Michelle said as she seized on John's hope. "If we can find the number six clue, we can be the ones to open the door on this scam. Right?" She floated closer to John.

"Michelle! We *can't* prove it's a scam," Sean insisted. "Our material evidence—the metal shavings and a busted snow globe—don't constitute proof. So let it go."

"I can't. People are being misled. Many will make decisions that could profoundly change the course of history. I won't sit by and be idle." She stared at John. "And—I'm hoping—neither will *you*. Hawk, of all people, you could speak up and make a difference." Michelle knew her words would hit him like a slap in the face. Maybe that's what it was going to take.

MONT SAINT MICHEL, FRANCE

Why bring the spiders here today, of all days? Kerry wondered. The monster proxigean tide, a once-every-eighteen-months occurrence, had flooded all of the accesses to the island now that the century-old causeway was gone. Kerry's police boat was his transportation, and they were headed straight to the beach. Everyone else on the island was stuck until low tide.

"Helicopter," he yelled again at the captain. Then he pointed to himself. The captain understood and they raced for the landing.

Half an hour later, Kerry was on his way by air headed in the direction Ulrich's boat had taken, speaking over the radio on a frequency used today only by the French authorities and his own agents. "It's still going north?" he asked.

"Bouncing across those waves like a madman. We can see a person who fits his description. He's driving it."

"What do you mean 'fits his description'? Do you *see* him or not?" Kerry demanded, his spirits suddenly flagging. He'd been here before, in this very situation. Then it hit him. "When did you last get a good look at the guy? I mean *his face?*"

"Next to the island. Like I said, the boat took off right after that, and we've pretty much been watching his back."

"No!" Kerry yelled into the mike, spooking his pilot as they made their way across the open ocean. He pounded the dash in front of him. "This can't be happening. Not again."

"Did you copy my last? We've been looking at his back. He's still there."

Kerry swallowed his first words and waited a moment, seething. "No, he's not. He's gone."

Kerry radioed his men on the island. His only hope now was the divers searching the mooring area. And that was a very long shot.

"I doubt your divers will catch him," Dr. Pestorius said, his voice mysteriously joining those of the agents on their special frequency.

"Dr. Pestorius?" Kerry asked. "How'd you get on this net?"

"I have a satellite repeater on Mont Saint Michel. I have been following your progress. As to finding Ulrich, with a good submersible he could be far enough out to join the Kilo in—let's see—about an hour. Perhaps ten kilometers."

"He could *do* that?" he asked, amazed that the admiral had penetrated his operation.

"Yes, but there's one problem with that theory," Pestorius said.

Kerry froze. Even from thousands of kilometers away, Dr. Pestorius had that tone in his voice. Bad news was coming.

"The Kilo has surfaced, and we have boarded the vessel. I have the three American culprits in Navy custody."

"What?" Kerry said, breathless. "How? But—"

"I can imagine your surprise, Special Agent Kerry, and I'm most sorry for this chain of events. The good fortune of finding these men is, of course, offset by losing a chance to capture Ulrich. A failure for which the United States Navy takes full responsibility."

"How, Doc?" He could see the ocean racer on the horizon. *Please! Let Ulrich be on that racer.* A small British warship approaching from his right was on an intercept course, but it was no match for the lithe speedboat.

"You should be able to see the British Navy now, Agent Kerry. Just ahead of you."

"I can, but how—"

"I can see the *both* of you. Let's leave it there, shall we?" the doctor said from somewhere far across the ocean.

"And the sub? How did you board it?" Kerry asked as they drew closer to the boat.

"Our trail sub was in close pursuit—much too close. The Kilo stopped with their acoustic silencing system engaged. Our crew literally ran them over. Our sub's bow chewed up their propeller—or vice versa, depending on your point of view. The Kilo is dead in the water, and ours cannot dive. The U.S. crew boarded the Kilo when they surfaced and took armed control of Ulrich's boat. In international waters."

Kerry was stunned. Ahead of him he saw the British warship fire a shell across the bow of the ocean racer. The boat came to an immediate stop. *Be on there, Ulrich!* The helicopter pilot banked left to circle the boat, dropping low.

"The Americans? Tex. Cliff. Billy. You found them, right?"

"In one piece. They weren't too happy to see us, but they're in U.S. custody. The Russian commander has threatened us, but he has no grounds. It was not a Russian naval vessel."

Kerry could see the boarding of the ocean racer in progress below him. A single man stood aft of the cockpit, hands raised. Not Ulrich.

Kerry slammed the dashboard, startling the French pilot again. Kerry waved for him to keep circling. *Maybe he's below. But not likely.*

"The Captain of our sub had an interesting initial exchange with these men, Kerry. They did not know Ulrich's name. I believe them."

"Didn't know *Ulrich*?"

"Completely unaware. The man was a master — *is* a master — of disguise."

Kerry had heard all he could stand. He knew where Ulrich was. He was underwater, where he always went in times of trouble. Somewhere near the mount, perhaps on it, or on a long ride toward the ocean. But not to a Russian Kilo. That last prospect, at least, made some of this disaster palatable. Perhaps he'd surface when he realized he'd been abandoned. Kerry motioned the helicopter pilot back toward Mont Saint Michel — and the slim chance that his divers had found their mark.

"I understand," Kerry said six hours later. "Let's keep searching through Saturday morning." He put down the phone in his makeshift command center on the island.

Somewhere out there were six silver spiders on the bottom of the sea. The U.S. had the Kilo diesel submarine in custody, but the whale-like mini-sub was gone. After six hours of searching with helicopters, with Navy P-3C *Orion* aircraft, and a downward-looking sonar on a French research vessel, they were empty handed. No Ulrich. No spiders. And no clue.

Kerry looked out the window at the abbey spire rising above him. The archangel stood with one foot on the throat of a dragon, his sword raised to slay it. Portrayed in brilliant gold, gleaming for the entire world to see. How he wanted to be that heroic in real life, to capture the dragon and slay it. The dragon Nick.

PALM SUNDAY, MARCH 24, 2013:
EPSILON

"Did you like my brownies?" Michelle asked, preparing dinner in the galley.

"I loved 'em. Make some more! By the way, did you finish analyzing those bio samples?" John asked.

She nodded. "I've started, with some incredible results. I found more of the *methanogenium frigidum* per microgram than I did in the first sample." She smiled. "Those samples are the proof positive. I haven't told anyone at NASA about them yet—not even Sean. Figured I had a while to get all the images I need with the electron microscope and document my conclusions. Make sure it's ironclad. Then I'll pop the news. After all, we have eight months left, right?"

"You sure you want to do it that way? I mean . . . wait and tell them later? What if someone was depending on your information?"

"What do you mean, John?" Michelle said, giving him a strange look.

"I mean what I said. When you're dealing with an issue of life—life that no one thought existed—you don't keep that a secret from the people who depend on you to tell them." John shrugged. "Or maybe you do, depending on what impact you're trying to have. Like if you want to be really, really sure it's life."

Michelle stared at John, her mouth hanging open.

"Mich? Are you okay?"

She closed her mouth and turned suddenly, wiping at her face.

"Mich?"

She shook her head as if to discourage John from coming closer. He stayed back.

Michelle's sniffles gave her away. A few moments later, John slid up behind her with a napkin, handing it over her shoulder to preserve her privacy. She took the thin paper, nodded "thanks," and blew her nose.

"You want to talk about it?"

"You know?"

"Know what? I just asked if you wanted to talk. We used to do that, remember?"

Michelle turned, a smile creasing wet cheeks, two diamonds of tears floating off to the side of her head. He'd forgotten that sight. It had been a long time since he saw her cry the first time on the Space Station.

"We did talk a lot back then, didn't we?" she said, wiping her eyes. "I liked that."

John smiled, hanging on to the dining table, waiting. "Me too."

"But we didn't visit much on the way to Mars." She looked down at the deckplate, wringing the wet napkin. "Why?"

John felt cornered. "I—I don't know." He lied.

Michelle watched him a moment, tilting her head. "I don't believe you. Please. Why didn't we bond, or whatever?" The tears came back and she daubed at them. "You weren't there when I needed you."

John's heart was breaking. For Amy. For Michelle. For lost opportunity. "I couldn't." *Couldn't because I didn't trust myself to be just friends.*

"Couldn't?"

I wanted to. I really did. But Amy matters more. "Please, Mich. Let's not go there, okay? This hurts too much."

"You have no idea," she said, her voice cracking. More tears flowed.

John had fought this craving for months, thinking about Amy, remembering Michelle, wanting someone to hold or to hold him. This moment was about to break him. He could hold out no longer. Surely

Amy would understand. John reached out to her hand and squeezed it. "Let's talk."

Michelle looked at her hand, then into John's face, and the tears began to run full stream. She choked repeatedly on words she couldn't fully form. She pulled on his hand. John took Michelle in his arms, the two floating in the dining area, alone. Michelle buried her head into his shoulder and sobbed.

For a long five minutes, John held her, the warmth of her body and the pain she released making him feel human again. He was silent as he held her, stroking the back of her neck, alternately feeling deep empathy for his close friend and horrible guilt for embracing another woman.

John pulled another napkin from the pocket of his cargo pants and handed it to Michelle. She gripped him tighter than he'd been held since Amy rolled with him in the sand at Cocoa Beach, saying good-bye two days before the launch. Again, the guilt swept over him, but he held on. It felt so good to be needed.

Michelle loosened her grip as she regained her breath, and her control. She pushed away just in front of him, as though unwilling to get far away.

"Just a minute." She blew her nose, wiped her eyes, and tried to smile. "There's something—something very important I need to tell you. Please promise me your confidence."

John nodded, puzzled. "My word's always been good."

"Yeah. I know, you Boy Scout." She smiled, then chuckled and took both of his hands in hers.

His heart was racing. His head said "run," and his heart said "stay." He held on.

"What I'm about to say—this is so hard—is *not* your fault. You told me once, a long time ago, that confession is good for the soul. So . . . I have something I need to confess—and you're the only person I can tell."

"You always have God. He wants to hear from you. Every day."

"Trust me, he's *been* hearing from me. Many nights and days. I even went so far as to write what I'm about to say on a card and tie it to Viking. Sort of like a confession tree or something, you know? But when you said what you did a while ago about life, about not keeping secrets, well—I—Please forgive me, John. I made a terrible mistake. And I don't know where to turn."

"Can it be all that bad, Michelle?"

Michelle nodded, kneading his fingers for a minute or more. Then she bowed her head, her whole body shuddering as though fighting to quell a raging inner battle. Her voice was weak but clear.

"I'm pregnant."

26

"BUT — HOW?" JOHN BLUSHED, realizing that was a stupid question. "I mean—when did you know? And what about Sean?"

"He has no idea. I figured it out halfway through the lander mission—by the end of the second week." She smiled through the tears floating about her. "Raines was right. I was the first mother on Mars. 'Eve and the womb of mankind,' remember?" She raised an eyebrow. "Little did he know."

"I wish I'd known. I could've done something."

"You tried to warn me, remember? And you know what's sad? I didn't—I mean, I don't—really love Sean. I *needed* him—that skin-hunger thing the shrinks warned us about. Now he's falling for me." She shook her head. "This is so complex."

John held her hand. "I'm sorry, Michelle. I don't know what else to say."

She wiped at her eyes. "What *can* you say? I blew it. I should have listened to you a long time ago. By the time I found out, it was too late. I couldn't abort it, not by myself. Not on Mars."

"You'd do that?"

She sighed and squeezed his hands. "It wouldn't be the first time, John."

He was sure his shock would upset her. It didn't.

"You're so pure sometimes, you know?" she said. "Like you think I'm some perfect little woman. Well, I'm sorry to disappoint you, John. But I'm not perfect." She paused. "And neither are you, by the way."

His red face intensified. He shook his head.

"I terminated a pregnancy in college. The father ran off, and I wouldn't have been able to raise the kid." She lowered her head. "And again, the summer after I came back from the Space Station—when you were stuck in orbit. Keith was a dream. But the relationship went too fast, and I didn't take precautions. He doesn't know, by the way." She looked up at John. "I'd like to keep it that way."

As she looked away, he could feel her shivering. "What am I going to do, John? About the baby? The radiation? The whole prenatal thing? I'll probably deliver just before we land." She looked back at John, her hazel eyes wet, yet deep with a strange new longing—or perhaps a peace—he'd never sensed before. "I want to care for this child," she said.

John released her, rubbed his face, and got her a soft cloth from the galley. "We'll take it together, Michelle. One step at a time."

"How will I tell Keith?" she asked, wringing her hands.

John grimaced. He could feel the horrible burden crushing Michelle. She carried another man's child; she had to share the news with Sean *and* her husband. John's entire gut ached. There were no easy solutions.

"I hate to ask you this," John began, red-faced again, "but since we're being so frank—I thought you were taking some—well, you know—"

"You are such a prude, you know? It's called the *Pill*. And *yes*, I was on it. Ever since I terminated that other pregnancy."

John sighed, his eyes locked with hers.

"I thought I missed a cycle a few weeks before we landed on Mars," she said. "That happens to me sometimes. I thought maybe it was because of the stress. But I missed *another* cycle halfway through the mission on Mars. I took a test . . ."

"I thought those pills were—you know—perfect."

"Not always. And it's my fault. I was on antibiotics for a throat infection, remember? I forgot that antibiotics cancel the Pill's effect." She hung her head. "I was hurting during the flight to Mars, John. I needed attention—physical attention. You should remember," she said, her lower lip quivering. "I came to you first."

MONT SAINT MICHEL, FRANCE

Nick shivered in the cold catacombs deep in the granite below Mont Saint Michel's ancient abbey. The space was cramped and cold, but considering what she—his benefactor for the past many years—had accomplished in so little time, Nick had no complaints. She was ready to swing into action when he'd called needing help, as though she were already here on the island. In no time, a forgotten room deep in the bowels of the island became his home, directly below the very men seeking to bring him in. Who she was would remain a mystery for him to solve yet another day. He pulled a thick sweater over his shirt and returned to the bench.

Nick bent over a tiny clamshell-shaped device, careful to keep it under a thick copper cage as he handled it. No signal could emanate from this grounded copper electromagnetic shield, and if it did, the signal would never penetrate the dense rock above. He pressed a pointed tool into the edge of the device, and it snapped open.

Elias Ulrich—Nick, to his men—was a man of many talents. And he'd need all those talents now, stranded far from his Central American base of support, chased across the Atlantic into the Baltic, resupplied by those he trusted and abandoned by the same. Days ago there'd been no pickup, no submarine waiting. For hours he'd floated in the waters off Mont Saint Michel, waiting. A cold and harrowing night return by undersea scooter brought him back to the rock. He was alone for the first time in years.

Nick prodded the electronics with a digital multimeter, then a logic probe. He found what he was searching for and disconnected a critical wire. It would work now, but not transmit. Nick pulled the silver clam from the copper cage and inspected it under an eyepiece.

"NSA," he said, admiring the fine micro-miniature electronics. "Quite nice." He put the device on the bench and turned to a computer monitor in his lab-in-a-tomb facility. Well-muscled and with little fat insulating him from the cold damp, he shivered again, then stood and pulled on a jacket. He opened his Internet browser and searched the news for some notice about him or his men. Nothing. He clicked his way through a series of cover sites into an alias within Colorado Springs' Northern Command, an unlikely place to find him, and through it, queried another computer server in the Pentagon.

"Just as I thought," he said out loud. "You got lucky. You got Tex."

He scowled. "We're on our own now, Nick. Just you and me."

Michelle wasn't sure how John would take that last comment. It was as direct as she dared to be. *If he'd been there for me then, this might be* our *problem.* That thought broke her heart. She knew his wife well; she was a friend. Now she understood Amy's comment months ago over lunch in Galveston—that she trusted John, despite his foibles. Amy trusted him because her husband was honest about his weaknesses, and she knew where he stood on issues of temptation.

What was it you said to me on the Station? You build a wall around your relationship with Amy to protect your marriage? You said you'd do it no matter how silly it makes you look.

Michelle continued to stare into John's blue eyes, deep-set orbs shaded by an awning of bushy eyebrows. *That relationship wall of yours worked, John. And I'm so glad you're here for me now.*

"I'm sorry about the other pregnancies," John said after a long silence. "I didn't realize . . ."

She was sure he was avoiding her comment about her temptations, and her confession about pursuing him.

How could John be so shy around women—even with someone he knew well? It fascinated her. And how could a man be so—simple? Like an astronaut version of Forrest Gump. She frowned. *And what does that make me? Jenny?*

"Don't apologize," she said. "After all, how could you have known? Keith didn't. I didn't tell the docs at NASA either. It was my decision." She took a deep breath, reliving that day last year at the Women's Health Center. "It was a choice, John. Accept a slot on the first mission to Mars—or be tied down with a child."

John frowned.

"Don't judge me, John Wells. Not now."

"I'm not judging you, Michelle. I was thinking about the baby."

"They weren't *babies*. They were pregnancies."

"Is that so? Why is it a 'baby' if you want the child, but it's just a 'pregnancy' if you don't?"

"There you go—being judgmental!"

"You're right. I'm sorry." John touched her shoulder. "I care for you, Michelle—as a close friend. And I'm here to love and support you through this tough time. Whatever it takes. You owe that child your best shot."

Michelle squeezed her eyes shut, grateful that he understood her need. "Thank you so much. I need your help, John. And your prayers."

"I'm here for you every step of the way." He took a deep breath. "So—how far along are you?"

Her heart lifted. John had shifted into his "Mr. Fixit" voice. She could see the wheels turning. He'd figure this out.

"Almost ten weeks."

He wrinkled his eyebrows. "I don't have all the answers, Michelle, but I can think of some options. If you're ten weeks, you'll be full term two to four weeks before we get home."

She nodded, glad for someone else to share the pain . . . and the planning.

"Whatever option we choose, we'll get you through this pregnancy, and when the baby comes, it comes. One possibility is to keep it a secret—not tell NASA. We could keep you off camera, only do head shots on the video conferences, perhaps even deliver the baby secretly. That'd be hard to do, particularly if there are complications. But we might pull it off." He smiled. "I've been there for three deliveries with Amy. I could be your midwife, in a pinch."

"I don't know what you call a male astronaut labor and delivery nurse," Michelle said. "But we'd never get away with it. NASA can watch us all the time."

"Second option. You tell Keith, and a few days later come clean with NASA. We'll all get some raw attention, particularly Keith—as well as Amy and Debra. But that's life. NASA will be bombarded, and they'll probably fire some of our friends. But the space program and our friends will survive." John rubbed his chin. "Of course, the rest of the astronaut corps will kill us."

Michelle forced a weak smile. "No doubt. And they'll probably never send another woman on a long-duration mission. Unless it's an all-woman crew. Other options?"

"Don't be so sure. About sending women, that is. There were compelling reasons to send just one woman on this mission. There will be in the future, too."

"Third option?" she asked.

"You do something stupid—damaging to you and the baby. Please, Michelle—don't take us down that path." John squeezed her hand, his long bony fingers warm in her cold, sweaty hands.

Michelle wagged her head. "I won't. I made that decision on Mars."

"What decision?"

"To have the baby. I intend to take responsibility for my actions this time."

John nodded. "Something we *all* need to do. Including Sean."

"Maybe. But the burden's all on me right now, isn't it?" She frowned. "Any other ideas, Miracle Man?" she asked, releasing John's hands.

"The only other option is to lie. I don't recommend that. You have to tell him—and NASA—soon. And you've got to tell Sean. The best option is always to be frank and honest, Michelle. Admit you made a mistake and then pray for compassion and understanding."

Suddenly the look in John's eyes changed, and he frowned, his head jerking to the side as if listening for something. "What was that?" he said.

"What?" Michelle asked, wondering how anything could divert John's attention at a time like this.

"Didn't you feel it? Like running over a squirrel on a freeway." He turned from Michelle to a nearby plasma panel and called up the ship's diagnostic program, his lifeblood as the flight engineer.

"Should I tell Keith first—or Sean?" Michelle asked, desperately wanting closure with John on this issue.

"Your call. I'd tell Sean first if I were in your shoes," John said as he scanned the information and turned toward the hatch. "We need to go to the flight deck right away, Mich. Come on." John moved toward the exit.

"Can't we finish this first?"

John turned, a little red-faced. He took her hands again. "Mich, I'll be here for you every step of the way. I'll do as much heavy lifting as you need. But right now something else is very wrong, and I need to go." He turned and disappeared before she had a chance to respond.

Maybe that was best. Michelle needed some time alone. She was trapped—as she had been twice before, but this time she had to deal with the root issue—with herself. She had to level with her husband—and Sean—then admit her mistakes and move on.

What was that insane thing John said two years ago on the Space Station that made her so mad? *It's hard for a man and a woman to be close friends because, sooner or later, sex gets in the way.* How had John managed to maintain his professional distance all this time, yet she'd given in? She floated in the galley compartment, trying to recall the day she'd been offended by his pulling back from her touch.

I remember now, she thought. *He said, "I pray for the strength that I don't possess."* She pulled herself over to the portal, staring out at the darkness of space above the Milky Way. She whispered a prayer, like she'd seen John do as he hovered in front of the Space Station cupola, praying for his family—and praying for her. *I need some of that strength right now, God. Please help me through this.*

Half an hour later, Michelle moved to the flight deck, her face washed and some of the puffiness gone. John was working on the communication control panel with a puzzled expression.

"What was it, John? Did we hit a space squirrel?"

"Don't get in too big a hurry to call Keith," he answered without looking up.

"What's the problem?" Michelle moved closer to him.

"Can't get a signal on the S-band antenna. Or the X-band. Not even the low-data-rate system. All circuits are dead, as they say. And it's not an electrical fault."

"Why?"

He shrugged, canceling a flashing alarm on the panel, a warning that the ship's telemetry link with Houston was severed. That, she already knew, would send Mission Control into a huge panic and an eruption of activity as soon as they found out.

"If I didn't know better, I'd say our antennas fell off. Every one of them," he said, looking up at the ship's curved bulkhead above him.

"That's not possible."

"I know," John replied, "but the indications are that we have good electronics—and no way for the signal to get out. Therefore, no antennas."

"But I need to call Keith—"

John crossed his arms, scowling at the communication panel and the flashing yellow warning. "We need to wake Sean." John put a lingering hand on her shoulder. "Got to tell him about this—and about you."

"I'll wake him," she said. "But I want to ask you one more favor." She watched John's face. "Let me tell Sean in my own time, okay? Not today. I've dealt with all the pain I can handle for a while." She laid her hand on his. "Please?"

John nodded. "Your timing, Mich. I won't say anything to him." He looked back at the control panel. "And until I figure out this equipment problem, we won't be telling anyone back home, either."

27

AMY LAY IN BED praying, the day's events swirling in her mind — images of Palm Sunday service and the procession with fronds, and shocking images of spiders marching up Mont Saint Michel three days earlier. Images of crowds welcoming Jesus, and six spiders. Purple-robed Remnant priests accepting the glowing sphere, and images of round communion wafers and purple wine. Malcolm Raines proclaiming the great visitation of an unknowable God and Pastor McGehee proclaiming the arrival of the Son of God. Amy prayed for discernment.

The quiet, dark house screamed at her. She rose and turned on a small fan, creating some background noise.

Alice knocked and poked her head in. "Mom?"

"I'm awake, sweetie. You okay?"

Alice ran to the bed and jumped in. "Why didn't Dad call tonight?"

"Your dad has lots of important things to do."

"He calls *every* Sunday. No matter what."

Amy caressed her daughter's cheek. "I know. He'll call soon, sweetheart. I promise."

＊

"Amy? It's Jake."

It was early Monday morning of Holy Week, and the children weren't yet awake. "Hi, Jake. We didn't hear from John last night."

"That's why I'm calling."

"What?" She sat straight up.

"We wondered if you had your teleconference last night. We've had some technical difficulties with communications."

"Stop it, Jake. 'Technical difficulties' is a euphemism for 'trouble.'" Amy sprang out of the bed and pulled on her robe, the phone pinned between ear and shoulder. "So don't try to be cute."

"I won't. We lost our telemetry link to Epsilon last night about the time John usually calls home. Just like that. Something's on the fritz with their transmitter — with *all* of them, to tell you the truth."

"That's all? No other indications?"

"No. I'll call again when we know more."

"I won't sleep 'til you do, Jake. Please — call me soon."

"I will. Don't worry. It's most likely a very simple electrical issue."

MONDAY, MARCH 25, 2013: EPSILON

"Nothing since yesterday, Sean. No data in or out." John shook his head, pointing at the communication system interconnects on the large plasma screen.

"Backups?" Sean asked.

"Been through that. I plugged directly into the communication front panels in system control. Doesn't matter. The antenna doesn't respond. *None* of them do. My guess is we've completely lost the antenna farm, like every one of them fell off—or someone stole them."

"Very funny," Sean replied. "What else?"

"I felt a bump, kind of like hitting a rabbit on the road, about the time we lost comms. I'd bet my paycheck something hit us. Might've knocked our antenna field out of alignment. Whatever it was, we need to inspect it—do an EVA. The only way to fix this problem is to go outside."

LONDON, UNITED KINGDOM

The office entrance was low key, with only a brass plaque on the old building to indicate the address. But when Special Agent Kerry stepped through that door, he felt like he'd stepped through a magic portal from London into the Pentagon. Behind a burly young Marine, a large sign announced "Commander, Naval Forces Europe." Military personnel moved through the old halls despite the early hour.

"This way, Sir," a young woman said. Her nametag said "IT-1 Bell." She obviously knew where she was going, and why he was here.

"What's an IT-1, Petty Officer Bell?" he asked as they threaded through the maze of offices in the hub of naval warfare near London's main thoroughfares.

"An Information Systems Technician First Class, Sir. I operate satellite and cryptographic equipment. I've been tracking that sub you were chasing."

The petty officer led him to the operations core of the cleverly disguised building, scanning each of their handprints as he had done in Suitland. The door opened with the familiar hiss of positive pressure, preventing gas and biologic attacks from seeping into the critical space.

She said good-bye and left Kerry at the door, closing the vault. It seemed like the exact duplicate of the Navy's classified operations center back in Maryland—or else he truly had been transported back to the states. Kerry was beginning to question his own sanity.

"Welcome, Special Agent Kerry. Thank you for coming."

Dr. Pestorius, seated at the head of the table just as he would have been ten thousand kilometers away in Maryland, extended his hand. "We have much to show you."

EPSILON

"EVA?" Sean asked. "Why risk that?"

"I've tried everything I can, Sean. It isn't just the antenna farm that isn't responding—neither are the cameras showing us the antenna farm. My only option is to inspect the problem. That, or—" John paused.

"Or what?"

"Or accept the loss of comms. Somehow I don't think you can adopt that second option."

Sean punched a nearby bulkhead. "Bad choices, both of them."

"Why?" Michelle asked. "We can do an EVA. Heaven knows we did enough of them on Mars."

"Not the same," Sean insisted. "We could always sit down, walk back to the hab, even suffer a small leak and survive. Not the same here in deep space. And there's no one to back us up—no one to call if we need help."

"Your logic's flawed, Sean," John said. "We did EVAs all the time on the Station. I don't see where we've got a choice."

"Exactly," Michelle said, her eyes sparkling at the prospect of an EVA on an interplanetary mission.

"No!" John objected. "I mean, it's too dangerous for us *both* to go out."

Michelle glared at him. He ducked the stare.

"Any EVAs have to include both of you," Sean said. "That's always been the plan. I stay behind to fly this bucket of bolts."

LONDON

After three hours in the locked vault, photos of Ulrich's submarine were strewn on the conference table. Kerry put down the last photograph and leaned back. "It's hard to imagine, Doc. Absolutely phenomenal."

"I agree," Dr. Pestorius said, struggling to stand with his cane. "You've led us," he said, wheezing, "to Elias Ulrich, and through your pursuit, we've now gotten our hands on the most advanced submarine known outside of the United States. As well as three of the four remaining culprits in the terrorist attacks. Congratulations." Dr. Pestorius stood at the head of the table, wobbly, but dominating the room.

"I don't feel like celebrating, sir. Ulrich is still out there," Kerry said. "This sub you caught. How long can it stay underwater with that special propulsion system?"

Dr. Pestorius waved to a technician. Pictures of Ulrich's Kilo came up on the screen. "This system is probably good for thirty days. Liquid oxygen and diesel drive a Stirling engine that's encased in a special acoustic and vibration damping enclosure. No wonder we lost them when we tailed Ulrich off the coast of Africa. This sub is more silent than even the Swedish Gotland Class, type A-19. It can transit for a month underwater at almost ten knots, with absolutely no acoustic signature. Remarkable. And deadly. If there are more of these, they could put us out of business in antisubmarine warfare. Our nuclear craft are no match for something this quiet. At least, not yet."

"Now what?" Kerry asked.

"Ulrich. We have a theory."

"I hope you do, because I sure don't," Kerry said. "Have you been able to track the tag I put on the last alien?"

"No. We've monitored that frequency since they went into the water. Nothing under or above the water. Either it's dead, or it was found."

"Too bad. It was worth a try."

"Remember the whale-shaped feature we saw in satellite photos, the one that was missing when our sub ran into the boat?"

Kerry nodded.

"The Swedes developed a system known as *Sea Dagger*. It looks just like a small submarine and comes in several variants, one of which is an autonomous swimmer delivery vehicle. Our theory," he began, pointing to charts of a strange craft similar to that which they'd seen on the sub's back, "is that the alien craft were staged in a similar vehicle—like a garage or a hangar. It may have been designed to maneuver in shallow waters and retrieve the six spiders. It was supposed to retrieve Ulrich as well, escaping under water while you—we—chased the red ocean racer. But—"

"But," Kerry said, "you ran into the Kilo from behind because it was so silent, forcing it to the surface, and capture, before they could link back up with the *Sea Dagger* thing."

"Exactly. And since the *Dagger* is probably a titanium alloy, we wouldn't be able to see it with our Magnetic Anomaly Detectors during the aircraft sweep of the area."

"What about active sonar?" Kerry asked. "Something that big should stand out in any sonar survey."

"My guess is the craft was gone by the time we got there."

"My men searched the island. Three times. So where are we now?" Kerry asked. "If that Russian captain won't talk about his rendezvous plans, and if Ulrich's three men won't sing, we're stuck."

"Perhaps. But there's another variable in this equation we've not yet defined."

Kerry cocked his head.

"Recall Kilo Nine Six Three? The other sub we tracked from Nicaragua to the Netherland Antilles before they threw us off with an underwater transfer?"

"Yes."

Dr. Pestorius pointed to a map of the Atlantic. "He's back. We found him, transiting the North Atlantic, on a direct course for the UK. My guess is that Ulrich has help on the way." He shook his head. "And that means there are at least two of these deadly boats in existence."

TUESDAY, MARCH 26, 2013: EPSILON

"I'm going, John. Besides—you need me." *And you're the only friend I have right now. I'm not letting you take this risk alone.*

"I wish you'd reconsider," he said, helping Michelle don her glove, then cinch down the seal to the arm of her space suit. "You don't need to do this."

Michelle smiled and rubbed John's flattop with her other gloved hand. "You're too protective, Father John. I'm pregnant, but I won't break. And if you don't lay off the nesting comments, Sean's gonna figure this out." She knocked him on the head to get his attention.

"And that would be a *bad* thing?"

"It would. I want to set the time and place to tell him. Let me do it my own way, okay?" She put both hands on John's suit collar. She demanded an answer.

"Okay," he said, smiling slightly. "You win. But for the record—"

"I know. You object. Now, let's get outside. We have a job to do. And unless we brought a maternity space suit, I won't be able to do this job in a few months. I'm not about to miss the chance to be the first mother on an interplanetary EVA."

John and Michelle exited the airlock one at a time, John the first man ever to emerge into the vast openness of interplanetary space. After months in Epsilon, unable to roam the surface or go EVA, the experience made his head spin. He was free.

Emerging from the airlock, he could see the entire length of Epsilon's living and working area, as though looking out the door of a 747 airliner, eyelevel with the aircraft skin. The immense cylindrical spacecraft stretched out forever beyond him. To his right was the ship's forward end, the storage area for the Mars and Earth landers. Inside that cylinder lay his return ride to Earth.

Awed, John hung above the massive ship as Michelle emerged. Her head pivoted like a top, taking it all in. Unlike their EVA activities together on the International Space Station, there was no Earth rotating below them. No sun peeking over the limb of the Earth once every ninety minutes. Only the grand background of stars and spinning galaxies, distinct points of light in a virgin black expanse of space. And the Sun far away.

"Sort of takes your breath away, doesn't it?" John asked as Michelle stared in wonder at the immense ship and the grand universe beyond it.

"Words can't describe this. It's too much for me to fathom. I need to sketch this, but how?"

"I get the picture," Sean said over the radio. "I'm jealous. So get to work."

"Yes sir!" John replied, offering a hand to Michelle as they began the long trip down the ship's length to the antenna farm, their collection of low- and high-data-rate dish antennae that routed precious communications to Earth. From here, John thought they looked fine.

For the next forty minutes, the two white-clad explorers carefully clipped and unclipped their way along a series of handholds, moving aft toward the rocket and antenna end of the ship. Gingerly at first, as they grew accustomed to EVA, and then with more confidence, they advanced along Epsilon's length, nearly a football field long.

"I wonder if my sketch pencils would work in a vacuum," she said.

"Probably."

"Wouldn't that be a kick, to sit out here and draw the Milky Way?"

As they drew closer to the antennae, poised directly above Epsilon's System Control deck, John saw the problem. It looked as though they'd been fired upon.

"I don't remember making those antenna parts out of Swiss cheese," Michelle said. "Do you?"

John shook his head, amazed. "I think I know what that bump was. We took a pretty nasty meteoroid hit back here. D'you copy that, Sean?"

"I did. What're you seeing?"

John was about ten meters away, but the damage was clear. "Miniature perforations all over the high-data-rate antenna. Looks like someone popped it with buck shot. From here, I'd say that the control stanchion and pointing assembly are smashed. That's why we couldn't point it—and Houston can't hear us."

"And vice versa. But what about the low-data-rate antenna pair?"

"Ditto," Michelle said, reaching two small dish antennae, also elevated on a mast above the ship's cylindrical side. "Shredded. Including the waveguides—and the cameras."

"What amazes me," John said, reaching the large five-meter-diameter dish for their high-data-rate communications, "is I don't see any micrometeoroid damage to the ship's skin. Like we caught the blast's very edge."

"Lucky," Sean said. "Can we fix any of them?"

"Not the low-data-rate. And the ones we used for Mars to Epsilon comms are full of holes, including the pointing motors and waveguides. The high-data-rate is a total loss. The waveguide feed out in front of the dish is sheared off. I'll need a couple of hours for a full assessment."

"Not good."

Michelle pulled herself further aft to the engine compartment. "We need to inspect this area too, John. No telling the impacts the engines took."

"I hate to look," John said. "We can live without comms. But without engines, it's gonna be one very fast, blistering hot aerocapture at Earth."

"Copy."

As John looked down the length of the ship, toward the flight deck segment and the airlock just beyond it, he heard a sound so out of place, so bone-chilling, that in the first split-second he was sure he'd heard the blood-curdling cry of a dying rabbit. But that wasn't possible. Gradually, over the next second that seemed like sixty, John's mind processed the sound and acknowledged what it was. He'd heard Michelle scream.

John spun around, sure she was only two meters to his left. She was gone.

"Michelle!" Sean called. "What happened?"

There was no response.

John pulled quickly toward the engine compartment, frustrated with the clips and his slow speed, then peered over the end of the ship at the massive nozzles. No Michelle.

"Michelle!" John shouted. "Where are you?"

"She's gone?" Sean asked. "What's happening?"

John looked up, fearing the worst, and he saw her, floating about twenty meters above him, a small stream of red spewing from her suit and freezing in the perfect cold vacuum. Her tether was sheared, a ragged line dangling behind her as she drifted away from the ship.

"Michelle's been hit! Micrometeoroids! She's drifting off!"

Before Sean could respond, John had unclipped from Epsilon and fired his maneuvering jet, a fancy version of the SAFER unit—Simplified Aid for EVA Rescue—he'd used to rescue Sergei on the Space Station.

His backpack roared to life as Sean called out, "Get her! Now!"

Only later did John realize what he'd done, flying free of the safety of an Epsilon tether clip, now drifting, like Michelle, in interplanetary space with no buddy backup. His focus was on Michelle, and he fired the backpack again, pointing in a beeline for his dear friend. A line of tiny frozen blood balls trailed behind her, reaching beyond the end of the shredded tether.

"Michelle! I'm just behind you. Hang on. Sean, d'you copy?"

There was no response. From either astronaut.

28

JOHN GUIDED HIMSELF UP behind Michelle, flying more than fifty meters from Epsilon. Her tether trailed behind her, severed where a meteoroid had ripped through her thin Kevlar cable. As John guided in to grab her, he tried to focus on his trajectory, and not the improbability of her tiny line being hit by a flying rock in the middle of nowhere.

Dark purple blood, frozen in near spherical globules, ricocheted off his visor as he reached for the short tether. Her cable in hand, he pulled Michelle slowly toward him, the two drifting even further from Epsilon. He had to get them both back with whatever gas was left in his own unit.

"I've got her, Sean!" John said into his helmet microphone, wondering why Sean hadn't responded to the first call. *He's probably coming to help.* Sean had been pre-breathing oxygen and could be outside in as little as fifteen minutes—if he could suit up fast enough.

Michelle felt lifeless when John got hold of her waist. The dark blood oozed out near her midriff, a purple venous flow. It was a tiny hole, no larger than a BB in diameter, hissing gas with occasional spurts of blood. She was decompressing.

John pulled Michelle's helmet in front of his own. Visor to visor, he could see, through her brilliant gold reflective shield, her face illuminated by the helmet's interior lights. Michelle's eyes were shut. He could barely make out her labored breathing.

John wrapped his arms around her in a bear hug and directed his SAFER control to turn the two of them around. Once they faced Epsilon, he lifted her right arm and read her wrist monitor. Three-quarter pressure! So little time.

With his left arm across the front of her suit, John directed the SAFER with his right hand using his chest controller. He shot as much of the nitrogen gas as he dared, now seventy meters from Epsilon and on the far side of the ship from the airlock.

"I've got her, Sean. Headed in. Venous bleeding. Suit pressure going down. Get ready!"

Again, no response.

"Sean. I'm headed in." *He must be suiting up.* The ship was tumbling in a slow circle as though Sean had commanded some sort of attitude control maneuver. *Why would he do that now?*

John had been here before, two years ago, with Sergei. Flying across the void in a rescue that had saved his Russian friend's life. Michelle had resuscitated their Station commander when John got him inside. Now John was depending on Sean to be there to save Michelle. *Where is he? Why doesn't he stabilize the ship?*

Fifteen meters from the ship, John fired a counter-pulse to slow their approach, then a redirect to circle the tumbling ship. "Sean! Pop the lock if it's shut. We'll be there in sixty seconds."

The comm link was silent.

Half a minute later, John was five meters from the skin of the ship and maneuvering to place the two of them on the far side adjacent to the airlock. He struggled to match Epsilon's rotation while flying an intercept.

Michelle's internal pressurization was dropping a little each minute. He had perhaps three minutes left. After that she'd be decompressed too far to save her. *Move, John!*

As he prepared to fire a final pulse, John saw the massive hole, a ragged gash across the face of the ship's cylindrical surface where a meteoroid had torn through the flight deck. His skin went to ice as he unconsciously directed himself and Michelle toward the open airlock door, his eyes glued to the awesome destruction below.

When had the ship been hit? Then he remembered the last time he heard from Sean, just after he unclipped and headed to save Michelle. Leaving to catch her might have saved his own life. Below him he could see through the half-meter-wide gash in Epsilon's white shell that exposed the ship's interior—and he could see Sean's exploded body.

The jagged hole had instantly depressurized the compartment. Sean's eyes, ears, nose, and mouth exuded a frozen trail of blood. His distended abdomen, bulging under his clothes, was blown up tight. The body twisted in the tumbling ship amidst a cloud of frozen purple globules.

The momentary glimpse of his friend made him gag. John lowered his head and forced himself to concentrate as he guided Michelle to a gentle bump with the airlock. "Two minutes left," he said out loud, trying to calm himself. The meteoroid had torn away the pressure wall of the flight deck and destabilized the ship before Sean could save himself. Another rock could be hurtling their way now.

John pushed her down into the exit they'd emerged from barely an hour ago. Unresponsive, she bumped off the floor of the lock. He shot the last of his nitrogen in the SAFER, forcing himself on top of her in the two-person air lock. He slid the hatch into place and hit the command button to pressurize; that would take about a minute. It occurred to him that the bloody ooze, frozen in the hole in Michelle's suit, may have saved her life.

Sixty seconds later, the air lock's pressurization proved it had been spared the calamity of the flight deck. John forced himself into a tight bend to face Michelle. He popped her helmet and set it adrift, then removed his own.

"Michelle!"

She didn't respond. He ripped his gloves off and checked her neck for a pulse. He could see a slight throbbing in her temple and felt the same weak throb. Her breathing was almost imperceptible.

John worked in the tight space to free her waist seal. A blaring siren and warning lights announced what he already knew. The flight deck had depressurized, and only the central access tunnel was safe—for now. He could barely maneuver as he opened the hatch to enter the two-meter-diameter "cave," then pulled Michelle inside and began working on her.

He pulled her suit pants off and exposed the blood flow. A tiny hole entered the middle of her back and exited through her abdomen just above her right hip. Dark purple-red blood oozed from the wound. It might be her liver. Perhaps a major vein. John pulled his own suit off, laboring for two precious minutes to get free and move around her. To revive her if he could.

Free of the suit, John pulled closer to Michelle's face, stroking the floating auburn hair away from her hazel eyes. Why was she unconscious? The blood loss wasn't enough to knock her out. But the pain, or perhaps the loss of pressurization, might have done it.

Then he saw the cause—a long gash on her left temple, like a slash from a flathead screwdriver ripping through the top of her eyebrow. As he turned her head, he could see where the tiny rock had pierced the top of her ear before striking her brow. Moving through her helmet at thirty thousand kilometers per hour, that speck of rock had the wallop of a major league baseball bat.

Michelle moaned.

"I'm here, Mich. It's John. You're safe."

She moaned again, eyelids fluttering. She coughed dark blood onto her lips.

"Michelle. I'm here."

Her eyes opened.

"John?" She tasted something copper-like in her mouth. Thick and warm. Blood. She tried to spit it out, nearly a mouthful.

"I'm here, Michelle. I've got you."

"My head—" She groaned.

"You've been hit. Twice. A lucky glance to the temple that almost killed you. And a second meteoroid through your abdomen. Your liver, maybe. What do you feel?"

She forced a thin smile. "I'm the doc. . . . Don't do my job . . . for me."

She wanted to laugh, to be happy, to be with him. Somehow she felt she'd been here before. In this situation. With John.

"You're bleeding internally, Michelle. I don't know what to do about that."

She grimaced, not wanting to admit she could feel what he observed. "Not much you *can* do . . . Is what it is . . . No surgery." She reached down and placed a finger on the bloody spot of her cooling garment. "Rip this off—Get a HemCon—Stop the flow."

John nodded and turned to an emergency medical kit pinned to the cave's wall. She helped him hold supplies while he prepared the magical HemCon battlefield dressing for her wound. Its shrimp cell extract would staunch the flow of blood in seconds.

"Blood pressure next. Cuff behind you . . . in the bag." She coached him through the procedure. "Must . . . know . . . the pressure," she said, beginning to stammer.

She watched John pull the auto-cuff over her arm and inflate, deflate, and then beep her pressure. She knew from the sound what her problem was. John couldn't lie about this.

"Eighty over sixty five. Pulse eighty nine, Mich."

"On the edge . . . Get some Ringers," she commanded between shallow breaths. "IV."

She'd taught him herself, volunteering to be his lab rat months ago. She hoped he remembered. John ripped open the plastic pouch with his teeth and slipped a sharp needle into her right arm. She winced. He'd lost his touch.

"Now," she said, handing him the line to the Ringers, "squeeze the bag lightly—body needs the fluid." She looked around the cave. "Where's Sean?"

John hung his head.

"Sean . . . where *is* he?"

The bare shake of his head, the look of pain, and the tears forming around his eyes told her Sean was gone.

"How?" she said, choking on blood.

"Meteorite," he said. "Big one took out the flight deck."

She squeezed her eyes shut, hoping this pain in her heart and her midriff was a dream. But this pain was too intense for sleep. She looked at John, floating above her.

"He never knew—" she said in a hoarse voice, blood gurgling in her throat—"about the baby."

John nodded, working to connect her IV and tape it down to her arm. "Perhaps that was best," he said, his voice cracking.

"Check BP . . . five minutes. . . . Let me squeeze," she said, feeling more lucid as she took the Ringer's bag from his hand. Perhaps she'd make it through this. Her eyes began to mist, then to fill with tears, as the impact of Sean's loss settled on her.

After John got the blood pressure cuff started again, she took his hands in hers, the IV bag tucked under her armpit. She gripped him hard enough to show him that she was strong.

"Can you forgive me? For my mistakes?"

John looked at her with the same deep longing she'd seen in Keith's eyes when they first met. Lonely eyes that screamed for comfort and companionship. He nodded. "I do, Michelle. Jesus forgives you too—if you ask Him."

She hesitated. She didn't know how to express this, but she knew what she felt and had experienced. A warm glow radiated deep inside her—with a peace and a certainty that buoyed her. Just as John had described to her so many times before.

"I *have* asked Him," she said with emphasis despite the pain that seared her insides. "On the night when . . . I almost died . . . trying to get back to Columbus." She fought for a deep breath. She couldn't seem to get enough air.

"I wanted to . . . tell you the night . . . we talked . . . about my pregnancy." She was suddenly faint as she fought back images of space rocks ripping holes through her guts.

John's mouth was agape.

"We were . . . interrupted," she said, trying to smile now that she knew her body was getting some of the precious fluid. "I know He heard me. . . . I can *feel* it. . . . I didn't want to . . . slip away . . . without some . . . of your spark."

Two hours later, John cradled her in front of him, gently stroking her hair as she took each new painful breath. He'd opened his heart to her, doing most of the talking as she tried to hang on.

"Thank you . . . for your . . . honesty," she said. "For sharing. I feel much . . . closer . . . to you." She coughed up more blood. John wiped it gently from her mouth.

"And for yours," John said, tears in his eyes. "It took guts to tell me about the pregnancies. And Sean."

Michelle slowly brought her arm across her abdomen, patting her belly. "Two of us," she said with a weak smile.

John nodded. "You're a mom."

"I've made some . . . awesome . . . mistakes, John."

"The slate's clean," John said, wiping the tears from his eyes, then hers. "Jesus forgives and forgets."

"I like that. Clean." She winced when she touched the bandage over her exit wound. "What will . . . you do?" Tears welled in her eyes, her face close enough to his he could feel her breath.

"What do you mean?" John said as he choked back sobs. He could see she was slipping away.

"It's so . . . far . . . home."

John looked into her eyes for a long time, just that moment realizing the gravity of his situation: Eight months from Earth, in a horribly damaged spaceship. Alone.

"I don't know. I'll take care of *you*."

The barest of smiles crossed her lips. "No." She fought for another breath. "I'm going . . . somewhere else. Somewhere *new*."

John stroked her hair, running his hands through the wonderful, silky auburn strands he'd so long admired. "Yes, you are, Michelle Caskey. You're going somewhere wondrous and majestic."

She reached up and took his hand in a feeble grip. "One more . . . confession."

"Shhh. Conserve your breath," he said, tears clouding his vision.

"No . . . your problem . . . being alone. Brownies . . . chocolate."

"Shhh. It's okay. I'll make some. I promise."

She shook her head. "My stash . . . dark chocolate . . . guitar case." She forced a smile again. "Just for you." She coughed up more blood.

John stared at her in disbelief, realizing in that moment the great depths of her care for him. With hardly the strength to speak, she was determined to tell him about her treasured hoard of chocolate. Her natural medicine to help him endure that which he was too proud to admit he feared most—loneliness.

She'd once told him that the reason women craved chocolate at certain times of the month was because it naturally stimulated the secretion of endorphins — the brain's "happy chemical." She was medicating him — even now.

"It's . . . time." Michelle put her hand on his while he cradled her. More tears broke free, like so many years before on the Space Station, encircling her head in a starry wreath of diamond-like liquid joy and pain. His own tears flowed freely.

"I love you, John—I always have." She coughed and sucked in a wheezing breath. "Just never told you." Michelle gave his hand a faint squeeze. "Two favors?"

He nodded, dislodging a flow of liquid gems from his eyes.

"Tell Keith," she began, laboring against her pain, "how much I love him."

She squeezed his hand one last time. "And please . . . let my secret . . . die with me." Michelle closed her eyes and exhaled one last time, her face frozen in a sudden expression of joyous wonder.

John pulled her cheek to his, their tears mixing as he cried out her name.

29

ASK FORGIVENESS, NOT PERMISSION. Those were John's watch words, and that's just what she'd do. It was time for action. Amy rang the doorbell of the old home on Shady Lane in La Marque. The "820" house number hung askew on the doorframe, one of the nails corroded from Galveston Bay's salt air.

A heavy-set, gray-haired woman in her early sixties came to the weathered screen door. From the look of her simple dress, Amy guessed she sewed her own clothes. Her curled hair and familiar face reminded Amy of a Norman Rockwell painting of someone's grandmother. "Can I help you?" she asked through the screen.

"Hi, I'm Amy Wells. I'm looking for the home of Ronnie Williams. Does he live here?"

"Yes!" the older woman said, her face brightening. "You're Amy Wells—as in *American Moms Magazine* and John Wells, the astronaut?"

She pushed open the screen door, wiping her hands on a faded blue apron, and then pushing at her gray curls in an attempt to arrange her hair. "Oh my!"

Amy smiled. "Yes, ma'am. The very same. I—"

"Oh, I'm so sorry," the older woman blurted. "My name is Martha. Martha Williams. I've wanted to meet you for the longest time. I love your articles."

Amy extended her hand as Martha joined her on the door stoop. "Thank you. How do you do, Martha?"

"Gracious! You're just like I thought you'd be! I mean, you're not ashamed to meet me or anything."

"I beg your pardon?"

"Oh, I'm being so silly. But I always thought no one like you would want to meet someone like me. Old. Gray. And fuddy."

"Fuddy?" Amy smiled.

"Fuddy duddy. Washed up. Worn out. Old timer. That's me."

"No. That's not you. I'm sure of it," Amy squeezed her hand. "I'm very glad to meet you. I guess I found the right place?"

"You sure did, dear. Ronnie and I have been here long as I can remember. He grew up in this house." She waved at the land around them. "Used to be lots of horse pasture and no people sixty years ago—when his parents were young. Town grew up around him, we got married—and life moved on." Her smile faded and she looked off into the distance for a moment. "Everyone went north or south. We stayed here."

Amy nodded. "I live in Clear Lake."

Martha brightened. "Oh my, yes. I know. I've been after Ronnie for twenty years to move us up there. But he won't leave." She waved toward the fields behind the house. "Says we'd have to leave all this. And he won't budge. So," she adjusted the errant house numbers while she spoke, "we hang on here. Ronnie has his radios. And I have Ronnie."

"Actually—that's why I came, Martha," Amy said. "I wanted to ask for his help."

"But why, dear?"

Amy looked down, then back at her car parked on the Williams's crushed shell driveway. "We haven't heard from Epsilon in nearly a week. I wondered if Ronnie had heard anything."

Martha touched Amy's arm. "You poor dear. Yes, I know. I'm so sorry. I dithered on and forgot your pain. It must be so hard. But listen to me. My my." She pulled the door open. "You come in right now and we'll talk. Ronnie works day shift. He'll be home tonight. But we can visit. Please," she said, her plump face alive with emotion, "come in and let's visit."

"I—I didn't want to bother you—please. I just wondered if, well—" Amy felt her eyes watering—"if Ronnie had heard anything. NASA won't tell me much right now."

Martha turned back toward Amy. Her face said, "I want to help," but she shook her head. "He's tried every night. Not a word, dear. But no one's as determined as my Ronnie. Please," she said, pushing the screen door open wide. "Come in and let's talk."

"None for me, please," Amy said as Martha offered her a sweet roll. "I'm diabetic. Have to watch my carbs." She stirred her coffee at the kitchen counter.

"Oh yes. I heard. Sorry about that." Martha busied about the kitchen. "Well, anyway, Ronnie's been listening in on the mission since the day they left. He does it just for fun, you know? NASA won't let him post any Web images from the mission like he does for the Mars landers, but he can see it all."

"All of it? I mean, even listen to our calls?"

"Gracious, no!" Martha said, waving her hand and smiling. "John does that over the Internet with a privacy password. Ronnie says he's one smart guy, your husband. My, my, how he'd like to meet Captain Wells."

Amy sighed, relieved that a space voyeur wasn't listening in on their family conversations. "That's John. And I know he'd like to meet Ronnie. He'll be back in eight months. A long time."

"Well, I know just the thing to help that time pass. Yes, I do." Martha pointed Amy toward an old oak dining table. "You bring those kids over here and we'll let 'em play with the horses. I'll cook you a good meal and we'll all visit. I mean, if you'd like that. Would you? Like it?"

"Horses? The kids would die for that. You have horses here?"

"A whole pasture of 'em," she said, waving toward the window. "Three old nags. And your children are welcome at my house any time, Amy. Please," she said, sitting down and slicing the sweet roll. "You let me know when. Ronnie and I'll put on a horse ride and dinner you'll never forget." She pressed Amy's arm again. "I know this is a difficult time, dear. Let us be family to you, okay?"

Amy smiled and nodded. "I could use that. How about Saturday? We'll be pretty busy on Easter Sunday."

"Saturday it is! And tell your little ones to wear jeans. They'll need 'em."

"I will, Martha. And thank you," Amy said, grasping Martha's hand. "Thank you *so* much. You are truly an answer to prayer."

WEDNESDAY, MARCH 27, 2013: MONT SAINT MICHEL, FRANCE

Nick swam with the night current away from the mount, unnerved by the proximity of naval forces still searching the waters near Mont Saint

Michel. After a week on the rock, hiding in long-forgotten catacombs, it felt good to be in the water again and headed out to sea. The swimmer delivery vehicle pulled him along at a good clip toward deep water and his waiting ride to freedom.

Until recently, he'd never been alone. For years he'd been surrounded by his fellow airmen in the Air Force and by others when fighting the legal battle of his life with lawyers to retain his honor—a battle he'd lost. Then followed years in St. Petersburg, immersed in a new country and a new language, plunging into his passion, the Russian circus. And finally, the years of planning and executing the attacks with his hand-picked men. But for the past week, he'd been truly isolated. And now, he was alone, in the Gulf of Saint-Malo off the coast of France. Immersed in a dark cold sea. For the first time in his life, he wondered if he'd survive. This isolation, far out to sea at night with limited oxygen and power, suddenly consumed him. He fought back the demons of fear and forged on.

Fifteen kilometers and three hours later, Nick took the sea scooter to sixty meters depth and deployed a drogue, pulling free a long thin cable that spooled off his craft and sank in the black depths below. He trolled along slowly, awaiting contact. Within minutes he had his prize, a deployed wire deep in the ocean signaling his waiting craft to rise on its own.

An hour later, Nick was dry, nestled in the small control room of the only submarine of its kind in the world. A strange variant of the Swedish *Sea Dagger*, his craft held six flying craft in a watertight compartment behind him. The vehicle was configured with autonomous navigation capability for unmanned operations when he was away and a small but adequate control room, bunk, miniature galley, and head. Nick guided the modified *Sea Dagger* down into the thermal layer, setting the autonomous navigation to motor southwest. Behind him, the unique craft's ultra-silent air-independent propulsion made no observable acoustic signature as he spirited away, concealed in the Atlantic Ocean's thermocline.

Five kilometers north, the attack submarine Virginia (SSN 774) fell into a distant trail on Nick's craft.

"He's hugging the layer, Skipper. We're tracking him using transients. Propulsion acoustics are nonexistent. Probably air-independent propulsion, like Kilo Niner-Six-Zero. He's headed south, Sir."

Captain Kelly leaned over the acoustic operator, peering at the faint signature, the squiggly lines barely observable above the background noise of freighters, shrimp, whales, and fish. They could lose contact with this target at any moment, if Ulrich went to one side of the thermal layer and Kelly's sub to the other.

"You won't chase a more wary foe in the next decade," he said to the two Petty Officers at the acoustic station. "We're the elite of the fleet—the fastest, quietest, most capable attack submarine on the face of the earth. Do *not* lose him."

He turned to an older gentleman to his right who leaned on a cane, an unusual sight on an attack sub.

"As you predicted, Dr. Pestorius," Captain Kelly said. "He came in on a swimmer delivery vehicle and is underway now with the big craft. How'd you know he'd swim out when he did?"

"Signals intelligence, Captain. And steganography. Our target loves symbolism, encryption, and coded Internet communications. We exploit those weaknesses. Elias Ulrich is the law enforcement target of the millennium. And his submarine's spider payload may change history. If we can catch him, that is."

"We'll catch him," said another observer standing next to the man using the cane. The trim African American fondled a pocket watch. "I've been on his trail two years, and we've almost got him in our grasp."

EPSILON

John threw up a third time. Between the sight of Sean's body and the vomit's vile odor filling his space suit, he was barely able to continue cleaning Epsilon's flight deck. An entire wall and a fourth of the big screens were sheared away by a meteoroid that could have destroyed the ship. Sean hadn't had a chance to respond, his body subjected to an immediate vacuum, and his sinuses, ear drums, and abdomen exploding in the sudden transition to zero pressure.

Worse, Sean and he had never come to closure about what John felt mattered most in life. Sean may have ridiculed John's faith, but John would have given anything to have time with Sean before he died to share his faith, as he had with Michelle. It was too late now.

John zipped Sean's body bag shut and pulled it through the hatch into the central access tunnel, now at zero pressure. Tears he couldn't wipe stung his eyes, mixing with bile and chunks of food floating inside his helmet. His misery from losing his friends and enduring his space suit's putrid microclimate was overwhelming. He tried to stop the tears, but a choking wave of pain burst out as he left the demolished flight deck. Sean would never see home, never make that Earth landing he'd talked of so often. He'd never know he was a father. There were no more chances for John to explain God to the rough-and-tumble mission commander. It was over.

Despite his intense personal pain, John found himself dwelling on Rex Edwards's genius in setting up hatches in the central access tunnel, one at every deck. John could isolate cave portions into individual air-locks, as he had just done for this section between the flight and science decks, without evacuating the rest of the cave's air. He commanded the hatch shut to the flight deck, pressurized the tunnel's isolated portion, and escaped the reeking suit.

With the tunnel at full pressure, John opened all the mid-deck hatches and floated to the galley. He stripped off his clothes, wiping down with towelettes to clean off the worst of his vomit. A shower would have to wait. He couldn't seem to stop the tears, but he didn't care. No one was here to see him. Months of isolation from his family, compounded by the loss of his only companions, ripped his heart in two.

An hour later, spent from the emotional fury of the past twenty-four hours, John floated at the end of two black body bags, the complete inventory of the ship's funeral materials. They'd only sent two, presum-ing, he supposed, a third person would be there to use them. NASA efficiency. His friends lay inside these two bags, their lives ended much too soon, and in such a strange way. Despite decades of spaceflight expe-rience, no U.S. Shuttle or Station module had ever been incapacitated by a meteoroid, much less had a human been killed by one. Today, they'd nearly lost it all.

John looked down on the two bags, trying to imagine his friends' faces in joyous times, sharing a meal on the way to Mars. He fought to purge the visions of Sean's exploded sinuses and bloated gut, remember-ing him as the solid commander of the first human exploration of Mars. And Michelle, the first human—and woman—to reach another planet.

CLEAR LAKE CITY, TEXAS

Amy jerked upright in bed, nerves on edge. Was it an intruder? The kids walking in their sleep? The clock showed nearly midnight, but she felt like she'd been asleep for hours, so alive were her senses. Something was wrong.

She listened a long moment. Only the little fan's purring disturbed her home's silence. Victoria the cat lay at the foot of her bed, oblivious to whatever had roused Amy.

Lying under the comforter, Amy began to pray. She thanked and praised God for His peace in past weeks, for Christ's sacrifice, for her children, and for John. Then she felt an odd gnawing—a doubt growing like a fanned flame.

As she prayed for John and the mysterious loss of communications, and for Sean and Michelle, it hit her again—that seed of a dark, unanswered question. Amy sat upright.

It wasn't a sound that had alerted her. She'd *felt* this—like she did once before when speaking to a close friend expecting her husband's arrival from deployment overseas; Amy had discerned a horrible dread. The husband never returned, his plane lost at sea. Praying for Sean and Michelle had that same eerie feel of finality. And she sensed a horrible pain for John—but no finality. None of this made any sense.

Amy arose and knelt at their antique wingback chair, settling onto a crocheted kneeler, and began reciting the twenty Scripture verses she'd memorized over the past months. She poured them out of her heart as prayers.

She knew that somehow, against all odds and with God's help, John would endure.

Haggard and reeking of dried vomit, John stared at what remained of his crew, two lumpy black plastic bags stuffed at the back of one of Epsilon's freezer units. For the last three hours, he'd unloaded all of the frozen goods meant to sustain the three of them for the long trip home. Nearly a hundred packages drifted in the space outside the man-sized door. With a mover's skill, he'd carefully squeezed Michelle and Sean into the closet-sized cold space, and then repacked frozen goods around them until the unit was filled.

The food that wouldn't fit back in the freezer would thaw. He didn't care. Right now, all he could think of was feeling their bodies through the thick plastic, forcing them into a seated position before they froze. He'd find a way, somehow, to return them to Earth. For a proper burial on their home planet.

John remembered Michelle's last moments and the amazed look on her face as she passed into the next life—*as a believer.* Her memory tore at him. She'd been so concerned in her last moments about how he'd survive. Even he had no idea. Except to take each moment a step at a time. A voice deep inside him said *trust.*

John stared absently at the frozen food packets drifting all around him. He'd operated on adrenaline for hours. The floating food annoyed him as he floated aimlessly in the galley deck.

Blank-faced, John pushed into the central access tunnel and sealed all of the hatches to the decks, additional protection in case of more impacts—and deadly holes in the outer skin. He wrapped himself in a reflective space blanket and closed his eyes, overcome with grief and fatigue.

His body drifted slowly in the short tube, surrounded by hatches and the protective skin of the central access tunnel, as a re-stabilized Epsilon raced across the solar system toward home. Somewhere in the midst of the tormenting memories of the past twenty-four hours, John fell asleep.

30

"AGAIN!" ALICE SCREAMED, HANGING onto a lazy old mare's mane and circling bareback around the pasture.

Amy leaned on the gray oak rail fence behind Martha and Ronnie Williams's little home. This experience was a throwback to another era for her: white-haired people isolated from the twenty-first century in gray old homes under the shade of ancient moss-draped live oaks. Incredible peace, away from crazed Clear Lake City—and the space program. She put a hand on Martha's arm as her new friend rested with her against the fence.

"The kids love it here," Amy said. "Thank you so much for the invitation."

"We're honored to have you," Martha said with a broad smile. "Ronnie and I never ride anymore, but he won't get rid of those horses. This is a treat for *us*."

"She's right. Wouldn't have it any other way, Mrs. Wells," Ronnie said, feeding sugar cubes to a mare.

"Please, Ronnie. It's *Amy*. You know, John would give anything to be here right now. Months ago, we watched those images of the spider alien craft on television—images that came through your house. Your radios and antennas, listening to Mars. You were famous to us . . . especially to John."

Ronnie nodded. "It's been a wild ride. Martha crawled out of her skin the first time we saw those spiders on Mars." He held a carrot out and the mare gobbled it out of his open palm. "Tell you what's really strange, though. I don't understand this communication gap. Haven't heard hide nor hair from 'em all week. NASA won't come clean, and that Rex Edwards guy is hopping mad. All of which tells me none of 'em has the slightest idea what's wrong."

"Ronnie!" Martha blurted. "That's no way to talk!"

"Sorry, Mrs. Wells—I mean, *Amy*. I didn't mean that in a bad way."

Amy smiled slightly. "It's okay. But I admit this has been on my mind all week. Especially after last night."

"What happened last night?" Martha's eyebrows furrowed and she touched Amy's hand. "If you don't mind me asking, that is."

Amy tried to compose herself.

Ronnie slapped the fence rails. "Martha. Quit poking around in people's business."

Amy lifted her hand. "No, Ronnie. It's a legitimate question. I can explain." She took a deep breath and let it out slowly. "I woke up with a start last night, like there was a sound in the house. But it wasn't a *sound*."

"What was it, dear?" Martha asked, putting her hand to her mouth.

"You might find this hard to believe," Amy began. "I think something's very wrong on the ship. When I prayed about it, I got this strong sense that John and the crew were in serious trouble, but at the same time, a real peace that the situation was in God's hands." Amy waved at Alice as she rode up. "Does any of that make sense?"

"Don't know about the peace part," Ronnie began, "but waking up with some premonition or something I *do* understand. Been there, done that."

Martha nodded. "Ronnie's had those spells. Always right too. Saved our lives once. He woke up just before we had a big lightning strike on a tree behind the house. Fell through the bedroom and nearly killed us."

Ronnie shrugged. "So—I believe you, Amy. Got a new bed out of it, too," he said with a wry smile.

Martha looked down at the ground. "But we're not the praying kind, Amy. I don't know why—we're just not."

"Anyway, Amy," Ronnie said, "I've been listening for them. When their equipment gets fixed, I'll be the first to let you know."

Amy's eyes widened. "Can you initiate contact? Call them, I mean? I'd always assumed you just listened." Alice waved as she rode up, but Amy never noticed her.

"Sure!" Ronnie said, grabbing the mare's mane and helping Alice down. "Called that lady doctor once a week all the way to Mars. Even swapped a bunch of radio calls with your husband when he was orbiting Mars. You know—ham radio." He winked. "Very *special* ham radio."

"Can you try to call them again? Today?" She pressed against the rail, her eyes wide.

Ronnie turned to face her. "Sure. I mean—I thought that's why you came over."

"Did you know that John and Ronnie are ham buddies?" Martha asked.

"What?"

Ronnie pulled the horse closer toward the fence and approached Amy. "John. He contacted me months ago. Asked me for help."

"He did?" Amy frowned. "He never told me about it, and we talked every week. He e-mailed me every day." She cocked her head as she leaned against the railing. "Are you sure?"

A huge smile crossed Ronnie's face. "Absolutely! John wanted me to teach him about ham radio. Said he was looking for a new hobby—that the bike riding was getting a little boring and he wanted a challenge."

"Well—yes. He told me that three hours a day on a stationary bike was driving him nuts." She shook her head in wonder. *Why wouldn't he share this with me?*

"I e-mailed him the study materials," Ronnie continued. "He wants to take the certification exam. Smart man, your husband. Picked up that radio theory right away." He leaned over the top rail. "If anyone can figure that radio problem out, he can."

THE CELTIC SEA, SOUTH OF LAND'S END

Nick paced in the small cockpit of his whale-shaped, titanium craft, a compartment the size of a modern home's den, configured with kitchen, bath, control room, workout equipment, bed, and engine access. He'd intended to be docked to his special diesel submarine, Kilo 960, several days ago. His backup, Kilo 963, was headed to St. Petersburg—and safety—if his crew could slip past the Americans. Now he was on his own, matching wits with the magical adversary that continued tailing him somewhere in his baffles, at least ten kilometers behind.

Nick had once believed that no one could track him. A hundred meters below the surface of a stormy ocean, he navigated at the imprecise boundary of different-temperature waters, trying to remain in the center of that thin margin, not ducting his sound above or below. Of all submarines on the planet, only his unique craft was configured to accomplish this remarkable feat, climbing and descending autonomously to stay sandwiched in the acoustic dead zone between the warmer upper waters and cold deep.

He lifted a glass of red wine to toast the skipper of the unseen boat that seemed to hold his acoustic signal despite Nick's best efforts to evade. "Congratulations!" he said, clinking the glass against the titanium bulkhead. "It's been fun, Captain. But now it's time for me to go."

Nick set the glass down and commanded a series of maneuvers on a computer terminal, his special craft's version of a dive control. The hum of equipment around him ended as he shut down the special engine, suspended in its soundproof capsule. Running only on fuel cells, he reduced his electrical load to the absolute minimum, and the lights faded to a dull orange glow. The whale-like craft was absolutely silent, drifting in a slight current as the Gulf Stream ended, headed west-southwest.

"My batteries against your brains, Captain. If you can find me, I'm yours."

An hour later, the USS Virginia glided past Nick's chubby submarine as the Americans headed due west, following the last known course of their quarry. Nick's acoustic suite recorded every signal of their passage, less than two hundred meters off his port bow. A fraction of a degree of course correction a few kilometers back, and the USS Virginia would have plowed directly into him.

Nick padded from the acoustic suite to his computer in stocking feet, commanding his automatic target recognition algorithms to watch for the special signature he had just recorded as the USS Virginia passed abeam. With a hydrophone floating fifty meters above his craft in the surface duct, and another weighted one hundred meters below in the deep water duct below the layer, he watched and waited, tracking the passage of his foe with remarkable precision.

Nick drained the wine glass, then stripped to the waist. A chin-up bar, welded to the titanium frame, was his exercise passion. Ninety minutes later, as Nick ground away toward the thousand mark, his signature recognition system beeped faintly, illuminating a red warning light.

His pursuer was headed back his way.

LA MARQUE, TEXAS

Martha finished serving the supper of chicken-fried steak, mashed potatoes, green beans, and coleslaw. Amy hadn't eaten chicken-fried steak in decades. She suspected her children *never* had.

The tiny old frame house seemed so inviting. These people were real. Simple in an elegant way, not caught up in the frantic lifestyle of so many families she knew in Clear Lake City. Faded curtains, outdated carpet, harvest gold paint, and rickety chairs adorned the house, but every aspect of the aging home was clean and tidy. It was clear that Ronnie put his time into radio and Martha into being a homemaker.

"If I wanted to call him—like right now—could I do that?" Amy asked.

"Sure," Ronnie said. "When they get that radio running again—the S-band satellite rig—I can dial 'em up and tag on the frequency any time. NASA hates it, but there's no law against it. All we can do is talk, of course. I can't control the spaceship or anything. And you gotta wait a while between 'how are you?' and 'I'm fine.'"

"I know, but that's okay," Amy said excitedly. "I wonder why he didn't ever tell me. About the radio thing—and about you?"

"Actually—he did, Mom," Abe said, poking at a large puck of fried meat. "Remember? He said he was studying something neat and that he'd tell us more about it when he passed the test. Said it was a surprise."

"There's a test?" Amy asked, holding a fork of potatoes in midair. "Is this what he meant—the ham radio?"

Ronnie smiled and nodded. "John was getting ready to take the General Class License amateur radio exam. He's up to ten words per minute on Morse code. And he nailed the theory sample exam last week. Scheduled for his final theory exam April 7. If the radios are back up, that is."

Amy shook her head in wonder. John *had* mentioned this. She'd thought it was some technical thing—and had mentally tuned out that bit of news. Now she understood.

"You know, Ronnie, until now, I didn't realize how close you were to my husband and the mission. I came looking for help, but never dreamed I'd meet one of John's friends." She smiled and looked at Martha. "And make *new* friends."

Martha nodded. "Our lucky day!"

"Maybe," Arthur said with a mouthful of chicken-fried steak, "it *wasn't* luck."

Amy smiled, hoping that her second son was about to say what she'd been thinking. "You like the steak, son?"

"Mmm-hmmm," he responded, swallowing a huge gulp. "Love it! Maybe tonight was supposed to be, you know—like dad says."

"What does your dad say?" Martha asked.

Arthur shrugged and looked at his brothers, as though they all knew.

Martha caught the looks and laughed. "What am I missing?"

Amy chuckled at the telling glances of all four kids, each stifling a laugh. "Go ahead, Arthur," Amy said. "You tell her. Before the rest join in."

"Okay. Mrs. Williams. My dad says that everybody has a purpose, and—" he paused to cut into another bite of crunchy fried steak—"God has a marvelous plan for your life. So," he said, lifting a fork full of meat, "Mom finding you guys must've been part of that plan, don't you think?"

EASTER SUNDAY, MARCH 31, 2013: EPSILON

John stared out the portal toward the distant Sun. Still so far away—almost eight months of travel, three hundred million kilometers to Earth. Somewhere out there his family waited. He glanced at his watch; it was nearly ten in the morning Houston time. Tears welled in his red eyes, eyes sore since the loss of Sean and Michelle.

Easter Sunday. His kids would be spiffed up, shoes shined and Alice's dress pressed. Amy would be in her usual pink two-piece suit, and Alice in ruffles and white sandals. The boys would be pushing and shoving to get away from Amy's stiff brush, and everyone would be running late.

Or maybe not. Perhaps in the difficult week since they'd lost contact with Earth, the kids would be helping her to make it all work amidst the stress. He could imagine Abe taking over as the dad, cajoling Albert and nodding at Arthur as they left Alice to their mom. Yes. They'd be on time. And surely they'd be in prayer for him, as he was for them.

Easter. He'd been home for the last one—and on the Space

Station the Easter before that, just after the attack on Washington. This would be the *last* Easter he would ever miss, the last in space, the last time he'd leave his family. "I promise," he said out loud, surprised at the anguish in his voice.

John looked at the distant Sun and the beauty of the universe that framed it, but the scenery barely registered. He felt unable to move. Diagnoses of his condition flashed through his mind: "Passive and withdrawn," Michelle would say in her amateur psychiatrist manner. "In the shock phase of grief, you will experience low self-esteem and expect more bad things to happen. Just when some say it can't get any worse, you'll say it will."

Some distant part of him wanted to laugh, putting words in Michelle's mouth.

Michelle was dead.

"It's my fault," he cried. He no longer cared if he talked to himself. There was no one to hear, and there never would be. He was destined to float in space until he ran out of food or oxygen. "Don the Astronaut, damned to drift alone forever," John said, remembering a favorite author's depiction of hell: a stranded astronaut circling the Earth all by himself, never to set foot among people again. And here he was. Don the Astronaut, in real life.

"This can only get worse." He slapped the portal hard, half of him wanting to force the glass out and end this nightmare. "And I'm helpless to do anything about it."

John grabbed at his ragged flattop, unable to even pull his own hair in frustration. He slammed the glass portal again and again. The impact forced him back away from the wall into the middle of the compartment, beyond any handhold. All he could do now was wait to drift into something he could grab. He couldn't swim through the air to a bulkhead. He was stuck in the middle of his compartment, beyond help. Don the Astronaut, adrift inside his own ship.

"Jesus!" he screamed, grief-stricken, at the dead walls.

"Christ is risen!"

"The Lord is risen indeed!" the congregation responded as Pastor McGehee opened the service on Easter morning.

Four well-scrubbed and nicely dressed children were lined up to her left and right. All around her, elated voices lifted in song, celebrating this day. Sharon and Mike Walters and their three children were seated in front of her, and Mom and Dad were farther down the pew. On any other Easter, Amy would be celebrating along with her friends and family, but the uncertainty of John's situation threw a damper on her spirits she couldn't escape.

Easter was all about resurrection.

At the refrain of the hymn, Amy choked. The words stuck in her mouth. Tears streamed across her powdered cheeks as she tried to block out a thousand cheery voices celebrating the fact that God might have John in His hands after all — in Heaven.

> *Up from the grave He arose!*
> *With a mighty power o'er His foes.*
> *He arose the victor from the dark domain*
> *And He lives forever with His saints to reign.*

31

SPECIAL AGENT KERRY STOOD on a pier looking across Her Majesty's Naval Base in Devonport, Plymouth, Western Europe's largest naval base.

A temporary scaffolding covered in dense black cloth shrouded the dry-dock holding the damaged hull of Kilo 960. Her propeller and steerage were smashed, crushed by the bow of the attack submarine USS Cheyenne (SSN 773). Crews clambered over the American boat in the adjacent dry-dock in a round-the-clock rush to repair her sonar dome, gouged and sliced by the propeller of Nick's submarine when the two collided after the alien landing at Mont Saint Michel.

Kerry badged through the security gate and into the shrouded pier-side area. This mysterious Russian quarry fascinated him. He walked along the black beast's length, marveling at the specially configured deck aft of the sail. Sculpted mating adapters appeared tailor-made for a bulbous payload like the whale contraption he'd seen in overhead satellite photos.

"What's next?" a voice asked behind him. Kerry turned to see Dr. Pestorius and Lieutenant Commander Slagle walking from the guard station toward him. "Figure it out?" the tall doctor asked.

"Your guess is as good as mine, Doc. I can see how he evaded us, with the super-quiet diesel and liquid oxygen engine. But I'm wondering about what's *missing*— the minisub that fits on the back— or whatever it was."

"Our quarry's out there," Dr. Pestorius said, waving a cane toward the sea. "But you and I gave it our best. Two weeks chasing him on the USS Virginia, and not a signal. He's either dead or one very capable adversary."

"He's *not* dead," Kerry said, looking at the Kilo. "Not Ulrich. He's just smarter than we are— for now."

"That's the spirit," Dr. Pestorius said, moving alongside Kerry. His height was so much greater that it made Kerry self-conscious. Lieutenant Commander Slagle stepped between them, a good balance.

"We've finished the interrogations," she said. "Do you still want all the crew extradited to the United States?"

Kerry nodded. "The Russian government won't claim them. Seems they're the naval variant of soldiers of fortune. The skipper in particular. An infamous rogue. Hails from St. Petersburg."

"One of Ulrich's old haunts," Dr. Pestorius said. "I'm not surprised."

"I just left their holding facility," Slagle continued. "The Russians, except for the skipper, claim to know nothing. The three Americans don't deny working for a guy named Nick, but no one's talking beyond that. They demand lawyers. We can't refuse that right much longer."

"We could," Kerry replied, turning toward her. "They're terrorists. But we won't. I've arranged for a special security flight out of the UK tomorrow. We'll take them to the detention facility in the Pearl Islands off Panama. As for the skipper, I think he's the connection we need to Ulrich's past in Russia. He might help us connect the dots for what happened after Ulrich's dishonorable discharge from the Air Force."

"Agreed," Dr. Pestorius said. "I plan to stay a little longer to check some Swedish sources. Are you going home with the prisoners?"

"Yes," Kerry said. "What's in Sweden?"

"Friends who know things. Fellow submariners." Dr. Pestorius pointed at the empty docking fixture on the Russian submarine's aft end. "Whatever went there is what we were chasing for two weeks on the Virginia. And when we find it, my guess is we'll find six alien spiders huddled on board. If we don't—"

"If we don't," Kerry said, "we're at a standstill. Without Ulrich and those spiders, we have no proof."

TUESDAY, APRIL 16, 2013: JOHNSON SPACE CENTER, HOUSTON, TEXAS

Director Greg Church took another swallow of water, wishing he was anywhere but here.

"We have no idea what caused the communication failure. But no data support the conclusion that the crew or vessel are lost," Church said to a packed crowd of media and VIPs at the Mars Press Center. "In fact, just the opposite. Deep space telescopes can see Epsilon's white hull, and it's progressing on course—toward home."

"If the signal failed suddenly," asked a television reporter near the front, "isn't it just as likely something catastrophic happened on Epsilon? I mean, like a cell phone quitting in the midst of an auto crash. Isn't that a possibility?"

"Why inflame this situation?" Church asked angrily. "It's much more likely that your cell phone signal died for lack of a battery or cellular coverage than that the driver crashed the car."

The crowd murmured, his answer connecting with a few of them.

"So do me a favor," Church said, jaw clenched. "Let's not scare the public when we don't know one way or the other."

A woman in back raised her hand. "Director Church?"

"Yes, Cynthia."

"What communication options could they be working on?"

Church relaxed a bit, able to speak to what NASA understood. "If the antenna for the S-band high-data-rate is busted, they could try the low-data-rate system. But we haven't heard from either one. So either both antennas are gone or shot. If the low-data-rate and high-data-rate are both on the fritz, then there's the option of turning the vessel around, removing the Columbus module from the storage bay, and directing her antenna toward Earth. That S-band unit is strong enough. Barring that, there are no other options. We only built the craft to be triply redundant."

"And that was adequate," Rex Edwards blurted out from his chair on the speaker's stage. Both hands were flexing a pen so far it appeared ready to break, and his beet red face matched his bow tie. "You can't build in protection against every possible contingency. This is space flight—it's risky business."

Church wouldn't blame Rex for shooting every reporter in the room. This was a set-up—against NASA and Rex. They couldn't win.

"Nothing else?" Cynthia asked Church.

"No. They have tools to repair some flaws in the electronics. And Captain Wells can accomplish miracle repairs—with enough time. They can rebuild the antennae with some pretty basic fixes, like a space version of duct tape, or pointing the ship to point the antenna. But since we haven't seen any signals yet, I suspect the flaw is more fundamental. Such as a major electronic or computer fault they're trying to patch."

"Director!" shouted another reporter. Church pointed at him in silence.

"Sir, I understand you can patch directly into the S-band control box in the system control deck. If that's true, then wouldn't a computer fault be ruled out?"

Church's face reddened. These reporters were more resourceful than he'd given them credit for. "It's possible. That patch would feed directly to the antenna from the S-band control."

Rex shook his head, burying his face in his hands.

"Then if it's not a computer problem," the reporter continued, "it must be a complete loss of power, or a triple failure of three independent electronic systems—which is a mathematical improbability according to Mr. Edwards. So, tell us, if they lost all power, what would their chances be at this point, three weeks into the crisis?"

Church developed a sudden hatred for this reporter. He'd brought Church to the brink of admitting on national television that there had to be a catastrophic problem. He'd hoped to avoid that. But now here it was, staring him in the face.

"Without power, after three weeks, their chances would be grim. However," he said, both hands raised to quell the murmurs, "I'm sure there are other explanations, Mr.—"

"Rodale. John Rodale, Fox News. If there are other explanations, sir, please—do share them with us. Believe me, we all want something to hope for. We're on your side."

Church stared in silence, Rex Edwards sat tight lipped, and his flight director shrugged, confirming what everyone knew: *nothing.*

"There are no other explanations, Mr. Rodale. You've summed it up. Power, antennas, electronics, or—God forbid—an unknown catastrophe. I promise, we will not give up our search for their signal."

"Could it be the Father Race?" Malcolm Raines asked his audience of twenty thousand faithful packing the coliseum at a weekly service. He shrugged his big shoulders in an exaggerated motion. "Perhaps. But I think not."

At six foot eight, Raines was an imposing religious figure in his floor-length purple robe, cinched at the waist by a gold braided rope. It was a fancy version of those worn by the priests of Saint Michael's Remnant. The white clerical collar stood stark between the purple field and his dark neck. He waved toward the large video screens behind him. Images of spider craft, Mont Saint Michel, and quotes of his prophecies scrolled as he spoke.

Every slide had a common banner on the top: "Embrace the unknowable God."

"Some media and many nonbelievers have proposed that the Father Race has perpetuated a catastrophe. But this cannot be! Trust me! The Father Race will reveal how we must respond."

He raised his hands. "We cannot give up! We *must not* sit still. We are called to seek the inner hidden knowledge and follow the Father's call."

He swept a hand toward six purple-robed associates. "What is their number—*our* number?"

"SIX!" the crowd thundered in unison. "Our number is *six*!"

High in the coliseum's gallery, a young woman headed for an exit before Raines started the closing hymn. Her hair fell to the middle of her back, jet black and straight, pulled into a single ponytail under a black rodeo hat. A tight black western-cut top, with silver buttons, met at her waist, tucked into tight black jeans with a large silver buckle on a hand tooled belt. Black snakeskin boots completed her cowgirl outfit. Only the red of her lips and tanned face broke the dark field of her striking appearance.

She walked down exit ramps to the coliseum's rear and flashed a badge to enter a secure area behind the stage. Soon she stood in Raines's private dressing room with the lights off.

Five minutes later, Raines stepped into his suite. "Monique?"

"Here I am, Father." She shook her black tresses free of the ponytail clasp and hat.

Raines pushed the door closed with his foot and the room went dark.

THURSDAY, APRIL 25, 2013: EPSILON

"Remember the good old days?" John asked himself as he puttered about the lonely space ship. In the past month he'd grown accustomed to holding one-person conversations. He hated the silence, often turning on a movie and piping the audio throughout Epsilon to make it sound inhabited. *Galaxy Quest* droned in the background as he surveyed a bank of instruments.

System control was his home now. With the flight deck demolished almost a month ago, John had shifted complete electronic control of the ship to "after steering," as he liked to call it, reminiscent of his Navy shipboard terminology for an emergency steering compartment directly above the rudder. From here, he could run all of Epsilon, and excepting the communications, the ship ran well.

The steady *ping ping* he could hear on 381 megahertz in system control was supposed to be foolproof—like the spacecraft version of an emergency locator transmitter, or ELT, on a plane. If nothing else would work, this should. He watched the small green LED illuminate each time that the transmission went out, carrying a short burst of sound that would tell the world the ship was headed for Earth. And now it would share his story. John was proud of his latest accomplishment, finding a way to put a very little bit of information in every one of those *pings*. As NASA and the deep space network listened, his story would be told. It would take days, but at least he had a link home now. He could only hope that it worked. He had no way to know for sure.

Besides the flight deck, the science deck and the Columbus lander had been destroyed. Four small meteoroids had ripped through the skin of Michelle's private compartment, rendering it off limits. He'd done an IVA—an intra-vehicular activity—in a space suit to recover her books, sleeping sack, computer, guitar—and a massive stash of five kilograms of expensive dark chocolate hidden in her guitar case. The meteoroids lost so much energy penetrating her compartment's hull that they'd failed to puncture the central access tunnel. The aluminum bulkhead of her bathroom vanity had stopped the flight of the marble-sized rocks through the solar system. Her vanity had probably saved his life.

A large meteoroid had sheared through the bulkhead of the flight deck, leaving an oblong banana-shaped gash in the hull. An even larger rock had blasted through Columbus in the parking bay just forward of the airlock. He'd surveyed the devastation of Columbus during an EVA a few days after the impact—wondering all the time when the next impact would be. There was no one left to save *him*.

As the big rock flew through their trusty Martian lander, it had fragmented the metal on the lander's insides like an armor-penetrating shell spraying molten metal inside a tank turret. Most of the inside of the lander was destroyed, along with their Martian samples and three orbs—the two given to Rover and one presented to Michelle. The impact eviscerated the storage bay and only a few Mars rocks remained. All of the control and communication equipment was gone—along with a man-sized hole in the hull. That impact had sent the ship tumbling just after John unclipped to save Michelle.

The space rock that sliced through science deck had vaporized equipment, samples, computers, and their wonderful deep-space telescope. His last survey had proved that he had everything he needed to survive, but most of their studies, their explorations—and *all* of Michelle's biological samples, along with the deep freeze and her precious bacteria from Mickey Mouse—were gone. It was as though the history of Epsilon, and the Columbus expedition on Mars, had been wiped away in an instant.

Despite that, he was still alive.

"At least we can fly this thing," John said, adjusting a vernier thruster to point the ship. "And we're still on course. Headed home. Only seven months to go, right, John?"

"Right, Hawk. One down, seven to go." He chuckled at the conversation with himself. "Just focus on the good old days, buddy, and we'll get this piece of Swiss cheese home."

Dear Michelle would have advised him that he was nuts, talking to himself and reliving the past. She'd have said, "You're wallowing in nostalgia, Captain Wells. Your brain no longer cares about the future. You are mentally constructing stories that transform the past into the present." Actually, she'd said that very thing to him once before, after the devastating attacks of March 21. Something like "nostalgia is a form of adaptation."

Adaptation or not, it felt good to ponder the times together with Sean and Michelle on their way to Mars, reliving their technical conversations about exploring the planet and the great debate about alien life. But it all seemed so distant now.

John tuned the vernier control a bit more, watching a pen he'd left floating in front of him jerk to the side as the ship's attitude control made a minute adjustment. The ship moved around the pen and the instrument drifted toward a bulkhead. Despite the ship's gashes and the lost materials and systems, Epsilon was flying well.

Thank goodness for that. An automatic vernier firing got him out of a frustrating jam in his compartment three weeks ago, moving the ship around him so he could reach a handhold and get on with his life. After a shower, and days of blank stares at the bulkheads, he finally got a handle on his grief and his situation. Now John was back in form. He was a survivor, and he would find a way—somehow—to take this ship home.

"Gonna get fat, John boy," he said, finishing off another square of Michelle's dark chocolate. After a couple of morose weeks, he'd admitted his depression was real. Michelle had cared enough for him to prescribe her natural antidepressants—bitterly rich semi-sweet chocolate bars. "A stable brain serotonin level enhances a positive mood state," she'd said once about mood-food relationships. In remembrance of her, he followed the doctor's advice. And the chocolate made a world of difference. His serotonin and endorphin levels were up; he felt better, and he was Mr. Fixit again. Optimal brain happiness, thanks to Michelle's chocolate stash.

In the past two weeks, John had completely surveyed the ship, strategically positioning space suits where he could reach one in moments if there was a minor puncture. He'd spent hours inspecting Epsilon's external skin. Those were magical EVA excursions, hanging by himself in the midst of the solar system, just one man against the universe and a backdrop of brilliant stars.

John sealed the chocolate pouch and slid it into the pocket of his cargo pants. "No more euphoria today, John. Time for a bike ride."

Whistling an old country tune, he headed for the exercise deck, a punishing three-hour ride on the exercise bike, a short shower, and then dinner.

"Two hundred thirteen days to go!" he shouted, bouncing off the walls as he headed down the central access tunnel.

"Two one three!"

32

three months later

PARKER HANNIFIN AND FOSTER Williams dueled in front of fifty million listeners with words as their weapons. Neither gave the other an opportunity to conclude his point. Yet, both managed to claim victory, like best friends fighting to the death and shaking hands as they stopped short of the final plunge of the knife.

Three minutes after breaking for an advertisement, the two were civilized, with their next guests queued up. Malcolm Raines, principal mentor of Saint Michael's Remnant, sat preening onstage, his wave of greased black hair perfected with each touch of a large comb. Amy Wells sat opposite him, enduring a last-minute powder.

Why did I agree to this circus? she wondered.

"Forty seconds," someone said behind a bank of lights. Amy began praying under her breath for patience and for calm—and for the right words. The last one hundred twenty days had been hellish. The public finger-pointing was in high gear, blaming Rex Edwards, blaming NASA, and blaming the aliens. Some even blamed the crew for the lost communications. Amy sought to remove herself from the acrimony, devoting herself to family and friends, to prayer—and to the occasional trip to the Williams's home. There she could use Ronnie's radio to talk to the cosmos—just in case John was listening. NASA never offered her such an opportunity.

"Five seconds!" the voice said. Her heart skipped when the red light came on above the camera.

"Welcome back to the second half-hour of our special midweek segment! Tonight, we're taking a deeper look at the mysterious Mars mission, silent since March. On my left," said Parker Hannifin, "Amy Wells, outspoken wife of Captain John Wells, flight engineer for the Epsilon craft."

"And on my right," Foster Williams countered, "Father Malcolm Raines, chief priest of the World Inclusive Faith Church in Phoenix, Arizona. Welcome, Mrs. Wells and Father Raines."

Amy nodded, tight-lipped.

"It is my great pleasure to join you again," said Raines, smiling broadly.

"Mrs. Wells, we'd like to start with you," said Parker. "You've been a vocal opponent of some recent criticism of the mission. Can you tell us more about that?"

Peace, dear Lord. Give me the words.

"Yes, thank you, Parker. Let's all be part of the solution, not part of the problem. The finger-pointing about what went wrong—and who's to blame—needs to stop. Good people have done their level best to make this mission a success—and those people are still working hard to talk to Epsilon. Let's remember the crew will fly around the back of Venus in little over a month. We need to be committed to prayer—not dissension."

"Prayer cannot change the past, Mrs. Wells," Raines said. "Whatever has happened has happened. Someone disappearing for this long usually implies disaster."

"Prayer is always effective," Amy countered, "if you're praying to the right God. And we don't know what happened, Mr. Raines. This much we do know: you can't say 'usually.' No one's ever returned from Mars—not even a robotic mission. We must trust, as you say so often. Trust that our crew is fine and simply out of touch. We must trust God."

"I wish it were that simple, Mrs. Wells. But with all due respect, it sounds to me as if it is you who are out of touch—with reality. Perhaps there are no other missions against which to gauge this singular event, but it is highly unlikely that, with engineers of your husband's caliber, the crew has been unable to find any way to communicate."

"My reality is grounded in Scripture, Mr. Raines."

"I prefer to be addressed as *Father* Raines."

"'Father' is a term I reserve for my dad and for my Lord. And as for the true reality—Scripture says I should be anxious for nothing, but in everything through prayer let my requests be made known to God. He will meet our every need, and He cares infinitely more for John and the crew than we can imagine."

"Well! How about it, Father Raines?" Foster Williams said. "Tell us—what's your perspective?"

"Foster, I believe what I can see. I saw—even spoke with—representatives of the Father Race at Mont Saint Michel four months ago. Trust me; I want this mission to succeed. It is a test of our ability to discover the inner knowledge and move beyond Earth to a higher plane."

Amy laughed quietly and shook her head.

"Did I say something to amuse you, Mrs. Wells?" Raines asked.

"I'm sorry. I interrupted."

"Then interrupt again—please," Raines said. Parker Hannifin seemed to stifle a laugh over the standoff. Maybe because no one was shouting.

"Very well. You speak in generalities. What is this 'inner knowledge' and 'higher plane' that you speak of? You suspect my husband is dead because you can't see any proof of his existence, but in the same breath you exhort us to trust in an 'unknowable god' and 'hidden knowledge'—your words—neither of which we can see. Speak plainly, Mr. Raines. And practice what you preach."

His scowl intensified, and she could see his right hand clench into a fist. "I do, Mrs. Wells. Perhaps I did not explain myself—"

Amy decided it was time to adopt techniques she'd seen used on this show. She didn't let him finish his sentence.

"Jesus said that 'blessed are those who believe, but have not seen.' He was not unknowable. He came among us and shared knowledge openly—not in secret."

"True. He was a great teacher, and he—"

"He *is* a great teacher, but He is also the Son of God, who lived among us, was crucified, died for our sins, and rose again. People saw him, ate with him, and even touched Him after His Resurrection."

Raines waved a hand dismissively. "Stories. Ancient history."

"Eyewitness accounts, Mr. Raines. A better witness than your assertions that you hear voices—voices that no one else has heard."

Parker and Foster had been silent, marveling, Amy imagined, at the spiritual conflict developing on their set. Foster spoke first.

"Father Raines? Your shot."

The tall priest seemed to force a smile through his clenched jaw.

Amy was sure she'd touched a raw nerve; she could feel the pressure, on her and on Raines, as everyone waited.

"The gospel I preach is not my own, Mrs. Wells," he said, jaw twitching. "My words are those of the Father Race—the true gods."

"The Lord our God is *one*," she shot back. "And He doesn't need spaceships to reach us."

"You are hopelessly immersed in orthodoxy, madam. Open your mind."

"I've tried. I've tried to open it to all your teachings, Mr. Raines, but I've found they have the spiritual food value of cotton candy."

Both of Raines's hands clenched into giant fists. Amy was glad he was on the other side of the table. "Your faith is misplaced. You will be overcome with grief when you realize just how shallow your god is. Your husband has perished—of that I am sure."

Amy took a deep breath, praying as she spoke. "Is that another of your prophecies? Because it sounds like one to me." She looked at Parker Hannifin who nodded. Next to Raines, Foster Williams was frowning. "And as for *faith,* that is being sure of what we hope for and certain of what we do not yet see. But it's not faith that sustains me for the day I will see my husband again. It's *hope*—a quality of our spiritual lives I've never heard you speak about. Hope sustains us in our darkest hour."

Raines scowled. "I base my expectations on what I can see and measure. Hope is empty. In what state do you expect to see him next, madam? Dead or alive?"

Amy seethed. "Alive, Mr. Raines. I will not—under any circumstance—ever give up hope."

Privacy. Unspoiled Caribbean territory. An exquisite retreat from civilization. Mysterious beauty once open only to the most privileged.

Nick flipped the brochure onto a rattan stand in his luxury bungalow on remote Mustique Island south of St. Vincent and the Grenadines. He picked up a set of binoculars, training them on a large fishing boat off the coast of his private beach on the tiny resort island. With maximum magnification, he could see a large hose draped over the fishing boat's stern, a diesel fuel line leading to the shallow inlet's bottom. He checked his watch. Four hours gone. Another two and the fuel would be completely transferred. A few more days resting in the sun and he'd be ready to move on.

Nick picked up a map and made a red mark on the tiny island. After four long months of isolation under water, punishing but necessary seclusion in the embrace of his ocean, he was almost back to where he'd started a year ago. Four months adrift in the *Sea Dagger*, the perfect acoustic ploy—as hard as it was to endure. With hydrophones listening above and below the thermal gradient, Nick took the slow route, observing the passage of hundreds of ships, many whales, and the occasional transit of a submarine, perhaps on the hunt for him. But it was a big ocean, and drifting, on battery and fuel cells, he had no acoustic signature. Nick's craft was absolutely invisible.

Four months of letting the Earth deliver him safely back to North America. Four months in the dark, with only occasional night trips to the surface to recharge, and only then when he'd calculated that American thermal imaging and photo intelligence satellites had passed. Four months wishing he could see the sun, or drink in the salt air of a moonlit night at sea. Sometimes he snorkeled in the wake of a loud ship at night. But mostly he tried to relax, riding age-old currents to his destination. Currents, he knew, that would take him exactly where he needed to go. And in plenty of time.

First he rode the Canary current—the southern branch of the North Atlantic Drift, and the Gulf Stream's last vestige. Off the western coast of Africa, he turned due west, joining the North Equatorial Current and tranquilly riding that across the Atlantic. Once, decades ago, a sailor had been lost at sea in the Canary Islands and had drifted for seventy-six days from western Africa to these same islands. Dehydrated, burned, a survivor of hunger, sharks, storms, and scurvy, the man walked off his patched rubber raft into the hands of local fishermen. He'd barely survived. Nick, on the other hand, had transited with every luxury. No longer pursued, with plenty of wine, food, and hours of gymnastic exercise in his tiny room, he'd arrived at the precise spot he'd planned.

Nick mentally gauged his remaining days. With a full load of diesel and riding the fast-moving Gulf Stream, he could easily transit the Gulf of Mexico and be off the coast of Virginia within weeks. There would be no more four-month journeys.

He sipped a tall drink and watched his rented fishing boat bob on sparkling blue waves against the backdrop of sugar-white beaches and swaying coconut trees. This would be his final mission. The culmination of years of preparation. Despite all manners of trials, Nick had endured.

Finishing the last of the concoction, he stripped to his swim trunks, then jogged to the shore. He dove into the warm turquoise water, his strong strokes pulling him quickly across a kilometer of ocean to his rented boat.

At the vessel, he did a free dive nearly twenty meters down to the submarine, his eyes open in the bright waters. Patting his small craft's titanium hull, he pushed off and headed for the surface, reveling in the burning sensation of lungs fighting for air. It made him feel so alive — the crushing pressure of the water, the great chase, and the imperative: his mission to change history.

This challenge enthralled him so much more than the money.

TUESDAY, JULY 30, 2013: EPSILON

John kicked the makeshift bench he'd constructed in the central access tunnel. This was his focus: hours and hours hunkered over electronic equipment, determined to rebuild the crippled radio system. He was hidden away, as much as he could stand it, in the safe confines of the cave. The closer he came to Venus and the Sun, the more imperative it was to protect himself from dangerous radiation. He craved freedom, a look at the stars, and open spaces.

A small fan blew the smoke of burning solder flux away as he squinted at his work. The solder joint had failed—again—and he'd fried three tiny resistors near the failure. John ripped the board from its vise and flung it against the bulkhead, splintering the electronics. It was useless now.

"Why me?" he screamed at lifeless cylindrical walls.

The parts scattered, floating in the tunnel, yet another in his many failures to repair the failed S-band transmitter. After three dangerous one-man EVAs, he'd repaired all the antenna parts. He'd patched the dish, constructed a crude waveguide, and rebuilt the stanchion. But the communication system still didn't function. Maybe it was a polarization problem. Perhaps a timing signal or a bad preamp. He'd exhausted everything he knew of electronic design, and had consumed all of the reading material in Rex's digital system files. Even Ronnie Williams's ham radio instruction was of no value at this point.

John had finally pared the problem down to the circuit boards, a daunting microelectronics repair task beyond his soldering skill. He felt nostalgic for his childhood, when he'd built his own radios with man-sized components—big brown resistors, huge capacitors you could get your hands around, and tubes—beautiful tubes filled with all sorts of unknown magical plates and wires that made his radios hum. But those days were gone. Assembling this hypersensitive microelectronics stuff was like stacking sand grains on the head of a pin.

John grabbed the roll of solder and threw it at the wall.

"I need *help!*" he screamed, anger rising like a shaken soda ready to spew. Anger renewed with each fresh memory of lost friends and lost family opportunities. As much as he prayed—and trusted in the God on the other end of those prayers—there were times when he felt he was surviving on empty hope. John wanted action.

He hurled an epithet at his space prison's white bulkhead, eighty million kilometers from another human being, regretting the vile word as soon as he said it. He'd found himself losing his temper often lately, mad at the world . . . mad at God . . . mad at himself as soon as his outburst was over—mad at himself for cursing, and mad about being mad. A furious cycle of anger and repentance had engulfed him.

If Jesus really cared about me, He'd point the way out of this godforsaken mess.

The frequency of this cycle of fury followed by penitent prayer seemed to increase daily. That worried him, and he feared he might end up like the Ancient Mariner, with a circuit board—his albatross—hanging about his neck as he lost his mind. "Circuits, circuits everywhere and not a one that works," he parodied. A thin smile played at one corner of his mouth.

He remembered Amy approaching him fearfully after a rare

chair-throwing tirade a month before leaving on this mission. "You weren't always like this, John," she'd said with that pained tone that pierced him so. "There was a day when we had to pry an ugly word out of you. Now—well, you blow up a lot. And I think I know why. It's the *stress*. Let it go, John, or it will kill you—and us."

John laughed, the first funny thought he could remember in months of eighteen-hour days trying to rebuild Epsilon. "Relax," she'd said. It was like Amy was here, lecturing him again. He laughed again, his renewed voice bouncing off the curved inner walls of his pressurized sanctum.

Maybe it was time to do just that. Follow Amy's advice. Relax.

He knew just what would do the trick.

33

| **WEDNESDAY, JULY 31, 2013:**
| **LA MARQUE, TEXAS**

"I NEEDED TO ESCAPE," Amy said, hugging her new friend at the doorstep of the old home on Shady Lane in La Marque. Cicadas chirped, hidden in the stately live oaks that surrounded the mildewed white wood-and-brick rancher. "Thanks for having us over."

"You're welcome here any time," Martha said as she hustled the children toward the den. "And I don't blame you. I know everyone wants a piece of you today—the one-year anniversary." She held Amy's hand. "Any word?"

Amy shook her head, hanging it in defeat. "Nothing new."

Martha put an arm around her shoulders. "It's time for lemonade, Amy. When life hands you lemons . . ."

Amy smiled. "Pitch 'em and grab the powder mix."

"You know that's not what I meant, girl. Meet me in the kitchen. I'll get Ronnie."

Ten minutes later, her youngest children outside exploring and the two older boys planted in front of the television, Amy was in the kitchen scrubbing lemons when Martha returned.

"That's my job!" Martha protested.

"No. I want to help. Hi, Ronnie," she said, hugging him while holding onto the wet citrus.

"Glad you're here. We have something special to show you," Ronnie said.

Amy cocked her head, pushing her long bangs aside. "For me?"

"For *all* of us. Come see."

Ronnie led Amy to radio central, his special room with walls of electronic equipment, his connection with the radio world. Abe followed. Two chairs were arranged in front of a makeshift desk, a door that rested on sawhorses. A rack of equipment stacked on the door rose to the ceiling, arranged in an arch of sorts over two old computer monitors.

"Those are old," Abe said, pointing at the tube monitors. "I thought everybody had flat screens."

Amy nudged her oldest boy in the side. "Shhh!"

"It's okay, Amy. He's right. But they're cheap. My money's invested in the antennas out there," he said, gesturing out the only window toward the pasture. "And I just added some new ones. That's what I wanted to show you."

Amy squinted, having a hard time understanding what this was all about.

"Look at this," Ronnie said, pointing at a picture of John in a space suit on the International Space Station. "Got my idea for this the last time you visited me, Abe. How does your dad talk to NASA when he's in that suit?"

"Radio, I guess," Abe said.

"Yes, sir! A UHF radio, in fact. Ultra High Frequency. The military band runs from about 199 megahertz up to 399 meg. His suit, it turns out, has a radio set on 321 megahertz. NASA used 312 megahertz for suits on the Space Station."

"Can you hear him on that frequency—from this far away?" Amy asked, afraid to hope where this conversation was leading.

"I can't. But NASA can, with that deep space telescope thing. That hasn't worked so far, though—has it?"

Amy shook her head. "No. It hasn't." She hesitated. "They quit trying with the deep space network after three months. Said there were higher priorities for science." She fought back the tears.

"But there's something they haven't tried, you know?" Ronnie said. "So I decided to give it a whirl. Might get fined for it, but what the heck, you know? 'Live a little,' Martha tells me. So I did. Look!"

Ronnie pointed out the window at a series of eight tall antennas that looked like corkscrews. Albert and Alice, playing in the pasture, stood around the base, staring up at the massive contraption.

"High gain quad helix UHF," Ronnie said, smiling from cheek to cheek. "Got both quads and the transmitters that go with 'em off an old aircraft carrier decommissioned in Corpus Christi last month. Satellite communications. They suck the power, let me tell you. Seventeen decibels of gain and circular polarization. I could fry a seagull if it flew too close."

Abe whistled. "Mr. Williams, do you think—"

Ronnie nodded excitedly, gesturing Abe on. "Yeah, Abe, I can."

Abe punched the air. "Yes!"

Amy looked in astonishment at the two. "What? Do what?"

Ronnie walked up and put a hand on Abe's shoulder. "We'll try 'em tonight, son. I figured out all the angles."

"Mom!" Abe turned to Amy and grabbed her by the shoulders.

"Do you understand what he's saying?"

"Afraid not."

"It's just like music, mom. Amps and all. Those antennas work at the same frequency as Dad's space suit radio. But they can crank out some awesome—and I mean wicked *awesome*—power. You measure that in decibels. Like sound. That's why they look so cool, you know? And he's saying that in a couple of hours, those quad helixes will be pointed toward dad. So, just in case he's wearing his suit—I mean, it's a long shot, you know—we can send a blast out to space that might get to him. We can't hear his radios this far out, but—"

Amy looked at Ronnie for confirmation, his smile all the answer she needed. He nodded his head feverishly.

"We can't hear him, Amy," Ronnie said, putting a hand on Abe's shoulder, "but there's always a chance—a very distant chance—he could hear us. It's worth a try!"

GEORGETOWN, DISTRICT OF COLUMBIA

"This place is pricey, Terrance. You sure it's okay?" Shawnda perused the dinner menu of an exclusive French bistro on M street in Georgetown.

"My special treat," Special Agent Kerry said, dressed casually for the first time in many days. "You've done a lot for me these last months down at the Agency. I wanted to say 'thanks,'" he said, taking her hand and leaning far across the table toward this beautiful, available, interesting, and incredibly well-connected analyst, a contractor he'd met more than a year ago at the CIA.

Shawnda smiled. Her wet brown eyes seemed to sparkle in the low light. "You're welcome! So let's split something. Otherwise you'll have to mortgage your condo to pay for dinner."

"Deal."

An evening with Shawnda was just the distraction Kerry needed. Months of disappointment after losing Ulrich and months of interrogating his newest prisoners had sapped much of his energy. There were days, and today was one of them, when he felt like he'd come to the brink of arresting those responsible for the biggest terrorist attack in the history of the United States, yet fallen short of the critical win.

As if it had been planned that way—and Kerry was sure it was—no one in Ulrich's organization knew enough about the overall plan to rat out the ultimate culprit. The identity of the person or organization who had paid for the terrorist attack remained the great unknown. Even with Tex's admission of telephone calls from "a mature woman, kind of cultured" when asked about who commanded Ulrich's attacks, they were no closer to understanding who was ultimately responsible. They had to find Ulrich. Or lose.

Shawnda prodded him with a fork. "Earth to Terrance. You there?"

"Yeah," he said, snapping back to the present. "Can't get Ulrich off my mind."

"I understand," she said. "I have a little present for you tonight. Interested?"

Kerry's face lit up. She whispered in his ear and Kerry's eyes went wide. "When?" he gasped.

"Thirty minutes ago. I got a call on the way over from Langley."

"We've gotta get over there! Now!" Kerry said as he jumped up from the table.

Shawnda placed a hand on his arm. "No. We don't. We need to sit right here and chill a little. They're running the analysis for the next hour," she said, urging him toward his seat, "so we eat."

Kerry sat down, his pulse racing, beads of sweat on his forehead.

"How'd you do it?"

"I didn't. Our Virginia friends did. I had a standing priority request for some space imagery in the vicinity of Grenada. The satellite was over Saint Vincent's at the time it started the photo run. An analyst got lucky and happened to be screening the downlink of the earliest images in the run, as the satellite headed for Grenada. And poof."

"Poof?" he asked.

"Poof. One heck of a metal whale, moving in the shallow waters off Mustique Island. That rich man's resort. If it hadn't been night time, if he'd been deeper, if it had been any time other than just then—we'd have never seen him. There's no doubt, Terrance—"

"Doubt about what?" he asked, breathless.

"It's the *Sea Dagger*. Stood out like a sore thumb. Headed due west," she said, grabbing his hands and squeezing them. "Toward Nicaragua."

Kerry started to sit up, pulling against her grip. "Have to call Pestorius. Let him know!" She held on tight and tugged Kerry back to the table as he chattered. "Ulrich is headed back to where I found him!"

Shawnda grinned. "Already done! The Navy's all over it. So sit. Let's eat!"

LA MARQUE, TEXAS

"Now?" Amy asked, her heart atwitter on this special night, one year to the day after John's departure. "I just hold down this button and talk?"

Ronnie nodded. "We've got three hours of line-of-sight visibility to Venus. Starting now. We'll talk as long as we have a view. No promises — but we can't just sit around and do nothing, can we?"

Amy smiled. "No. We can't. I doubt he'd go outside, though — so close to Venus. But here goes."

The four children sat on the floor of Ronnie's radio central, and Martha plopped down in the second chair. Ronnie offered his seat to Amy. She turned to her kids and hosts. "Before we do this, we need to pray. Is that okay?"

Martha shrugged. "I guess. It sure can't hurt." Ronnie nodded, silent.

Amy reached out to Abe and Alice, and they all made a circle of seven.

Amy bowed her head, tears forming as she spoke, her heart filled with thanks for these friends and their efforts to fill her day with joy and filled with awe at the hand of God working — a hand she felt moving in this little group. She prayed for John, for the kids, and for Ronnie and Martha. She prayed for the radio signal to reach John. "Thank you, Father," she concluded.

Before they opened their eyes and broke the circle, Alice continued. "And bless daddy, Jesus. He needs you lots more than we do. Amen."

Amy's tears flowed freely as she released her daughter and son. Abe handed her a tissue.

"Ready?" Ronnie asked as he pushed the microphone in front of her.

"Okay. We'll take turns. We've got three hours, right?" she asked, sniffling.

Ronnie nodded. "Just push and talk. Five minutes from now, who knows? Maybe he'll hear us."

Amy lifted the microphone toward her lips. She pressed the black button on the base, and the lights in the room dimmed noticeably. She released the button, alarmed, but Ronnie smiled and waved her on. "That's normal. It takes a boatload of electricity to power those babies."

"Cool!" Abe said. "Brownout!"

Amy pressed the switch again and spoke into the wire-mesh device before her lips. "John? It's Amy. Can you hear me? We're all praying for you." She choked back a sob, determined to stay with it. Ronnie had offered her hope tonight, and she would take full advantage of it. "John? Please let us know you're all right. I love you."

EPSILON

"Amy said to relax. So that's what we're gonna do. Tiger Woods, eat your heart out. We're celebrating our one-year anniversary!"

John stood atop the brilliant white cylindrical vessel, his boots strapped to a handhold with a tie-down rigged for just this occasion. His white suit seemed to blend in with the shiny white of Epsilon's skin, stretching out fifty meters to his left and right. Brilliant galaxies burned like perfect lightbulbs in every direction, points of light with billions of suns, millions of billions of kilometers away. John was standing with feet locked into the skin of his space home, taking it all in. His hand gripped the ultimate toy.

He pulled a dimpled ball from the pocket of his suit pants. "NASA would freak if they could see me now! You hear me, Houston?" he said into his microphone, as if someone were listening. "I'm standing outside while we fly past Venus. You hear me? I'm sick and tired of being cooped up. I'm gonna play through."

He laughed as he knelt and stuck the golf ball on a wad of space duct tape that he'd affixed to the top of a hand hold. He stood up, a golf club in his hand, and flexed his knees, moving his hips as if he were

Tiger Woods settling in for the game of his life. "Sean would be proud that I gave his driver some use," he said chuckling.

John took three practice swings above the ball, having almost no idea how to do this. He'd never hit a golf ball. "First time for everything," he said, conversing as if Sean were by his side and Michelle watching along with him.

John pointed to the distance, lifting his club in the direction of Venus, its roiling sulfuric acid clouds visible from half a million kilometers away. "Now *there's* a target," he said, settling in again with some practice strokes. "Can't miss it."

John reared back with one last twist of his body, the club raised above his head, and yelled for all he was worth. "Fore!"

Even in the clumsy confines of the suit, John's swing was dead on, the wood driver connecting with the ball in utter silence. The white sphere blasted away from Epsilon like a rocket. John nearly lost hold of Sean's precious driver in the follow-through, his boots jerking at their restraints without the benefit of gravity to hold him on the ground.

John tried to watch the ball as it disappeared toward the bright cloud-shrouded planet. "Give it a year," he said. He took another ball out of his pocket. As he did, the speaker in his helmet crackled, the first radio noise he'd heard in what was now five EVAs and months of solitude. He froze in place, hair rising on the back of his neck. Was it just his imagination? Or radiation affecting the radio circuits?

The speaker crackled again. He strained to hear. This could not be. He was too far. *It's impossible—the suit's radios could never communicate that distance.*

"—can you . . . me . . ."

John's heart pounded. He was millions of kilometers from Earth. Could it be? He reached for his wrist control, turning up the reception gain and volume to the maximum. A steady hiss told him he'd saturated the signal, that there was nothing there.

His heart sank; he was sure he'd heard a voice. But maybe that's what he *wanted* to hear, not truly heard. John threw the golf ball into space, frustrated to have been so stupid, to have fallen for such a false—and long-shot—hope.

He shrugged, then reached for a third ball, when he heard it. The steady hiss ceased, and the voice was strong, but scratchy. For one brief moment, his heart stopped.

"John?"

He dared not breathe and miss a word. The static cut in and out.

"—you're all right. I love you."

John jerked at his foot restraint, struggling to turn around and face Earth, a dim blue point of light behind him. He pulled one boot free, then the other, and spun about, yelling the one word closest to his heart in that special moment.

"Amy!"

34

WEDNESDAY, JULY 31, 2013:
NAVAL OBSERVATORY, WASHINGTON, DC

"THAT'S RIGHT, DR. DIAMOND. This is the vice president. I'm calling from my office in Washington. I'm sorry to have bothered you tonight, but this issue is of national importance."

Dr. Diamond was only half awake, the vice president was sure, and the fact that he'd been asleep so early just added to the veep's growing frustration. The request he'd received fifteen minutes ago from a critical constituent in Phoenix could not go unfulfilled. "We need to talk, Diamond. Right now."

"I'm sorry, sir," Diamond said, sounding drowsy. "How can I help?"

"Information, doctor. I need to know what you've heard at SETI—the latest on the Mars Mission. Has the Search for Extraterrestrial Intelligence heard any signal from Epsilon?"

"Sir, I made a complete report to the administrator after we—"

"I asked you a direct question. Is there a signal out there—anything—that would indicate our astronauts are alive?"

Diamond hesitated. "None, Sir. We listened for three months. I wouldn't hold out much hope."

"Only three months? They've been out of touch for *five*. Is the deep space network broken?"

"No, sir. But we had higher priority assignments, including—"

"Bad move, Diamond. You should have kept those radios running. I want them back on. As in the next hour. Understand?"

"Sir—and I assume you are who you say you are—I set our priorities for data collection based on many factors. There's no chance the crew is alive. I monitored every possible frequency. Five of them. They're all silent."

"You want to set priorities? Go right ahead. And as the chairman of the National Space Council, I'll set some too. Your budget will dry up before you can climb back in bed."

"With all due respect, Sir, the SETI is predominantly funded by private donations."

Vice President Ryan coughed. "Change those scanning priorities, Diamond. Or your National Science Foundation grants will be canceled before dawn." He paused, smiling at the sudden brainstorm. "And I will personally call on every one of your corporate donors. That won't be pretty."

| EPSILON

John checked his oxygen level as he listened. He had more than an hour of air left, but he was still out of time. He'd come out to hit a few balls and then scoot back in, mindful of the Sun's heavier radiation doses as he whipped around the backside of Venus. Any other time, he could stay and listen. Not today.

"Don't go!" he said to Abe in the silence between his oldest son's breaths. He was sure they couldn't hear him, but he talked anyway as he headed for the airlock.

"Here's Mom. She wanted to sign off. I miss you, Dad. Can't wait to go hiking when you get back." John was sure he heard a sniffle, out of character for this oldest son who never cried.

"I love you, son! I'm fine!" he said, reaching the lock. "You take care of your mom for—"

"John?"

"Amy!" He stopped his progress into the airlock.

"The lights dim here when I push the button on the microphone. Ronnie has a very strong transmitter. I hope you can hear it."

John heard her cough like she always did when she was trying not to cry.

"I miss you so much, John. I don't know if you can hear us, but I trust that God has you in His hands. This chance to talk—to try to reach you—has been good for all of us. Ronnie said we could come over and try again tomorrow night. He said you'd know when you could see Houston and to tell you—let me read this to get it right—to build a right-hand circularly polarized helical antenna. Yes, that's it. We're supposed to remind you of that often, he says—just in case you're dialing in at the last minute."

"I will! I'll be ready tomorrow, Amy. I—"

"I love you, John. I always have. Maybe you can't hear this, but I need to say it anyway. For a long time I was mad at you—for going to Mars, for leaving me alone. Mad because I didn't have this same calling that you did. But God got me through that, you know? He showed me how much He needed you—and needed me. I understand your sense of mission now—it's like we're *both* called, in a way. I'm really proud of you. Please forgive me for being mad. Just get home. You mean everything to me—to us."

"Amy!" he yelled over the beeping alarm in his suit. He'd reached maximum time for radiation exposure.

"Good-bye," she said.

John wiped the tears away before they could go floating around the ship. The sound of Amy's scratchy voice, and that of each of his children, filled his memory as he zipped through the cave toward system control. *They didn't know! The beacon was supposed to be foolproof!* But from what Abe said, they'd had no contact since March. New tears welled up as he realized the horrible grief his wife and kids must have suffered, not knowing. And it brought all his pain back to the surface. For the past months he'd uploaded the entire story of the busted antennas, the EVAs, Epsilon's destruction by the meteoroids, and his recovery and restoration of the vehicle. It had been therapeutic, sharing the pain, telling his story on a very low-data-rate link back to Earth. He'd kept the world informed for months of his progress, each day uploading a few hundred words to the low-data-rate signal. Now he knew for sure. *No one had any idea he was alive.* He shook off the hurt as he bolted through the hatch into system control. The light on the beacon transmitter was still flashing green. *Why?*

An hour later, with only twenty hours to go until his next window opened to talk to Houston and Ronnie Williams, he'd discovered the fault. The beacon antenna was busted too. It looked fine, the radio tested fine, but for whatever reason, the system had been transmitting into dummy load for the past five months. And there was nothing he could do now to make it work. John stared at the bulkhead, stunned.

Months of sending his story, months of hope that others were following his progress, were dashed in an instant. No one knew where he was or that he was alive.

Twenty hours remained. Images of his radio theory notes and memories of Ronnie's ham radio coaching came to mind, reminders that there was always a solution. What had Amy said, undoubtedly coached by Ronnie— "a right-hand circularly polarized helical antenna." John raced back to the airlock. He needed that old suit. The one with the vomit in it. There was just enough time. He would not fail this time.

JOHNSON SPACE CENTER, HOUSTON, TEXAS

"This breaking news from our affiliate in Phoenix, Arizona, reporting by phone from the international headquarters of the World Inclusive Faith Church and Father Malcolm Raines. Go ahead, Brownlee."

Director Church's pulse raced as he watched the Fox News feed in Mission Control late at night. He hated that space prophet.

"From Phoenix, this is Brownlee Roberts, with Fox News channel 23. Reporting live from the home of Father Malcolm Raines. Father Raines announced tonight—these are his words—'a confidence that the mission to Mars has survived.' He says, 'I felt their presence. The Father Race welcomes home all who persevere.'"

"What?" Church said. "That's all? Where's he getting this tripe?"

The reporter continued. "Raines believes—he told me in private discussions—that the Mars crew is *alive*. And he says we'll soon see proof of this new prophecy."

"Double talk. 'Felt their presence'? 'All who persevere?' What's that supposed to mean?" Director Church swore and threw a soda can into a wastebasket in Mission Control. "Did you get SETI on the line yet?" he asked the flight director.

Dan Jefferson nodded, setting down the telephone receiver with a puzzled look. "Just did. Seems there've been some recent developments."

"What? Did they finally give us that sweep we've been asking for?"

"SETI came up thirty-seven minutes ago. They got a snatch of a UHF signal, then it disappeared. 321 megahertz."

The director's jaw dropped, his eyes wide. "321?"

"Yeah. Can you believe it? EVA intercom frequency. Someone was outside—while approaching Venus!"

Director Church was speechless. After so many months of wondering and a pitched battle with SETI to keep the deep-space network dedicated to watching the Epsilon orbit, why the sudden decision to scan again, why Raines's sudden decision to go public with a prognostication, and why a space suit—not high- or even low-data-rate comms? And why was someone on EVA during the Venus flyby? That was nuts.

"Did SETI patch the file over to us?" Church asked, taking a chair as his legs began to feel weak.

"Sure did," Dan said, holding an earphone tightly to his head, trying to make out a faint sound. "Got it cued up now. Only two seconds of comms. No voice, just—well, just a weird sound."

"Weird? Like weird how?"

He shrugged, offering the headphones to Director Church. "Sounds like someone's crying."

✳

"I will not raise the hopes of a nation based on the evidence of a two-second signal!" Director Church exclaimed in the telephone conference. Half a dozen senior NASA managers sat in the stark white room, lined with old Apollo posters and dusty NASA memorabilia. The NASA Administrator sighed, and everyone heard it over the speakerphone.

"I'm inclined to agree," the Administrator said. "I don't want to play into Raines's hands. Not now."

"Give us a couple of days to work with SETI, sir. We'll keep our ears open, and keep blasting Epsilon with S-band and X-band comms. They're bound to fix those radios sooner or later. If they're alive."

"You don't sound too convinced," the NASA administrator said. All heads turned to face Director Church.

"After five months, no one wants this more than I do. But no. I'm not optimistic." He paused. "I don't trust Raines any farther than I can spit, and he's in this somehow. I advise caution, Sir."

"Caution, how?"

"SETI's watch standers told us something else, Sir. Ours was the *second* call they placed tonight about the results on 321 megahertz. The first call went to Vice President Ryan. About an hour before the news report from Phoenix."

THURSDAY, AUGUST 1, 2013: EPSILON

John gobbled another chocolate square and downed a Pepsi from the special stash of canned sodas he'd kept for months, awaiting that special day when they entered Earth orbit. Today was special above all. And he needed the caffeine jolt. He hated coffee.

John's nose wrinkled at the old suit's odor of ancient bile and cleanser. He'd cleaned it out as best he could months ago, but vomit was vomit. You couldn't turn a suit inside out to clean it. Today, the old suit and its radio were each getting a new life.

After fifteen hours of work, he realized he'd gone all night—and into the next day—with no sleep. With three hours to go he had everything ready. It was time to test the rig; MacGyver would be so proud.

A rotary cutter and two storage lockers provided all the material he needed. With the spinning grinder blade, he'd sliced away strips of aluminum from the sides of tall lockers to form the helical portion of his antenna. Metal dust tried to float away and he vacuumed it up, cut a little more, vacuumed, and so on for three hours, generating twelve meters of narrow aluminum strip.

He'd use the space suits' transmitters. They were the only radios he had that worked, as far as he knew. A helical directional antenna might amplify his signal enough to cross the millions of kilometers of space. He *had* to try.

Helical antenna. It was a strange name, but it worked. He'd used them in the Navy to communicate with satellites. With a long aluminum pole cut from the exercise deck and a base plate taken from a metal table top, he'd created a pole stuck on a platter. Aluminum strips rolled in a broad spiral surrounded the pole, from the base to the end. It looked like a corkscrew with a nail threaded down the middle, all mounted to a flat plate. He mounted the antenna on another section of pole with a vise to clamp it to an external mounting bracket. The spiral would send out a circularly polarized signal, tuned for Ronnie's antenna field. It wasn't ideal for the suit transmitters, but it would have to do.

John rigged the last of the suit batteries together, putting enough spares in the crusty old barf suit to power the radios for hours. He hooked the antenna to the old suit, then rigged a UHF automatic relay to his own suit. If it worked—and it had to—he'd secure the suit and antenna to the ship's skin like a space-suited scarecrow pointing a giant corkscrew toward Earth and talk until he reached his maximum radiation dose. With Michelle's tether, he could tie the contraption to the airlock adapter ring, where he could reach it easily for maintenance. Beyond that, he'd find some way to make the power source permanent so that he could talk any time from inside the ship.

An hour later, he'd proven at least one thing. He could talk to himself within the ship. But sending a signal the length of Epsilon's central access tunnel was one thing. Calling Amy and his kids in Texas from Venus was quite another.

LA MARQUE, TEXAS

Martha and Amy cleared the dinner plates an hour before Ronnie said they might have a view toward the ship. After a day of waiting, Amy was more excited than ever. "Who knows?" she'd said to Alice. "Dad might hear us but can't talk back. We at least owe it to him to try."

"Shouldn't we tell NASA?" Abe had asked earlier in the day, wanting to hurry back to the Williams's home. "They could be trying to help us."

"They have been, I'm sure," Amy said. "But this seems so much more—personal. And it's *fun*. Let's try it a few more times, first. Okay?"

Fifteen minutes before the communications window opened, the entire family crammed into Ronnie's radio central. More people, Amy was sure, than Ronnie had ever hosted in his little room full of communication equipment, wires, and books. The walls were plastered with things he called QSL cards. They were postcards from strange, faraway places, each with a group of letters and numbers—their call signs—

designating who he'd talked to. Ronnie's identifier was AK4WO — Alpha
Kilo Four Whiskey Oscar, as he said it.

"It's time," Ronnie said. "We have a bit of a problem, though."

Amy's face fell.

"It's not serious, but we need to make a decision. We have a sim-
plex link. That means we can talk . . . or we can listen . . . but we can't
do both at the same time. Kind of like an old-style cell phone. So," he
said, hesitating, "do we listen first — or talk?"

Amy looked at the kids, then to Ronnie. "It depends on what John
might be doing. What do you recommend?"

He smiled. "Talk first. Tell him you love him. That's a message
that's sure to get through."

35

NICK ENGAGED HIS SPECIAL craft in drift mode, with a hydrophone fifty meters above and below him and a tiny antenna floating on the surface for Global Positioning System location data and satellite radio. Relaxed from two weeks of sun and fresh air, he prepared for another three months under water. He didn't have to be anywhere until November.

Nick opened up the first of a few dozen good books and settled into his reclining captain's chair. But within minutes of engaging his autonomous navigation, a unique system that trimmed the *Sea Dagger* precisely in the middle of the Gulf Stream's headwaters, his automatic target recognition system registered the presence of a key acoustic signature.

Nick bounded from his chair, scanning the screen. He let the system auto-classify the target, one of thousands in his digital library. It provided only one suggestion. Nick took in a long breath as he read the message in the dialog box.

"Target: USS Virginia, SSN 774. Confidence level 92%."

ABOARD THE USS VIRGINIA

"Signal *was* bearing 263 degrees, Sir. It was there, then it did its usual thing. Poof! It's gone," the acoustic operator said.

"I'm not buyin' that this time, Sonar. Did he punch up through the layer?"

"No, sir. We're above the thermal layer right now, and it's quiet as a church."

"Don't know about you, Petty Officer Nathan, but it's loud where I worship."

"So I've heard, Captain. Anyway, it's silent *above* the layer, Sir."

"Very well. Diving Officer of the Watch. Take the boat below the layer. Sonar, give me an answer fast once we're down there. If he's not above it, and he's not below it, then . . ."

"He's in it, Sir."

"Bingo. What lines are you tracking him on, Sonar?"

"I had a fuel pump, a fifty-hertz Russian generator, and one more for what's probably his air-independent propulsion system. But they're all gone now." The young man tapped his screen. "He's turned on that blasted adaptive acoustic camouflage."

"We'll change depth and see if that helps," Captain Kelly said, his eyebrows furrowed. "Stay sharp, Sonar. We're not going home empty-handed this time."

✴

After three hours, Nick's system confirmed his hopes. The Virginia was moving beyond him. It was as if they'd passed by at glacial speed and were following his projected path far into the distance. He could rest easy now. He picked up the novel and took his seat. With his headphones plugged into Tchaikovsky and a glass of stout red wine, he leaned back and immersed himself in H.G. Wells. *The Invisible Man.*

EPSILON

Everything was in place. John tested the strap holding him to the ship's skin and tugged on his crude helical antenna, secured to the edge of the airlock adapter ring. A passerby might see it as an astronaut sitting on the ship's skin holding up a giant corkscrew. John still had a sense of humor; the astronaut scarecrow was securely lashed in place holding the antenna pole.

John checked his wrist control. The watch counted less than a minute to the opening of the communication window to Houston. His heart pounded out of control, it seemed, blood slamming his ears as he strained to hear any sound. Galactic noise filled his head, every burp and hiss in his speaker a possible garbled word from home.

As the clock counted below a minute, he spoke. "Amy. I'm alive!"

LA MARQUE, TEXAS

"We can start talking any time," Ronnie said. "The comm window opened about five or six minutes ago, but I wanted you to see what we're talking to before we start. Venus is rising above the pasture. There it is," Ronnie said, pointing out the window at the bright planet low on the horizon. "Have you decided what to say?"

Amy watched the point of light near the Moon, imagining John approaching the planet's swirling mass of sulfuric acid clouds. She wondered what he must feel to have seen three planets in this marvelous tour of the solar system. Then the doubt she never showed crept back, if only for a moment. She turned to the kids. "We need to pray first."

Ronnie shrugged as Abe and his brothers and Alice joined hands. "Hurry, Mom," Abe said. "I want a chance to talk."

"Me too!" Alice said as she squirmed.

Amy smiled, bent her head, eyes closed, and began. "Thank you for—"

The radio suddenly crackled with background static, but Amy could make out a distant voice. She screamed, jumping up from her prayer and grabbing for the mike. Ronnie pulled it back before she could hit the wide black button and interrupt the transmission. She listened, wide-eyed.

"—I'm alive!"

"He's okay!" Amy yelled, dancing in the tiny radio room with Alice and the boys. Jumping and hooting, they hugged in the moment's magic. Ronnie turned up the volume.

"Amy and Ronnie, this is John. I heard you yesterday during an EVA. Tell Ronnie I built a helical RHCP and hooked it to a spacesuit transmitter. I'm standing outside on the skin of the ship, pointing the antenna in your direction. I'll be quiet now. I will begin transmitting again at 1930 hours your time. Over!"

Shouts of joy consumed the family. Martha dashed through the house, hands raised, her ample body jiggling as she bounced and shrieked. Ronnie patted his equipment with reverence. At last he handed the microphone to Amy.

"Here you go!" he said, touching her arm and handing over the microphone. "Someone heard your prayers."

JOHNSON SPACE CENTER, HOUSTON, TEXAS

"This is *who*?" asked a voice identified as Dan Jefferson, the flight director.

"Ronnie Williams, Sir. You may have heard of me."

"Yeah. Sure I have. You're that guy in La Marque with all the antennas who used to put the alien images on the Web. Wish you could help us figure out this comm dilemma."

"I have a big surprise for you tonight, Sir." Ronnie was afraid his surprise would somehow vanish before he could describe it. Behind him, Amy poured out her heart to her husband.

"Lay it on me, Ronnie. It's pretty quiet here tonight in Mission Control."

"It won't be for long. I have John Wells on the line. Would you like to talk to him?"

Sixty seconds after Ronnie's words, John's recorded greeting played over the speakerphone for everyone to hear. Mars Mission Control was pandemonium.

"They're alive!" someone yelled.

"On UHF. Talking with a space suit and a homemade helical!" said another. Applause, whistles, and shouts broke out around the room.

The flight director waved to quiet his team. "How, Ronnie? Can we patch him in live?"

"As soon as he starts talking. Right now, Amy is telling him some things. In private."

"*Amy Wells* is over there?" Dan asked, amazed.

"Yes, sir. The whole family's here. Want to join us?"

"Are you kidding?" the flight director said, waving at his logistics coordinator to hurry over. "Where are you?"

"820 Shady Lane. In La Marque."

"Can you patch your comms into our center?"

"I will, but later. When this pass is over."

"Then we're on our way!"

Dan barked at his capsule communicator. "Jake. Get over to Ronnie Williams's place in La Marque. Take the helo. I'll have air ops waiting with the rotors spinning and a map!"

EPSILON

". . . and I told Raines I'd never give up hope. Oops! Ronnie says I have to get off. It's time to hear from you." Amy coughed and sniffled, a sure sign she was near tears. "I love you so much. Here's Ronnie."

The audio quality wasn't great on his end, and John was sure Ronnie must be burning holes in the atmosphere with his transmitter to make this link. But he heard her. Every word. They were *finally* in touch.

John shifted in his foothold, watching his clock for just the right time to talk. Ten minutes for his message, then back to Ronnie. He struggled with his next words, his heart breaking as he stood atop Epsilon and watched Venus in the distance. He had to let loved ones on Earth know the news they'd been denied for months. It was time.

"My dear Amy," he began. "I love you and the kids so much. There are so many things I want to tell you and so many more things I want to hear about. But I have some important news I have to share first." John coughed, working hard to maintain control.

"Michelle and Sean are dead. Epsilon is severely damaged. We flew through a meteoroid field just after we left Mars. It shredded all our antennas. The science deck, Columbus lander, and Michelle's compartment are all destroyed, along with most of our Martian rock and soil samples. A large meteoroid ripped through the flight deck killing Sean, and a small meteoroid pierced Michelle. She was on EVA helping me fix the antenna. I managed to get her inside before she died, and I was with her the last hours. Sean died immediately. There is so much more to share."

John choked back sobs now, desperate to control himself inside the sealed suit. He wished, for the hundredth time, that he'd spent more time sharing his testimony with Sean. It was too late now.

"It's been a horrible five months, Amy. But I'm coming home. Just like I promised."

LA MARQUE, TEXAS

Amy heard the *whump-whump-whump* of a NASA helicopter move over the house as her family, Ronnie, and Martha sat, rapt, listening to John's story. She could hear him choke with emotion as he shared the story of Sean's and Michelle's deaths and their extraordinary experiences on Mars—and of Michelle's spiritual renewal that John only learned as she died in his arms. Amy, Martha, and Alice shared a box of tissues as John poured out the painful account. Ronnie ran out the back door with a flashlight to mark the landing area in his pasture.

Two minutes later, Jake Cook was huddled by the radio as John finished speaking. Amy handed the microphone to him. "We're glad you're here, Jake," Amy said. "But there's something you need to know. Sean and Michelle are dead, and the ship is severely crippled. John's talking to us with a homemade antenna and a space suit, standing outside and pointing his antenna our way. Let him know you're here. Okay?"

Jake nodded, a veteran of space hardships and bad news. He took the mike.

"Hawk, this is Jake. For the time being, we've moved Mission Control to Ronnie Williams's place." Ronnie flashed a thumbs up, and Jake continued.

"Amy's briefed me on the ship and the crew. I'll want to know more, but for now, I'm an intruder. Your family wants to talk to you. I'll be back. Here's Amy."

The diminutive brunette took the mike and tried to start her words, each one seeming to stick in her throat. "What do I say, John? I am so sorry for your loss, for Sean, for Michelle, for the damage to the ship. Oh, John, I want you home so bad. I know you did all you could, and I'm so glad for Michelle's decision. We've been in constant prayer for you." She paused. "Somehow, I knew this all along—that you were okay, but the others might not be. As though God gave me a sense of peace about you." She wiped her eyes and turned toward her son. "We can talk more later. Here's Abe."

And so it went, each child with a minute or so to say hello, then a seven-minute wait for him to hear and another seven for his response to reach them. Ten minutes of talking or listening and fourteen of waiting—a nerve-wracking but joy-filled experience for them all. Forty-five minutes after Ronnie's call to NASA, several cars pulled up in the front yard and nearly a dozen NASA officials and reporters joined the fray. Even Sharon Walters, whom Amy had phoned moments after they reached John, was here, sharing in the joy of the night. Neighbors began gathering, wondering what had happened at the Williams's. In moments, the small home was a madhouse.

Amy looked at the growing throng and then raised her voice: "We need ten more minutes of privacy with John before you get him. *Please.*"

Ronnie escorted the NASA crew to the den while Amy and the kids each took the microphone for a minute to say their good-byes. Amy finished.

"We've got to go now, John. Half of Mission Control's here, and they need to talk to you." She paused, drawing a deep breath. "Thank you, John. For working so hard to keep your promise to me. I'm so proud of you. We all are."

An hour later, John was complaining of the cold as he stood outside the ship. Jake knew he was past his allotted radiation exposure. "We need to get you inside," Jake told John in his last transmissiom.

"We'll have a radio design ready for you by this time tomorrow, Hawk. Plan for one more EVA and we'll give you some options to communicate from inside the ship after that. We're proud as punch of what you've accomplished against incredible odds. I will personally convey your message to Keith Caskey and Debra O'Brien. I'm gonna stop now and give you the last word."

Moments later, John's voice echoed through the house, filled with NASA controllers, media personnel, and the Wells and Williams families. Awestruck, Jake watched, all of NASA dependent on Ronnie Williams's homegrown communications. They'd figured out how to answer questions and talk at just the right time so that their transmissions passed each other, and there was no dead time. After tonight, Ronnie would be alone again. But for now, his radio central was at the center of the universe.

"Houston, this is Epsilon. Orbit is nominal. ETA Earth orbit intercept in one hundred and eight days. Get ready, guys. I'm gonna bring this baby home."

SATURDAY, AUGUST 3, 2013:
ABOARD THE USS VIRGINIA

"We've been drifting in this current forty-eight hours, XO. No contact." Captain Kelly pushed a cold mug of coffee toward the mess steward who refilled the Skipper's cup and then left the wardroom of one of America's most advanced attack submarines.

When the two senior officers were alone, the captain pushed a red file folder across the table to his second in command. "Our secret orders. Arrived an hour ago. Says 'Stay on his tail.' What's your take on the tactical situation?"

"Only two possibilities. Maybe he eluded us just before we punched through the layer and he really *was* headed into the distance. That's the most obvious answer. Or he's trickier than we thought and he degraded the acoustic signal of his propulsion equipment over time to make it look like he was moving away from us."

"Impact?"

"Option one, he's long gone — we'd probably never find him if we went back. Option two — we're drifting into the Gulf Stream together. Which means — ?"

"Which means," the captain continued, "that we may as well keep doing what we're doing." Captain Kelly stared at a digital chart of the currents and bottom topography. "We can't search the entire Caribbean Sea, so we hang tight and see what happens. Trim the ship in the layer, XO. We'll play this game a while longer."

CLEAR LAKE CITY, TEXAS

The *Houston Chronicle*'s headline sickened Amy as she read it, fresh from its plastic wrapper on a muggy summer Saturday morning.

"Two die. Wells perseveres. Epsilon coming home." The subhead made her blood boil. "*Raines is right again.*" Malcolm Raines got billing, yet the astronaut heroes were anonymous until you read the story below. She hit the paper with her fist. "You did *not* predict this," she yelled at the paper. "Not *ever!*"

Amy's eyes were still red and puffy from a long night with Keith Caskey and Sean's ex-wife, Debra, at Mission Control where they listened to the recordings of John's call. They were hours of relief for Amy and painful closure for the other two after months of silence.

The headline simmered below her, dragging up all sorts of hateful thoughts about Malcolm Raines. Then the phone rang, a blessed distraction from the space prophet. Not until she answered did she think about how many calls she might get today.

"Hi, this is Amy."

"Amy? This is Special Agent Terrance Kerry with the FBI."

"Hello, Terrance! Did you hear the news about John?"

"I did. I wanted to tell you how happy I am for you. And terribly saddened for the other families."

"Thanks. I know that John would be happy to hear you've called. And he'd appreciate your concern."

"Well, ma'am, there's another reason I've tried to reach you so early on a weekend. We need John's help. Now that you can talk to him, I wondered if you'd let him know for me."

It was happening. Everyone would want to get a piece of John.

He'd never get a moment's rest. But this was important.

"All right. I'll tell him. It's kind of hard for him to talk. He has to stand outside and hold the antenna."

"You're joking?"

"I'm not. We'll be talking tonight from Mission Control."

"Great. Tell him this: we're down to one—the big one. And I need his help with some codes."

"Codes?" Amy asked.

"Yes, ma'am. Codes. Tell him I need his help to break a tough one. 321."

36

three months later

THREE MONTHS AFTER LEAVING the Caribbean, Nick rested. He wiped down with a towel and peered over his acoustic suite, checking for any activity since beginning his workout—hundreds of grueling reps with his chin-up bar. His biceps and shoulder muscles were taut from months of gym activity as he'd drifted, then driven, to this long-awaited spot downriver from the nation's capital.

Twenty-five meters below the surface of the Potomac River, in the historic tributary's deepest hole, Nick waited. His acoustic sensors showed that a few pleasure boats, and at least two federal police craft, had plied the waters above him during the last hour. The tide was headed in. Some kayakers would be emerging from Piscataway Creek to the east.

To the west, the first tourists might be headed into Mount Vernon after a three-day weekend. "No estate in United America is more pleasantly situated than this," George Washington had said. Nick remembered the words from his days scouting out this location years ago.

Satisfied that no one significant was moving on the murky river, Nick checked his connection to the real world, a thin cable running to the special dinner barge moored above, which had accompanied him upriver for the past week of preparations.

Nick marked an "X" on a calendar above the submarine's control suite, lining out yet another day since entering the Gulf Stream west of Saint Vincent's and the Grenadines. It had been months since he'd silently drifted side by side for days with the hulking USS Virginia, whose crew never suspected he was only a few hundred meters away.

As days had merged into weeks, he'd edged along the coast of Florida, then headed north, free of the hunter-killer submarine menace that had given up the search after three weeks.

Nick was almost home, just a few kilometers south of his destination. Only at high tide did he dare press his luck bringing the *Sea Dagger* farther up the sediment-clogged river. It was a feat, he was sure, that no one suspected a submersible could accomplish.

Five more days until a full moon, high tide, and the fulfillment of years of planning.

| EPSILON

"You have no idea how nice it is to be able to hold a relatively normal conversation again," John said, cradling the microphone as he talked to Amy. The time delay now, three months after they'd re-established contact, was only a second or two—virtually instantaneous, in John's mind.

"Wish we had some video to go with your voice," Amy said. "I really do miss those teleconferences."

John ran his hand through the close-cropped flattop. "You probably wouldn't notice any difference," he said. "Except I'm a lot skinnier than I was when I left."

"You've lost that much weight?"

John chuckled. "Haven't weighed *anything* since I left, to tell you the truth."

"You know what I mean."

"I can't get too excited about eating, Amy. Every time I open that freezer—"

"I understand." No one spoke for a while.

Amy broke the silence. "Did you hear about Raines and the prophecy stuff?"

"I did. Wondered if you'd bring it up. Did he ever apologize?" John asked.

"Not yet. He's making a big splash in all of his 'gatherings,' he calls them. Says that his prophecy about a successful mission was fulfilled. You showed up only a day after he made the prophecy. His people are convinced he's a clairvoyant."

"He was right," John said in jest. "I came back right after he predicted I would. I owe him!"

"I hope you're joking." Amy's voice was subdued. "Everyone but me seems to have forgotten that he predicted you were dead—on national television. The world hears what they want to hear and forgets the rest—which makes it hard to argue with his assertions." She paused, her voice shifting tone, becoming even more serious. "You know he's got a big thing planned on the day you arrive, right?"

John coughed, holding the microphone tighter. "What?"

"A celebration, John. He says he wants to thank the Father Race in a special way for bringing back an explorer from another planet. He's going to hold a big party to 'commemorate the full completion of our Father's plan.'"

"On November 17? Are you sure? Where?"

"In Washington. I'm surprised NASA hasn't told you. He made the big announcement this morning."

John nearly yelled into the mike. "November 17 in Washington? *Where?*"

"Are you okay, John? It's at RFK. Starts at 6:00 p.m. He rented the entire stadium just for this event."

John was silent a moment as the gears wound in his head, mentally connecting the dots.

"Amy. Call Terrance Kerry. You have his number. Then call Ronnie. Tell him I need some help with a temporary encryption, and I need him to patch Kerry in, wherever you find him. It's very important you get Kerry on the line. Immediately."

LA MARQUE, TEXAS

"Hey there, Ron."

"Hello, Captain Wells. How can I help tonight? Amy sounded scared when she called."

"I need a covered circuit, Ronnie. Can you do it?"

Ronnie Williams was in ham radio heaven. Not only had he found a way to communicate with Epsilon and reach John, now John was calling for help, making him part of an inner communication circle. All those years of ridicule about his radio and antenna farm in a horse pasture were worth enduring for this very moment.

"When do you need it?" he asked. The short pause waiting for

John's response—a couple of seconds—was nothing compared to the forty-minute delays of Mars exploration.

"Right away. And I need to patch in an old friend," John replied.

"Good news, captain. Mr. Kerry is flying to Houston. He and Amy will both arrive here in about two hours. Martha's making dinner, and I've already got your system ready to go."

Ronnie detailed how John should set up his communications on the far end, including a program Ronnie would send by e-mail over the UHF circuit. Ten minutes later, the explanation was complete. "Any questions?"

"One, Ron. Even though we're not on the normal UHF channel for NASA comms, we have to assume that someone's monitoring this conversation."

"They probably are, Sir. But when you enter that seed—the magic number and word string that only you and Amy know—there wouldn't be enough massive parallel processors on Earth to break my encryption in five weeks of work. Someone could figure it out eventually—but it would take a *very, very* long time."

"Good job, Ron. Call me on our offset frequency. I've got a NASA conference in five minutes, but I'll be ready whenever Amy arrives."

Special Agent Kerry marveled at the array of radios in Ronnie's radio central, and John's grasp of an obvious numeric clue that his agents—and the CIA—had completely overlooked. Like Ronnie with this encrypted communication to John, sometimes the best answers weren't the most complex or expensive ones.

"The number 321 could be code for dates or locations or times, Kerry," John said. "And it fits for every one of them. Take locations, for example. If you use 321 as a location—3 degrees, 2 minutes, 1 second for latitude and longitude—you get the position south of Ivory Coast where Ulrich had his sub during the African alien landings. It's like Ulrich was subtly giving us a code for his location. But we missed the cue."

Kerry saw Amy cringe on the edge of their little group, huddled in the stuffy radio room.

"It gets better—or worse, depending how you look at it," John said. "November 17 has been planned as our arrival date on Earth since this program's beginning. It's no accident we're landing that day. Rex Edwards and NASA *planned* this mission just this way. Now look at a calendar or call up a date calculator on the computer. What day of the year is November 17, Kerry? I'm looking for a numeric value."

Ronnie handed him a calendar, an American Radio Relay League 2013 version with pictures of old tube radios on each page. He found the date, with a little number printed in the lower left of the date box. Kerry's mouth fell open in astonishment.

"What number *is* it?" Amy asked.

"321," Kerry said, pressing the microphone switch. He was silent for a moment.

"Something big is going to happen that day. I'm sure of it," John said after a pause. "And I'd bet my paycheck that Ulrich will play, that the submarine is in the Potomac or nearby to launch and recover the spiders, and that he will reveal himself. He likes to live dangerously." John paused, letting all that sink in. "This is your chance. You want to find Ulrich? He'll be in your neck of the woods—Washington—very soon."

"We can be ready for that," Kerry said. "Although I'd wager he's already there—in DC. The key question is how does NASA play in this? If NASA modeled November 17 as the ideal return date, and it wasn't Rex's idea, then our pool of potential conspirators just got much larger."

"That's why we're on a secure net," John said. "This one could run deep."

SATURDAY, NOVEMBER 16, 2013: EPSILON

Epsilon and John Wells raced toward a blue Earth, its clouds and continents visible for the last few days as the distance from home grew smaller by the second. John's only views were from the portal of his compartment, or portals in the galley area and exercise deck. He longed for the flight deck's surround video and its panoramic view of the universe. He strained to see Earth at the edge of his view, Epsilon's nozzle end pointed toward his destination in preparation for the final firing maneuver—slowing down to capture Earth.

An hour later, John floated into system control, just a few meters forward of the nozzles, preparing for the big moment. His extensive EVA inspections, conducted months ago, along with NASA's communication support, gave everyone a sense of confidence about the engines' integrity. There was no apparent damage to the rocket system.

"All systems are GO," John said over UHF, his one and only radio link to Earth. "We're ready."

"Copy, Epsilon. Houston is also GO. Downrange tracking has you on vector for retro thrust in three-zero minutes."

"Copy, Houston. Three-zero to retro."

John drifted in the silence of his lonely home for a few minutes, perhaps his last moment of peace before the great return. Four hundred seventy-five days in zero-G, and nearly nine months of that alone, eight of it in solitary since losing Michelle and Sean. He'd endured more in those eight months than he wanted to remember. And through it all,

God had sustained him, helping him through the hard times, the shock and grief, nostalgia, the desperation and depression, and the anger, to this moment. True to God's Word, John had endured the trials, and none beyond his ability to cope.

"You ready for this, John?" a voice asked, breaking him from his daydream of the mission.

"Yeah. We're ready."

"We're?"

John wiped at his eyes, determined to get through this day and stay in control of his emotions. "Houston, Epsilon, *we* are ready for retro burn. Three of us are coming home."

WASHINGTON, DC

"Yes, Father!" Malcolm Raines fell to his knees, his hands to his temples as if in pain. His aides swooped in from left and right to catch the tall man before his face hit the pavement outside Robert F. Kennedy stadium—RFK.

The purple-robed priests, normally docile, also rushed to Raines's side. "Your grace. What is it?" One priest held Raines by the forearm, his own eyes wide with surprise.

"The Father Race speaks! I have not heard them since we were in France. Amazing words!" Raines squinted, as if he could almost see the words. "Words of promise," he said, struggling to his feet. He held his hands to his ears to capture the faint words that continued to ring in his head and his heart.

You shall be my Guardian of the Mother Seed.

EPSILON

With not a moment's hesitation, the two silver rocket nozzles at Epsilon's aft end roared to life. The boom of the powerful engines was a muffled roar for John, standing less than thirty meters from the inferno, just beyond the tanks and pumps at his station in system control.

"Ignition!" John announced into the portable headset microphone as he monitored system performance. For the first time since their launch from Martian orbit, he felt the familiar tug of a G-load, the craft decelerating as it approached Earth. Millions of pounds of thrust fired in the direction of travel as John and Epsilon sought to slow their blistering speed for entry into Earth's orbit. The engines roared for three minutes with John strapped into the emergency seat to prevent the change in speed from slamming him against the bulkhead. The craft rumbled below him. He knew every nuance of this special home, and the powerful force that shook Epsilon calmed him, embracing him in gut-shaking rumble and acceleration.

John was coming home.

JOHNSON SPACE CENTER, HOUSTON, TEXAS

"Epsilon's retro fire has just completed," the voice of NASA began, "and downrange tracking shows the craft passing through perigee of its new elliptical orbit about Earth. Epsilon has returned!"

A cheer erupted in Mars Mission Control, dozens of men and women raising their hands in triumph as they sat at their control stations. Behind them, Amy and her children hugged in silence in the glassed-in VIP lounge overlooking the control room. Debra O'Brien and Keith Caskey, standing to Amy's left, touched hands. Amy turned, eyes brimming with tears, and took a frail Debra O'Brien in her arms. The two hugged for a long time.

"I'm sorry for your loss, Mr. Caskey," Abe said, approaching Keith, hand extended. "Mrs. Caskey was a good friend of my dad."

Keith managed a slight smile in return, taking the hand of the teenage boy and gripping it tightly. "I know, Abe. I'm really glad your dad made it. Thanks for all you've done for us these past months. I won't ever forget it."

Amy's heart warmed, watching her son reach out in solace to a much older man. Abe had grown up so much in the past year and a half. This mission had transformed him. It had transformed them all. Amy put an arm on Alice's shoulder, sure that her little girl had grown six inches in the past five hundred days. John would hardly recognize this growing brood. They had all been refined—Amy in particular—in this crucible called Mission to Mars.

"When will Dad be home?" Alice asked, holding Amy's hand.

"Tomorrow, Alice. We leave tonight for Nevada. To watch the landing."

37

JOHN STRUGGLED WITH THE frozen black bag, trying hard to avoid thinking about the icy shape beneath the plastic as he guided it out of the freezer toward the airlock. This was his last task.

For days before his arrival in a high elliptical Earth orbit, John had prepared for his return home. After several EVAs to gather material from what remained of Columbus, the science and flight decks, and from Michelle's room, John had the crew return vehicle packed.

All that remained was to stow his crewmates. The plastic body bags shed ice crystals as he maneuvered them through the ship, frozen months ago in the shape of the seats he would use to carry them home. John buckled Sean's black bag in and patted the frozen shoulder. "You're riding copilot today, pal."

Minutes later, every task complete except this one, John paused at the door of the freezer compartment. He dreaded touching this final bag, connecting with such a close friend, and reliving such a painful loss.

John lifted Michelle gently from her frozen seat in the cold room and maneuvered her toward the ERV. This was his last trip through Epsilon. The familiar walls seemed to tell his story as he passed down the central access tunnel, past all the decks that had been his home for the past five hundred days, now strangely silent.

"Good-bye, old friend," he said to the ship. "Someone will be back for you—one day."

RFK STADIUM, WASHINGTON, DC

Ten thousand cars jammed the parking lot of Washington, DC's only stadium, home to the Nationals baseball team and past home to the Redskins. Sitting low near the Anacostia River, the arena overflowed with 43,000 worshipers celebrating the return of the manned mission to Mars. A mission that Malcolm Raines was sure, as he watched the stadium fill, could not have been accomplished without his involvement and support. This was his day.

Fifteen minutes after sunset, a huge full moon began rising, cresting the stadium's top decks around 5:30 p.m. Raines took the stage draped in a brilliant purple robe and a golden rope sash. The full moon hung above him like a galactic spotlight as he raised his hands.

"The Father Race has spoken! To me! Today!" Cheers erupted around the stadium, his followers hungry, Raines presumed, for more prophecy—and their first personal encounter with the progenitors.

"I bring wondrous news. Tonight we shall meet the Father Race. I have been promised that they will join us, that they are in our midst. Tonight—here at my side—you shall see them."

The crowd went wild. Raines let them revel for a minute or more. This was their night. And his. He scanned the crowd, wondering where in this throng of adoring followers representatives of the Father Race might be observing him this very minute. Years of toil and ridicule faded away as he stood on the precipice of the spiritual acclamation he had sought for so long. He was the Oracle of the Unknown and Unknowable god.

The crowd eventually fell silent again, and Raines spoke. "Open your hearts to their message, my people. Accept them as you have accepted me. I am one with the Father Race."

At those words, a blaze of fireworks erupted, blanketing the stadium's elliptical open top in exploding color. For over three minutes huge bursts drowned out the giant moon and stadium lights.

When Malcolm saw it, dropping from the sky under the hail of Technicolor fire, its silver sides reflecting the explosions, the object was almost invisible. Until the silver creature was below the stadium's highest galleries, he didn't believe his eyes. Silence gradually replaced the cheers and applause, and the last of the raucous booms faded away as a single silver spider dropped toward a landing on the stage in front of Malcolm Raines. The blast of its downdraft whipped Raines's robe and sash. He ducked his head, unable to watch as it settled a few meters away. Somewhere, a woman screamed. Otherwise the massive crowd was silent.

"Hear me!" a voice boomed, so loud and crushing that most people covered their ears. The deep tone, emanating so close to Raines, roiled his stomach, like a huge creature had crawled inside him and homogenized his insides. He crumpled to his knees, prostrating himself before the three-meter-tall creature. Behind him, six priests also fell to the floor.

"Well done, faithful servants," the voice said, surrounding everyone with ear-splitting volume. "You were called to Venture Forth, and you obeyed." The spider moved forward, placing a single spear-like leg onto Raines's back. "Rise."

Raines stumbled as he tried to stand, still feeling the imprint of the sharp tip where it had pressed against his shoulder blade.

Eight legs *clacking* on the stage's wood surface, the spider turned and walked toward the edge of the dais. The deep bass of its over-amplified voice rattled the stadium. Malcolm had never experienced such volume. The spider lifted a leg in his direction. "This man sought the god within him. He speaks for us—for the Father Race."

The spider walked across the stage to another corner, addressing the crowd just as Raines would have done. "This day, you have accomplished your mission. As I speak to you, one of your kind prepares to fall to the planet's surface. Now you are ready. The one who sent me to you brought his seed to this planet a thousand decades ago. *His* descendants carried *their* seed to other planets where your brothers and sisters reign today. Improve your seed as he did. Then Venture Forth and multiply."

Raines's robe began whipping in the first breeze of the spider's propulsive blast. It was powering up for flight! Raines recoiled, standing too close to the craft. The priests also backed up, holding their flapping garments against the strong wind. The spider lifted off the stage as Raines lifted his hands into the sky, finding his voice at last.

"Great one!" Raines cried out, desperation clutching him like a vise. "Reveal the Father Race! We beseech you! *Where are they?*"

The craft stopped its flight as if it understood him. The spider hovered thirty meters above the field, slowly spinning, the crazy head whipping about like it was looking over the entire mass of humanity.

"The Father Race lives among you, Malcolm," the spider bellowed. "Seed of our Mother! Come forth and make yourself known."

"Now!" Kerry yelled into a cuff microphone. "It's lifting off!"

"Copy. Dark Steel, flight of three, airborne."

Special Agent Kerry watched from the stadium's highest vantage in a control booth above the upper gallery. To the south, he saw the red beacons of a flight of three Special Forces Blackhawk helicopters, their dull paint dimly visible in the brilliant moonlight. In front of him, Kerry watched the gleaming silver spider rise out of the stadium and turn toward the Anacostia River.

"Spider's clear! Headed east," Kerry said into his cuff mike.

"Copy. Got him in sight."

John was right—again, thought Kerry. 321 had been a clue, the culmination of two-and-a-half years of symbolism. And the culmination of Raines's prophecies, in all their tawdry glory.

Kerry spun about in his perch when he noticed the silence. Below him he could see people—small ones, it seemed—making their way out of the stands toward the field. He glanced back at the spider, headed away from the stadium, and three red beacons of black Special Forces helicopters closing on the silver target. He saw the silver craft swoop low over the river and head south, past the Naval Research Laboratory and National Airport that flanked opposite sides of the Potomac. The silver body gleamed in the stark moonlight like a whitish gem. *We've got you now*, Kerry thought.

"Dark Steel base! Target headed under Woodrow Wilson bridge!" Kerry heard a pilot report in his earpiece. "Standing by to deploy divers."

"Under the bridge!" another pilot yelled. "Close in!"

"Divers away. Twelve in the water. Target's hovering under the eastern span."

Kerry's skin crawled, remembering the days off the coast of Nicaragua when Ulrich and his three men evaded hundreds of Special Forces, killed two dozen in the final chase, and left him empty-handed.

That must not happen tonight.

The enduring silence caught his attention. It was as if the entire stadium had been evacuated. Kerry scanned the field with binoculars. A shiver ran down his spine as he trained the glasses on the infield and saw hundreds of short people milling about. Raines was standing in the midst of them.

Hundreds and hundreds of girls, all dressed in black, long black hair on every one, each with a ponytail falling to the middle of the back, bound by a red bow. Every one in a black sweat top and tight black pants—and all of them facing Raines. The circle of girls was perhaps thirty meters in diameter about him. The crowd was hushed.

Kerry zoomed in on a few faces. They were all the same! From this distance he would swear they were identical girls, about eight or nine years of age, standing rigid before the Priest of the Heavenlies. It reminded him of Muslim throngs surrounding the stone pillar in Mecca—but all these girls were still, not milling about. They were facing the tall priest, who stood in the middle of a sports field, his arms outstretched over the massive throng of young females.

Raines swept his hand above them. "The Father Race lives among us. This is the perfect egg of our Mother."

As if they'd been cued by Raines, the girls began to chant in unison. Raines's microphone picked up the chilling words, sending shivers down Kerry's spine. The spider was temporarily forgotten.

"We hold the keys to the germ of life. We are the Mother seed."

"It's gone."

Kerry swore out loud. Dumbfounded, he watched the eerie scene on the field below while listening to the radio report.

"This is Dark Steel base. Repeat your last, over." The voice on the other end of the link sounded like Kerry felt—livid and dumbstruck.

"Diver report, sir. Twelve men in the water. No target. Boats and more divers en route."

"Nothing?" the voice said. "It *vanished*?"

"Continuing the search. No contact yet."

Kerry shook his head in amazement as he watched hundreds of girls move in step with Raines toward the six Remnant priests. Where had these young women come from?

They won't find the spider, Kerry realized as the night darkened. *Ulrich thought of everything.* He leaned his head against a rusted steel rail.

Maybe all this Father Race business is for real.

EPSILON

John fired the first burst of hydrazine thrusters to guide the ERV out of Epsilon's parking bay. Like an Apollo capsule lifting out of a grain silo, John guided his lifeboat free.

"Houston, this is Magellan," John said, invoking for the first time Michelle's pet name for the Earth Return Vehicle. "Maneuvering to safe standoff distance in preparation for retro."

"Copy, Magellan. Insertion T minus sixty minutes."

An hour later, John touched a plasma panel, his final step in the ignition sequence. Above him, at the top of the cone-shaped capsule, a solid rocket engine fired to slow the craft in its orbit ten thousand kilometers above Earth. When the engine was expended, John pitched the craft over and pointed Magellan's blunt end in a final plunge toward Earth.

Minutes later, orange tongues of flame raged around the ablative shield as John and his fellow explorers fell toward Earth in a cocoon of fire. The force of three gravities crushed him as he plummeted toward home.

Amy stood with the children next to Jake Cook in the VIP area of Mars Mission Recovery. She fought off memories of the Columbia mission, her friends streaking across the sky in a ball of flame over California, and then in a hail of debris over Texas. For the first time in the history of the U.S. space program, a capsule mission would come down over land. It had never been attempted, but it was no tougher than landing on Mars—and it was the only way the Russians had ever landed. Amy prayed silently for safety—and for her own peace.

The attention of Mars Mission Control was divided. Those who could afford to divert their attention from the landing were glued to cable news broadcasts from Washington, DC. Media were flooded with images of the hundreds of identical girls following Raines like lemmings around the field. Amy glanced back at the news, trying to force herself to remain focused on John. But she couldn't resist. The scene in Washington was pandemonium. She turned to watch the broadcast.

Almost a hundred metro police were separating the stadium crowd from the flock of more than three hundred identical girls in black. The girls were exact duplicates. Amy shivered when she first heard the word spoken during John's descent.

Clones. She'd never seen one—and neither had any other human, as far as she knew. But how else do you explain so many exact copies of one person?

Jake's voice brought her out of the news trance and she spun around. "Good approach vector over Hawaii." He pulled her arm and pointed at the large Mission Control screen. "Some great pictures coming from the Big Island. He's looking great!" Jake pointed at an image of the superheated capsule ripping into the atmosphere.

"How much longer?"

"Half an hour. He's in a comm blackout; high temperature plasmas surround the capsule. We'll pick him up over the coast."

Amy glanced back at the news monitor. Replays of the rising silver spider were followed by live feeds from television choppers near a large bridge. The news ticker said "spider disappears in Potomac." The broadcast cut back to the stadium and the police protection around the young girls. They looked Alice's age, none scared, all surrounding Raines and his Remnant. Police pushed away those in the stadium's crowd seeking to touch the girls. The ticker made her shiver.

"We hold the keys to the germ of life. We are the Mother Seed."

Jake's forecast came true. A scratchy but definable voice broke through as John emerged from his fiery descent.

"Houston, Magellan. We're over land. Passing San Francisco. How copy, over?" Amy let go the tears she'd tried so hard to quell. He was on the final leg!

Minutes later, three billowing chutes blossomed above the large Magellan capsule, red, white, and blue against a clear late afternoon California sky. Long-range imaging cameras caught the parachutes opening, and a cheer erupted in Mission Control. Raines was forgotten. Fifty thousand observers lining the runways cheered en masse. The family rushed out onto a platform to watch the chutes high above. Bright parachutes bringing John home.

A short, muscular man next to her touched her elbow. "It looks like everything has performed according to plan, Mrs. Wells," he said.

"I'm sure you're proud of your husband. I know that I am."

"Thank you, Mr. Edwards," Amy said. "We're all proud." She put an arm on Albert and Alice. "I believe you've met my family."

"I have. And allow me to introduce Adrienne Packard. Adrienne, this is Amy Wells and her 'A-team.' It's good to have you here today, Amy."

Rex stared back up toward the chutes descending before a brilliant sunset. "This was the challenge of a lifetime."

Amy nodded. "Yes. And I hope it's the last one."

"One hundred meters!"

"Fifty!"

John made the sign of the cross on his chest as the count headed to zero. It was all in God's hands now.

"Twenty! Stand by for impact—three, two, one!"

The next thing John heard was akin to what he imagined a car crash would sound like in slow motion. The capsule slammed into the dry lake bed of Edwards Air Force Base, cushioned by monster Vectran air bags that could take a bullet's impact and not rip. Like falling into a massive pole-vault bag, the huge cushion below him deflated, pitching him back and forth as the craft creaked and groaned. Michelle and Sean's bodies bounced in their seats but held fast. After a few seconds of motion, the craft settled to the ground.

I'm home.

"Magellan has landed!" the voice on the speaker said. "The first manned mission to Mars has returned!"

Amy wept for joy, bouncing on her toes, hoping to see farther. She watched the quarantine vehicles racing out to the landing site, dust rising behind a fleet of trucks and support personnel headed three kilometers to the south where John's capsule sat on the desert floor.

"Are you ready to go, Mrs. Wells?" Rex Edwards asked.

"I beg your pardon?" Amy asked, gathering the children to her.

"We're headed out to the landing," Rex said, pointing to a van. He led Adrienne by the hand and motioned Amy to follow. "I thought you might want to join us. *All of you*," he said, sweeping a hand across her brood. "Let's go meet John and welcome him home. He's the hero of the century."

A tall young woman in a black jumpsuit, ebony hair cascading down her back in a single ponytail, opened the door to the van for the children and Amy to step in.

"Thank you, Antoinette," Rex said as she shut the door. "Please, Amy, join us. We are headed out to meet history."

38

"REMEMBER ME?" JOHN ASKED, as he stood wobbly-legged, supported by two men in yellow biohazard suits. Amy gazed across the plastic tent boundary at her lanky husband. A temporary barrier draped over the top of Magellan separated John and his ship from Earth's atmosphere—a biohazard precaution. She put her hand to the plastic, and his hand met hers. Her insides screamed to fall into his arms.

"You bear a resemblance to someone I knew once," she said. "A little skinnier, a little grayer, but no worse for wear."

John leaned into the quarantine boundary, arms outstretched, and she grabbed for him, hugging as though through a shower curtain. John took her face, plastic and all, and gave her the best kiss he could. She grabbed his hands and squeezed hard, unwilling to let go.

"It's been so long—and so far," John said. "I need to come

home."

Amy smiled with a faint nod. "Yes. I'm so glad it's over."

John's knees weakened and he stumbled, the handlers steadying him. "I have one more thing I have to do. You guys wait for me, okay?"

Amy nodded again and watched as John turned and spoke quietly to his support crew. They returned to the capsule.

"You're in no shape for this, sir," one technician said. The yellow-suited NASA employee tried to escort him toward a transport van.

"Don't lecture me," John said defiantly. "I owe it to them. I will *not* leave."

John struggled to hold himself erect as the men passed the first of two heavy body bags out Magellan's hatch. John held on to the capsule skin with his left hand and lifted a rigid salute with his right. A somber honor guard of four men, each in yellow biohazard suits, took separate corners of the large bag and walked the frozen body of Navy Captain Sean O'Brien, mission commander, to a transport vehicle. A fifth technician, also yellow garbed, guarded John, offering him his arm, but John refused. He struggled to maintain his erect posture for the second bag, Dr. Michelle Caskey, chief mission scientist, as she passed through the hatch. He saluted again. Four more men carried Michelle's remains with reverence toward another van.

How he wanted to reach out and touch Michelle, somehow to gain closure as she passed him, the last contact he would ever have with her. In a macabre way, she and Sean had been with him for months, even in death. No more. They passed into the hands of NASA, yellow-garbed nameless men who took their bodies to prepare them for burial. The pain in his chest grew by the moment as memories of days in space with

Michelle seemed to play in fast-forward while he watched the men set her remains in the back of the van. Like she was a sack of feed. Nausea overwhelmed him, thoughts of her and years of friendship, now contained in a frosty sheath of opaque black plastic. His knees buckled, his head light, as they closed the door on her. He'd fulfilled his duty. He'd brought them both home.

"John!" Amy screamed as he wilted to the ground. The technician missed him and John slumped in an awkward pile.

He lifted a weak arm to the technician. "Sorry." John waved to his family as the handlers lifted him into a wheelchair and rolled him to a waiting transport. He tried to get them to divert toward Amy and the plastic. The yellow men refused. He waved feebly. "Amy! Kids! I love you!"

As his stoic family waved in return, John felt his heart about to break. He was so close to a homecoming, and then suddenly whisked away, to quarantine, more delays, lengthy studies, and hours of debriefs. He'd had no time with his family, not even a moment to greet his kids before starting to faint. Just a momentary kiss through some plastic.

He was so ready for all of this to be over. For good.

FORT WASHINGTON, MARYLAND

Nick moved with practiced skill in the black murky water of the Potomac, loading his cargo in the massive underwater hold of his *Sea Dagger* craft. With the unique contraption lashed down, he commanded broad clamshell doors to close, and repressurized the compartment, forcing out all the water. Alongside the spider craft, a modified scooter was also lashed to the deck, his special conveyance to quickly move the spider out of the area when it settled into the dark Potomac. Divers and sonar-equipped boats were still scanning the river bridge area looking for the "alien."

Half an hour later, Nick had dried off and was on the *Sea Dagger's* control deck. He commanded the vessel to rise under the specially adapted hull of a large dinner barge moored above him, nestling the submarine into a sculpted hold. Fifteen minutes after stowing the spider, Nick was on the bridge of a packed dinner boat, headed downriver under a brilliant full moon with more than three hundred hungry guests. He dialed a satellite telephone registered in India, with no idea where it would ring, or who would pick up. A mature, cultured female voice answered, the response he'd grown accustomed to.

"Cargo's secure," Nick said. "Awaiting further orders."

"Well done. You have accomplished our final objective. Every detail was choreographed perfectly. Now proceed to Galveston," she said. "Download your next assignment in the usual way."

WASHINGTON, DC

"These young women are in *my* care," Raines asserted, three hours after the stadium cleared. The girls seemed tired but well behaved, seated outside in the upper gallery, waiting. *They are mine. They were promised to me. Copies of the perfect seed.*

"Father Raines," said a large African-American woman, her ample rolls spilling over in an overly tight business dress. "I respect your position. And I want to trust you, but the law is the law. These children are clearly not yours, and they're unclaimed by anyone in that crowd. Therefore, they are wards of the District of Columbia."

"Which ultimately makes them wards of the federal government.

Correct?" a short well-dressed man asked from the back of the large conference room where Raines, the police, and District child protective service officials continued their standoff. The man coughed. "I asked you a question. Am I correct, madam?"

The plump woman scowled, then nodded. "According to recent federal law—yes. But District statute conflicts in this case."

"Effective last year, the federal law in child protective custody matters overrides District statute, isn't that true?" asked the Hispanic man. His red bow tie stood out above a tailored shirt and suit, like he'd just stepped out of a fashion advertisement. "Why are you bullying my client? You knew that your office and the police have no jurisdiction over those girls. Please, may I have your card?"

The woman huffed, waved to the metro policeman standing at her side, and left without speaking another word. The police waited until she'd gone, then came up together and asked for Malcolm's autograph. He signed the insides of their hats with permanent marker and shook each policeman's hand. The short, well-dressed lawyer stood in the background until they'd left.

"Good move," he said, extending his own hand to Raines. "You carry that pen with you all the time?" he asked, a mouth full of bleached teeth showing through his smile.

"Everywhere. My autograph can move mountains," Raines said with a wink. "That, and a little basketball talk works wonders with my older fans." He motioned the man to a chair. "Nice bluff. Did Rex send you?"

"Yes, he did. I am Manuel Rivera, sir. Of Rivera, Gonzalez, and Fitch. Los Angeles." He presented a gold-embossed card, then opened a brass-and-leather briefcase, removing a handful of folders. "And that was no bluff, Father Raines. Rex asked me to stand by—just in case. He wanted to be with you tonight, but of course . . ."

Raines waved a hand. "No apologies. Today was his capstone in Nevada." He waved toward the girls and the stadium. "And this was *mine.*"

"As I said, this was no bluff. With our lobbyist support, the law I referenced passed last year. In preparation for this very day."

Raines jaw dropped. "You saw this coming?"

"It's not so hard to understand, actually. We were retained nearly two years ago by Mr. Edwards for your support. Just in case. He gave us complete latitude. As a result, we've been following your prophecies. Some of our firm wagered that eventually the Father Race might materialize—gambling you might be right. You were, of course." He continued to dig papers out of the voluminous case, setting them on a table in front of Raines.

"A small group within that subset also maintained that if you *were* right, you might actually meet the Father Race—and if you did, they would probably look like us. On that assumption, the Father Race might ultimately need legal representation to ensure that they—shall we say—fit into our legal system. Do you understand?"

"I do. So here we are. Your timing was impeccable."

"It always is. And here we are," the man said, gesturing to the stack of papers. "It seems you now have a very large family."

"Yes. I do. But your engagement from this point forward has me concerned, Mr. Rivera. You bailed me out of a jam, and for that I am in your debt."

"Rex Edwards's debt, sir."

"Very well. But these papers—"

"These, sir, are birth certificates. Live birth documentation for every young woman waiting in the box seats before you. My staff and I fingerprinted each girl during the past two hours while the District's finest were busy parlaying a deal. You almost succeeded with them, by the way. They are consummate bureaucrats. I'm very impressed with your negotiating skills."

Raines furrowed his brow, staring down the young lawyer. "And who is the legal guardian for these young women?"

The man raised an eyebrow. "*You* are, sir. Of course. You are the Guardian of the Mother Seed, are you not?"

Raines glanced out the box window at the hundreds of girls waiting patiently, then turned toward the lawyer. "Indeed. I am."

"Sir, I have been commissioned to ensure that your every need is met with whatever challenge this evening presented. I have a plan in place, when you are ready to execute."

Raines saw the opportunity of a lifetime staring him in the face. He'd been chosen as the Oracle of the Unknown God, and now, Guardian of the Mother Seed. He could not fail.

"We have an amazing legacy to protect, Mr. Rivera." He waved at the girls through the glass, and a few waved back. "If you represent Mr. Edwards, I am open to your support. But you must realize, I exist for the pleasure of the Father Race, and these young women must remain in my care. Whatever the cost. Do we understand?"

"Perfectly," the lawyer said as he snapped his case shut. "We would not want any other arrangement than to ensure that you succeed. Five motor coaches are standing by now sir, and two hotels in Silver Spring await our arrival. Shall we go?"

"Yes, but before we go, Mr. Rivera . . . are you acquainted with my prophecies?"

"Every one, Sir. Committed to memory."

"Have you completed an accounting of *all* our young ladies tonight?"

"I have sir. Your prophecy has been fulfilled." The lawyer stood and walked to the window, overlooking a crowd of girls, most sitting quietly, as if they'd been well prepared for this tumultuous night. "We are the Father Race. Our number is six," Rivera said as he waved his hand in the direction of a sea of tanned faces, all with perfect black ponytails bound in tight red bows. "There are 321 of them, Father Raines. The Mother Seed is now safely in your hands."

Raines walked to the window with the lawyer, staring out in silence for a long moment. "Genetic perfection," Raines said at last, drawing out each word slowly, like he was tasting the sound of them. "Of incalculable value." He put his hands together, raising them to his lips as if in prayer.

"Mr. Rivera, you are gazing upon Eve reborn."

39

"SURPRISE!" JOHN SAID. He stood on the front stoop of his home in Clear Lake, a finger poised above the doorbell as Amy opened the door.

Amy's scream alerted the household just before dinnertime. Minutes from now, she and the kids would have been praying, before they ate, for John's last week in quarantine. Praying for an end to their hours on either side of glass walls and yellow-suited guards.

Amy fell into his arms, the first time they'd touched in sixteen months. She buried her head in his shoulder and squeezed him hard. The familiar whiff of Old Spice brought back a flood of memories.

Amy heard Alice and Albert running up behind her but refused to let go.

"Dad!" Albert exclaimed, the first of the four to round the corner. Alice came on a dead run, from the feel of it, as she collided with Amy and John at the hip, tears streaming. The telltale sound of two big boys careening down the stairs two steps at a time was a sure sign Abe and Arthur were also on the way.

Amy looked up at last at John, a huge smile on her wet face, her heart racing but not skipping a beat—for the first time she could remember in a long time. She ran a hand through his freshly trimmed flattop, marveling at the feel of his little gray rug.

"You didn't warn me!" she said, laughing with the kids and refusing to give up her number-one spot in his arms. "Never ever do that again! I haven't cleaned yet or set for six." She gave him a playful tickle under his ribs. "You know better than to bring surprise guests for dinner!"

Amy pulled him into the house, waving at the NASA personnel who escorted him home to ensure he didn't fall. "He's mine now. You can go! Bye-bye!" She took his duffel bag and shut the door before anyone could object. With four kids looking on and moaning "Ick!" John twirled Amy around and kissed her. A very long time.

"You're smothering him, Mom! Give Dad some air," Abe joked.

"What about quarantine?" Albert asked. "Won't you give her some space disease doing that?"

John released Amy as she began choking with laughter. She wiped the back of her hand across her mouth and looked at her youngest son. "You're right! Yuk! Mars bugs. Quick!" she said to Alice. "Get my bottle of 409! We've got to clean him up before he can come in!"

Amy turned and took his head in her hands, caressing the stubble of a day's beard, a sensation she'd almost forgotten. "I am so glad you're here." She stood on tiptoes and kissed him gently again, her hands tracing the familiar lines of his face. "We're all so proud of you."

A single tear coursed down her right cheek, and John caught it with his thumb. She smiled under the embrace of his hand on her face, dropping her hands to his shoulders.

"You kept your promise, John. Against all the odds, you made it home."

SATURDAY, DECEMBER 7, 2013: VANDERPOOL, TEXAS

Except for the funeral parlor, an old clapboard storefront for a closed mom-and-pop hardware and a small cemetery marked the only sign of civilization in Vanderpool, Texas, forty kilometers west of Bandera. With the Sabinal River gurgling a few meters away, John and seven fellow astronauts served as pall bearers for Dr. Michelle Caskey. John faltered, struggling with the casket's weight and his recent return to gravity, but refused to step out of line with his buddies.

Four men and four women astronauts rested Michelle's casket on the burial platform, and John sat next to Amy and his children. Less than a hundred friends, family, and officials attended, at Keith Caskey's request. He wanted some privacy for his wife and—John suspected—for himself.

Warmer Texas temperatures and what John could best describe as joy among this funeral party replaced the dark dread and winter chill of Sean's funeral at Arlington National Cemetery in Washington two days earlier. Today was not the black pain he'd felt in Arlington, with black horses and a black lacquered caisson marching with a staccato *clop clop clop* and the chorus of soldiers' metal-tap shoes *clacking* on pavement. Rain had fallen on that funeral from black skies amid a dreary cold of early winter. Dark uniforms and black suits, and an ex-wife draped in black escorted by estranged relatives. John had never realized the depth of loss that could exist among those without hope.

He looked up at a cheery-faced young pastor, a man who'd grown up with Michelle, dressed in a jacket and sweater. Something about him was bright, distinctly casual in contrast to Sean's duty military chaplain at Arlington. He preached a short service and concluded as John had asked him to. Michelle would have wanted it this way.

"John Wells shared a story with me yesterday you all need to hear one day," the country pastor continued with a slow Texas drawl. "It's a story of redemption and renewal in Michelle's life. And it ends like this: Michelle shared her decision to give her heart over to the leadership and forgiveness of Jesus Christ. John told me that when Michelle died, her face had an expression of wonder, as though she'd just met her Maker on the way out of this world.

"Michelle nearly died on Mars. She was *fiercely* determined, like only Michelle could be, to bring back a biological sample from Mars that would revolutionize how we look at life in this universe. In her last minutes before Sean arrived to rescue her, Michelle asked Christ into her life and her heart. She knew she was at the brink of death, yet she was willing to risk her life to save something precious. It's the same way with Jesus."

As the pastor concluded, each astronaut stepped forward and placed a rose on Michelle's casket. The deep red of the long-stemmed roses was stark against the polished black casket's lacquered top. John, Amy, and Keith approached the casket with the last roses. John laid his bloom with the others, then produced a miniature white rose from his breast pocket and set it aside the red.

"Two roses?" Amy asked.

John nodded. "Yes, two. She would have wanted it that way."

John's hand lingered on her casket, tears welling as he gently laid a gift on top of the bouquet of delicate flowers. A small dark jagged rock rested in a field of red, green, and white. He pressed it into the greenery, holding a hand over what Michelle had considered most precious, and gave her life to retrieve.

A piece of Mars.

"This place is perfect for a getaway," John said. Amy rested her head on his knees while they sat on the stately old home's gray painted porch. "You say it survived the storm of 1900?"

"It did," she responded. "Everything you see in front of you, all the way to the ocean, was gone. 1204 Sealy Avenue was the first address left standing on the east end."

"I like it. Close to home, but it's still an escape. I'm glad you thought of it."

"You wouldn't have?" she asked, pinching his leg.

"Ouch! No. I mean, *yes*. But I'd have done something too expensive. And I don't want to be far from the kids. Ever again. This is just right." He took a deep breath of the Galveston air, laden with the scent of palms, saltwater, and fish. It was good to be able to smell again. "I'm glad that Sharon Walters could stay with the kids tonight," he said, watching Amy's face for a reaction.

"She's been the best of friends, John. I don't know what I'd have done without a girlfriend to lean on." She nudged John. "In case you're hinting around, the kids will be just fine. She's accustomed to them."

"Good."

John caressed Amy's long hair, fascinated as it rippled toward the floor like liquid, running through his fingers. "You know," he said, combing his fingers through her tresses once more, "gravity has some distinct advantages."

Amy giggled and took his hand in hers. "For example?"

"This," he replied. "You can't lie down in zero-G. Or sit in a chair or cross your legs. Hair goes everywhere—that used to drive poor Michelle nuts." He sighed. "It's really *good* to be home."

Amy sat up, her elbow resting on his knee. "Did you mean what you said earlier? You never want to be away from the kids and me again?"

"I meant it. There'll be business trips and all," he said, "but no more long trips and *no more space.*" He squeezed her hands. "I'm so sorry for all the pain that my calling—all those years of pressure and struggles—have put you through."

She returned the squeeze, a broad smile growing across her full lips. "Apology accepted. But to be fair, I knew what I was getting into. Well—*almost.*" She raised an eyebrow.

A few new wrinkles pushed up around her smile and eyes, the price, he was sure, she'd paid for his interminable pursuit of a career in space. He bent over and kissed her on the forehead, pulling her toward him as they lay back together in the deep wicker porch chair.

"I'm home, Amy. For good."

John snored.

The noise was a valuable cover as Nick slid the micro-miniature device into Amy's wallet. The size of a credit card, it would pick up conversations within three meters and broadcast over the best available wireless signal—cellular or Internet—that it could find. The little card could store hundreds of hours of conversation, just waiting on Amy to walk into the right digital environment—wherever that might be. Nick wore rubber-studded socks as he crept through the old house at 1204 Sealy and passed back out through the tall antique sliding window, just as he'd entered half an hour earlier.

The snoring continued uninterrupted.

In the alley behind 1204, Nick worked the lock to the one-car garage. In the cool December night, he heard the wail of distant sirens, ambulances making their way toward the John Sealy Hospital complex a dozen blocks away. The lock gave way. They always did.

The tracking beacon slid easily into the trunk compartment of the Wells's Chrysler minivan and Nick was out of the garage in minutes. He cursed the garage door, its hinges rusty from the seacoast's salt-laden air, then slipped back into the alley, skirted three blocks west, and found his vehicle.

Two hours later, the black-clad Nick crouched on the roof of a Clear Lake City address. Alice's bedroom window was unlatched.

FRIDAY, DECEMBER 13, 2013: TRIESTE, ITALY

"Slovenia is just beyond the edge of the city," Mr. Rivera said, standing at the front of the bus near Malcolm Raines's seat. "This location near the Adriatic suits all of your needs."

"Does the International Congress for Biogenetics know we have arrived?" Malcolm asked, raising his voice over the chatter of a busload of girls talking about the sights on this, the last leg of their odyssey traveling from Washington.

"I spoke to the Master Regent at ICB this morning, Father," Monique said. His aide sat to his left, setting a hand on Malcolm's knee to get his attention. "They will meet with us tomorrow."

Rivera nodded, then pointed ahead of the bus, the first of eight trams making their way down the narrow streets on the edge of the ancient city. "Your new home!"

A block ahead, Malcolm could see what he'd dreamt of his entire spiritual career—the retreat where he could separate himself from the bustle of the world—a place of contemplation to plumb the depths of hidden knowledge.

Actually, Mr. Rivera's company had found it. This convent had closed two years ago for lack of funds. Now it would serve as the new international headquarters for Raines's World Inclusive Faith Church—and three hundred plus young women who needed anonymity and a place to mature under his tutelage. Trieste, a city renowned for its advances in biotechnology and transgenics, was the perfect place to escape, to prepare, and to launch the next phase of his plan.

Here in northern Italy, with hundreds of young girls of Mediterranean complexion ensconced within the nunnery's walls, their long black hair tucked under the white scarves of Saint Michael's Remnant, his brood would barely stand out. It was the perfect retreat from a world of prying eyes and salacious gossips who wondered what he would do with so many young women in his charge.

"You have done quite well," Malcolm said as the bus slowed to creep through the convent gate and park in a spacious gravel courtyard. "It is beautiful—and well-protected. Exactly as I specified." The park-like setting was surrounded by tall walls that harbored white-washed cottages, a large main building reminding him of manor houses back home in Louisiana, two chapels, and numerous servant quarters. This complex would serve his needs perfectly.

Malcolm touched the hand of his aide, her thin hand warm in his grip. She returned the embrace. "Call the Master Regent at ICB, Monique. Let him know that we have arrived. I wish to schedule our initial meeting for this afternoon. We cannot tarry—there is so much to do in such a short amount of time."

Behind him, one of the girls called out, "Father! Will our mentors meet us here?" More of the girls joined in, talking rapidly about the long-anticipated reunion with people Malcolm had heard about, but never met—spiritual guides whom the girls discussed constantly, each referring to these beloved members of their lives only as "mentor."

"Yes," Malcolm said. "Soon. The Father Race will show us when—and how."

40

"THE CONGRESSIONAL GOLD MEDAL of Honor?"
John asked three months after his return.

"Uh-huh. The same one they presented to Rick Husband and the Columbia crew. It was approved yesterday by unanimous vote. Congratulations, Hawk." Jack Schmidt extended his hand across the desk and his large nameplate: Director, Manned Flight Operations.

John grasped his hand and stared in disbelief at the man who'd worked so hard with Marv Booker to get John a place as an alternate on the Mars crew. That mission, its glories and pains, were now history. In a month, he'd be on the road for a public relations tour—months of speaking. He only wished he could share this special moment with Michelle and Sean. His smile faded.

"What's the matter, Hawk?" Jack asked, rising and joining John at the window.

"I was thinking about what they're missing. People shouldn't have to die to win medals or get recognized."

"*You* didn't die."

"Came awful close. That space rock could have ripped through me just as easily as it got Michelle."

"And it *didn't*. You've told me a thousand times if you've told me once. We're here for a purpose. God has a plan. I might not buy all that, but I can at least remember what you said."

John suppressed a laugh. "I'm that persistent, huh?"

Jack nodded. "Some would say so. Persistence got you home, by the way. And it's why I got you on the crew in the first place. So, Captain Mars — persist. Get out there, accept what you deserve, and then tell the country all about it so that we can keep this program alive." He slapped John on the back and turned to his desk. "One day, maybe you'll share what was going on with Michelle," he said, taking a seat on the corner of the desk. "We followed her last wishes. No autopsy." He seemed to eye John as though looking for a crack in his story. "That *was* her last wish, correct?"

John held Jack's gaze without flinching. "It was. She was adamant about that one thing."

Jack shook his head and shrugged. "Everyone's got their hang-ups. Whatever." He moved behind his desk and sat down.

"One more thing — " he began. "You got a call today from that FBI agent. Wanted to congratulate you on the medal. Apparently, he has connections too and knew the medal was in the system. Wanted to know if you could come talk to him about his case someday."

John turned from the window, hands in his pockets, his lips forming a straight line, neither smile nor frown.

"It seems, Hawk, that your insights are needed by the Navy

again," Jack said. "So get up there and give them a hand. We'll start the roadshow after you're back."

✳

"Late next week, John," Special Agent Kerry said on the telephone. "You come up a day before the ceremony to consult with us on the Ulrich case. We've arranged for Amy and the kids to ride to Andrews Air Force Base on Air Force Two with Vice President Ryan and his wife. He'll be in Houston for a fundraiser early that week." Kerry paused a moment. "Believe it or not, I've already cleared their trip with the White House."

John whistled into the telephone. "You must have some pull up there. Pretty impressive."

"It was Rex Edwards. He pulled strings with the veep to bring *all* of you up, and then take you back the day after the ceremony. Admiral Pestorius—I mean, *Doctor* Pestorius—was the one with the idea to have you come up a day early. Edwards doesn't know about that wrinkle yet, but it helps us to keep a lid on things if we don't announce it. The bad news: You don't get to fly with the vice president."

"And the good news?"

"You get an extra night at the White House."

"The White House?" John exclaimed.

"Oh, yeah. Didn't I tell you? You and Amy get the Lincoln bedroom. So you'd better behave."

SATURDAY, FEBRUARY 22, 2014: SUITLAND, MARYLAND

"We think Ulrich came upriver in the *Sea Dagger*," Kerry said as he and John sat in the ultra-classified operations center in Suitland. "We started acoustic and active sonar sweeps of the Potomac right after you warned us, John, but it must not have been early enough. What I don't figure is, if we didn't see him for days afterward—where'd he go?"

John studied the Potomac bathymetric chart, his eyebrows raised. He tapped a finger on the Potomac River. "River's too shallow for him to drive that thing out reliably. But I'd be concerned about a different option. He could still be working the DC area—whether or not the sub is long gone. If you don't know where he is, then he could be anywhere. So DC's as good a place as any." John shook his head as he turned from the chart. "Maybe he never left."

Kerry slumped in his chair, rubbing his eyes. "Great. And that could mean 3/21 all over again."

"Amy?" John asked. "You sound funny."

"It's the cellular connection, John. We're on Air Force Two—about to take off. You can't imagine what a beautiful plane this is! And the children love it. They all met the vice president and his wife, Bunny. She's a riot. We wish you were here!"

Amy never used a term like "riot." Mrs. Ryan must be rubbing off on her, *and that's not a good thing,* John thought. *She's a notorious party animal.*

"Travel safe, sweetheart. I'm getting lots done with the Navy, and we'll be there when you arrive. Can't wait to see you. Is Alice enjoying the trip?"

"She is! She has the vice president's autograph on five coasters, a napkin, and three packages of mints. Her classmates insisted."

"Good. See you at the White House tonight, dear."

"I feel like one of those wives in the movie *The Right Stuff,* headed to DC for tea with Jackie Kennedy."

"Only better," John said. "I'll see you soon. I love you."

She said good-bye, and John hung up the phone, shaking his head. She'd never sounded so bubbly before. *Amy's not herself. But she's obviously having fun.*

✳

"Nice wheels," John said, admiring the custom leather interior of the stretch black limousine. Complete with bullet-proof windows.

"Courtesy of President Manchester," Dr. Pestorius said, seated across from John. "Your consolation prize for coming up early on such short notice while Amy takes the fancy ride north on Air Force Two."

"She called me a couple of hours ago. Didn't sound like herself—probably so excited. Said that the plane was beyond fancy."

Dr. Pestorius nodded. "It's a smaller version of Air Force One. I like it better, to tell you the truth."

John watched the winter woods drift by as they drove down the Suitland Parkway headed for the District of Columbia, his chin in his hand and elbow resting on the door. Both men were silent for almost a minute. "I have this theory," John began.

"That is?"

"The 321 thing, Admiral," John said. "There are so many options for how to interpret that number. I mean, you could come up with addresses, dates, locations—like the latitude/longitude I told Kerry about—or even the time of day. I did some checking, by the way. Kerry pulled some security tapes for me the other day. Did he tell you about this?"

"No. Why?"

"The tapes from the stadium showed the video of Raines standing in the middle of the infield with all those girls. He shut the lights off at exactly 7:42 p.m. and 14 seconds."

"Which is important because—?"

"Important because, it just so happens, if you convert that time to Julian date format, you get our favorite number."

"321?"

"The same. For that time of day on November 17, the Julian date's 2456614.321. The digits 321 are the Julian representation for that time of day on any day of the year. And the girls—321 of them, by the way— arrived on day number 321. *Each* of those number series adds up to six."

Dr. Pestorius tilted his head. "That analysis would have been a bit of a stretch in advance of the March 21 attacks, John. But after the fact—I admit, it's a little too perfect to dismiss as chance."

"Right. So humor me, okay? We could take it a step further. Back to that 'our number is six' thing, right?"

"Go on."

"Try today's date. 2/22. It also adds up to six." John stared out the window for a moment, lost in thought, then he sighed. "A years ago, it was our first full day on Mars. Strange, huh?"

"Sure, but you could take this numerology thing to extremes and look for codes everywhere, John. Nothing significant happened on 1/23 or 2/13. You could pick half a dozen dates and panic the entire country."

"Agreed," John replied. "You can't chase ghosts. Or weird number sequences. But we know this: Ulrich loves numbers. And it seems like he's leaving us—leaving you—a calling card. A message that we haven't yet figured out how to read."

| THE WHITE HOUSE

"It's an honor, Mr. President," John said as he shook President Manchester's hand when they met on the veranda overlooking the South

Lawn. "I wish my crewmates could be here to share this day with me."

"As do I, Captain Wells. I'm sorry for your loss. The entire country is." The president pointed off to the distance. "Vice President Ryan and your family will be coming in over the Lincoln Memorial around 3:20. In that direction." He pointed toward the reflecting pool and the World War II memorial. The president led the reception entourage onto the lawn under an overcast sky in the mid-afternoon.

President Manchester turned and responded to an aide who'd interrupted him from the far side. "Thank you, Rebeca. They're inbound now, Captain. Abeam the Watergate at this moment. By the way, Vice President and Mrs. Ryan will be joining us for dinner tonight."

He was a genuinely pleasing man, John thought, despite the president's reputation for being aloof or brusque. He turned toward John as they waited. "Have your children ever been to the White House before, Captain?"

"No, sir, and please — at NASA we usually drop the titles. I'd rather just be John."

"Very well. John."

His heart swelled as he watched the red beacon of the Marine Corps' Presidential helicopter peek over the tops of the trees in the distance. For a moment, he forgot the pain of months on a crippled Epsilon, unable to communicate. The warmth he felt in that moment swept away the recurring fear of being alone, or losing close friends — fears that tormented him every time he closed his eyes. John fought back a daydream of his second night in the Lincoln Bedroom. His family focused on the president, and the welcome the two of them would give Amy in just a few minutes.

The president tugged on John's blue astronaut jumpsuit sleeve. He'd worn the classic blue flight suit at the insistence of the Commander in Chief. "Better for signing autographs in," the president had said.

"Here they come!"

Those were the last words John remembered hearing. His eyes, always more capable of distant vision than his fellow pilots, made out the telltale white trail of a missile inbound to the large helicopter as it crested the Lincoln Memorial in the distance. Flares spewed from the belly of the sleek craft just before the missile impacted, and for an instant, the helicopter pitched nose-up in a steep climb, as though the pilot had a one-second notice to evade the weapon. The missile impacted the starboard engine near the blades in a sickening fireball, and the loss of symmetry in the fast-moving rotor subjected the crippled craft to hundreds of lateral G's that would shred the airframe and its occupants like a giant coleslaw machine.

"NO!" John screamed, helplessly watching the aircraft tumble to the ground in fiery segments, cascading off the Lincoln Memorial's dome. "Amy!" He ran down the South Lawn toward the disaster. Someone caught him from behind and threw him to the ground. John fought him fiercely—until he realized that the one who had tackled him was a secret service agent, who was now covering him. Protecting him. John looked back toward the White House. The president was nowhere to be seen.

The agent pulled John to his feet and toward the White House without a word. As they ran, John yelled, "I have to get to them!"

"Can't—do that—Sir," the agent huffed. They dashed into a corridor of the White House.

John shook off his grip. "My family was in that chopper!"

The agent stopped, his eyes connecting with John's, then glancing left and right. He grabbed John's arm and pulled him. "This way, Captain."

✳

The Suburban's brilliant blue lights pulsated on top of the black vehicle and on the dashboard. John rode in the front seat as his escort roared out of the White House compound toward the Ellipse. John's stomach lurched as he saw trees aflame in the distance.

Half a minute later, they raced down Constitution Avenue toward the Lincoln Memorial, whipping past dazed motorists who stood next to their cars watching fires burning around them. Only three minutes after the attack, John was rounding the backside of Abraham Lincoln, at the east entry to Memorial Bridge—rebuilt after 3/21. The streets were littered with burning debris. The agent swerved suddenly to miss a helicopter seat with a charred body—part of one—still strapped in. He stomped on the brake, the rear end sliding out from under the SUV on the jet fuel-slicked roadway. John leapt out before the vehicle stopped moving, racing to the bloody VIP seat that lay on its side in the roadway.

John fell on the pavement before the chair and its cargo. Only a leg and part of the lower torso remained. The charred pants and shoe were those of Amy, his patient, enduring, godly wife.

John collapsed to his knees, vomiting in the street.

41

"WE SHOULD GO, CAPTAIN WELLS," a female police officer said, pulling gently on his right arm. John looked up through bleary eyes, noticing the setting sun. He nodded, wondering where the time had gone.

John knew why he was here, but had no idea where here was, other than in Washington, DC—amidst the carnage of his family. Family members he could not bear to identify. He was seated on a stone bench. A statue rose above him, a tall golden half-nude woman with her back to a massive golden horse and its rider. The flared nostrils of the animal towered over him. Memorial Bridge began here.

A very tall man was screaming a few feet away to his left. John looked up, past the gentle policewoman who encouraged him to follow her.

"I must get through now!" the tall African-American man yelled, his face blocked from view. "I am a personal friend of the vice president of the United States, and I insist on coming through."

"Not today you ain't, Reverend," a capitol policeman said. "This crash site is off limits. To everyone." He shook his head as he stiff-armed the big man. "The veep's dead. So go home. There's nothing you can do."

"I know he is dead, you imbecile. I have come to pray for him—and for the rest of the victims."

John's senses suddenly engaged. He knew that voice. Malcolm Raines. *I thought he'd moved to Italy.*

As John watched, the tall, powerful Raines pushed the policeman. When the cop yelled for backup, the policewoman ran to help. John followed, his blood pounding, a red rage blocking all sights except the big man in the ridiculous purple robe.

"Raines!" the policeman yelled, raising his gun. "Leave peacefully or leave with cuffs. But leave."

"I will not!"

"Yes, you *will*," John said, stepping behind Raines amid the confusion and pulling the man's right arm up high behind him and pinning his wrist. Raines sank to his knees with a guttural scream. "You will *not* desecrate the site of my family's death," John growled, bending the wrist further. He felt the bones break as he forced the man's palm all the way to his wrist.

Raines howled in pain and rolled to his side, spinning John off his back and free of the wrist-snapping grip. The policeman lowered his weapon in the melee as Raines tried to get to his feet and John regained his own balance. While Raines was still bent over, John jerked his knee into the preacher's jaw, snapping his head upward. John followed the knee with a right hook square into the preacher's left jaw. The punch landed with a loud crack.

Raines's head snapped to his right and he tumbled to the pavement, blood streaming from his mouth and his wrist hanging limp at the end of his right arm. Standing over the jumble of purple robe and busted gold chain hanging around Raines's neck, John drew his foot back to launch a kick to the downed man's face.

The policewoman grabbed John's arm and pulled him back, her voice soothing. John was suddenly aware that he wasn't sitting at the base of the big horse any longer. His right hand shot fire up his arm, like he'd slammed it into a brick wall.

"I told you, Raines," the policeman grunted as he threw a set of cuffs on Raines's broken wrist. "You're goin' home."

Raines lay on his side and spat blood on the street, cringing from the ache of what John was sure was a broken jaw. His own hand felt Raines's pain. *It must've been a wallop.*

The tall man struggled to his feet, eyeing his assailant and the weapon in the policeman's hand. "Release the cuffs. I will leave." He spat more blood at the foot of the cop. The bloody puddle had parts of a shiny tooth in the red spittle. Once free of the bracelets, he turned, cursing, and headed for his limousine, where two ashen-faced, purple-robed attendant priests waited. They seemed in no hurry to join the fray.

As Raines moved away, the policeman put a hand on John's shoulder. "Didn't need that—but thanks anyway. Nice roundhouse."

John shrugged as he nursed his hand. "I think I need to sit down." Another wave of nausea overwhelmed him and his vision blurred. The policewoman escorted him back to the stone seat below the golden horse.

Ten minutes later, John was alone. The nausea was subsiding, but every time he took a breath he could smell death. The greasy odor of jet fuel, a scent he used to love when fueling and flying planes, was now the perfume of macabre destruction. Burned flesh, fuel, and the cool winter odor of the dank Potomac mixed in a gruesome aroma. He heard more noise, this time from above him, on the bridge to his left. Agents and police were swarming to the railing.

"There! Headed downriver." Radio calls began crackling all about him and two helicopters flew overhead, their spots focused on a sleek racing craft. As the helos closed in, the craft roared to life and sped in the direction of the Fourteenth Street Bridge.

"Suspect was photographing the crash site from the river," John heard over a radio held by a policeman ten meters to his left. "Now fleeing southeast, pursued by harbor police."

John stood and looked around the base of the big statue. In the gathering dusk, a sleek racing boat cut a deep wake as it sped in the direction of Washington National Airport. The image of that boat clicked for John. *An ocean racer.* As the craft disappeared under the Fourteenth Street Bridge, rage grabbed John again, with an even tighter clutch than when he'd pummeled Malcolm Raines.

If Ulrich had been on that ocean racer, he was gone now. He'd be in the water, just like all the other times Kerry had told John about, headed for another boat, or a way off the river. They needed divers, not helicopters. Then John remembered the ideal location for Ulrich to escape, a familiar landmark John had passed often as he jogged the river trail from the Pentagon for many months early in his Navy career. The Pentagon marina!

He set his eyes on the river, all other sights fading into the background. He saw but didn't acknowledge the expression of the young man whose craft he stole off the bank as capitol police interrogated a rubbernecking canoeist at riverside. Nor did he acknowledge the calls of police to come back to shore.

John ripped the water with the paddle he'd found in the canoe as he pointed toward Lady Bird Johnson Park and the marina canal on the far side of the Potomac.

This time he would *kill.*

The first thing John noticed was the smell.

Or more accurately, the lack of the haunting aroma of jet fuel and charred flesh. As he pulled with all his strength, the fresh air on the river brought back the reality that he'd avoided for the past many minutes, all of it a blur since he'd clocked the purple priest. Gone was the stench of death.

He pulled long strokes with the paddle, getting the hang of the "J" stroke after two years away from a canoe. The physical effort refreshed him, and he tore at the water with the paddle, weeping as he pulled. The cold February wind blew the tears back to his ears. He made no attempt to wipe them away as he crossed the first third of the river, angled downstream.

"I trusted you, Lord!" he shouted into the wind, sure his voice would die out across the water in the same way his wife had slipped away from him this night. He could see her again, alive with emotion . . . color . . . fragrance . . . life. The vision of Amy snapped, and the images of the crash site returned. Gruesome images of what remained of her lower body.

"Amy!" he croaked, yanking the paddle hard, skimming across the river, nearly halfway to Lady Bird Johnson Park. "I'm so sorry."

Close to shore, John saw what he'd set out to find. Downstream of the canoe he caught a flash of light in the water. Deep in the water, and moving too fast for a swimmer. It pointed toward the marina canal.

John dipped his paddle and pulled without a ripple. The canoe scooted forward, headed behind the statue of a wave and seagulls at the Navy and Marine Memorial—dedicated to men and women lost at sea—as he moved up channel toward the Columbia Island Powerboat marina. The Pentagon marina. The light flashed again under water. He kept pace with the occasional blinks, staying back five meters.

A swimmer-assist vehicle. That's what Kerry had called it. Surfacing in the Pentagon marina. Who would be diving in the Potomac in February? After sunset?

John made an extra hard pull with the paddle, gliding within two meters of the rear of what looked like a short torpedo in front of a swimmer, running just below the surface. No bubbles. *A rebreather.*

The swimmer slowed, and John could barely see him in the dusk. Only a single bulb on a pole at the end of the first dock illuminated the water in the early evening. John prayed for invisibility as he glided forward, stalking his prey. The swimmer released the short torpedo-like unit, and it sank into blackness. His back crested the surface of the dark water.

John dipped the paddle one last time, stopping his progress. He'd only get one chance at this. The masked swimmer surfaced without a ripple, staring directly at the light pole, away from John. He lifted the paddle, his heart pounding as images of Amy and the children swirled in his mind. The red rage consumed him now, his pulse pounding in his temples as he cocked the paddle behind him as if preparing to hit a homerun. The head pivoted in the water as he swung the paddle, and John saw the face of death.

Sweeping like a two-meter long broadax, the edge of the wooden paddle connected with a sharp crack and sliced into the man's skull and left ear. The wooden handle broke with the tremendous impact, shattering the glass plate of the diver's mask. John saw blood spurt across the water.

The diver fell forward, lifeless, and sank out of sight, a slight crimson stream swirling behind him.

John peered over the edge of the canoe, reaching down to touch the dissipating blood. His heart slammed against the walls of his chest while verses about vengeance rang in his ears.

"You're not getting off this easy," John yelled, ripping off his leather flight jacket. He rolled from the canoe into the water, tipping the boat.

The frigid water crushed him like an icy vise, and he fought the urge to gasp as he kicked to the bottom of the dark harbor. His body shivered immediately as hot sweating skin met the chill of the Potomac.

John's head pounded as he struggled in his flight boots to kick toward the bottom, groping in the dark where he thought the diver might have gone down.

Out of air, his lungs screaming for relief, he finally turned in the darkness and tried to push off the bottom. Instead of mud, his foot planted on something firm.

John reversed, struggling to stay alive, but was determined not to lose his quarry as he reached down. He felt a strap, perhaps a weight belt. He grabbed it, pushed his boots into the soft muck below him, and shoved off. A tiny glimmer of light beckoned above him. The bulb on the pole at the end of the dock glowed dimly, far above.

John exhaled as he rose, praying for air, fighting with one hand to swim and with the other to pull the dead weight behind him. Images of free-dive tanks and warm water came to mind, twenty-meter deep Navy dives where he had to plunge to the bottom and complete a task on one breath. Red splotches swam before his eyes as he groped for the surface.

His arm flailed in midair as John popped from the cold water like a cork. He gasped for a breath, the frigid air searing his lungs as he sucked it in. With the dead weight in his hands, he lay back, one hand sculling to keep the two of them afloat as he kicked toward the end of the dock. John tugged at the weight below him, trying to find a head in the dark, to get it to the surface. He found skin, then a face, and pulled it out of the water.

Blood ran from a deep wound above the man's left ear, and splinters of wood lodged in a deep gash running from the back of his skull to his left cheekbone. John pulled the diver over on his back, threw his right arm over the man's chest, pulled the head back with his left hand, and kicked. And kicked. He pulled the bloody mouth closer and began to breathe for him.

For what seemed half an hour, John struggled in the clumsy flight boots, headed for the marina ramp, breathing for this man who, he was sure, had stolen away the most precious part of John's life. His family.

John shivered in the freezing night air, hands shaking from exhaustion, cold, and fear as he stripped the rebreather from the swimmer's chest where he lay on the grass near the dock and boat ramp. How he'd pulled the man up here, John couldn't remember. In the distance, he was sure he could hear sirens. His teeth chattered so hard he couldn't get a full breath, but he breathed into the bloody mouth again and then pushed on the man's chest.

"Jesus, forgive me. But this man deserves to die," John said, his voice faint and vibrating as he shivered violently. He pushed on the chest again and breathed once more. Pain was like fire in his head, dizzy from so many exhales, his chest constricted from lack of oxygen and rest. John gasped, faltering as he tried to compress the diver's chest once more.

The swimmer coughed at last, spitting out blood and water. John wheezed, arms shaking, and he rolled the man on his right side. Blood oozed from the swimmer's deep gash, directly below John's face. The swimmer coughed again, then vomited up water and bile.

John could hear riverboat sirens closing in, but his head was reeling. Dazed by the lack of air, he tried to stand, then fell to his knees, trembling. He reached a shaky hand forward to steady himself and tried again to push up to a standing position. He needed to get some distance from the swimmer—just in case.

It was too late. A diver's knife plunged deep into his right thigh, and John fell forward, screaming.

A black-gloved hand jerked the jagged knife free as John rolled downhill toward the dock, the only direction he could move with his leg immobile from pain. The black neoprene hand slashed at him again, nicking John's arm as he rolled onto his back, lying on dock planks. In the dim light, John looked up into bloodshot eyes, a rivulet of crimson running down the left cheek. The swimmer stood over him on wobbly legs, shifting the knife from a slashing to a thrust grip.

John kicked upward, his boot connecting with the swimmer's ribs. Then he rolled again, clawing for the edge of the dock, where he pulled himself over the edge.

When he hit the icy water, the slap of water on John's face mixed with what sounded like a clap of thunder. Moments later, a body tumbled into the water beside him, and John struggled to swim away from his attacker.

The body was still and sank into dark water. John let it disappear. He was aware, vaguely, of things slowly going black, of cold water rising over his face. He surrendered to an irresistible craving to sleep.

John opened his eyes to bright lights and muffled sirens. The world was bumping along below him. He fought to clear his head, to regain his bearings. His leg felt like it had fallen asleep and was coming to life again, with deep stabs of pain like a million needles in his thigh. He blinked.

"Welcome back, John. Thought I'd lost you there for a minute."

The voice was familiar. "Amy?"

There was no response. He tried to open his eyes in the glare of a light directly over him. "Where are we?" He was vaguely aware that he should be sad. *But why?*

"We're somewhere between the Pentagon and Bethesda Naval Hospital. It's me, Kerry. You've lost a lot of blood, buddy. So rest up, okay?"

John nodded, his head propped on a warm pillow. His whole body felt warm, encased in something soft. Then he remembered. Nightmarish images of body parts and the stench of burning death. The crushing pain of utter loss, of the death of his bride. And all his children. Forgotten were all memories of space or career. Or Mars. John looked up into the familiar face of his FBI friend. It jarred him back to the moment.

"Ulrich?"

"You found him, man. I mean, I can't believe it. But you nailed him. He nearly killed you, by the way."

"Shouldn't have . . . pulled him out . . . of the water."

"You did *what*?"

"You didn't know?"

"How could I? You were unconcious when I yanked you out of the drink. You put that nasty gash in the side of his head?"

John smiled meekly. "Yup. He still alive?"

"'Fraid not, pal. He was about to run you through when my boat came into the marina. I plugged him. One shot."

John shook his head, the pain stabbing him with every movement. The ache in his chest wasn't a wound, he was sure. The deep stabbing anguish was loss. Debilitating loss.

"No more Ulrich," Kerry said.

"Why would he do it?" John asked with a bitter sigh, trying to forget this night, and forget why he was here. "I cost you your last suspect," he said. He didn't want to talk.

"Don't be too sure," Kerry said. John fought to focus on his friend in the bright lights of the ambulance bay. A plump woman sat adjacent to Kerry, checking John's blood pressure. Kerry put his hand out over John's chest. "This might help," Kerry said, dropping a minuscule object into John's hand.

It felt like a tiny pebble. "What is it?" John asked, raising it and trying to focus in the bright lights.

"Malcolm Raines left it behind. Thanks to you. It's part of a tooth that he spit out when you K-O'd him on the bridge. Policewoman there picked it up. Gave it to me when I came looking for you."

John turned the small silver object over in his fingers. "It's not a tooth. Looks like a filling."

"Bingo. A very special filling, John. Thanks to you, we're back in business."

John tried to shake his head "no," but it hurt too much. "I don't understand."

"You brought me *two* prizes tonight, buddy. Ulrich was prize one. He's dead now, but that's the price we paid to save you." John could see him turn the pea-sized item over in his hand, a big smile growing on his face. "But this—well, I'd certainly call it a great consolation prize."

"You've seen it before?" John asked.

Kerry nodded. "Sure have. I'm gonna deputize you, Wells—after you get some rest."

"What *is* it?" John insisted.

"It's a bug. An advanced cellular telephone, in short, designed to fit inside a molar. The FBI invented it three years ago. Limited use, mind you. You can receive signals but you can't send."

"The Father Race—" John began, putting a hand to his pounding temple.

"Bingo," Kerry replied. "If you had one of these in your head, you'd be convinced you were hearing voices. It might be just the evidence we needed."

"Maybe," John said, wishing that the dizziness and grief clouding his thoughts would clear. There was something—a breakthrough—he needed to express. "Two options," he said at last.

"There you go again, Spock," Kerry responded with a little laugh.

John shrugged. "Can't help it . . . that's the way I think," he said, panting. He took a deep breath. "If that's a bug but Raines didn't know—" He paused and breathed twice. "Someone will make sure it gets replaced."

"Exactly. Or he knows it's missing and he'll fix it himself."

"Second option doesn't scare me as much as the first," John said, realizing now what the point was that he needed to force through the mental fog brought on by grief and fluid loss. "This entire mess . . . might be directed by someone else."

Kerry closed his hand around the silver pea. "Touchdown!" He put a hand on John's shoulder. "This jewel just might help us to find him."

"Or *her*," John said, groaning as he tried to move his aching leg. "Remember what Ulrich taught us."

Kerry took a deep breath, shaking his head. "Which lesson of many are you referring to?"

"Everything's not what it first appears."

EPILOGUE

| SATURDAY, MAY 16, 2015:
| WASHINGTON, DC

fifteen months later

ON A BRIGHT SATURDAY morning in May, Special Agent Kerry watched his friend place five long-stemmed roses at the northeast end of Washington DC's Memorial Bridge. John knelt for a long time in prayer on the sidewalk, burying his head in his hands—although John would not weep, Kerry knew, until he was by himself. Kerry had seen his astronaut friend walk through horrendous grief these past fifteen months. There were days—sometimes weeks—when John was utterly helpless, so deep did the raw despair run in the first months after they had buried John's family.

Today was a necessary closure for John. "I need you, Kerry," John had told him when he'd called a week ago. "I want us to go together."

Kerry shielded John from gawking passersby for the few minutes he spent in prayer, then John rose from the sidewalk and took a seat at the base of a statue near the Lincoln Memorial entrance to the bridge.

Together the two men sat and watched, without a word, as the world moved by. Cars whizzed past, tour buses rounded the Lincoln Memorial, and runners streamed across the bridge into and out of the District.

John eventually broke the silence, still staring straight ahead. "I wouldn't be here today if it weren't for you, Kerry. I want to make sure I thank you for that — often." No thanks were necessary, but it made Kerry feel good nonetheless.

"If you'd told me to leave you alone on the Space Station four years ago, John, you'd have never been in this mess. I owe *you*."

John laughed for the first time in the two days Kerry had been with him. "You've got a point. Let's call it even."

"I got some news this morning," Kerry said. "You interested?" They continued to stare at the stream of people, all of Washington ignoring these two men sitting at the base of a gold-gilded monument of a tall horse with a well-muscled male rider and a woman standing by the horse's side.

"Sure. I'm all ears."

"We got a line on Raines. Got an x-ray of his head. Don't ask me how — it was ingenious. Somehow, he has the telephone implant back in his tooth. We're trying to find a way to intercept the signal and track its source."

"Raines? Really? You doing that in Trieste? Anything new on those identical girls — the ones he calls the 'Mother Seed'?"

"CIA's certain they're clones, but I'm not convinced. Raines keeps them tucked away. No one can get at 'em. Which is weird for a guy like him who makes a profession out of showing off. If it's true that they're clones, he's sitting on the biotech news of the century — but won't talk."

"He's overseas for a reason," John replied, staring straight ahead at the stream of runners and traffic. "He has something to hide."

The two men sat quietly for fifteen minutes. John spoke at last, as if he'd been forming the thought for a long time. "NASA plans to announce a third manned mission to Mars. The crew leaves three years from tomorrow. It's a short trajectory, only four months each way. Gonna stay twenty-two months. The second mission, the one that leaves next year, will be headed home before the third group arrives." He took a deep breath. "We *had* to go back. We couldn't let all that sacrifice be for nothing."

John's face seemed to brighten as he talked, Kerry noticed, as if John could imagine the adventure others would have as they returned to Mars—to stay.

John looked at Kerry. "And you'll eventually break that code on Ulrich. The unknown boss who paid him, and the motive—and the *Sea Dagger*, and the spiders, and Raines with all those identical girls. We'll figure it all out over time."

"That's the spirit, John," Kerry said, patting his friend's shoulder. The two leaned back against the monument in silence.

Five minutes later, a large tour group approached. Kerry thought at first that a sandy-haired youth in the group was looking attentively at him—then he realized that the boy was looking at John. He spoke urgently to the red-haired woman beside him, who smiled and nodded when he pointed toward the two men. She waved him on.

"Are you Captain Wells, the astronaut?" the young man asked as he jogged up, out of breath and wide-eyed.

John looked up, a thin smile showing. "That's me."

"This is so amazing! I can't believe you're here. *Today*."

"Why's that?" John asked.

"Our middle school came all the way from Minnesota for a field trip. I've always wanted to meet you. I never dreamed—"

John stuck out his hand. "It's a pleasure. What's your name?"

The boy thrust out a Washington tour book. "Can I get your autograph?"

"Sure. Who should I make it out to?"

The student ignored the question and held on to the guide while he spoke, rapid fire. "You know what's really cool is that I found you right *here*. I mean, at *the* statue—my absolute favorite."

John and Kerry both looked up. "You mean this big horse?" John asked after a pause, pointing above him. The young man couldn't possibly know what pain John had suffered at the foot of this bridge.

"Yeah. You know what it is, right?" the boy asked, his freckled face alive with emotion. He fascinated Kerry, who'd always wanted a son.

"No. Actually, I don't," John said, leaning back against the limestone base of the beast, his hands wrapped around an upraised knee. John's smile grew as he connected with the boy. "Tell me about it," he said.

"It's called *The Sacrifice*, Sir. A man named Friedlander carved it sixty-four years ago." He pointed straight up, his mouth forming an O in amazement at the golden likeness of a powerful horse, a warrior, and a woman. "The half-naked lady is Earth. Her back is turned to the rider. His name is Mars."

Kerry coughed; he watched John's mouth fall open in surprise.

"She looks up into the warrior's eyes with longing, as the God of War rides off. He's headed away to do battle, to make the great sacrifice. She stays home."

John seemed barely able to talk. "How—" he began, choking on his words. "How did you learn this? I never knew."

The youth looked John in the eye, blushing a little, looking down at the ground for a moment. "Because I love everything about Mars, Sir," he said, clutching his tour book and rolling it nervously. "When I was nine years old, I decided I wanted to be a Navy pilot, become an astronaut—and go to Mars. *Just like you.*"

He handed the rolled-up Washington tour guide to John with a pen. "Would you sign this for me, Captain Wells?" he asked, looking down at the pavement again. "You probably think I'm just being stupid."

John moved forward on the bench, eye to eye with the young man as he put a hand on his shoulder. "No, I don't. Not at all. When I was twelve—about your age—I made the same decision. And I did it." Tears welled in John's eyes as he squeezed the boy's shoulder. "You can too. I believe in you, son."

"You think so? I mean—you do?" he asked as he looked up, his voice rising, a smile creasing his face from ear to ear. "Oh, yeah! Here. Sign this. I gotta go tell the guys."

John took the guide and started to write on it. "By the way, how do you want me to autograph this? I still don't know your name."

"Oh, yeah," the boy said, looking back at his friends, waiting in the distance. He waved them over. "My name's Simon. Simon Kanewski. I watched you take off for Mars." A broad smile grew across the boy's freckled face as John's eyes widened in surprise.

Now Kerry knew where he'd seen the boy before. He spoke up before a shocked John could form the words. "You're that brave fella who roped those alien spiders, aren't you?"

Simon nodded toward Kerry, his chin held high. "Yes, sir. I am. That's when I knew I wanted to be an astronaut."

**SUNDAY, MAY 17, 2015:
NAZARJE, SLOVENIA**

The ancient stone walls towered ten meters above the garden, creating the unforgiving confines of this new life of hers: twenty meters by twenty meters. A patch of clear blue sky stretched out above her. Besides this garden and her daughter, the heavens were the only color in her life. She smiled, praying silently in thanksgiving for her blessings.

The woman pulled her knees close to her chest, seated on a patch of grass in the far corner of the food plot, her arm around the shoulders of a young girl. Both wore simple grey shifts and plain black leather shoes. Peasant garb. They stared together across the patch of soil and vegetables they'd been working since sunup. In silence, she pointed at the only sight visible above the colossal wall that surrounded them: A cross thrust into the sky, poised at the top of a sharp spire on a gray, slate-roofed steeple. She could only see the tip of the spire, and only from this corner of her garden, peering through the crenellated ramparts of the far wall.

"I love the Sunday bells," the girl said quietly. "I wish they rang every day—like they used to."

The woman squeezed the young girl's shoulder, in wonder at the cool of the morning and the bells of all timbre resounding about them. Every Sunday morning, no matter how cold or wet, and particularly in the wondrous spring, this their second in this place, they would come here and sit. Tucked into the corner of the steeply walled garden, the only place where she could see the cross. Her hope.

The bells lifted her heart, part of a collection of sounds that told her of life beyond the moss-covered stones that isolated her and her daughter from the rest of the world. Sounds seemed to waft up to her, as if she were perched somewhere on a hill. And the sounds echoed and blended as though mountains rose just beyond her sight, their slopes reflecting all of life back her way.

She would sit outside at night, listening to the gurgle and tinkle of a distant river, wondering where this place was. And why she was here.

Tall trees stood somewhere just beyond her view. She could hear them sigh in the near-constant wind that burbled over the top of the crenellated wall. Theirs were sad songs in the gentle breezes of spring, and powerful screams when driven by a tempest.

A small town came alive by day, somewhere far away. The *rat-tat-tat* of jackhammers, clanging of equipment, and staccato sounds of workmen led her to think they were preparing something big. The toots and beeps of small cars, deep-throated horns calling workers to factories of some kind, and sometimes a siren—the European warbling kind—drifted up to her from what she imagined was a steep mountainous valley below.

She could also hear the voices of children, always girls. They were happy voices, blending from some source inside a nearby building, frequently singing songs she didn't recognize.

Together, the woman and child listened, their eyes on the cross. The melody of a dozen church bells and carillons ringing in their steeples filled the moment. The bells would peal only half an hour, then her week of labor in the walled garden would start again. She looked at the dirt and stains on her daughter's hands, remembering brighter days, family times, far away from this grey torment. She held her daughter close, caressing the girl's long blonde hair as they listened together.

"Keep your eyes on the cross, sweetheart. God hasn't forgotten us," the woman said as she hugged the child. She nodded toward the tip of the steeple, barely visible through the ramparts on the far wall. "Hope sustains us in our darkest hour."

She closed her eyes, taking the girl's rough hands in her own. "Let's pray for your brothers—and your dad." Both bowed their heads, and the woman whispered as she poured out her heart for the sons stripped away from her, and a husband who must, by now, have given her up for dead.

"Lord Jesus, please bring my boys back to me. And bring us all back to John."

etc.

bonus content includes:

1. Soon after their launch on the Space Shuttle Endeavor, John looks back at Earth and feels that he spent too little time communicating with his family about the mission.

   a. Have you ever been in John's situation, caught up in an important project or mission in life, and once at the pinnacle of success or accomplishment, you realize that you spent too little time focused on the real priority—family?

   b. Is there a proper balance between God's calling to a life mission and God's calling to family? Is it possible to hold the family in such a high position in your heart that it could actually become an idol? Have you ever known someone who worshiped his or her family, perhaps to the neglect of God's calling on his or her life?

2. On the way to Mars, John realizes that there may be an affair brewing between Sean and Michelle.

   a. Have you ever found yourself in a situation where, due to prolonged activity or isolation with a person of the opposite sex, you felt a growing attraction to (and/or from) this person? How did you deal with that situation?

   b. Dr. James Dobson, Rev. Billy Graham, and other leaders in the Christian community advocate building "hedges" around a relationship to be sure the relationship stays within its proper boundaries. How can you build hedges around your relationships to avoid temptation in situations where you might be tempted?

3. John confronted Sean and Michelle about the signs of their illicit relationship. His blunt approach made both of the other astronauts mad at him.

    a. Was John too brusque? Or did he not push far enough?

    b. How would you have dealt with this if you'd been in John's place? Would you have dealt with it or hoped and prayed God would resolve it without confrontation?

4. When Amy was diagnosed with obsessive compulsive disorder (OCD) she prayed about whether to take medication or to seek God's healing hand in the cure of the disease and its impact on her life.

    a. For problems like OCD, what do you think about pursuing a treatment path of doctors and medication as opposed to calling upon and trusting in God's healing power?

    b. Does God ever work hand-in-hand with doctors and medicine?

5. Malcolm Raines repeatedly advocated finding the inner god within you.

    a. Do you agree with Malcolm that experience is the ultimate arbiter of truth? Why or why not?

    b. Can you truly understand truth without experiencing it? Explain.

6. Michelle became pregnant during the trip from Earth to Mars.

    a. Would it be right for NASA to send one woman and two men to Mars?

    b. Should all crews to other planets be composed of the same gender? If so, which gender?

7. John killed Elias Ulrich in a fit of rage after a gruesome aircraft crash that apparently killed John's entire family.

    a. Was John justified in this killing? Why or why not? How would you have handled the situation?

b. Why did John jump into the water to save Ulrich after he tried to kill him?

8. When Sean, the mission commander, died, John regretted not sharing his faith more openly with him.

a. Are there people in your life whom you know you need to talk to about Christ but haven't, for whatever reason? What are some ways you might begin that conversation?

b. Have you ever been in John's situation, faced with a person who is reluctant to discuss spiritual issues, and you put off the opportunity — only to regret it later because there are no more chances to share?

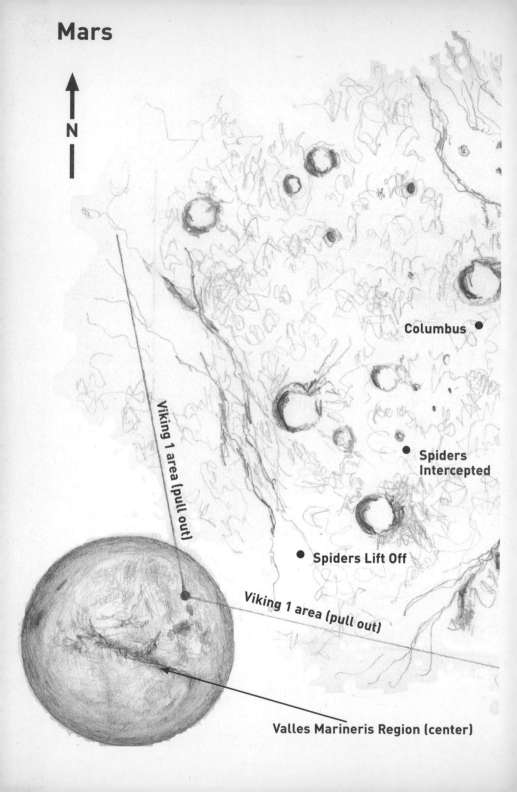

Mars

N

Columbus

Spiders Intercepted

Viking 1 area (pull out)

Spiders Lift Off

Viking 1 area (pull out)

Valles Marineris Region (center)

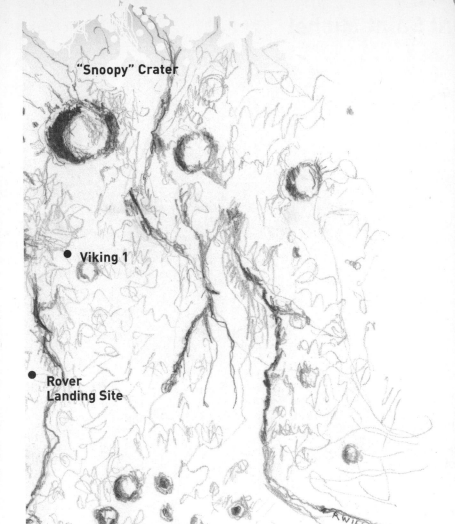

"Snoopy" Crater

Viking 1

Rover
Landing Site

R.WILLIAMS

Illustrated by: Rosemary Williams

etc.

Mont Saint Michel

View from the South

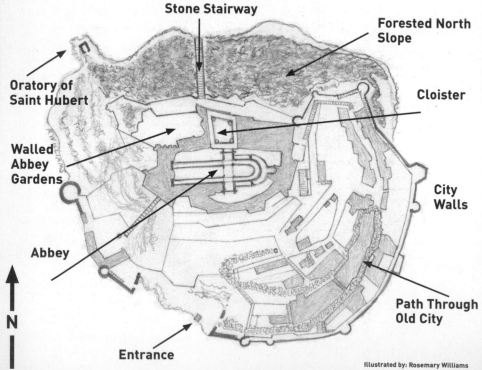

Stone Stairway

Forested North Slope

Oratory of Saint Hubert

Cloister

Walled Abbey Gardens

City Walls

Abbey

Path Through Old City

N

Entrance

Illustrated by: Rosemary Williams

THE RETURN

 BOOK THREE

1

THE SMALL POINT OF LIGHT moved toward them, an unhurried but relentless advance across a lifeless red plain. Not an out-of-the-ordinary sight on Earth, perhaps—a slow vehicle crossing the high desert. But this was Mars. And until moments ago, eight Martian astronauts, along with all of mankind, had thought those explorers were the sole living beings on this forsaken, desiccated planet.

"The glint's still headed straight for us." Rear Admiral John Wells, known to his crew as "Hawk," pointed at the computer display, consternation knitting his brow. "At the current speed of advance, it'll be here in three days. Tops."

John heard the quickened breathing of the seven other astronauts gathered around him in the quiet of the Martian morning. Hemmed inside their tight cylindrical home, the crew formed a tense circle in the mission operations center of their laboratory module.

"You've only seen those reflections at sunrise, right?" Martin Oswald, their lanky flight engineer, better known as "Oz," winced as he plucked hair from the side of his head. The guy's nerves had gotten so bad the bald spot was hard to miss now.

Colonel Melanie Knox nodded and looked up from a data terminal, her small frame bristling with energy. "Satellite surveillance picks up a glint as it crosses the horizon every morning. But only at low sun angles. There's no mistake—something's out there. I woke you because I wanted you all to see for yourselves." She studied her wide-eyed crewmates and waved a hand across the screen. "Whatever it is, guys, it's closing in on us."

John's crew conferred an hour later in the dining area of the habitation module. Everyone but John nursed a mug of coffee as they debated the next step.

"Houston's probably flipping out right now. And no one knows what we're dealing with." Dr. Deborah Readdy sighed and pushed a frazzled jumble of wiry strawberry hair over her shoulder. "It looks like a vehicle in this image. But it's too blurry to be sure."

Deborah tossed a glossy printout onto the scuffed plastic of their eight-person dinner table. All eyes riveted on the photo's fuzzy detail of what looked like a silver box. Behind her, a large wall monitor displayed expanded video images of the silver thing overlaid on a map of the deeply eroded Nirgal Vallis region of Mars.

This was their home, a rugged land of ravines and gullies, hundreds of miniature Grand Canyons coursing across the pockmarked face of bone-dry Mars. A lonely planet, distant from all John had ever known and loved, and proving more barren by the day—until now.

"That thing's blurry because we're taking the pictures with a *weather* bird, Deborah," Oz said as he peered at the photo. "The satellite's twenty-one thousand kilometers above the planet. It's not designed for high-resolution imagery." He slumped in his seat, bony shoulders spiking up under a loose, blue NASA jumpsuit. "Shoot, I'm surprised Melanie saw that reflection at all. We're alone, right, John? No secret manned missions?" He tossed a crumpled juice packet at their commander. "And no aliens?"

John caught the trash ball one-handed and shook his head. "You know as much about this as I do, Oz." He stared at the glossy photo. "Deborah's right. NASA freaked when I told 'em."

"Is it any wonder?" Melanie said. "We've got no idea what we're dealing with."

"There won't be any better imagery to help us. Mars Surveyor won't be in orbit 'til we're long gone." Jake Cook spoke for the first time that morning. The big man's deep voice reverberated like a bass drum in the gleaming white habitation module. "So, what do we know? Something big, of unknown origin, is headed our way."

Jake pulled the glossy image toward him, then leaned over the table, resting his large frame on his elbows. "We have two choices. Either we intercept this thing and deal with it. Or we sit on our hands and wait for it to arrive. In either event, we have to make some quick decisions when we meet it . . . them . . . whatever." Jake sat up, leaned back in his chair, and waved a hand at the airlock. "Remember, we aren't armed, and our only transportation off this planet is unguarded, a kilometer away."

His comment touched a nerve. No one ever considered guarding anything on Mars. They all started to talk at once.

"Jake's got a point." Melanie stood up to focus the group's attention. They quieted as she pointed a cursor at the track prediction on the screen. "We can't even lock the doors. I'd rather *act* than wait." She turned toward John, her gentle brown eyes demanding a response.

The crew geologist, Dr. Robert Witt, spoke with an aggravating nasal tone. "You're delusional. All of you. We know we're alone, right?

It's probably a glint in the camera lens at sunrise." He huffed. "Just a blip. Nothing to get excited about."

John raised a hand for silence as the others railed at "Geo," their crew skeptic. He surveyed the four men and three women waiting for his pronouncement. *Navy Rear Admiral John Wells, commander of the third manned mission to Mars—"Hawk," America's most experienced astronaut.* That's what the news ticker said once when he was on camera. It was time to command. "Put a lid on it, folks. Geo's point's as valid as any other right now."

John turned toward the blurry silver image on the big screen, resting both elbows on the table, his chin perched on his folded hands. The crew waited for him to speak. It was a tense silence.

Maybe it is *a figment of our imagination,* he thought. A noisy ventilation fan rattled in the background, distracting him. After five hundred dusty days on the Red Planet, things broke down much too often. *Can't afford major failures now. Four more months to go . . .*

When they'd begun this odyssey nearly seventeen months ago, everyone dreamed of water and ice on Mars, assuming they were alone on a planet shaped eons ago by rivers and lakes. They came looking for microscopic life, fully expecting to find it. The equipment functioned perfectly and failures were minimal. Lately, however, John spent half his time fixing broken stuff, the planet was bone dry and devoid of life everywhere they'd drilled, and now a vehicle appeared to be crossing this dusty rock headed toward them. Somehow, he sensed, their mission was about to be severely tested—much like it was the first time he'd come here.

"I agree with Mel," John said at last. "If something's out there, we can't let it get to us first. I'll coordinate the details with Houston and we'll head out today to investigate. Blue team, suit up. Gold team stays here."

He looked at Melanie, his second in command. "Be prepared to get your team out of here fast, Mel. You might not get much notice."

John moved slowly down the ten steps from the airlock, thinking about the next ten hours. His foot settled into the sugar-like dust of Mars, a familiar squishy sensation that affirmed he was outside. His hard bulky suit fit like a well-worn glove, and he took a deep breath of the dry recycled air, glad to be outdoors despite the circumstances.

It felt good to be afoot again for the first time in a week. The inside of his Mars suit smelled like a locker room after a year and a half of hard use, but the rigid torso fit like he was born into it. And, in a manner of speaking, he *was* born for this—space exploration, his lifelong passion. He looked into the distant amber sky above a rust-red rocky plain pocked with craters and ridges. A deep gorge ran west. He never wanted to forget this experience—standing on the face of another planet nearly two hundred million kilometers from Earth.

Seven years ago, John had floated in his suit, attached to his crippled ship, Epsilon, staring into the void of space as he passed Venus. Alone. A terrifying isolation. Yet the chill of the loneliness back then couldn't compare to the apprehension that gripped him now. He prayed for calm, but an inner voice, the quiet whisper of God's guidance, urged him on: *Go!*

A salmon-colored disc, surrounded by a halo of fine dust particles, shone in the morning sky. John stared beyond the team of four astronauts, his eyes on a distant, rugged, and increasingly ominous horizon.

"You ready, old man?" Jake let out a belly laugh as John gazed into the sun. "If you're not up to this, we can grab you a wheelchair."

John smiled, knowing his old friend couldn't see his grin. The sun's reflection glinting off the gold-tinted visor of his helmet was too bright. "I'm older, Mr. Cook, but definitely wiser. Be glad the shrinks gave me a thumbs-up to keep an eye on you pups. You'd have never made it this far without me."

"You're probably right, Methuselah." Jake patted John's backpack.

"Methuselah?"

"Yeah. Like that old geezer in the Bible. You're the oldest man on Mars."

Methuselah. Noah's grandfather. A sudden rush of memories ripped at John's heart, and he saw Amy, a petite brunette with a Bible picture book, reading about the ark with his young sons on a late summer morning while they all watched a torrential rainstorm. Baby Alice rolled on the floor in a layette, and the aroma of Saturday's breakfast of bacon and biscuits lingered in the air. That recollection of family warmth turned to ice in an instant, replaced by memories of their funeral. His wife and four children, ripped from him six years ago next month. Body parts raining down in a hail of burning aircraft wreckage.

John grunted as if he'd been kicked in the gut. Gritting his teeth, he shoved the pain of this daily mental hell deep inside. His raw grief compartmentalized yet again, the old pilot joined his team.

"You okay, pal?" Jake studied John from his position beside the rest of the crew.

"Yeah. Fine. I'm ready." John stepped forward, a checklist in his gloved hand. His loss was like acid rising in his throat. Forcing it back down didn't soothe the burn. "We've got a unique mission today, ladies and gentlemen." Three suited astronauts stood before him next to a large rover that reminded John of a California strawberry packer, six huge wheels suspending a glass-walled cab two meters above the ground.

John read from the miniature video screen on his data tablet. "Eighty kilometers round trip. Our primary target is probably some kind of vehicle, based on the image. Should take us ten hours, give or take an hour. That, plus—" he paused—"whatever we'll need to respond to the approaching visitor."

"Visitor?" Oz exclaimed. "Thought you said we're alone, Hawk?"

John shrugged. "Call it a target, then."

"Yeah. 'Target.' I like that." Oz sounded both pleased and anxious. "Are we armed?"

"You know we aren't. So give it a rest, Oz." Jake was tense, too. "We need to get going. Oxygen supplies and fuel checked out fine, John. Melanie did the rover preflight for us."

Melanie nudged John in the side. "I'd be glad to lead the team and let *you* stay here."

John smiled. "Thanks, Mel, but I need you to stay and hold down the fort." If John gave her the word, Melanie would leave without them, taking half of the Mars crew aloft to their return vessel in orbit—to safety. "You got the keys?"

Melanie nodded at his playful question, then laid a gloved hand on his arm, the top of her helmet barely as high as his shoulder. She held on for a long moment, her shiny visor hiding a normally expressive face. "Be careful, John. I want us to leave this rock *as a team*."

"Twelve o'clock!" Jake exclaimed loudly as they crested a low berm four hours later. He leaned between Deborah and John, pointing toward a bright object that lay directly in front of the rover.

John's heart skipped a beat. *It can't be!*

Startled, Deborah braked hard, pitching John forward. Jake grabbed at the seats to keep from spilling over the control console. Oz held onto the back of John's seat, craning his long neck to see the brilliant point of light fifty meters beyond them.

"Closer?" Deborah asked as Jake urged her to continue.

John nodded, unable to form a word.

Vertigo gripped him; his head spun. A tsunami of nausea rolled through John's gut. Everything he'd held sacred, including proof of the alien fakeries he thought he'd exposed long ago, all exploded before the glowing object just beyond the ridge's crest. A familiar golden sphere lay in the dust, shimmering with an intense luster. There could be no doubt now.

We're not alone. . . .

✦

Jake and Oz stood with John outside the rover, near an orb the size of a large orange, shimmering gold. The glow intensified as John approached it. No one spoke; even talkative Deborah was silent, sitting at the controls of the rover behind them.

Impossible.

"There's no dust on it, Hawk." Oz photographed the scene, kneeling to get within a couple of meters from the globe. "No tracks that I can see."

Maybe it landed here, John thought. Of all places on Mars, for whatever reason, the globe lay directly in his path.

John's heart beat so hard he was sure Jake, Oz, and Deborah could hear it pounding. He fought to breathe deep, to calm down—but failed. He'd convinced himself years ago that these orbs were part of a complex tapestry of deception, instruments of someone or some nation, capitalizing on a perpetual spiritual hunger in generations of questioning people. Self-deluded people scattered across the Earth who wanted to believe in an alien race. He forced a shallow breath and shuddered.

Was I wrong?

"Looks just like those orbs you guys tried to bring back from Mars on your first mission, John." Jake stood across from him. John kneeled, his hand reaching toward but not touching the glowing sphere.

It was like the others. A perfect duplicate of the gifts that purported "aliens" had left seven years ago on Earth to announce a mysterious coming Father Race—a race that supposedly had seeded human life long ago throughout the galaxy—and on Earth.

They were a ruse, weren't they? The aliens and that weird religion burgeoning on Earth? He'd been convinced then. But here was more proof on Mars.

John leaned toward the beautiful sphere. His gloved hand hovered above the mystical ball, his heart racing.

"Don't touch it, Hawk!" He heard Deborah's voice, but her message didn't register.

I have to know.

"No, Hawk!" someone yelled on his comm link as he reached closer to the radiant sphere. "We don't know if it's safe."

It never harmed the others. John's glove shook as he lowered it, oblivious to Deborah's screams and the slam of frantic heartbeats in his ears.

Oz put a gloved hand on his shoulder to restrain him, but John shook it off.

This is my chance.

John's rubber-tipped fingers touched the orb and it exploded with a piercing blue radiance.

✴

"Don't touch it!" Amy cried as little Abe crawled toward their meager Christmas tree. Before she could reach him, their crawling baby had grabbed a low branch, and the holiday decorations were crashing down upon him.

Springing from the rug in the center of their den, John barely missed getting a hand under the toppling fir and the star atop it. Like diving for a football in the end zone, he'd only managed to get a hand on one ornament, a precious blue glass ball he'd bought for his mother years earlier that she had recently donated to their collection. The remainder of Amy's ancient handblown ornaments splintered on the floor around their babe.

"John!"

Deborah's piercing scream brought him back to Mars. Knee-deep in red dust, he grasped the blue globe between white-gloved hands. An adrenaline-driven blue jolt shot through John's eyes and down his neck, exploding shivers through his shoulder and spine. Gooseflesh rose on his arms and legs as his muscles tensed for fight—or flight.

He was now the sixth.

The first blue explosions had occurred when two silver spider crafts presented their orbs to Mars Rover eight years ago, a thousand kilometers north-northwest of where he was now. Barb Kanewski said it happened the same way when her late brother accepted the third orb from Earth's first spider visitors only twelve days later in a swamp at Cape Canaveral.

On Mars seven years ago, his late friend and Martian explorer, Dr. Michelle Caskey, had experienced the blue explosion of light as she accepted the fourth orb from alien spiders. Aliens who met her landing craft on the day she was the first human to touch the Red Planet. A month later, a fifth orb blazed in the hands of Father Malcolm Raines, greeting a group of silver spiders in the cloister of a Benedictine abbey on France's Mont Saint Michel.

Five brilliant golden orbs, each presented by tall silver spider-like visitors, followed by five blinding blue flashes when the orbs were first touched. The blaze of this sixth orb was too brilliant to watch, and John turned his head as he grasped the sphere tightly with both hands. In a moment, the blue outburst faded to an azure glow.

Why here? Why now? The inside of his clammy Mars suit suddenly felt icy cold.

John stood still, clutching the blue globe. He fully expected a towering silver spider to materialize out of thin air and spear him through the chest with its sharp-tipped leg. Alien robot landers, three meters tall, should be flying in for an eight-legged landing, or walking up single file, their deep bass voices booming at him from nowhere. That's the way it usually happened. Or maybe he should expect the tall space preacher, Father Malcolm Raines, to saunter up in flowing purple robes as he had on Mont Saint Michel, hands raised to the sky exclaiming, "Father! Our number is six!"

The events of the past eight years on Earth and Mars had seen every fashion of strange occurrence with the presentation of these mysterious orbs. He had no idea what to expect next. And no idea why he'd found one here, in the middle of nowhere on Mars.

Something would happen soon. It always did.

Moments later, John stood in response to a tug on his arm, probably Oz trying to get his attention.

"Over there!" Jake yelled on the comm link.

"I see him. But—" Deborah gasped.

"John?" Oz's voice was strangely low and subdued.

John turned toward Oz and held up the ball. "Number six!"

"No." His friend's voice was stern. "Turn around, Hawk. *Now*."

John shuffled around, then flinched. The orb slipped from his grasp and fell into the dust at his feet.

For a moment he was back in Clear Lake City, in late October, cleaning windows for Amy. His oldest son Abe had crept through the living room in a ghoulish Halloween mask, then pressed his face against the glass. When John turned back to his task with a fresh paper towel, he'd met the bloody face with a scream—like the scream he'd just stifled.

A short humanoid stood one hundred meters away. It was dressed in what appeared to be a brilliant silver suit, like none John had ever seen before, topped with a strange trapezoidal helmet sporting two vertical antennae. The humanoid raised what looked like a hand, perhaps in greeting.

"Heart rate 145, John! Breathe!" Deborah's words pricked him, and he gasped for the breaths he'd missed. He couldn't make himself move.

Fifty years of alien images from picture books and movies mingled with pure wonder, rekindling childhood hopes that he might, of all humans, be the first to meet another life form. His dreams played at once like a mental movie in this historic encounter.

It's true. We're not alone.

In a flash, the movie strip broke, his mental film reel spinning out of control as the implication slapped him repeatedly:

I was wrong. There is life here . . . intelligent alien life.

The silver-clad humanoid kept its hand high, palm facing him. John's radio crackled, but it wasn't the usual clear radio link from his crew. The voice was like none he'd ever heard. It was high-pitched, almost girlish.

"We've been searching for you. My mother and I."

AUSTIN BOYD IS AN award-winning novelist who writes about faith issues related to technology, and spiritual allegories that represent a fresh approach to Christian fiction. He creates stories that encourage readers to wrestle with dilemmas of faith through what he calls "a novel approach to truth." Austin is a Christy Gold Medal finalist (*The Proof,* 2007) and winner of multiple writing honors, including the Mount Hermon Christian Writers' "Pacesetter Award."

Austin writes from his experience as a decorated Navy pilot, spacecraft engineer, and as an astronaut candidate finalist. He and his wife Cindy are the parents of four children and live in America's "Rocket City," Huntsville, Alabama, where he serves as the Senior Vice President of a product engineering company that supports NASA, the Department of Defense, and commercial entrepreneurs.

Austin's creative talents include inspirational fiction, poetry, and finely crafted reproduction colonial furniture. In addition to his writing, he is active outdoors as an avid archer, cyclist, and hiker. He serves Huntsville's First Baptist Church and his community as an advocate for crisis pregnancy centers, and as a speaker on issues of lifestyle evangelism through a popular series entitled "Understanding Islam."

Learn more about the author at www.austinboyd.com and www.amgpublishers.com

EXPERIENCE THE OTHER TITLES IN THE MARS HILL CLASSIFIED SERIES.

The Evidence

ISBN: 978-0-89957-828-6

The call to space for NASA Commander John Wells had been almost as strong as his call to serve God. Now, catapulted into the midst of a global controversy, he will face the ultimate test of both his training and his faith. The MARS HILL CLASSIFIED series opens with this highly acclaimed first novel from Austin Boyd.

The Return

ISBN: 978-0-89957-830-9

John Wells accepts the call to return to the Red Planet a second time. But this time, he goes to the surface to explore the planet, not simply to spend thirty days in orbit. Can he reach out to those he has discovered? Faced with immense personal loss, can he forgive? Why did God call him to this place, to grievous loss, and then force him to confront his tormentors face-to-face? The alien trilogy of MARS HILL CLASSIFIED comes to a surprising close.

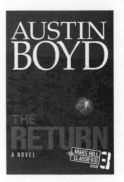

Visit your local Christian bookstore, call AMG at 1-800-266-4977, or log on to www.AMGPublishers.com to purchase.

Living Ink Books
An Imprint of AMG Publishers